"Th— —ur next work-
out. —rning America

"Warm, fuzzy, and ridiculously cute, *The Fastest Way to Fall* is the perfect feel-good read. Britta is an absolute breath of fresh air, and Wes is everything I love in a romantic lead. It's been weeks since I read this book, and I still smile every time I think about it. If you're looking for a novel that feels like a hug, this is it!"

—Emily Henry, #1 *New York Times* bestselling author of *People We Meet on Vacation*

"Funny, flirtatious, and full of heart, *The Fastest Way to Fall* is an absolute winner! I loved tagging along with upbeat and utterly relatable Britta as she tries new things, gets strong, and meets her perfect match in Wes. I fell head over heels and never wanted it to end."

—Libby Hubscher, author of *Meet Me in Paradise*

"An addictive romance filled with hilarious banter, sharp and engaging dialogue, heartfelt moments, and a real and empowering heroine worth cheering for. The love between Britta and Wes blooms gradually and realistically and is sure to utterly capture your heart."

—Jane Igharo, author of *The Sweetest Remedy*

"This charming, sexy novel pairs two people who likely would never have connected outside of an app. . . . Their slow-burn romance feels delightfully old-fashioned." —Washington Independent Review of Books

"Williams follows *How to Fail at Flirting* with another delightfully engaging romance full of humor and surprises. Fans of Jennifer Weiner may like this one." —*Booklist*

"A body-positive, feel-good romance with highly relatable protagonists."

—*Library Journal* (starred review)

"There's a lot to like in this romance with its supportive leading man, delightful heroine, and dynamic secondary cast. There's more than just romance going on, and Williams excels at juggling all the parts. . . . An emotionally resonant and thoughtful novel."
—*Kirkus Reviews*

"*The Fastest Way to Fall* is not a story about weight loss, but about learning to love who you are and about falling in love with someone who helps you feel strong. Britta's triumphs over her former insecurities concerning her body, her goals, and her job are transcendent moments thanks to Williams's sensitive and masterful storytelling."
—*BookPage*

Praise for
How to Fail at Flirting

"In this steamy romance, Naya Turner is an overachieving math professor blowing off work stress with a night on the town, which leads to a night with a dapper stranger. And then another, and another. She's smitten by the time she realizes there's a professional complication, and the relationship could put her job at risk. Williams blends rom-com fun with more weighty topics in her winsome debut."
—*The Washington Post*

"Denise Williams's *How to Fail at Flirting* is absolutely SPECTACULAR! Ripe with serious, real-life drama; teeming with playful banter; rich with toe-curling passion; full of heart-melting romance. . . . Her debut grabbed me on page one and held me enthralled until the end, when I promptly started rereading to enjoy the deliciousness again."
—Priscilla Oliveras, *USA Today* bestselling author of *Anchored Hearts*

"*How to Fail at Flirting* is a charming and compelling debut from Denise Williams that's as moving as it is romantic. Williams brings the banter, heat, and swoons, while also giving us a character who learns that standing up for herself is as important—and terrifying—as allowing herself to fall in love. Put 'Read *How to Fail at Flirting*' at the top of your to-do list!"
—Jen DeLuca, *USA Today* bestselling author of *Well Matched*

"Naya and Jake's relationship is both sexy and sweet as these two people, who love their work but are not skilled at socializing or romance, find their way forward. Academia is vividly portrayed, and readers will await the next book from Williams, a talented debut author and a PhD herself."

—*Booklist*

"*How to Fail at Flirting* is a powerhouse romance. Not only is it funny and charming and steamy, but it possesses an emotional depth that touched my heart. Naya is a beautiful and relatable main character who is hardworking, loyal, spirited, and determined to move on from an abusive relationship. It was thrilling to see her find her power in her personal life, her career, and through her romance with Jake. And I cheered when she claimed the happily ever after she so deserved."

—Sarah Echavarre Smith, author of *On Location*

"Williams's debut weaves a charming, romantic love story about a heroine rediscovering her voice and standing up for her passions."

—Andie J. Christopher, *USA Today* bestselling author
of *Hot Under His Collar*

"*How to Fail at Flirting* delivers on every level. It's funny, sexy, heartwarming, and emotional. With its engaging, lovable characters, fresh plot, and compelling narrative, I did not want to put it down! It's in my top reads of the year for sure!"

—Samantha Young, *New York Times* bestselling author
of *Much Ado about You*

"The warmth in Denise Williams's writing is unmistakable, as is her wit. She tackles difficult subjects, difficult emotions, with such empathy and thoughtfulness. Best of all: Jake is just the type of hero I love—sexy, smart, sweet, and smitten."

—Olivia Dade, national bestselling author of *All the Feels*

DO YOU TAKE THIS MAN

Denise Williams

BERKLEY ROMANCE
·····································
New York

Berkley Romance
Published by Berkley
An imprint of Penguin Random House LLC
penguinrandomhouse.com

LIBRARY OF CONGRESS CATALOGING-IN-PUBLICATION DATA

Names: Williams, Denise, 1982– author.
Title: Do you take this man / Denise Williams.
Description: First Edition. | New York: Berkley Romance, 2022.
Identifiers: LCCN 2021062531 (print) | LCCN 2021062532 (ebook) | ISBN
9780593437193 (trade paperback) | ISBN 9780593437209 (ebook)
Subjects: LCGFT: Romance fiction. | Novels.
Classification: LCC PS3623.I556497 D6 2022 (print) | LCC PS3623.I556497
(ebook) | DDC 813/.6—dc23/eng/20220208
LC record available at https://lccn.loc.gov/2021062531
LC ebook record available at https://lccn.loc.gov/2021062532

First Edition: September 2022

Printed in the United States of America
1st Printing

BOOK DESIGN BY KATY RIEGEL

For the ones who think

they're hard to love

Chapter 1

RJ

I DIDN'T BLAME Maddie Anderson for scowling at her soon-to-be ex-husband.

He appeared calm and collected in a somber Italian suit, remaining quiet and deferent, and seeming reasonable. He almost looked bored by the proceedings and the minutiae of his marriage ending. I made note of the gray at his temples and supposed it was easy to look dignified as a fifty-seven-year-old sitting next to one's twenty-three-year-old wife, and probably easy to look bored when you'd done this a time or two before.

Behind the makeup, Maddie's eyes were puffy, and the cuticle on her thumb looked shredded, like she'd been nervously scratching it. Since walking in on her husband with not one but two women during their son's first birthday party, she'd been through a lot. The hurt and embarrassment were clear in the woman's mannerisms, but Mr. Anderson didn't seem to care.

I'd never been in Ms. Anderson's shoes—today, a pair of crystal-encrusted pink stilettos. I'd learned young that people were rarely worth trusting, and baring your teeth was easier than baring your soul only to be shown you weren't worth someone's time. It didn't make me bitter, but it made me careful. It also made me enjoy these little moments when I could help someone else bare their teeth.

Granted, my client huffed anytime opposing counsel spoke. I glanced at the clock on the far side of the wall and estimated how long this would take. Despite the eye-rolling, gum popping, and faint smell of a perfume probably marketed to teenagers, Maddie Anderson was going to leave this office a very rich woman.

Twenty-five minutes later and before rushing back to my desk, I smiled at Maddie, whose philandering ex-husband was not as covert in his affairs as he'd hoped, and who'd chosen the wrong woman to underestimate.

"Everything should be finalized by the end of the month." I shook Maddie's hand to interrupt the hug coming my way and shared her smile. One point for the wronged woman and one more win for me. I rushed down the hall, trying not to look like I was in a hurry even though it was five fifteen and there was no way I was going to be on time.

"RJ." The smoky voice of one of the senior partners left me cursing in my head as I turned to greet her. Gretchen Vanderkin-Shaw would have scared the crap out of me if I didn't admire her so much. Really, she still scared the crap out of me, but as a named partner before forty with a success rate through the roof, she was a force to be reckoned with, and she liked me. Gretchen was the lawyer I wanted to be, and I was gathering my courage to ask her to be my mentor.

She nodded toward the conference room. "The Anderson case?"

"We were able to come to a resolution that worked in our favor." That was code for crushing them like tiny little bugs and then doing a victory dance that might involve some light professional twerking.

She nodded, a faint smile on her lips because I'd learned the victory dance from her. "Excellent. Eric mentioned you wanting to talk to me. I have a free hour now."

I stole a quick glance at my watch, because nine times out of ten, if Gretchen asked to meet, we did. Hell, if she'd asked me to hop, I'd have gone full Cha Cha Slide.

"Do you have somewhere to be?"

I could have lied and said a conference call or a client meeting, but what was the point? Everything I was doing was happening because the firm wanted to keep a client happy. Well, mostly. "I have to be downtown at six."

Her mouth formed into a thin line, and I knew she'd decoded my reason for needing to be downtown. She nodded. "Well, you'd better go. You know how I feel about this, though, RJ. You're better than some publicity stunt."

I fumbled for a response, biting my lower lip. That wasn't characteristic of me—I held my shoulders back and chin up on the regular, and I never backed down from anything. I made powerful people want to cower, and I was good at it. She was right, and I was better than a publicity stunt, but I had to admit, I enjoyed this particular stunt. "Thank you for checking in. I'll talk to your assistant and make an appointment."

I hurried into the back of a waiting Uber, with plans to change clothes modestly in the back seat. Was I telling myself I would be modest, knowing that I was about to give anyone looking a bit of a show? Absolutely.

PENNY: Where are you?

RJ: On my way. There's traffic.

PENNY: You're killing me.

I sent her the knife emoji. *Top of my class in law school and this is my life now. Event planners harassing me as I strip down in the back of an Uber.* My phone buzzed again from the seat as I brushed powder onto my cheeks and checked my edges in a compact.

PENNY: But I love you.

RJ: I know.
RJ: You have the mic set up how I like?

PENNY: Yes, but if you're late, you're getting a handheld with a tangled cord.

I pulled out the binder where I'd prepared my script. All the pages were in plastic covers with labeled tabs just in case, a copy of all pertinent information in the back folder and a Post-it Note reminding me of everyone's names and pronouns tucked in the front. I climbed from the car and repeated the opening phrase to myself as I hurried toward the stairs of the venue. I spoke part of the line to myself. ". . . the promise of hope between two people who love each other sincerely, who—"

Suddenly, I was hurtling toward the sidewalk, not sure whether I should try to save myself, my bag, or the notes. I clutched the binder to my chest as I hit the concrete, scraping my leg, my palm stinging with the impact. The clothes I'd hurriedly shoved in my bag after changing fluttered around me, and I took in the large form who'd been blocking the sidewalk.

In a movie, this would be the start of a how-we-met story. The tall guy, his features obscured by the sun at his back, would lean down and help me up. Our eyes would meet. He'd apologize, I'd note something like the depth of his voice or the tickle of the hair on his forearms, and we'd be off. That might have happened for other people, but though our eyes met, I was not in the market for cute, and now I was about to arrive late and bruised to perform this couple's wedding rehearsal.

Chapter 2

LEAR

I STEPPED OUT of my car and stood looking up at the wedding venue as if I was standing on some great precipice. My phone buzzed again and, against my better judgment, I looked at the screen.

SARAH: I just need to know you're okay.

She hadn't texted for a while. Someone must have told her I'd gone home. I'd never planned to return to Asheville, North Carolina, and yet there I was, living in my cousin's basement after doing my best impression of someone trying to self-destruct for the better part of a year.

I tapped the delete icon with more force than it needed. I imagined the sympathetic face she'd probably made while typing the text, with her lower lip out, eyes soft. When I didn't respond, she'd sigh in exasperation. She told me once that nothing drove her crazier than when someone didn't respond to texts, and I made it a point from then on to never leave her hanging. One of the many things I did to make sure I was everything she wanted, something I'd done with everyone since I was a teenager.

Done with her sympathy. Done with her. Done with being a nice guy. My phone buzzed again, but this time it was my cousin.

PENNY: Did you go back to LA or
something? Can you still cover this?

LEAR: Got held up. There in a sec.

PENNY: You're killing me.

I shoved my phone into my pocket, clearing my head so I could take on my first task as Penny's assistant wedding planner. The title required a second deep breath, because my old job, planning events for a professional football team—my dream job—was across the country, and it wasn't mine anymore. With Sarah's text fresh on my mind as a reminder that falling in love was the first step off a cliff, I headed into my first day as a wedding professional. I'd helped my cousin with setup earlier in the day, but now my only task was to woo a prospective client and her mother. I sucked in a breath. *Here goes my new life.*

A fast-moving body stopped my progress when it rammed into me, the voice of its owner high pitched as she cried "Motherf—" but hit the ground before completing the expletive.

The woman was sprawled on the pavement, the contents of what looked to be her entire life strewn around her. Her shocked expression quickly shifted, lips pursed and brow furrowed.

"Dammit," I muttered.

She was dressed professionally, but the grass near her thigh was littered with a few tampons, a balled-up shirt, a stick of deodorant, a small bottle of maple syrup, and nine rolls of butter rum Life Savers. I lost focus on her haughty expression and tried to figure out why a person would have these things just with her. If she hadn't still been muttering curse words under her breath, I would have really taken a moment to appreciate the randomness of the maple syrup and the audacity of that many Life Savers.

She looked up at me like I owed her something, eyes narrowed and expression incredulous, and I lost interest in the contents of her bag. I didn't have time for this, but I tried to sand the edge from my voice. "You should watch where you're going," I said in what I hoped was a playful tone, holding out a hand only to be met with a deeper scowl.

"Speak for yourself," she said in a huff, pushing away my hand and scrambling for balance. Her face was pinched, annoyed, and she turned in a flash to collect her things. "And manners. Have you heard of them?"

"You ran into me."

"Because you were standing in the middle of the sidewalk, not moving."

I still held out my hand to help her. Ten years in LA hadn't completely robbed me of my Southern home training, but this random angry little woman was pissing me off. I reminded myself that I left the nice-guy thing back in California, along with everything else. I shook my outstretched hand at her, letting any veil of politeness slip. "Will you take my damn hand so we can both get going?"

She scowled again, and the entitlement running off her petite frame in this brief exchange hit me in waves, even from a few feet away. "This is not what I needed today." As she pushed herself to her feet, she ignored my outstretched hand, and I stepped back.

Her hands flew frantically over her clothes and swiped at her hips. She muttered to herself as she tried to pick everything up, swatting my hand away when I tried to help. "Assholes just standing in the middle of the sidewalk," she muttered to herself. "The last damn thing I needed today . . ."

I'd never heard that combination of whisper-quiet cursing. My instinct was to offer help again, to apologize again, and to smile until she walked away, but if the last several months had taught me anything, it was that my instincts weren't all that great.

"Good luck with that." Without another word, I turned to walk away, but not before deciding I could truly go against everything my gut told me to do, to hammer that last nail in the coffin of the old me. I called over my shoulder, "You know, you should smile more."

I regretted it immediately. My sister would have my ass on a plate if she knew I'd uttered those words. I thought briefly about turning back to apologize, but I was already pressing my luck after getting lost. My phone buzzed in my pocket again, no doubt my cousin.

I pushed the woman from the sidewalk out of my mind and reminded myself that being a nice guy was not on my priority list anymore. I'd probably never see her again anyway.

THE VENUE HAD been a bank once upon a time, and the old architecture framed the entryway. Following a complete renovation years ago, it was an event space now and today would host a wedding rehearsal. I wondered if the vault was still in place and if anyone held parties there.

LEAR: I'm here and waiting for them. Fear not.

PENNY: You're my favorite cousin, but if you fuck this up, I'll end you.

LEAR: Noted. Love you, too.

The door opened, letting in a swath of sunlight. A pang of anxiety hit me that it might be the woman from outside, and I ducked my head, intent on examining the pattern on the marble floor. Instead of the angry growl someone had briefly introduced me to outside, a voice that sounded more like chirping filled the space.

A stylish younger woman chatted with an older woman, both adjusting their blond hair. Catching my eye, the younger woman beamed. "Are you Penny's cousin? She said you'd be tall and well dressed and, oh my, you are. How lovely. She didn't say you'd be so good looking, but of course you are." She talked without pause, her words flowing from her nervous laughter. I flashed an easy smile at Melinda and Victoria Matthews, daughter and wife of Richard Matthews. The family apparently owned one-third of North Carolina.

"Nice to meet you," I said smoothly, taking the younger woman's hand. "Lear Campbell." I wanted to make a good first impression, but I also wanted her to stop rambling. From what Penny said, the bride wanted to copy and paste that next day's wedding, but we wanted her to feel like she was just getting inspiration. Her wedding was over a year away and it seemed silly to be concerned with how the rehearsal venue's lobby and gardens might work, but Penny's words played in my head. *Make them feel special. Don't disparage any idea they love, no matter how bad the idea is. Make it seem like you can move mountains.* She'd also added *Don't make that face*, but I was fairly certain that was her being my older cousin and not my boss.

"This is so beautiful!" Melinda twirled around in a circle, looking at the space. She also seemed to end every sentence with an exclamation point, her voice high and excited. She reminded me of a teenager or a terrier.

"It's a beautiful venue. You chose well." My compliment on her excellent taste was met with a beaming smile from both mother and daughter. Penny didn't give me quite enough credit. It wasn't like I didn't have to schmooze and make people feel important working in professional sports. "We can visit the gardens. That space isn't in use now."

"We are just so excited. I can't believe—" Her voice halted and her eyes grew wide.

Over my shoulder, I saw the woman from the sidewalk hurry out of the restroom across the vestibule. I snapped my head down before she caught my face. She'd put herself back together, clothes straightened and her hair, which had come loose when she fell, pulled back into a bun that showed off her neck. She had a nice neck. She was short but in sky-high heels and a black dress that subtly highlighted her rounded curves. She looked better when she wasn't scowling at me from the ground. It was a wonder I hadn't seen any of that outside. *Well, maybe not a wonder. She was pretty adamantly insisting I was an asshole at the time.*

"Mom," the girl hissed. "That's her! The woman who performed Alejandro's wedding! I love her." Mrs. Matthews followed her daughter's gaze.

"Who is Alejandro?" Her voice was sweet and slow. Her accent reminded me of my aunt, and I smiled, also interested to learn why the bride knew who the woman from outside was.

"Alejandro Calderón proposed to George O'Toole in the park and it was totes cute, just, like, all the feels. Their families were there, and he said all these nice things. Mom, I was seriously bawling." The woman bounced on her heels, her energy like a gale force wind.

"Melly, you know I don't know who those people are," her mother interjected.

I'd been in a hole for almost a year and even I knew who they were. The two men had played opposite each other in a superhero epic a couple years earlier, and when the country's new favorite hero and most reviled fictional villain started dating, it was big news.

Melinda fiddled with her phone and held it out to her mom. "You remember. They were in the Interstellar Man movies. I had the biggest crush on Alejandro when I was a kid and had all these posters." She took a breath, and I slid into the conversation, because this was taking us way off course.

"Weren't those movies great?" I asked smoothly, sidestepping Melinda's trip down Middle School Crush Lane. "So, they got married?"

"Anyway, this woman was in the park where it happened and could perform weddings, so they did it that day. She was amazing, like, such a beautiful ceremony that she wrote on the fly. Absolutely everyone has seen the video. Mom, we have to get her. Can you imagine if the same woman who married the hottest couple in Hollywood married me and Sam?"

I peeked over my shoulder again as the woman strode toward where the wedding would be held, hands smoothing down the front of her outfit.

"Well, you know your father and I would prefer you use our pastor, but it's your day, and if you want this woman, it's fine with us." She turned to me. "Can you check on that?" I did not know the answer to her question and would rather have talked up an antideodorant activist with a new multilevel marketing obsession than show my face to that woman, but Penny had told me to make them think we could move mountains, so I nodded.

"She's completely popular, but everyone on the wedding websites says she doesn't take new clients. How cool is it that she's attending this wedding?" the younger woman exclaimed, her smile spreading. "If you could get her, I would be the happiest bride in all North Carolina."

As the woman I'd left scowling on the sidewalk reached the door, a slip of paper fell out of her binder, and I jogged over to her. *Turn on the charm. Apologize. Move mountains.*

"Excuse me?" I bent to pick up the yellow Post-it Note from the ground. "You dropped this."

At my voice, she turned, her smile genuine. "Oh, thank—" She stopped when she saw my face, her soft eyes snapping into cold daggers and her smile turning into a tight line of full, pressed lips.

I held out the note and smiled anyway.

"Thank you," she said coolly, taking the slip of paper but being careful not to touch my hand, as if I'd peed on it or something.

"Listen, I'm sorry about what I said outside. I was way out of line and—"

She interrupted me with practiced skill. "Can I help you with something? I'm in a hurry."

"Yes, I just wanted to apologize. I'm Lear Campbell," I said, holding out my hand.

She looked at it like I'd just offered her an old gym sock. "Lear? Like King Lear?"

"It's a nickname," I said, pulling my hand back for a moment. "My client over there is interested in working with you on a wedding." I motioned to the embodiment of fangirling, her blond ponytail bobbing while she bounced on her heels. "Do you have a card, or can I call you about your availability?"

"Did you hear me say I'm in a hurry?"

"Sure—"

She interrupted me again. "Are you familiar with the phrase?" She arched one eyebrow in a way that made me feel two inches tall despite having a good eight on her.

This might be the least pleasant person I've ever met, beautiful body and stunning smile be damned. "I am," I gritted out. "If I could just get your card."

The door to the anteroom pushed open, and Penny slipped out. "RJ. Thank God. I was about to send out a search party. You're never actually late." She glanced between us. "And you met Lear," she said to her with a sideways glance at me. "He's just starting out with me. Lear, RJ Brooks is the officiant."

Oh, shit.

I noted the binder RJ held, the one she'd clutched to her chest outside. The officiant for this wedding. That made sense and was so much worse for me. "It's nice to formally meet you," I said, holding out a hand again.

She raised that eyebrow again and then turned away from me, a fast-moving polar vortex taking over the space where she'd stood. "I ran into something unpleasant on the way in. Sorry. I'm ready." She flashed a smile to my cousin and didn't give me a second glance.

Penny flicked her eyes to me in a way I knew meant *What the hell did you do?*

My first day was off to a great start.

Chapter 3

RJ

ERIC POPPED HIS head into my office. "Lunch? I need to get out of here."

I glanced at my watch. It was three fifteen, and I had eaten nothing since a bagel at nine that morning. "I have a ton of work to do," I said, unconvincingly nudging the pile of folders on my desk.

"I'll rephrase. This is a senior associate telling a junior associate to leave her office for thirty minutes."

I grabbed my purse from my desk drawer because I was hungry. "Does your husband know you're this annoying?"

"As a matter of fact, he does." Eric leaned against the door frame. "But my charm and good looks more than make up for any shortcomings."

We walked down the hall, side by side. Streaks of afternoon sunlight flowed from open doors into the hallway. "I know that's not true," I said with a laugh. I liked Eric. He and his husband had become fast friends of mine when I moved to North Carolina. "I seem to remember him definitively disliking your brief but memorable obsession with fur-lined Crocs."

"We don't speak of that period in our relationship," he said, pushing open the door. "And I thank you not to bring it up."

We laughed as we stepped out into the sunshine. The deli down the street was a frequent stop, though lately I'd been ordering in more than leaving the building.

Eric rolled the sleeves on his shirt as we walked. "Did you talk to Gretchen yet?"

"We met a few days ago, and she agreed to be my mentor."

"And you're . . . happy about this? You look like she agreed to be your *tor*mentor."

"No, I'm excited." I'd been nervous as hell to tell Gretchen she had the career I wanted and to ask her to mentor me. She'd grilled me about my goals and plans in a way that made every job interview I'd ever had feel like practice runs. "I admire the hell out of her, but you know she's terrifying. It was like asking the goddess of war for a favor."

Eric chuckled. "She does have a *few* Athena qualities, but I don't think she's quite as intimidating as you assume."

I leveled him with a stare.

"Fine. She is, but she's a person. She's got flaws and skeletons, just like everyone else, and, believe it or not, she has a soft side, too."

"Well, as long as she can help me have the career she's had, I don't need to see her soft side." I didn't know the full story, but Eric and Gretchen had known each other socially. He'd mentioned casually once that Gretchen had introduced him to Tyson years earlier. Still, I didn't really believe she shed her veneer of power and poise when she left the office, which was part of what I admired. "She hates this wedding thing."

"That's not shocking," he said, pushing through the door into the space crowded with other professionals who had forgotten to take lunch on time. "What's going on with that? I was out on parental leave when it happened, and everything after that is a little blurry. You performed this wedding in the park and it turned out he was a client of ours?"

The smells of the deli made my mouth water and I made a mental note to order an extra sandwich to have for dinner later in my office. "A big client with the LA branch. After it went viral, they were interviewed constantly, and every time, they talked about the ceremony I wrote for them on the fly, how it was original and beautiful. Add to that, he told some friends who told other friends, and suddenly . . ." I paused as we stepped forward.

"Suddenly you're a divorce attorney who performs weddings." Eric shook his head. "Why did you get ordained in the first place?"

I sighed. "My best friend is getting married and asked me to perform the ceremony, so I did it online."

"Got it," Eric said. "So, now you have a side hustle."

"Exactly," I said, stepping to the counter and ordering my sandwiches. "I got the impression we should keep the clients happy and then I got in over my head. I am booked to do them through the summer. Gretchen doesn't like it, but the other partners appreciate that clients are happy."

"Clients? More than one?"

I raised an eyebrow and blew out a slow breath. "You'd be surprised how many of our wealthy and powerful clients have children getting married who are dying to be one degree closer to a celebrity." I didn't add how surprised he'd be to learn I kind of enjoyed doing it, or how much of a sucker I was when hearing the stories of other couples not related to the firm. I'd said yes to too many of them.

Eric chuckled, thanking the woman at the counter for his food. "I'd pay to see this."

"See me do a wedding? You don't have to. The video of Alejandro and George's went viral." That had been slightly less fun than a root canal.

"Well, I saw that already. I was up at three a.m. with an infant. I think I saw everything on YouTube." Eric sipped from his straw, making me wait for whatever he was going to say next. It was one of his more endearing and annoying habits. "Honestly, it was amazing, especially if you pulled it together on the fly. You're just so unromantic. It was kind of shocking to see you out there, waxing poetic about love," he mused. "I teared up. I mean, I was sleep deprived and my shirt was stained with either poop or Coke Zero, but still. I didn't know you had it in you."

"Unromantic" was one word for it. Romantic love wasn't meant to last. I'd never questioned that. It didn't for my parents, it never had for me, and I made a good living at watching it not last for others. "You know I love being in charge of a room," I deflected, even though it was a little more than that. It was easy to pretend love *could* last for other people, even if just for those few hours. That's what I'd tapped into when I wrote that first ceremony. I thought about the kinds of things my best friends Britta and Kat would want to hear with their soft, love-receptive hearts. I thought about the things I'd wanted a guy to say to my mom when she started dating again. I thought about the way Eric looked at his husband, and the words came. I was pretending to believe, but I'd come to enjoy the pretending, though no one needed to know that. I'd thought about my last relationship and the peace I secretly wanted and never found and, on the fly, I'd added a line about finding a home inside someone else's heart. My friends teased me, saying that was the line that made them suspect my anti-romance stance wasn't as strong as I thought. I assured them I'd googled it even though I hadn't. Eric didn't need to know that, though, and he still eyed me. "Plus, maybe I'll pick up some future clients."

The woman at the counter handed me the two giant sandwiches, only one of which would fit in my purse and that I could save for dinner. Eric's tone had shifted to cautious. "You're being careful, though, right?"

"Yes. I always have condoms handy." The woman at the counter did a double take before looking away. "Are you worried I'll go soft being around the weddings?"

Eric barked a laugh. "No. Do you even have a soft setting?"

I knew why he asked. You couldn't look soft in this job, especially as a woman and definitely as a Black woman. We had to seem intimidating to co-counsel, but not to the judge or jury; we had to convey not only competence but unassailable ruthlessness on behalf of our clients. So maybe having this brief escape where I could be a little soft was a novelty.

I lifted one shoulder. "I only agreed to do them through the end of the summer," I said. "It's mostly people connected to Alejandro or the firm. Children of clients. That kind of thing." Also, several people who Penny talked me into. She was my favorite of the wedding planners I'd worked with, and we'd met shortly after the viral video when the officiant for a real estate developer represented by our firm had to cancel at the last minute. Penny won me over immediately with a no-nonsense approach and a good sense of humor. Penny, who I normally adored, was now on my shit list for hiring that asshole cousin of hers who I ran into in the parking lot.

Eric looked unconvinced, and I added, "Most people spend a few hours a week on a hobby or loved ones." I shrugged again. "Consider this my puppy."

"There's a reason most junior associates don't have dogs," he said, but smiled. Eric had a pleasant smile, the reassuring kind. "I know you're on top of it, though."

Fifteen minutes later, we hurried back into the building, Eric needing to make a call and me eager to get back to work. I waved as Eric took off toward the stairs, wanting to get the workout, then turned to the elevator, but someone obscured my path and we slammed into each other. My sandwich fell as I stumbled, but another hand saved it from the floor.

"Sorry," I said, taking a step back and glancing at the sandwich before meeting the man's face. I noticed his shoes before I saw him. Stylish, but not overly fancy. "Sorry," I repeated, straightening. "I—"

"We really need to stop meeting like this," he said, still holding my sandwich in his large, not completely unattractive hand.

"What are you doing here?" I held out my palm to take the sandwich, but he ignored me.

"Well, it's a law firm." He gestured around the lobby. "I'm meeting with a lawyer."

I held out my hand again, moving it toward his, though he didn't budge.

"Glad to run into you, though. Could we discuss your availability to perform my client's wedding?"

We can discuss hell freezing over, but it will be a quick conversation. "I'm not taking on any new couples. Penny knows that."

"We got off on the wrong foot, but my client would really love to work with you. I watched some of your videos and you're an impressive speaker." He smiled this kind of charming frat boy smile, and I fought the urge to kick him. I didn't because I was an adult and a professional . . . and there were cameras in the lobby.

"I'm busy," I said, making a last motion for my sandwich. "You, once again, seem not to know the meaning of that word."

"I am crystal clear on the meaning," he said, obviously faking his charming smile now. "I also wanted to apologize again for the other day, and since we are both standing here anyway, we could—"

I dragged my eyes from him, noticing Gretchen striding toward us, her heels clicking on the tile floor. *Shit.* I had a sudden blast of panic about all the things I should have been doing in my office instead of going to lunch with Eric and getting waylaid by this guy. Gretchen had made it clear she wasn't supportive of the wedding thing, that it could in no way interfere with my work, so I really didn't need her to catch me talking to this wedding planner. I made a grab for my sandwich as she stopped.

"Lear," she said, a wide smile brightening her entire expression. She opened her arms and pulled him into a hug. "You're early."

I stood by, stunned, as Gretchen smiled, held him by both shoulders, and hugged him again. I'd barely ever seen her smile, let alone emote like this.

"You can't stomach tardiness," he joked, pulling away from her.

"I absolutely cannot," she said, dropping her hands and glancing over to me. "RJ, this is Lear Campbell, my best friend's younger brother. Lear, RJ Brooks is one of our top associates. You've met?"

Lear's eyes fell on me, and I had the sudden worry I'd forgotten to get dressed that morning and that he was looking at me naked, and the idea wasn't completely unpleasant.

When I didn't speak up, he did, and I kicked myself again. "Yes. I'm working with my cousin planning weddings now. Ms. Brooks was so kind to give me a moment of her time. I'm trying to talk her into working with me."

Gretchen arched an eyebrow. "Well, if you're doing weddings, you can't do better than working with someone like Lear."

She smiled warmly at him, and my cheeks heated. *Shit. How do I turn him down now?*

He had a dimple, a small one in his annoyingly handsome cheek, and it popped when he smiled. "Is email or a phone call best?"

I gritted my teeth. "Your cousin can give you my phone number."

"Excellent." Gretchen motioned toward the elevator and glanced between Lear and me. "Shall we?"

It took every ounce of focus to not run a hand down my dress to make sure it was there. "I'm going to take the stairs, actually, getting my steps in and all," I said, wondering if the words sounded as flustered to them as they did in my head. I was running calculations about how much it might screw me over with Gretchen if I continued to blow off the guy who was apparently the brother she never had.

Lear nodded, a smile on his lips. "I'll call with the date for the ceremony, Ms. Brooks. I'm looking forward to working with you."

Stab, stab, stab. "Looking forward to it."

I turned toward the stairs, fuming with each step that I'd probably have to work with this annoying jerk.

"Ms. Brooks!" His voice startled me, and I almost tripped as I stopped abruptly. He jogged toward me and, dammit, he looked good when he ran, his body held straight, well-developed shoulders filling out the shirt. "RJ."

"Yes?"

Gretchen stood near the elevator across the lobby checking her phone, but I had a feeling if I held up two middle fingers dramatically in his face, she might look up at the wrong moment.

"Don't forget your sandwich." Lear held out his hand, winked, and I grabbed it, our fingers brushing for a moment and an unwelcome warm tingle radiating up my arm. "I'd hate for you to go hungry." He smiled again—no, it wasn't a smile. He smirked and then returned to Gretchen and the now-open elevator doors.

Shit.

Chapter 4

LEAR

"HEY, TINA." I shared a smile with my cousin's assistant. "Penny around?"

She shook her head. "Hasn't been in all morning. She wasn't at the house?"

"She and Kelly went to Charleston to visit Kelly's parents for the weekend. I thought she was planning to come straight here." I glanced at my watch. Penny was usually in the office early on Tuesdays. "Thanks, T. I'll just wait in her office and try her cell." We were supposed to be meeting to talk through the next several months and create a working plan. Settling in the chair opposite Penny's desk, I glanced around the office. The exposed brick and industrial look fit her, and black-and-white photos covered the walls. Penny had carved out a niche for herself as someone versatile by taking on small offbeat ceremonies and then, after making connections, earning the trust of people wanting larger, more elaborate events.

I hadn't grown up with my cousin. She'd graduated high school a few months after Caitlin and I moved to Sybel following our parents' death. But before she left for college, she'd given us the lay of the land, showed us how to navigate the deep political waters of a small-town high school, and she'd been right. I'd held tight to those reminders ever since.

1. If no one sees what bothers you, no one can really mess with you.
2. Be nice to everyone.
3. If you can't control it, roll with it.

It was ironic that that last bit of advice came from someone who grew up to be so in control of every detail that I sometimes thought she understood the world to bend at her insistence.

My sister had added a fourth: Date someone nice who doesn't bring drama to your doorstep.

All four had been in the back of my head since then.

Photos of Penny and her wife lined the window ledge. The two of them together on trips around the world dotted the space. It had been the two of them for a long time. They'd been trying to adopt for years with no luck. Still, I wasn't the third member of the household they planned on, and I ran through calculations in my head of when I could afford to get my own place and move out of their basement.

My phone buzzed on the desk, and I smiled as I flipped over the device. "Hey, loser."

"Speak for yourself," my sister said with a laugh. "How's North Carolina treating you?" She'd moved to Southern California two years earlier to begin her residency.

"You know. It's home," I said, sitting back in the chair. "Need to stop in to see Uncle Harold still."

She was biting back a comment about me not going to see him yet but, uncharacteristically, she didn't say it, which was how I knew what her next question would be. "How you doing?"

I glanced out the window, planning to ignore her question. The same question she'd been asking me for months. "I'm fine."

"Do better," she said. There were muffled voices in the background that sounded like the coffee shop we used to frequent together. "All you've said is 'fine' for months."

"Yeah, you'd think a doctor like yourself would be smart enough to take the hint." I glanced at my watch again, wondering where the hell Penny was.

"I take hints very well. They're often disconnected from what someone says out loud. Anyway, when have you ever known me to just let something go?"

"Not once in your life."

"So . . . ?"

"I'm fine."

"You're impossible." The background noise changed as she stepped outside, and I immediately missed the incessant sunshine of LA, the noise and energy. Things were different in North Carolina—Southern hospitality, but I missed the shine and smiles, even the fake ones. Sarah popped into my mind, and my face shifted into a drawn expression. Her insistence on how happy she was. I shook my head, pushing the image away.

I drummed my fingers on the desk. "What's up?"

Can you hear an eye roll over the phone? "Well, my brother got screwed over, lost his job, and ran away from his life, so I'm getting coffee on my break and asking him to let go of this toxic masculinity, keep-everything-inside shit and talk about his feelings." As Cait spoke, Sarah fell out of my head and RJ Brooks popped into my mind, her flustered expression, just the flash of it, when I handed her back her sandwich.

"I think my toxic masculinity is serving me fine."

"Weird flex," she muttered, sounds of traffic behind her. "You're spending too much time alone."

"How do you know I'm alone? Maybe I'm the swipe-left king of Asheville."

"Again, weird flex." The sounds of the hospital filled her end of the conversation, and I knew she'd have to be off the phone soon. "I know you. You're alone."

"I enjoy being alone. Alone is good. I don't need another person dragging me down."

She sighed again, and I knew she was biting her lip before deciding to respond again.

Luckily, my phone buzzed with another call. "Penny's on the line. I'll talk to you later."

"You better!"

I clicked over. "Hey. Where are you?"

Penny laughed in a high-pitched, kind of disconnected way, and I sat up straighter. "Well, long story, but I'm in Texas."

"Um . . . why?"

"We got a call late last night," she said, voice shaky. "It was all so fast, but we have a son!"

My jaw hit the floor. "Whoa! What happened? Texas?"

"He's two and a half months premature and in the NICU, he's so tiny, but he's . . . perfect." Her voice broke, and I felt a lump in my throat but coughed to cover it.

"Congratulations, Pen. That's amazing." I crossed and uncrossed my ankle over my knee. "I'm really happy for you."

"Yeah, it's . . . I can't believe it. He needs a lot of care and there's all the legal stuff, but it's so . . . I can't believe . . ."

I smiled, not even needing to force it.

Penny sucked in a deep breath. "So, yeah, I'm . . . It's a lot, and I have to be here for a while."

"Just tell me what you need. I got you." I moved to the other side of her desk, searching for a notepad.

"There are only a few things that need immediate attention. We can get everything else squared away tomorrow or in a couple days, but there's a rehearsal tonight for the Jameson/Lopez wedding tomorrow."

"Their wedding is on a Wednesday?"

"They're nontraditional. Tina can get you all my notes and files and make sure you're caught up. Everything is ready to go. It's a small event and RJ Brooks is officiating. Shouldn't be too much to pick up on late notice."

I paused a beat too long before saying "Okay."

"Be nice to her."

"I'm always professional."

"I'm serious. I love working with that woman and she means more to me than you. Just let her handle things and run the show for the rehearsal. Let's see . . . Tina will get you everything you need. But be nice to RJ."

"I can handle it," I mumbled, not liking her implications. They were fair, since during our first meeting I'd suggested RJ smile more, but still. "Hard to believe, but you actually like me, too."

"I do . . . but not as much as I love a rock-solid and popular officiant." Penny's voice was muffled as she said something to someone nearby. "Look at the notes and call me later with questions. I already emailed the couple and gave them your cell number. They're laid-back. I gotta go, but call me if you need me."

I navigated to the file and notes on Penny's computer. I was organized—Penny's hard drive was other-level organized. I glanced through the detailed day-of schedule. I was still new to weddings, but it looked straightforward. Confirm with caterer, florist, and transportation. The guest list was small—fewer than fifty people—and the ceremony was being held in the public library midweek. This was such a different world from professional football, but I kept telling myself this wasn't a different job. It was an event I had to run, making sure things went well. "No problem. I'm on it. Go take care of my little nephew."

"I think technically the baby is your first cousin once removed."

"Well, tell me a name and I'll stick with that." I made a few notes on the notepad, trying to organize a to-do list. "I'm really happy for you two. You're going to be great parents. Let me know what you need and we'll talk later." We hung up, and I wrote furiously on the pad, combining my own to-do list with the things noted for the upcoming rehearsal. My phone buzzed and Sarah's name flashed on the screen. I clicked to ignore and kept writing, knowing if I maintained focus on this, I could block out everything else.

I wondered how many of Penny's upcoming ceremonies had RJ Brooks officiating. It had surprised me to see her in the lobby when I'd gone to meet Gretchen about some things I'd left unsettled in California. She'd been almost nervous to run into me and then was kind of an ice queen, but that had melted when she saw Gretchen. I wondered what the deal was there, but whatever it was, RJ had agreed to help me. I wasn't sure why I couldn't get her out of my head. When I scrolled over to the YouTube app, the video of her viral wedding ceremony was paused, and I tapped the play button. Her voice and the slight rustling noise of the breeze filled the office. "Repeat after me. I take you to be none other than yourself." George O'Toole repeated her words, but I kept my eyes trained on her. "I trust you to be my home and I promise to be yours." The rising tide of reaction I felt to those words had me tapping the screen to pause the video and staring at RJ's face again.

She was hot, but I was used to being around beautiful women— LA had a higher than average population of would-be models and actresses—so it was something else. I chuckled to myself in the open office and ignored my reaction to the video. *She doesn't like me.* And that felt like a very normal and well-adjusted reaction.

Caitlin gave me crap all the time about wanting to be liked, about charming people. I couldn't help it. I'd always been that way—a people pleaser. It served me well, usually. It hadn't really gone my way with Sarah. I reminded myself why I needed to cut that part of my personality away with a hacksaw if necessary. *Nice guy* wasn't getting me anywhere. RJ Brooks could dislike me all she wanted and it wouldn't matter.

I kept scribbling, moving on to the second page of a to-do list, shifting focus to what I needed to do for Melinda Matthews, besides how I'd get up to speed on Penny's event plans. My mind jumped again to RJ's narrowed eyes and wondered if they'd widen when I touched her, if her lips might part when she felt the spark of desire. *Dammit.* I shook my head and dotted an *i* with too much force, ripping the paper. Maybe my sister was right and being alone was messing with me.

Tina walked in just then, and I welcomed the reprieve from my fantasy about the woman who couldn't stand me. I set my notes aside and gave her the good news about the baby.

Chapter 5

I TOOK THE exit leading toward the venue, listening to my friend Kat's voice filling the car. "So, she agreed to be your mentor?"

That discussion with Gretchen had been grueling, but I thought I'd held my own until she asked me what I was willing to sacrifice to be a top attorney. "Anything," I'd said. I'd watched her unmoving expression and rushed to explain. "I know you don't like the wedding gig, but I'll be done by the end of summer, and I bill more hours than anyone at my level. I am one hundred percent committed."

"She agreed," I said to Kat, glancing at the unfamiliar streets and letting my voice trail off. I'd be spending a late night back at the office after this was over, and driving all the way across town on a Tuesday was not helping the mood I'd been in since that morning when Penny called me.

"Why do you say it like that?"

"Like what?"

"Like you're not sure what the word 'agreed' means."

I'd been distracted thinking about tonight and having to work with the dude-bro after all since Penny was in Texas. "I had a run-in with this jackass I have to work with, and it turns out he's buddy-buddy with Gretchen."

"Mommy! Mommy! Mommy!" Ethan's little voice interrupting made me smile despite the notes of exasperation in Kat's exhale. "I need juice!"

I bit my tongue when he said his dad told him she was better at pouring it. Kat had married an asshole, and I'd stopped bringing it up a long time ago. She was one of many examples I had of amazing women settling for guys who didn't deserve them. Our friend Britta was the exception, but the world wasn't filled with guys like Wes just waiting to be wonderful. My GPS led me to the library, and ahead I saw an SUV with California plates that I assumed belonged to Lear. *The world is filled with guys like that guy.*

"Sorry," she said, returning to the conversation as Ethan's voice faded away. "You're working with another lawyer who is friends with her?"

"Not a lawyer. It's for wedding stuff." I had surprised my friends when I started officiating ceremonies, especially Kat, who reminded me that I'd shared my views on how detrimental marriage could be. "A wedding planner."

"Do you have to work with them closely?"

I parked a few spots down from the SUV, popping a Life Saver from the open pack on the dashboard. "I hope not. I better go, though."

"Sure. Oh! While you're on the phone, can you still fly up for Britta's bridal shower?"

I scrolled through my phone, trying to remember if I'd booked a flight, because I was a horrible friend who had forgotten about her best friend's bridal shower. "Yes, I'll forward you my flight plans."

After we hung up, I gripped the steering wheel and took a few deep breaths. My search had turned up little—Lear Campbell had been an event planner for a football team and lived on the West Coast since graduating high school. I didn't see any red flags, so all

I had to go on was the pull I'd felt to shoulder-check him the first two times we'd met and the oddly sexy curve of his cocky grin, which kept my thoughts wandering.

INSIDE, THE COUPLE and their guests mingled. The library was old, with personality and history covering every surface like a fine dust. I breathed in the scent, so familiar from childhood. I didn't have time to read much anymore, but I'd spent every Saturday morning in the library near our house as a kid, finding new books and sneaking into the adult section when I thought I could get away with it. Some of my tension from the car faded with the smell of books. I saw the bride and groom, an older couple who were both marrying for the second time. This was one Penny had talked me into.

Fishing the ceremony binder from my bag, I walked toward them. I'd done my research, and officiants didn't usually spend much time, if any, at the rehearsals, but I didn't like the idea of leaving anything to chance. Penny and I had figured it out quickly, the good balance of me having control over things while she still kept things moving. I liked the time to get my couple on the same page. Veronica and Trevor were like sitcom parents—both librarians, and they'd been easy to work with. I was looking forward to their wedding, which definitely wasn't true for every one I had agreed to do.

"Hey, it's the lawyer I like the most!" Trevor reached out for my hand and smiled widely.

"I'm the only lawyer you like," I joked, volleying back. "Are you two ready?"

Veronica wrapped an arm around her fiancé's waist and rolled her eyes. "We could have been done with this months ago with a quick ceremony at the courthouse."

"I wasn't going to face the wrath of my daughters," Trevor said, motioning across the room to his three daughters, all in their early twenties, who huddled together around . . . *him.*

One woman touched his arm, giggling, and the other two stood close, which he didn't seem to mind. *Typical.*

Lear said something to the three women and they all laughed, then he stepped between them, striding toward us.

"And we heard Penny's good news," Veronica continued. I realized I hadn't been listening, focused instead on Lear's shameless flirting.

"Oh," I said, shifting my gaze back. "Yes! Wonderful news."

"Hi, RJ." Lear gave me the same smile he'd been giving the daughters, and I returned it with a tight grin. "Okay, you two," he said, turning to the couple. "You ready?"

I prickled. This was a rehearsal for the ceremony, and usually I led things.

"Obviously I'm stepping in late with Penny's absence, but she tells me RJ is an absolute pro." He flashed another smile my way, and my annoyance faded.

It was possible I was being too hard on him. We hadn't worked together before and he didn't know how this went, but his compliment was kind and maybe he'd back up and just let me take over.

"Thanks." I opened the ceremony booklet. "Before we start—"

"Actually," he said, "let's head up front. Easier to get everyone's attention from there." He motioned toward the space that would serve as the altar, and Veronica and Trevor nodded, following him.

Um . . . I was in the middle of a sentence.

Lear turned to me with a sheepish look and an apologetic smile. "Sorry, didn't mean to interrupt, just wanted to move them before you got going."

"Sure. I usually like to check in with the couple on a few things before everyone is involved."

"Sorry about that," he said, returning a wave and smile from one of Trevor's daughters walking by. "But we can do it up there, right?"

He's Gretchen's friend. He's Gretchen's friend. "Sure."

The wedding party was small and, as expected, everyone gathered around as soon as the couple made it to the front. I made a note in the book to adjust my plan without the early check-in. "Okay," I said, "let's get this show started. First things first, where—"

"Thanks, RJ. Can we start with a few introductions, so we know who is who? Carolyn mentioned you don't all know each other."

The tallest of Trevor's daughters, a lithe redhead, beamed at the attention, batting her eyes at the wedding planner, who was quickly becoming my least favorite person. I'd been an attorney for a long time and was on social media, so that was a significant designation.

I tightened my grip on the ceremony binder. "Yes, that's where I was heading."

"Great!" He motioned to the group and, I swear, Trevor's daughters all winked at him in sync. "Why don't you begin?"

He's Gretchen's friend. He's Gretchen's friend. As predicted, with no guidance for introductions, every person took far longer to introduce themselves than needed, and Lear periodically and subtly checked his watch. I gave him a pointed stare, which I was sure he missed. As the last person wound down, I stepped forward, physically taking over the space. "Wonderful. Now, I'd like to line everyone up so you know where you're standing."

I was sure I'd get an interruption from Lear, so I didn't pause before guiding Veronica and Trevor to their places.

"Aren't we going to practice walking in?" One of the other daughters raised a hand, directing the question to Lear. "Lear, we really are lost on who walks when."

Your dad talks about you a lot and I know you're earning a graduate degree in physics from MIT. I seriously doubt you're flummoxed by taking turns walking in a line.

"That's not a bad idea. Why don't we begin with the processional, RJ?"

"This works better," I said with a forced smile.

"Please? I'll feel so much better if I know how this part works." Violet spoke to Lear again, a hand on his biceps, and a few others around them nodded, murmuring agreement.

"This way they can practice coming down the aisle and knowing where to go at the same time. Win-win," he said to me as if he'd just figured out the secret to doing this and was ready to educate me. I was about to give myself the same refrain I had been: *He's Gretchen's friend. He's—*

"Everyone, gather at the back. I'll get you organized."

He's dead to me.

By the time everyone moved to the back of the space, we'd wasted another few minutes, and once Lear had everyone organized to practice walking in, time was running shorter, especially because I had to place each person at the front of the room, instead of them knowing where to go as I'd planned. Luckily, my "colleague" did not comment on the placement up front. If he had, I might have laid hands on him.

"Once everyone is in place, I'll give a few remarks," I said when everyone was finally in their places. I glanced at Lear, who stood watching from the aisle. For once, he was quiet and deferent, looking at his tablet and following along as I walked the couple through the vows, the exchange of rings, and the readings. I was in the homestretch, already calculating how late I'd end up being in the office as we ran long.

"RJ, do we need to run through the beginning again?" Veronica eyed the aisle.

"I'd say so. It's always good to practice one more time."

"Love it, but we're getting very close to when you should head to dinner," Lear said, clapping his hands and glancing at his watch unnecessarily. "Since you have others meeting you there, is everyone okay with the one walk-through?"

"I think we'll be fine," the daughters all chimed in, along with a chorus of voices.

Veronica looked unsure, and I stepped forward. "It won't take long. Let's practice one more—"

"So, everyone is good? Let's head out." Lear nodded toward the exit, and people fell out of line.

Something I perfected at a young age was camouflaging my resting bitch face. It came in handy with juries and when I spent any time with my ex's family, but the skill wasn't so honed that I could do much about the active version. I patted Veronica's arm. "Is there anything else you two want to talk through? They will wait for you." I shot a glance across the room to where Trevor's daughters again surrounded Lear, each of them somehow with a hand on him. That was fine, but he was lapping it up. *Like a dog.*

"It'll be fine," she reassured me. "They'll get it right or they won't—certainly wouldn't be the first time something didn't go as planned." She and Trevor shared a knowing smile and laughed together at their inside joke. The syncopation of their laugh struck me—they were so in tune. I just smiled. After going over a few last-minute things, they headed for the exit with their families.

"That went well," Lear said, clapping his hands together after getting them on their way. He looked like a cheerleader when he did that, and I always expected a head nod and loud "Ready? Okay!" to follow the movement.

I slid the binder holding the ceremony back into my bag after making a few notes in the margins. "Mm," I said, looking into the bag instead of at him. Reason and self-preservation were still trying to hold me back. *He's close with Gretchen. It's his first time doing this.*

"Penny said she rarely steps in much for the rehearsals, but I think us tag-teaming went well."

I paused, a slow blink kicking in. "So, she told you to step back and let me run things?"

"Yeah," he said, gathering a few things and glancing around the room, a half smile on his face. "But that's not really my style. I like to have my hands in things, you know?"

I stared at him. The smile created a dimple in his left cheek, and it stayed for the few moments before he realized I wasn't happy.

"What? Did I do something wrong?"

"One, I don't care where you like your hands to be." I ticked off the items on my fingers. "Two, you talked over me the entire night."

"What? No. We just jumped in at the same time a few times."

I stared at him again, a look my friends called my lawyering stare.

He held it for a moment longer than I was used to people withstanding but cut his eyes away.

"I don't enjoy 'tag-teaming.'" I added finger quotes to the phrase. "Please make note for future reference. As Penny told you, I prefer to run this part, since it relates to the ceremony."

"My fault," he said, holding his palms out to me, his half smile returning, like his charm would disarm me. "Mea culpa. Won't happen again."

"Good." I slung my bag over my shoulder, ready to head back to the office. I hadn't expected him to keep talking.

"But you have to admit it worked. I mean, we stayed on time and no one got too bored."

I ignored him, taking a few steps toward the exit, but he followed, his stride longer than mine, so we reached the doors to the space at the same time.

"It looks like we've got a lot of weddings to do while Penny's out, so it'll be good for us to figure out a give-and-take."

I turned on my heel, pausing at the door he held open. "There won't be give-and-take. I have a way I do things to best serve the couples. I run the ceremony. You're on top of all the other parts, but I'm on this, like Penny told you."

The smile fell off his face, and I stood with my hand resting on the door. "Whoa. Calm down. I understand."

I rolled my eyes and stepped out into the hall. "Good."

My well-timed and pointed exit was perfect, except for my stumble when I ran into one of Trevor's daughters just outside the door. I gave her a tight smile and headed for the parking lot.

Chapter 6

LEAR

WHAT THE HELL just happened? I stared at the door as RJ stormed out. Her scent—something sweet and enticing—lingered behind her. I rested my fist on the door frame, replaying the quick exchange in my head.

"Lear?"

My head shot up at the high voice. Trevor's daughter, the youngest, stepped tentatively toward me, tucking her hair behind her ear. *What's this one's name? Maybe Megan?* "Hey. Can I help you with something else?"

She glanced away and then back, sinking her teeth into her lower lip. "Actually, I'm hoping you can save me?" She stepped closer, draping a hand across my forearm, her fingers sliding against my skin in a way that left little question of her flirtation. "My car won't start."

I glanced over her shoulder, seeing RJ push through the exit. I dragged my eyes back to the woman in front of me, remembering to turn on the charm, and gave her a smile. "Sorry. Do you need a jump start?"

She shook her head, not moving her hand away. "I don't want to be late for my dad's dinner. Can you just give me a ride? I could call for a Lyft if you're busy, but I thought I'd ask."

I inhaled again, trying to place the scent RJ had left in the air, annoyed I cared, because her one-eighty from working with me to going off on me had left me unsteady, a feeling I wasn't fond of. I glanced at my watch and realized Megan was right—time was running short. "Sure," I said, remembering I was representing Penny. I slung my messenger bag higher on my shoulder and stepped back, motioning for her to lead the way.

Megan's arm brushed against mine a few times as we walked, and it was a few too many times to be completely accidental.

"Excited for tomorrow?" I held the door for her as we walked into the parking lot.

"Definitely! Veronica is a peach and Dad is really happy."

She was cute and perky, with a great smile. She and her sisters had stayed close to me all night. They were nice, funny, and there were worse people to be surrounded by at work. "It will be a good day," I said, holding the door for her again once we reached my SUV.

She flashed me another smile before I could close the door and walk to the driver's side. "I know it will. You seem to have such a good handle on everything."

Right? I handled all of that. RJ doesn't know what she's talking about. She just doesn't like me.

"I overheard that woman laying into you, which was totally out of line, if you ask me." When I closed my own door, she angled her body toward me, crossing her legs and flashing a lot of smooth, tan thigh. "You were great."

"Thank you," I said, pulling out of the parking lot, unease creeping through me as I thought through what RJ had said. "I appreciate you saying that." I eased into traffic and turned left. The route to the restaurant location in this older part of town came back to me like I'd never left, even though the rest of the town had grown and changed. My uncle Harold and aunt Bette had taken us to that restaurant all the time, saying their mashed potatoes were worth the drive.

"You really took charge," she said, angling even farther toward me, resting a hand over mine on the gearshift. "I appreciate a man who's comfortable taking charge."

My gaze shot to her as I hit the brakes at a red light. She looked up at me through heavily coated eyelashes.

She had big blue eyes with blond hair that fell around her shoulders. She was attractive, and her soft hand on mine made me realize how long it had been since someone had touched me.

I swallowed and pulled my hand from the gearshift, pointing to the restaurant in the distance. "Here?"

She nodded, dragging a manicured finger across her collarbone. "I'm serious, too. That woman was out of line. She was so uptight, and I don't remember you talking over her once."

"I appreciate it, but RJ is great." That was a lie—I had no idea how she was, but I wanted to shut this down, and something about her judging RJ rankled me. "We're new to working together, so just figuring out the kinks. I'm sure I talked over her a few times."

I pulled toward the restaurant, pleading with whoever was in charge of such things that the three stoplights ahead would stay green.

"Are you free later?" She returned her hand to mine, grazing her fingertips over my forearm. "You're attractive and there's no sense not being direct. Carpe diem."

Direct. RJ's face popped into my head, making me angry at the memory of our interactions, annoyed that she was on my mind, and curious about where she'd gone when she left the library.

I might kick myself for it later, but I wasn't tempted, despite Megan being sexy and clearly interested. Looking at her pretty face and impressive cleavage in her low-cut dress, I could imagine kissing her, going to bed with her, but I couldn't stop there—my mind fast-forwarded to lies, betrayal, and pain. "Normally, I would definitely want your number." She looked a little like Sarah, similar hair color and height, and I glanced back at the parking lot, scanning the rows of cars. *Nope. Nope. Nope.* "It's not really professional, though. I'm sure your dad would not appreciate it, and he's my client."

She pouted, pushing out her lower lip, which—upside—made her look less like Sarah, but also like a teenager. "It's not like I was going to brief him. He doesn't have to know."

I laughed uneasily, both hands resting on the steering wheel. "I'd know, but thank you for the offer."

"I get it." She winked and reached for the door handle and got out. "But . . ." She pulled a business card from her bag and scribbled on the back, all the while standing next to my open car door. "If you change your mind, I'm in town another few days."

I nodded and took the card from her. "I'll see you at the ceremony tomorrow. Good night."

She smiled over her shoulder and sauntered away, and I tossed the card on the passenger seat, waiting a respectable amount of time before getting the hell out of that parking lot. The night had been weird and awkward at every turn. *Not every turn. Just the ones involving women.*

As if summoned by my innermost thoughts, my phone buzzed, and I tapped the Bluetooth icon on the screen to answer. "Stop checking up on me."

"Then stop insisting you're fine all the time," Caitlin huffed into the phone, the background noise echoing around her.

"Are you in that parking garage?" It was connected to the hospital and there was security, but I'd never liked her walking there alone.

"Calm down. It's not even dark here." She called out something, holding the phone away, and I rolled my eyes. She was always in work mode. "How'd your first night as the new Penny go?"

"It was f—"

"If you say fine, I'll make it look like an accident. You know I can."

I laughed, merging onto the interstate, relief buoying my mood as I put more distance between me and Megan and RJ. "It was okay. Is that better?"

She let my joke hang, and I heard the ding of her car door opening and the shift from her phone to Bluetooth. "Oh, keep going. I'm just deciding where to inject the needle."

"I hear between the toes is good."

"True. So what happened?"

"Well, the groom's daughter propositioned me and I got into it with the officiant."

"Did you take the daughter up on it?"

"No." I glanced at the business card sitting faceup on the seat. Megan was some kind of sales consultant. I picked up the card, glancing closer. The header across the top read *Pleasure Crafts Unlimited*. "Maybe I should have, though. It looks like she sells Jet Skis or something. Maybe she could hook me up."

"Jet Skis?"

"Some place called Pleasure Crafts Unlimited."

She cackled into the phone, her voice filling my car. "Brother, you should have taken her up on the offer, but not to get a ride on a Jet Ski. That's a sex toy company."

I shot my gaze to the card again, reconciling that extra information and coughing out the words. "Why do you know that?"

"They make fantastic vibrators," she said, still laughing.

"Don't say shit like that to me. I don't want to know about your toys."

"You asked. Anyway, why did you turn her down?"

"I don't know. Wasn't feeling it?" I slowed, traffic stopped ahead of me. "She looked a lot like Sarah. I don't know."

"Lear . . ."

"Don't," I muttered.

For once, she listened and shifted gears. "Add to that you got into a fistfight with a minister? You're really not batting a thousand tonight."

"I didn't get into a fistfight with a minister. Just got told off by the officiant. She said I talked over her and undermined her or whatever."

"Did you?"

"Did I what?"

"Did you want to hear more about the vibrators? What do you think I meant? Did you talk over her?"

I thought back through the evening, replaying the events of the night. "Maybe a few times, but that's no reason to get bent out of shape. I was just keeping things moving. That's not a crime."

"Did she kick your ass?"

"A little, yeah."

"Good. Don't talk over women. We don't like it and it happens at work all the time."

"How do you know? She's not a doctor."

"It doesn't matter," she said, and I knew she was rolling her eyes. "Have I taught you nothing? Women deal with that all the time, everywhere. I'm glad she told you off."

"You would be." The traffic jam finally opened up, and I could hit the gas again. I chewed on the inside of my cheek, weighing my sister's words and looking at the rehearsal from that perspective. "Anyway, tonight aside, she's unpleasant, like she always needs to be right."

"That sounds familiar. Always needing to be right is one of your less charming flaws, of which there are many."

The desire to say "I know you are but what am I?" was always my signal to end a conversation with my sister, and I let her comment hang in the air.

"You're going to hang up on me, aren't you?"

"No, let's talk all night. I love this conversation."

"Apologize and don't do it again." I missed earning her exasperated sighs in person. Not that I didn't get them over the phone all the time. "Make it right and stop being a dick. You get along with everyone, like, compulsively. I know you must know how to apologize."

Chapter 7

RJ

"WHAT DO YOU think?" Britta asked. Her face took up the screen as she examined me closely, her voice from the speaker on my phone filling the dressing room like she was right in front of me.

"It's . . . something." The dress was Barbie pink with a halter neckline and a long, flowing skirt. I turned from side to side, but it didn't get less pink with any new angle.

"I like pink," she said with an eye roll. "It looks good on you, and I'm not letting you wear all black to my wedding."

My tablet dinged as Kat entered the call, her trademark upbeat expression slipping when the video connected and she could see the screen. "Sorry I'm late. Wow, Britt . . . that dress is . . . pink."

"I like pink! What do you two have against this color? All the bridesmaids can pull it off."

I ran a fingertip over the beading that lined the bodice. Britta was getting married early in the fall to her former-CEO-turned-PE-teacher fiancé. I was officiating, but she told me she didn't want me in black, which brought me to a dress shop during my lunch break on the Thursday the week after Trevor and Veronica's wedding.

"Oh, we'd help each other pull it off. It would be in order to throw it on the floor, but . . ." I shook my head. "I'll wear whatever you tell me to, but if you want my opinion, this is thumbs-down."

Kat nodded, eating a sandwich. She was on her lunch break at school, where she taught first grade. Brightly colored posters filled the background of her screen. Ever the peacekeeper, she added, "You're right, though. The color would look okay on everyone."

I turned, reaching a hand behind me to unzip the gown, which gave me a fresh view in the mirror of the layers and layers of cotton candy fabric surrounding me. The move to North Carolina was the right one professionally, maybe personally, too, but I missed being in the same room as those two. Kat would clap at every gown and Britta would make jokes while I was in my underwear changing. I missed them and I hadn't made time to make new friends locally. As I caught the zipper between my fingers and pulled it down, my expression frowned back at me in the mirror, and I shook it away. "Anyway, you haven't picked a dress yet. Why do we have to already?"

"I'm waiting until you come to visit. Stop whining and try the next one." Britta pointed at the wall where three dresses hung on decorative hooks that read *I Do* and *True Love* on the knobs.

I rolled my eyes at the store's cheesy hardware. "Yes, ma'am," I said, pulling a tea-length dress off the hanger, taffeta flowing from the waist in waves.

"How's work going, RJ? I never hear from you anymore!" Kat said as I was pulling the dress over my head with my hands poking out the top. I wasn't sure the bodice would make it over my hips, and that method felt safer until I had to work it down as my best friends laughed from their seats seven hundred miles away.

"Not bad. Busy." I twisted in circles, letting the skirt of the dress fan out. The soft peach color reminded me of summer and drinking fruity drinks on the patio at our favorite Puerto Rican restaurant back in Humboldt Park. "I like this one."

Britta cocked her head to the side. "Hmm. I thought I'd like it more, but isn't it kind of . . . young?"

"Well, yes." I placed a hand on my hip and turned to the tablet, where they both looked back at me. "The fluffy peach dress you asked me to try would appeal to a seven-year-old with a doll collection, but were you expecting something with this much taffeta to look some other way?" I glanced at myself in the mirror again, stifling the urge to twirl. I liked my reputation as the tough one in the group. I proudly wore black. It gave people the impression you weren't to be fucked with. In the end, my ex complained I wore too much black, that it was too severe. He did this unironically while dressed in dark suits. "I like it."

"You just never go for things like that," Kat said diplomatically. "It doesn't feel right for you."

I glanced away from my friends, facing the wall where the other dress hung. I didn't like that Kat's words evoked my ex, and I shrugged, unzipping the dress.

"It's cute on you, though," Britt said, backtracking. "Just . . . not the right one."

"No worries," I said, my back to them, pushing the uncomfortable thought away. I traced my fingertips over the taffeta as I hung the dress back on the hanger. I'd stopped buying pink years ago in favor of power colors, bold reds or blues to go with my closet full of black and gray.

Kat began pulling baby carrots from a small container, which reminded me I hadn't eaten anything since a bagel at eight. "Have things calmed down since the thing?"

The thing. The thing was turning out to be an albatross around the neck of my career. The *thing* was being swept away in the moment of the proposal I'd witnessed and the hurried wedding in the park. "Some of the press cooled off, and I'm working through this summer with multiple weddings, but then I'm done."

"It's so romantic," Kat said. "Getting to stand with people on their wedding day and help them declare their love."

"Mostly it's attempting to not roll my eyes when someone quotes song lyrics in their vows, because the photographer might catch it." I wrestled the fluffy green dress into submission and stepped into it. "But I know half of those couples will be in my office in a few years, unable to stand each other. It's hard to get too invested in love stories."

"Some love stories are real," Kat said, glancing at her ring finger.

I bit my lip. Kat's husband didn't cheat. He wasn't cruel, but he made her so unhappy. He never seemed to actually see her. I skirted it, though, not wanting to upset her. "I'm sure your love stories are real. Everyone else's . . ." I tipped my hand back and forth. "Doubtable."

"You're going to fall in love one day and have to eat those words," Britta said.

"I will never be hungry enough to make that meal worth it." I zipped the last dress up the side. It was lime green with little pink flowers, and I glowered at the camera. "You've got to be kidding me."

"It's . . . kind of cute," Kat said, a hitch in her voice.

"The flowers make a heart on the bodice, Britt." I was already unzipping it. "There is a limit to what I will do for you."

She laughed. I loved my friend's laugh, even through the phone, and my heart hurt at missing them both.

"As for falling in love, even if I wanted to, I don't have time to meet anyone. Work is my number one priority and I'm busy with the wedding stuff until the end of the summer. It's not like I'm going to meet anyone doing that."

THE RECEPTIONIST FLAGGED me as I walked into our offices. "RJ. You have a delivery."

I smiled at her, glancing between the woman and the response

I'd been crafting to an email on my phone. "Oh, those documents from Schuyler Williams?"

Patty beamed, glee on her face despite her hushed tone. "You got flowers!"

I abandoned the email. "From who?"

Patty shrugged, looking left and then right, lowering her voice further. "Not sure. I was on my break when they came, but they're in your office. Are you seeing someone? Jane said the man who brought them by was incredibly good looking, and he brought them himself. Very nice touch."

I racked my brain. "Maybe it was a client."

She shook her head. "I don't think so." Patty raised her eyebrows suggestively. "He left a card, but good on you, girl." She winked and smiled widely before returning to her regular staid expression and straight posture. "So many of you lawyers don't make time for dating."

I was thinking Jane must have made a mistake and that it was a shame I'd missed the good-looking delivery man, and was also debating if I wanted to give Tinder another try. I could manage things myself, but sometimes it was nice to have a second pair of hands. Something about putting Lear Campbell in his place the week before left a little pep in my step, and I felt an urge to pounce on something, more specifically someone. I'd even fantasized once about pouncing on him, provided he didn't talk. During the wedding, he'd looked good in a dark blue suit. My cheeks flushed as I passed the conference room. *You're a skilled attorney. Stop daydreaming about hate sex with a wedding planner.*

My assistant, Todd, approached before I got to my door. "Glad I caught you. Gretchen wants you in the conference room ASAP." Todd didn't exactly cower when Gretchen spoke, but I think he would have if his suit allowed more flexibility for him to curl into a ball. I handed him the things I'd been holding, asking him to put them in my office, and walked toward the meeting, a notepad in hand.

When I walked in, Gretchen nodded to me and motioned to an open seat across from her. "This one is big. Have a seat."

IT WAS AFTER dark when I finally got back to my desk after hours spent strategizing with Gretchen and the rest of the team. One of the wealthiest and most influential couples in the southeast was splitting, and tech billionaire Dina Mayfield had hired us. Gretchen had said this was big, but it wasn't big, it was career-making. The kind of complicated, high-stakes case I'd always wanted to work. Besides the couple's assets, which were many, their stockholders around the world would be nervous if word of their split got out, and their charitable foundation could suffer.

I fell into my desk chair and kicked off my heels under my desk, eyeing the bouquet. Sitting on the cluttered space was a vase filled with white and yellow flowers—daisies, lilies, and carnations. Despite the late hour and my utter exhaustion, they brightened the room. I traced a finger along the delicate petal of a carnation. They'd always been my favorites. When I was a kid, my dad would send Mom roses to apologize for some careless thing or another he'd done. They'd always be fresh and pretty and then wilt within days, much like his resolve to not disappoint her again. Carnations, though . . . they lasted a long time. After he left and Mom got on her feet, she opened her own flower shop, and I'd spent all my free time surrounded by every combination of flower. I stroked a petal of a lily. I liked this combination.

There was a card in one of those plastic holders, but I tried one last time to guess who might have sent them before I plucked it from the bouquet.

Ms. Brooks,

I'm sorry we got off on the wrong foot. It was my fault and I apologize for my rude behavior. I will do better in the future to show you the respect you deserve.

Can we start over?

Sincerely,

Lear Campbell

I slid my finger over the card and appreciated how the loopy handwriting was almost comically fanciful. I smiled despite myself, reconciling the loops over the *i*'s with the man's tough-guy schtick, with his kind of perfectly trimmed scruff and sleeves rolled up on those impressive forearms. I sat back in my chair and sighed. It was after nine and I still had work to do. I didn't need to be sitting here mooning over a dude-bro wedding planner's forearms, a dude-bro wedding planner I didn't even like.

I rested the card against the vase and opened my email, clicking through the most pressing messages. My eyes drifted to the loopy handwriting and my mind to the forearms and the stretch of Lear's large hands.

Shit. I needed to shut those thoughts down.

Chapter 8

LEAR

"THERE'S THAT BOY of mine." Uncle Harold waved from his porch as I stepped out of my car in his driveway. "Been waitin' for you to get your tail out here."

I waved back, the gravel under my feet giving me a weird feeling of being twelve again and spending the weekend at Harold and Aunt Bette's place, or being a teenager and figuring out the new rules when we moved in with them. I felt the tension in my shoulders begin to dissipate, being home. "Sorry it took me so long," I said, leaning down to give him a quick hug. He always pulled me close and mussed my hair or kissed my cheek.

"You look good, son. I like that car." He motioned to the seat next to him and then returned to tossing birdseed into the yard, where a cadre of birds pecked eagerly on the grass.

I eyed the almost-new SUV with the great safety rating and lots of room. "Thanks. It's alright." I reached into the bag next to him and took a handful of birdseed, settling into the seat and leaning back.

"Hm." He nodded in approval, and we sat in silence.

The sun hung low in the afternoon sky. The light diffused across the mountains, peeking through the trees at the top of the ridge behind his house. A tire swing that had been ancient when I was a kid hung from the massive oak tree. Harold lived alone now, after Aunt Bette died a few years earlier. I'd only been by a couple times since moving back. Something Penny and my sister had let me know in no uncertain terms was not cool. They were right, but Harold didn't know everything that had happened in California, and I hadn't wanted him to see how much my life had fallen apart.

"How's Penny?"

"She's good," I said, reaching for my phone. We'd gotten Uncle Harold a smartphone a few years earlier. As far as I could tell, he used it as a paperweight. I handed him mine, where a few photos of newborn Connor were stored. "The baby is doing better every day."

"What a face," he said, a smile lighting up his eyes. "I tell you, that sure is a good-looking baby. Those two'll be wonderful parents."

"Yeah," I said, glancing at the road winding up the hill. "They already are, I think."

Harold nodded, handing the phone back to me. "What about you?"

"Me?" I reached into the bag of birdseed again, tossing some to the spot to my right where a little cardinal pecked around. "Happy to be an uncle or second cousin once removed or whatever I am to the kid." I tried to ignore the way my chest felt hollow at his question and my stomach clenched at my answer.

We watched the birds again, the sounds of the evening filling the air so I didn't have to talk. The distant whirs of the highway were muted by the breeze blowing through the trees and crickets beginning their chirrups. Harold didn't look at me when he spoke this time.

"You doing good?"

"Oh," I said, relieved at the general question. "Sure. Yeah. I'm good."

"Tell me about the job."

Relief colored the edges of my mood and I pictured RJ Brooks. "It's alright. Little different from my last one for sure."

The birdseed bounced off the concrete and into the grass. "I never asked you what happened there."

My tongue was too big for my mouth and uneasiness roiled through me, that same feeling I had in high school when I'd messed up on a test. "You didn't."

A pickup truck rumbled down the road, the driver waving to Uncle Harold out the window. That kind of one-handed, smileless wave I imagined was common of neighbors across the country, like pleasantries weren't needed, just the acknowledgment of seeing and being seen. I'd never exactly fit in when my sister and I came to live there—I was too something and not enough something else, and everyone just kind of left me alone. That was before Penny gave me the advice for fitting in. After that, I got the waves. The literal ones in Sybel and the figurative ones elsewhere, though I wasn't sure I always felt really seen.

Uncle Harold had never treated me like I didn't fit in, just kissed my head and told me to treat people right. "I got fired," I said, sinking into my seat.

"Hm." He tossed a sunflower seed across the porch to where a more tentative bird paced, never getting close to us. "What did you do?"

That uneasy feeling returned. "A guy was being inappropriate to one of the waitstaff at a team event. Making comments, hitting on her, and I got into it with him."

"Doesn't seem like the type o' thing you'd be fired for."

I tossed the last of the seed in my hand into the grass and shoved my hands into my pockets. I hadn't heard what the guy said, but I remembered the look on the woman's face—irritation, frustration, annoyance—and the way she initially stepped back from him. They were the only two on that part of the veranda and she probably saw that kind of thing a lot, had to get used to leering assholes saying what they wanted and needing to keep her mouth shut to keep her job. Maybe that was why I stepped between them: the entitlement on his face, like he had the right. Maybe it was me being hungover and sleep deprived for months, too. How else to explain why I not only stepped between them, telling him the behavior was inappropriate, but then punched him in the jaw when he waved me off?

I glanced up at the sky where the colors tipped from blue to the faintest orange. "Guy is the team's star defensive end." I scratched my jaw. The punch I landed did little except surprise him before he calmly rolled up his sleeve and beat the hell out of me. My eye was still swollen shut and my lip split when they fired me.

"I see." Harold picked at a string on his jacket. "Seems the kind of thing that needed doing, though."

"The team didn't seem to think so," I answered Harold. I'd intervened all the time, getting the staff member out of the situation, calmly reminding the player or coach that social and traditional media were everywhere. Calling a star player a "lecherous fucking creep" whose "dick was so inadequate, he had to prey on servers trying to do their jobs and put up with his BS to keep those jobs" was decidedly outside of what I knew would be effective. It was the first time I'd ever actually punched someone, and I hadn't been prepared for the pain in my hand. Turns out, choosing a six-foot-four, three-hundred-pound professional athlete for your first physical altercation is ill advised.

Harold nodded again. "Not like you, though. The fightin'." A breeze blew the white hair around his ears, the rest of his head covered with a purple Western Carolina University baseball cap. "That girl of yours had you all twisted up, huh?"

I swallowed, remembering the flurry of texts from Sarah when someone told her, the way I'd wanted to toss my phone across the room every time it chirped with another message I'd have to delete because I couldn't bring myself to block her number. "Yeah, I guess."

"You gettin' yourself untwisted?"

I pictured RJ Brooks again, the way she'd looked at me when we bickered, the way she smiled when she was talking to someone else. "I'm trying."

Chapter 9

RJ

A SLIGHT BREEZE cut through the warm evening. I'd spent the entire day in the office, despite the Memorial Day holiday, and inhaled the fresh air as I walked from the parking lot toward the venue. The art museum's outdoor event space was modern, with white stone and concrete slabs fitting together at sharp angles. As I stepped into the space, I couldn't help but look around in awe. They'd strung overhead twinkle lights, and tasteful white ribbon lined the chairs leading toward an arched altar covered in flowers. White flowers, blocked slightly by Lear, who was standing in front of them talking into a phone with an expression that was clearly *I want to kill you but I can't lose my cool.*

"I don't care that it's a holiday. Your staff were two hours late and delivered the wrong flowers. How are you going to fix this?" He stepped aside, still speaking into the phone, and suddenly his expression made sense. The altar was covered with flowers . . . for a funeral. A large wreath held a banner reading *Gone but not forgotten,* and flowers on stands lingered on the periphery of the altar, along with a spray of roses, clearly meant to top a coffin, with calla lilies and greenery flowing from the middle.

Lear's cool demeanor had formally cracked, and he was all but hissing into the phone. "So, your staff mistook your instructions to create and deliver a wedding package for creating and delivering a funeral package and you can't do anything about it?" I examined the cut of his jaw as he nodded along with the response, the tense way he held his face, as if the person on the other end of the line could see it. I had a grudging admiration for others who could hold their cool. "A computer error. Are you kidding me?"

I glanced toward the back of the space, seeing Lear's tense, pacing body in my periphery. Penny's assistant, Tina, walked up the aisle toward us, eyeing the flowers and flashing a small smile of greeting to me. "Well, it's been a day," she said under her breath. "They dropped them off without saying anything. Haven't told the couple yet."

"Believe me, a full refund is only the beginning of your apology for this," Lear said into the phone before hanging up, the press of his finger against the icon on his phone lacking the impact he seemed to want. He added a "Fuck" under his breath for good measure before he caught my eyes. "Ms. Brooks. Sorry. I didn't see you."

"Well, what's the plan?" Tina ran a hand down the side of a cross made of roses, a tasteful *Rest in Peace* ribbon across the front.

"We have to get rid of these." He motioned to where a few potted flowering plants sat. "Maybe these can stay . . ." He ran a hand through his hair and let out a long breath before checking his watch. "Tina, I'll need you to get to the reception site . . . see what we can do about it, but the ceremony starts in an hour."

"We don't have a bouquet," Tina said, surveying the scene. "I think the bride is going to notice."

In that moment, it was hard to reconcile the man I'd met the first few times with the person in front of me who looked like he wanted to crawl into a hole and make a new home.

"I can help," I said, setting my bag on a chair. I stepped forward and began pulling white roses from the casket spray.

Lear and Tina looked at me, mouths open.

"My mom owns a flower shop," I said, turning back to the spray, pulling lilies and greenery along with more roses. I'd spent years behind the counter, working and learning the ins and outs of wedding flowers. Even then, I'd tell my mom and grandma the statistics on these being flowers for a wedding that didn't end in a divorce, but they always shushed me and told me I was too cynical. When my mom wasn't listening, my grandma would wink and tell me there was nothing wrong with assuming the worst as long as I could still spot the best. I slipped my fingers through the arrangement in front of me, mining it and giving in to dusty muscle memory for floral arrangement. I glanced up at Lear's cocky face. "Are you just going to stand there?"

Tina grinned and pulled up something on her tablet, reading through it. "One for the bride and three bridesmaids. Will some leftover ribbon from the chairs work?"

When I nodded, she hurried off to find it, and when I looked up, Lear was watching me intently. "You're staring. Planning to step in to do it yourself?"

"No. Sorry." He knelt, helping me free flowers from the wide arrangement. "Are you sure you know what you're doing?"

"Are you sure you want my help?"

"Yes," he said, cheeks tinted pink. "Sorry."

We worked in silence and he followed my lead, grouping roses, then adding lilies, a little greenery, and then tying it off with the ribbon Tina brought back. My mother would have sucked her teeth at the finished product, but it would work. I turned the largest bouquet in my hands, examining it from all angles. I handed it to Tina, who was delivering all of them to the bridal suite and breaking the news about the delivery.

Lear held out a hand for me as I rose to my feet, but I ignored it and stood on my own, brushing off my knees. I'd need some lotion before this ceremony started now. He'd already moved the flowering plants, the ones that didn't look exclusively like they belonged near a coffin, to the edges of the altar space, and we both looked at the wreath and the cross and the remains of the coffin spray. "Let's add a few flowers to the ribboned chairs along the aisle." He glanced over my shoulder. "If you're willing to help still, of course."

Goose bumps rose on my arms at his deferent tone. It was an improvement from the dude-bro, condescending one he'd seemed to fall into so easily in our other encounters, but it irked me. One thing I'd liked about the dude-bro was how easy he was to snap back at. "I can help."

He started grabbing the peach and red carnations from the wreath, stuffing them into his fist.

"How are we arranging them?"

"It doesn't matter, just a few in each ribbon."

I stood next to him, plucking flowers out. "Of course it matters. It still needs to look good."

"We're dismantling the well wishes for a nonexistent funeral. I'll be honest, it's not my top concern." He held up three carnations— two peach and one red—in his hand like a bouquet. "This is fine."

I arranged two carnations and bent to pull a white rose from the flower cross and a sprig of greenery from the spray on the ground. "This is better."

I wanted to grin when he gritted his teeth. *God, it's possible he might hate admitting he's wrong more than I do.*

"Fine," he said, copying my movements. "Thank you for your help."

We worked side by side for a few minutes, using the discarded floral wire to bind the flowers until we had enough to do the chairs. "I hope Tina isn't getting read the riot act," he said quietly, setting a bundle of flowers aside.

"Me, too." I finished the last twist on my floral wire and moved to the first row of chairs, wrapping the wire around the ribbon and admiring it. I heard the question in his voice, the *Should I have done it myself?*, but I didn't comment. "Tina can handle it," I said, not really sure what Tina could handle. I didn't know her well, but he made a humming sound. It made him sound vulnerable, and I stifled my instinct to tell him he should have been the one to deliver the news, because I didn't want him to feel bad.

"We only have twenty-five minutes," Lear said, his back to me.

I started on the next row of chairs. "Then you should move more quickly."

I kind of wanted him to volley something back, waited for it, but he stayed silent, moving a step up the aisle behind me, so I worked faster, stepping forward before him the next time and down the line. Back-to-back, we sped through the process, each clearly planning to win this unspoken race.

I tied off my last one and threw my hands in the air, declaring victory. "Done!"

I thought I heard him swear under his breath when I declared my win, but he didn't say anything directly to me. He was taking this professional and respectful thing too far, because it wasn't as fun to win when he wouldn't acknowledge he wanted to win. Instead, he nodded. "Thank you."

We walked back up the aisle, and he started gathering the remains of the coffin spray and setting it behind a concrete barrier out of the way. I followed with the rest of the cross and we cleared the altar. It was too quiet. "Maybe there will be a few bridesmaids you can regale with this story later."

I regretted it immediately. I didn't even know why I'd brought up that rehearsal and how he'd flirted with the groom's daughters. It wasn't like I really cared.

He dropped a heavy arrangement of purple and pink blossoms on top of the rest of the discarded flowers. "Excuse me?"

I was in it now. "I don't know if they're as keen on you as Trevor's daughters, but this could make a good story. Some women love a man with flower-arranging skills."

He looked away, scanning the venue and, again, clearly holding back what he wanted to say. "I don't flirt with women when I'm working."

"Sure." I dug through my bag for the ceremony script and began a quick read through the text. I raised one eyebrow, feeling his gaze on me. "Of course you don't."

"You know, you . . ."

"I . . . what?" I liked this better, the back-and-forth. I could win at this. Him just being distant and flatly kind was boring.

He shoved a hand in his pocket and looked at the watch on his other wrist, and I'd never wanted to make someone lose their cool more in my life. "Thank you for your help. You saved the day." With that, he turned on his heel and strode back up the aisle. One of the small bouquets I'd fastened had fallen and he dipped to pick it up, refastening it. "And I think that means I won."

Chapter 10

LEAR

TWO WEEKS LATER, I sat next to RJ, who shut her laptop where she'd been taking notes on the ceremony for Aubrey Morris and Thomas Goodman. "Is there anything else about the ceremony you'd like to talk through?"

I tapped my finger against my chair. We sat side by side, and I'd spent the better part of ninety minutes biting my tongue and letting RJ take the lead on this conversation like she wanted, even though I'd had a lot of thoughts. Penny's reminder to keep RJ happy played on a loop in my head, and I'd reminded myself twenty times to shut up like I had at the wedding with the funeral flowers. I'd never felt more grateful and annoyed with someone at the same time, especially thanks to RJ's little comment about flirting with Trevor's daughter, whose card was still somewhere in my glove compartment.

"Well," Aubrey said, raising her forefinger as if she needed to be called on, "we were thinking we wanted to have everyone dance down the aisle. Have you seen those YouTube videos?" She smiled wide and in my head I cringed—everyone had seen those videos, and I remembered laughing with Sarah, declaring we'd never do that in a hundred years, much to the relief of our close friends and family who would have been made to dance.

"Sure." I feigned interest and enthusiasm for the idea without encouraging it too much, and RJ's expression flattened, her lips moving into a straight line, her eyes unmoved.

"Well, we found this video. Honey, can you pull it up?"

Thomas pulled out his phone and fiddled with the screen, holding it up to RJ and me.

"It's this group doing the evolution of boy bands! Isn't that fun?" Aubrey beamed, her voice rising to a pitch I didn't know possible in the human vocal range. "Think of all the different dances, and it would be long enough for everyone to come down the aisle. It's totally us!"

I glanced at the four young Black men on the screen performing the multitude of songs and dance moves and had my doubts about this couple pulling it off at the last minute.

RJ chimed in before I could come up with a way to talk them out of it. "You know, those YouTube videos are cute, but it doesn't always turn out so well. Plus, you only have a week until the wedding. Can you get your wedding party in sync by then?" RJ's tone was definitive and parental and rankled me, even though she was trying to talk them out of it.

Aubrey's face fell, and Thomas placed his hand over hers. "They'd do it for us, don't you think?"

"Sure. They'll do it." Thomas patted her hand, and I noticed how RJ's eyes strayed to their supportive gesture.

"Great," I said, setting my palms on the table. "Well, let's talk logistics, then."

Aubrey's phone rang, and she excused herself.

"Lear, a moment?" RJ tapped my arm and nodded toward the hall. Since Thomas had opened an app on his phone the moment his fiancée walked away, I followed RJ and we met in Penny's conference room. She'd come from her office and wore a gray skirt that was tight enough to give me an idea of her shape. I tried not to feel too guilty about noticing or let my mind move too far from noticing to fantasizing as I wondered how my hands would fit against the curve of her hips.

She held a disposable coffee cup and a Danish, despite the hour, and she stood tall in her high heels. When we'd raced down the aisle, securing those flowers, I'd hoped the heels would slow her down. We'd never said we were racing, but since I knew I couldn't say anything, that was the only way to channel the energy she kept inspiring—this competitive, aroused, no-filter energy.

I motioned to her snack. "You do know it's seven at night and not seven in the morning?"

"I am versed on how to tell time, yes." Her voice was cool, which, oddly, was sexy as hell. "Not that you require an explanation, but I'm practically immune to caffeine at this point. I stay up late, and who can say no to a cheese Danish from Sid's?"

That comment left my mind wondering about what she got up to in the dead of night, but I tamped it down. "You're right. They're the best."

"This is a bad idea and you know it. Those two are going to pull together something foolish," she said in a hushed voice.

"Maybe, but it's what they want." I leaned against the wall, crossing my arms over my chest. "We'll make it work."

"You think it's a bad idea, too."

"Of course I do."

"I've seen that video—which of their grandmas is going to dance down the aisle to Boyz II Men's 'I'll Make Love to You,' and which of her sorority sisters is going to channel their inner New Edition?"

I chuckled, despite my desire to prove RJ wrong. "I'm a pretty good dancer. I'll help them."

She narrowed one eye.

"You don't believe me?"

She sipped her coffee. "I do not, but you should just follow along with me and I'll talk them out of it."

"No."

"Why not?"

Because I didn't want to give her the satisfaction. I didn't say that, of course, because it sounded petty and juvenile. I admired the way her shoulders squared, how her chin jutted out. "Couple wants it, we try it."

She glowered at me. "It's not like I really care, but I'm the one who has to stand in front of hundreds of people while this travesty goes down."

"I think you care. Not that I know why." *God, she's hot, especially when she's obstinate like this.*

"I don't *care.* It's not my wedding. You want your couple looking ridiculous at their own ceremony, be my guest." RJ moved to cross her arms, her eyes further narrowing and sarcasm dripping from her tone, and my body reacted like she'd said, "Go down on me right now? Be my guest!" For the briefest of moments, her eyes flicked down to my chest, and I swear her expression softened to something else. Her plump lips twitched.

"RJ?" I motioned to my face, drawing her eyes up. I imagined her getting flustered, her lips parting, giving away her secret. I'd always been with women who were careful and measured with their words, who would bite their tongue before snapping at me. RJ seemed ready to bite my head off most of the time, and that, paired with the hooded expression I saw a flash of, made me want to remove her panties with my teeth. The fantasy was short lived, though. The lip of her coffee cup caught on her blazer and coffee poured down her body. Insult to injury, her pastry fell to the floor and was immediately doused in the spilled beverage.

Yelping, she leaped backward, and her now-empty cup dropped to the tile floor in the puddle of coffee.

"Shit!" I'd jumped back, too, trying to avoid the mess.

She slid her hands down her dress, sluicing more coffee onto the floor, brushing at herself in that way someone does when they're not sure what to do with their hands. "Fuck me," she muttered and, again, my dick had no damn sense of context.

"Are you okay? Did you burn yourself?"

She held up a hand to stop me from stepping closer. "I'm fine." Her tone was frustrated, and she brushed at her skirt again, all the while muttering expletives under her breath. "I'm fine," she repeated after taking a deep breath. "Do you have paper towels or something?"

I realized I'd been standing still and also distracted by her hands moving over the wet fabric of her dress and, damn, did I wish she didn't despise me, because I'd never been that turned on by a coffee spill before. *And I just haven't gotten laid in a while.* "Yes, of course. The bathroom is down the hall," I said, pointing to the entrance of the office. "I'll clean this up."

"Thank you." RJ expressed the sentiment like she wasn't used to forming the words, at least not in my presence, and she turned on her heel.

"Oh, and, RJ?" She paused and glanced over her shoulder. I should have left well enough alone. "You're welcome to join us for the choreography planning. Do you want to dance in to 'I Want It That Way' by the Backstreet Boys or something slower?"

She didn't stop walking and held up her arm, flashing me a middle finger. Her walk was stiff—probably from the wet fabric clinging to her body, but she was clearly agitated, and I wasn't sure why I'd pushed it.

"Slow it is!" I called after her, turning to find paper towels in the small break room to clean up the coffee and the sad pastry on the floor.

Chapter 11

RJ

I POPPED THE last Life Saver from a pack into my mouth and glanced at the dry-cleaning bag hanging on the back of my door. Luckily, I'd been able to wipe down the coffee spill before any actual harm was done to the dress. Shame rose on my cheeks at the entire incident, because I'd been right about the dancing and he knew it, but I'd gotten distracted by his stupid chest, which looked extra broad and firm in the shirt he'd been wearing, and I'd always been a sucker for that. I shook my head, dragging my gaze back to my screen. *I have no time to think about Lear Campbell and his annoyingly hot body.* Of course he'd been a total asshole immediately after, giving me a hard time about the stupid dance. *And that's the memory that should be sparked from looking at the dry-cleaning bag.*

It was nearly eight and my stomach grumbled. The Life Saver wasn't going to cut it, and I should have let my assistant order me dinner when he'd offered. Now, two hours later, I was looking at another hour or two of reading, and a break to get food would just extend it. Dina and Andrew Mayfield had started Avente together, and what began as a small company supporting small-business web hosting had turned into a multinational tech powerhouse.

I hit play on the interview I'd pulled up, Dina and her husband sitting side by side a few years earlier. "We started this together.

We've been in this together our entire marriage." Her husband took her hand as if they'd done it a million times, and I tilted my head, wondering what had happened between them. It didn't really matter. We were going to make sure Dina Mayfield walked away from the marriage with as much as possible, but I was curious.

He had a serene smile. "She's always been the brains of the operation. It made so much more sense for her to be the face of the company. I have always been very happy in the background."

The interviewer continued asking questions about the scholarship foundation they'd started, one to rival the Gates Foundation, and their work helping high school students of color earn degrees. Andrew especially beamed when he talked about the program, and I made a note to look into it further. The interviewer closed by asking, "So what advice do you have for viewers about maintaining a happy marriage through the years?" I paused then, catching Dina's eyes looking so much like they wanted to roll, and Andrew's eyebrow quirking. It was a millisecond, a tiny peek into things gone wrong, but it was there.

I paused the video and rolled my shoulders, releasing some of the tension across my back. Those milliseconds added up, but sometimes one person didn't notice them. I never paid much attention to my parents' marriage—Dad screwed up, apologized; Mom forgave him; and the cycle continued until he left us both. My ex-boyfriend, Case, left, too. It wasn't as dramatic as with my dad—we weren't married, there wasn't a kid, but off he went. This case was bigger and more complex than others I'd worked on, but there was no reason it should have gotten to me, rankled me like it did. Andrew Mayfield hadn't left—the two of them had stayed together, living and working closely through their marriage, raising their children, but the milliseconds didn't lie. I hit play again.

His hand fell over Dina's again. "Advice? I think the best we ever received was that you both have to show up or nothing gets resolved."

Dina had alleged that her husband cheated, and he'd alleged the same, but everything was cloaked in secrecy, NDAs, and some history they weren't revealing. Publicly, they'd been a model couple for decades, making even me question if their love story wasn't something special. That level of public pretending wasn't uncommon when this amount of money and power was at stake. My stomach grumbled, and I paused the video. I was just hungry, that's why this case felt personal.

Before I could open an app to order something, Eric popped his head in my door. "I'm out of here. I'm going to be in trouble if I'm here any longer."

"Aww, Tyson doesn't want to be away from you?"

Eric snort-laughed. "No. I'm solo on darling daughter duty tonight. He plays some video game on Wednesday nights with his best friend."

"That's sort of adorable in a preteen way," I joked, rubbing the back of my neck.

He shrugged. "I don't get it, but they're happy. You going to be here much longer?"

I pointed at the screen, where I'd minimized the video. "Need to get through this research."

He winced. "Been there." Eric knocked twice on my door frame. "Take care of yourself!"

I gave him a wave and returned to the screen, scrolling and making notes.

"Ruthie." Eric was one of very few people who even knew my real first name, let alone who I allowed to use it. He walked back in and handed me a box. "Ran into a delivery person on my way out who said these were for you."

The box was pink with a sticker from Sid's, the bakery I went to most often when I didn't just grab something from the building's lobby.

"Pastries for dinner is a choice . . . Do you need me to bring you meat and vegetables?"

"Bite me," I said, running a finger over the box. "I didn't order these. Must be a gift. I helped the owner with a custody thing last month."

Eric nodded. "I'm out for real. Night, Ruthie."

I smiled, remembering the older woman's relieved and troubled expression when things were settled with her nephew. She'd reminded me of my grandma. My stomach growled again, and I flipped open the box. "Great timing, Mrs. Johnson," I said to my empty office. Inside were two cheese Danish, and a note was scrawled in loopy handwriting on the inside of the lid: *For RJ. Still not a meal. —Lear. P.S. Don't spill coffee on these.*

I stared at the handwriting, and the oddest sensation came over me as my lips tipped up in a smile. "Jackass," I said under my breath, inhaling the scent of one of my favorite foods second to waffles. I took a bite, letting my eyes fall closed for a moment. My frustration from working late, from embarrassing myself in front of him, even from him being a jerk, faded, and I reached for my phone.

RJ: Thank you for the Danish delivery.
Your note was so touching.

> LEAR: You're welcome.
> LEAR: I genuinely wanted to remind you to
> not pour coffee on them.

I sat back in my chair, because I should have ended the conversation there.

RJ: Noted.
RJ: To clarify, can I pour it on you?

> LEAR: I'm not the lawyer here, but I think
> that's assault.

RJ: I could make a case for mitigating circumstances.

> LEAR: What would those circumstances be?

That you'd have to take off your shirt, and what jury could fault me for that? I shook my head, because any jury vaguely conscious during the Me Too movement would surely find me at fault. I went with the next best option.

RJ: Self-defense.

> LEAR: In this imaginary scenario, I'm attacking you?

RJ: Maybe.

> LEAR: Is this your way of telling me you feel threatened by the idea of my dance moves?

I laughed, taking another bite of the Danish.

RJ: You know, I'm honestly not.

> LEAR: A little though, huh?

RJ: Not in the slightest.

> LEAR: Just threatened by my rougeish good looks, I guess.

RJ: Are you wearing rouge? I never
would have guessed—you're an artful
blender.

        LEAR: 💀 It's considered uncouth to make
        fun of typos.

RJ: All is fair in the wedding game.

        LEAR: Okay. Hey, have you been
        practicing?

He sent a GIF of New Kids on the Block performing their sig-nature Right Stuff dance, and I snorted, the sound ricocheting off the walls.

RJ: You're not as funny as you think you
are.

        LEAR: Yes I am.

RJ: Good night, Lear.

        LEAR: Good night, RJ.

I set my phone aside, taking another bite. I pulled my lower lip between my teeth, because I was still acting foolish and smiling from the stupid text exchange. I shook my head again and got back to work, determined to figure out how Dina Mayfield could walk away from this marriage with everything she wanted.

Chapter 12

LEAR

I STARED AT my watch pointedly before shifting my gaze to my phone, where the bride's text from twenty minutes earlier sat unchanged. I hadn't had anything major go wrong at a wedding since the funeral flowers, and even though I kept telling Penny to trust me, I also didn't want to disappoint her. The sun beat down, and the breeze I kept hoping for was shy at best or vindictive at worst. Either way, it was nowhere to be found. Nothing else to do, I tapped on the text thread with RJ from a couple days before. After I'd had the pastries delivered, I'd been surprised she messaged. The delivery I'd intended to be a dig seemed to open something between us.

LEAR: You'll be pleased to know the couple changed their minds on the dancing.

RJ: Disappointed?

LEAR: I was looking forward to making you eat your words even though you were still going to fake disdain.

RJ: You don't need to concern yourself
with what I fake.

LEAR: Would you ever fake it?

RJ: With you? Never.

LEAR: I promise you'd never have to. I'm
just that . . .

RJ: Annoying? Disdain-inspiring?

LEAR: I was going to say irresistible.

She hadn't responded, but now RJ strode toward me, a furrow
between her brows. Texting with her had felt flirtatious. In texts, I
was the guy she thought I was, so it was safe and like a game.

"What is going on?" RJ yanked on my arm, pulling me aside.
She looked pointedly around the courtyard filled with two hundred
of the couple's closest friends and family, the same two hundred
people who had been waiting for them to arrive for forty-five minutes.

"What do you think?" I lowered my voice. "They're late."

"People are getting restless."

I glanced over her shoulder and watched the flower girl rolling
on the floor and two ushers trying to slap each other's nuts. I sighed
and pinched the bridge of my nose. We hadn't seated anyone formally, but at a certain point, with nowhere else to go, people started
finding the chairs. I shifted my gaze back to RJ. "I'm aware people
are getting restless. What do you think I can do? She keeps telling
me they're almost here."

"Have the caterers open the bar so these people have something to do." She pointed to the reception area nearby.

I'd rolled with the flow in terms of other people my entire adult life, and the old me would have smiled, looked for a compromise, and made sure she still liked me when she walked away.

I shook my head. "No way. That would take too long, and the bride wants to start as soon as they arrive."

RJ narrowed her dark brown eyes, motioning to the crowd. Her voice was more a hiss than a whisper, but it still made parts of me take notice. "All well and good, except she left two hundred people waiting for an hour." She pulled at the neck of her simple black dress. Not that it did anything except make me want to follow her hand more than I wanted to take my next breath. The fabric clung to her skin, and a thin sheen of sweat made her chest glisten in the sunlight. "It's hot out here."

I stifled the urge to pull at my shirt because, yes, it was fucking hot, but I wouldn't give her the satisfaction. "I'm not opening the bar. They'll be here soon."

She growled, stepping closer. "You're being impossible. Just open the damn bar."

A few people sitting in the back row of chairs turned to stare at us, and I rolled my eyes. "Will you keep your voice down?" I wrapped an arm around her waist and pulled her into the shaded breezeway leading to where the reception would be held. On three sides, we were closed in, away from the eyes and ears of the guests.

"What the hell, Lear?"

"Oh, I'm sorry. Were you intending to have this conversation with the entire crowd?"

"Of course not."

"You could have fooled me with your volume."

"Are you saying I'm too loud?"

My eyes fell to her full mouth on instinct. "What?"

"How dare a woman raise her voice instead of just acquiescing to your charm," she hissed, donning a fake, waifish stance.

"I never said that, and you know it." I glanced at my watch again. "You have a job to do and so do I, and my job is to decide when to open the bar."

"Two hundred annoyed people sweating through their formal wear and an absent couple make my job hard to do. Maybe you could make both our lives easier."

"You're maddening," I said, shoving a hand in my pocket, then thinking better of it and scrubbing my jaw. "Opening the bar without food is a recipe for disaster. It's not happening, got it? It's not your call." I swiped my hand through the air, trying to hold my ground and make my point.

"I fully respect it's your role to coordinate the event, but in this case you're wrong," she muttered before meeting my eyes, hers filled with a steely resolve. "No one is going to pay attention to the ceremony if they're dehydrated and agitated."

Her condescending tone almost made me ignore how the dress covered her soft curves when she stood tall. Almost. "RJ. This may be hard to believe," I said, keeping my voice level. *I am the calm one and she'll hate that.* I patted my chest with both hands. "But I know what I'm doing here."

"You're going to have a revolt on your hands." She stepped forward, crowding me. "You," she said, raising her hands to push my chest, "are just too pigheaded to listen to a woman." Her eyes burned into mine.

"I listen to women all the time. I *happily* follow directions from women," I said, injecting a smirk into my tone. "I just don't listen to condescending, ball-busting, bossy know-it-alls like you."

She glanced around and gently pushed me close to the wall and even farther away from the guests. "I'm not bossy. I'm right."

"Maybe. Maybe not, but I don't care." We were inches apart, her palms still resting against my chest, and I hated how much I enjoyed the weight and warmth of her hands. Our gazes locked as if the first one to look away would lose some hidden struggle for dominance. I didn't care about the bar, and I couldn't imagine she did, either. This was about winning. We stared in silence as several moments ticked by and a slight breeze shifted the surrounding air. I softened my tone. *Shit, what am I even doing?* "RJ," I started, intending to apologize and de-escalate.

Her fingers tightened in my shirt. Her eyes stayed on mine, her expression shifting from annoyed to something else. If she tipped up her chin, even by an inch, our lips would be almost touching. Her palms flattened against my chest almost imperceptibly, her fingers spread over the fabric of my shirt.

"RJ," I said again, softer, not wanting to make her step back because, my God, the feel of her this close. I wanted to reach for her, to test the feel of her skin under my fingers. Her breath hitched when I took a half step toward her, and her chin tipped up. "Are you waiting for me to touch you?"

Her head whipped up, gaze sharpening like she was coming back from a powerful memory. A memory, it seemed, that was distracting. "No. You need to open the bar," she said, pressing her palm to me again.

I stiffened at her quick change in demeanor. "I'm not opening the damn—"

My phone buzzed in my pocket. The vibration made us both freeze. With her pressed so tightly, she must have felt it, too.

I caught my breath, and we pulled apart, just enough to meet each other's eyes. When it buzzed again, the vibration and sound echoed in the closed space. I pulled it from my pocket, only letting my eyes leave RJ's for a minute. It was a text from the bride. "They're going to be another fifteen minutes," I said, my voice scratchy as I tried to pull myself from the haze of that moment, which felt like it should have ended with a kiss.

RJ's hand loosened in my shirt abruptly and she stepped back, blinking furiously, one traitorous finger touching her lip before falling to her side.

She straightened her dress. Her expression started cooling to the neutral, cold one I'd gotten used to. "I'm going to tell people the wait will be a little longer." She stepped to the side and walked out of the breezeway, leaving me standing there, dumbfounded and fully aware of how incredible it felt to be that close to RJ.

Chapter 13

RJ

I WAITED FOR the call to connect, looking around the mostly empty coffee shop. I needed caffeine before heading to work on a Sunday morning. After a seventy-hour workweek focused on the case and distracted by thoughts of pressing against Lear, of wanting to kiss him, the caffeine wasn't just necessary, it was life affirming.

Britta's face filled the screen, and before she could finish her greeting, I blurted out what I'd needed to share all week. "I almost kissed him." I touched a fingertip to my lips before I could stop myself.

I pulled my fingers from my face to see Britta's eyes narrowed. "Almost kissed who?"

I hadn't stopped thinking about that moment in days, particularly how he'd felt so close to me. I'd imagined him backing me against the wall with an intoxicating blend of hard muscle and soft skin. I bit my lower lip.

"Not the hot dude-bro wedding planner," she said, eyes still narrowed in examination until they snapped open. "How did *that* happen? I thought you hated him."

I'd asked myself that a thousand times since last Saturday. "I do hate him! We were arguing like normal. He was annoying and not listening to me, but we were so close together, and he smelled so good, and then I just lost my head and I wanted to kiss him. I was about to kiss this man with two hundred people right there."

Britta's grin widened on the small screen of my phone. "So you didn't kiss, but you were close enough to? That's hot."

"It wasn't hot." Warmth rose up my chest. "I mean, it was fine," I said, schooling my expression and trying not to linger on how firm his chest had felt under my palms or how he'd pressed his tongue to the corner of his lip like he'd be good at sex. I clenched my thighs. "Maybe a little better than fine," I grumbled, still glancing around to make sure no one was nearby.

"A little better than fine?" Britta was in a park somewhere, stretching while talking to me. Her face was flushed and sweaty and she'd probably just finished a run. "It seems odd you'd be in a hurry to tell me about a slightly-more-than-adequate almost-kiss that happened a week ago."

"It was better than adequate," I said, sipping my macchiato. I lowered my voice and held the phone close. "It was hot, okay? I can't get him out of my head, and I absolutely can't let it happen again. I'm working a bunch of weddings with him this summer."

Britta laughed. "I'm still confused. What made you want to?"

I bit my lip, something unusual for me. I could usually play it cool, and I didn't enjoy feeling out of sorts. "I never would have before. He's not the kind of guy I go for."

"So, he has a job and *doesn't* live in his mom's basement until his YouTube following takes off?"

"That was one guy."

"Corey was awful, even for a booty call."

I waved my hand in front of the phone. Corey was safe—he let me call the shots, didn't demand anything, and walking away from him was as easy as sending a text and unsubscribing from his channel. "Corey was good for stress relief. Easy and uncomplicated."

"I think the word you're looking for is 'pothead.' Anyway, back to the dude-bro."

I sighed. "So, the night before, I'd had a dream about him."

She laughed. "What kind of dream?"

"You know the kind of dream." I woke grasping the ends of it, knowing only that we'd ended up in bed. In truth, I'd been seconds away from a powerful orgasm when I woke with the image of Lear's face between my legs, and I'd still been reeling from the flashbacks when I touched him in the alcove, the heat in his eyes from our argument feeling strangely erotic. I squeezed my thighs together again. "I've been under a lot of stress at work and I have a vivid imagination. It was a *detailed* dream. I think I just need to find someone to help me scratch the itch." I remembered the feel of his mouth in the dream and flushed. "There's no way Lear Campbell's that skilled in actual life, anyway."

Britta's expression changed, but before I could ask her what was wrong, I was interrupted.

"I don't know. I think I have *some* skills."

I froze at the deep voice behind me. Britta's eyes were saucers. "The guy you're talking about . . . is he tall with light brown hair? Kinda cute?"

Shit. Shit. Shit. "Yeah."

"Hi, I'm Lear," he said, waving over my shoulder. His hair was plastered to his head and some kind of workout shirt covered the expanse of his chest and shoulders.

Britta looked between him and me on the screen. I had AirPods in, so he couldn't hear her, but she waved back.

"I gotta go, Britt."

"Good luck," she said, clearly trying to hide a laugh. "Oh, and he's good-looking. Way better than Corey. Maybe you should see if these skills can help with that itch of yours."

I hoped when I hung up and raised my eyes from my phone, luck would have rained down on me and he'd be gone so I could figure out how to handle this, but no. My luck was the same as ever, and not only was he still there, he was sliding into the chair across from me, holding a bottle of water and two slices of the lemon loaf I'd drooled over at the counter. Damn, the cake looked good. He looked good, too, even sweaty. He pushed his hair back after setting the plates down, the muscles in his arm flexing at the movement and reminding me of how I'd wanted him to touch me in that alcove, how the stretch of his fingers would have felt against my skin.

He held out one slice, and I pushed the thought away. "I saw you over here and thought you might want a snack. It's not Life Savers, but . . ."

"Thank you." I should have refused and swept up the little pride I had left, but my stomach grumbled, and I reminded myself I had a lot of work ahead of me in the office. I accepted the cake. "How do you know about my Life Savers?" I'd never smoked, but one day I might need a patch for the candy.

"A bunch of them fell out of your purse the day we met."

"When you were running around the city, looking for women who might not be smiling?"

"I'm sorry I said that. I don't have an excuse, but I was way out of line." His cheeks reddened. Lear was careful not to touch me as he handed me the treat and immediately sat back in his chair. "I was beyond out of line."

His sincerity was jarring, the way he held eye contact unsettling some expectations I had of him. I didn't like being surprised, and I glanced away. I wasn't sure how I'd thought he'd respond, but that wasn't it. "It's not the worst thing anyone's ever said to me."

"Still. I am sorry," he said. Then silence descended on our table, and I was calculating how fast I could eat the cake and gulp my coffee and get out of there when Lear crossed his forearms, leaning forward on the table. "So, you, uh, had a dream about me? Is that why you almost jumped me last weekend?" His smirk was subtle, eyebrows raised, the humble expression from before gone.

"I apologize, too. For making you uncomfortable. That was unprofessional and inappropriate."

Lear chuckled and held out his palms. "Oh, I wasn't uncomfortable. I was very comfortable. Just surprised. I didn't think you liked me." He licked a crumb off his lip, and I threatened myself with a lifelong vibrator ban if I let my eyes linger on his tongue.

"I don't like you," I said before taking a big bite of the cake, which was sinfully good, a little too close to how I imagined it would be with Lear.

"Do you often cling to people you don't like?" He took another bite and, again, inside my head I snapped my fingers like a mom on the phone, quieting my thoughts.

"I wasn't clinging, and it's not a habit, no." *Please, for the love of God, just leave me alone.*

"For the record, I'd be okay with it being a habit."

I clenched my jaw and my thighs. "Well, it won't be. Again, I'm sorry. I don't know what came over me." I threw back the rest of my coffee, though it was still far too hot, but my throat would forgive me. I felt the caffeine working its way through my bloodstream.

I shifted in my seat, preparing to gather my things and get out of there, because the smell of his cologne took me back to being pressed against him.

"Sounds like you know what came over you." He shrugged. "Must have been a good dream."

I'm crawling into a hole and making a new life there. "How much of my conversation were you eavesdropping on?"

"You're in a coffee shop. It's not exactly private, but not much," he said, taking a last swig of his water before reaching for our trash. "Just the part where you said I was skillful in your sex dream." He walked away from the table to drop our things in the garbage can, leaving his words floating in his wake. He tipped his chin down as he returned, pitching his voice low. "What was I so good at, RJ?"

I hurriedly pushed my laptop into my bag and stood, dropping my phone and AirPods into the side pocket. Lear strolled back to the table, and I brushed crumbs down the front of my shirt, his gaze following the movement of my hand. Which, of course, set my mind off down the forbidden path. I ignored his question despite the memory of the dream playing at the edges of my thoughts. "I need to get to the office."

"On a Sunday? You're kind of a machine, huh?"

I'd heard that before, usually with some derision or sarcasm. Case, himself a devotee of corporate culture, said it as ammunition; my friends said it kindly, but always followed by the idea that I should take a break. Lear said it like he was genuinely interested, and maybe a little impressed. "Big case," I said, avoiding eye contact again. "Thank you for the cake."

"I'm heading out, too. Which way are you going?" He held out a hand, motioning for me to walk ahead. He didn't say more, which felt weightier than the questions at the table as we strolled toward the exit. But I didn't like loose ends, particularly those ends that meant Lear Campbell knew I'd fantasized about him.

Outside, the air was dewy, just on the comfortable side of humid, and Lear walked near me, our arms occasionally brushing. "Listen," I said as we reached the corner, "we work together. I shouldn't have touched you, and the dream was just a dream. We should drop this, okay?"

He met my eyes and slowed our pace. "Thank you for apologizing earlier and, to be clear, I was right there with you in that alcove, but, yes, we can drop it." He looked forward again, then surveyed the mostly quiet street. He smelled sweaty, with a hint of something inviting underneath.

"But, RJ, before we drop it," Lear said, pushing the button to cross the street opposite from me, his body still close to mine. My gaze lingered on the button—I hadn't pushed my own, since the streets were so empty. The heat from him was a subtle reminder we were standing too close, and I stepped back before he finished. "I'm just saying that . . . if you want to find out if the dream compares to reality, I'd be open to appeasing your curiosity."

The light changed, and he gave me another grin before taking two steps backward and jogging the length of the crosswalk, leaving me standing on the corner. "We're dropping it," I called after him.

He'd reached the other side of the street and waved. "See you next weekend, RJ!"

Chapter 14

LEAR

THE COUPLE KISSED, to the whoops and cheers of their friends and family. When Penny initially briefed me on the gas station wedding, I'd thought it was a metaphor. As I stood on the edge of the crowd near an ancient pump, I appreciated that it was unique. The couple had met while filling up in the rain, and they wanted their ceremony to take place right there. It was a small gas station in a rural area and backed up to an open field, where tables covered in board games and snacks sat under a tent. The couple wanted different. I had to hand it to Penny. This could have been cheesy and kitschy, but it was perfect.

RJ smiled as the couple broke their kiss and clasped hands. She was looking between the brides and the crowd, and her face changed a little when she did that, her smile natural. Somehow she softened. It was probably a calculated shift, but I imagined her looking at me that way.

"Marin and Lola invite you to enjoy Icees and snacks while they take photos."

I'd already checked that the signature flavors—blue raspberry, cola, and piña colada—were ready to go and the snack options—from cheese puffs to Cornnuts to jelly beans—were artfully arranged. I'd texted my sister a photo. I have a weird job. She'd sent back a photo of a paperweight molded to look like a human vulva weighing down a to-do list that began with *Buy cat food*. Tell me about it.

"Nice ceremony," I said, approaching RJ with the paperwork for the marriage license after Marin and Lola stepped away with the photographer.

She laughed, which made me grin despite myself. She had been her normal terse self the whole day, that cute flustered expression from the week before a distant memory. "It's really a gas station wedding. I just . . ."

I laughed, too, leaning against the gas pump. "I know," I said, handing her the paperwork organized the way she liked. "Fun, though."

"Definitely fun," she said, our fingers brushing when she took the folder from me. Her gaze shifted to the brides laughing with their wedding party as they posed near a stack of tires, and a silence fell between us. "I'm glad I let Penny talk me into taking this one."

I rubbed the back of my neck, glancing the other way as the small crowd filtered into the tent. "I—"

At the same time, RJ brushed her hands down the front of her red dress. She looked stunning, and I threw thanks out to Lola, who had insisted that no one wear black. RJ's dress hugged her curves more than her normal outfits, and I was transfixed. "Well—"

"I was wondering if you had plans after. Maybe we could grab a drink?" I glanced at my watch out of habit more than anything. The reception would wrap up by nine, and I'd been imagining how RJ and I might spend the rest of the night after first seeing her in that dress. I would not bring up the dream or that heated moment if she didn't want to talk about it, not that I was having any success pushing either out of my thoughts.

RJ rolled back her shoulders and looked down, reviewing the paperwork. "I don't have plans, but we shouldn't spend time together."

"Cool," I said, looking at my watch again for no reason.

"Just so we're clear," she added, meeting my eyes.

"Crystal clear." My dick hadn't gotten the message this thing was over before ever really starting, so I had a troubling mix of arousal and shame swirling through my body at the same time. "I better check in with the DJ. Are you sticking around?"

RJ looked visibly relieved to be talking about work. Her shoulders relaxed incrementally. "Just until they do the signing."

"Okay, then." I took two steps away, reminding myself I was a cool adult who was not trying to be a nice guy. "See you later," I said with a small wave, turning before I was tempted to take in another eyeful of her body in that dress because *damn, that red dress.*

The wedding had a small guest list, so I saw RJ constantly, even when I focused on the DJ—a hipster with an elaborate handlebar mustache and an astounding knowledge of hip-hop—or the caterer's questions about restocking the Funyun fountain. RJ was always in my periphery, and the brides, these funny, creative women, were killing me, because they first convinced her to stay and then convinced her to dance, so not only was RJ in my periphery in that red dress, but RJ's body moving in time to the beat in that red dress was also right there.

"Lear! You owe us a dance!" Lola's cousins pulled me onto the floor to join them as the DJ switched tracks. Bell Biv DeVoe's "Poison" played, and I immediately looked around for RJ at the throwback to the evolution-of-boy-bands video. She rolled her eyes and I winked, joining the cousins in their moves. A group crowded around us, including Marin, who proclaimed loudly to her new wife that she could be trusted, despite having a big butt and a smile.

A drop of sweat rolled down my back and I turned, looking for an exit from the heat of the dance floor. The DJ shifted to a slow one, a soulful melodic voice sounding out along with piano chords, and everyone around me was coupling off for the song. Standing in the middle of a dance floor alone as happy couples swarmed around me could have been awkward, but someone bumped me and then I was sprawled alone on the actual dance *floor* as happy couples swarmed around me.

"Sorry," RJ said, holding out a hand. "I was looking for an escape." The twinkle lights behind her framed her face in the twilight and I slowly took her hand, enjoying the soft warmth of her skin and letting her help me up. We were still boxed in, and she smelled like cinnamon, or maybe that was the churros nearby.

"Me, too." I hadn't let go of her hand yet, but she hadn't pulled away.

"But I guess this was payback for when we met."

I inched closer to her to avoid colliding with the couple behind me. "Not quite. You ran into me that time, too."

"Maybe, but that time I ended up on the ground." RJ's hand slipped from mine.

"You were falling for me from the beginning."

She laughed, a throaty, warm laugh at my expense. "I think you are falling for your own hype." RJ tapped my temple. "The odds of me falling for you are so nonexistent, you might as well be dreaming them."

I met her smug grin but didn't say anything, waiting for her to catch her own words. When she stopped tapping my temple, her finger grazed my cheek and I thought about asking her the same question I had when we fought about the bar, if she was waiting for me to touch her.

It clicked then, that she'd brought up dreams, and I raised an eyebrow at the subtle twist in her expression. "Don't even say it," she said, turning on her heel and sliding through the crowd.

I grinned to myself and walked to the other side of the dance floor, grabbing a handful of Skittles—*when in Rome*—before stepping away from the tent to check my messages. I had seventeen texts from Penny; so glad to see motherhood hadn't changed her. Instead of replying, I tapped the icon to dial her.

"How did it go?" Her voice was low, quiet, and almost rhythmic.

"Fine," I said, unsure. "Are you holding the baby, or do we need to have a talk about appropriate timbre for cousins?"

"Connor is asleep and I'm sitting next to the incubator."

"How is the little one?" I leaned against the side of the building, just out of view of the tent.

Penny sounded tired, despite the lullaby-like tone. "A fighter. Did the caterer get things right?"

I chuckled. I wasn't sure Marin and Lola had cared about the exact arrangements of their snacks, but Penny had drawn a map of what snacks should be placed where after meeting with the caterer. To say that caterer was stifling an eye roll during setup would be putting it mildly. "Perfect. Everything went fine—a few small hiccups, but Tina prepped most everything, and the couple is happy."

"Good. Good. And you and RJ got along?"

"We're professionals." *Also, I can't stop imagining what kissing her is like and if she's as ardent about winning in bed as she is everywhere else.* I pushed the thought from my head. "Stop checking up on me and go be a parent." I bit the inside of my cheek, shaking off the creeping emotion saying that had left in me.

"This business was my first baby."

"I'm an excellent babysitter," I said, peeking around the corner. "I gotta go, though. They're about to do their final dance and wrap things up."

"Okay," she said in a whisper I hoped was meant for the baby. "Tell RJ I love her."

"I'm not saying that."

Penny's tone changed but not the volume as she sweetly hissed into the phone. "Give her anything she wants."

Out of habit, I glanced around the corner, searching for a flash of red, RJ looking at something on her phone or her fingers drifting to her full lips, the same lips I'd been fantasizing about for a week, pretty much nonstop. "Anything she wants, got it." I shoved my phone back in my pocket and returned to the tent, happy to have something to keep me busy by making sure everything wrapped up well. I didn't see RJ anywhere, though. No more red dress. No more temptation to put myself out there. *Good, need to get her out of my head anyway.*

Chapter 15

RJ

MY STOMACH LURCHED as the car came to a soft stop and the slipping, sliding momentum finally stilled. The sound of mud and metal wasn't as dramatic as a crunch, but just as final. I tested the ground, seeing if giving the car gas would move me forward, but my tires just spun, probably making it worse.

"Shit, shit, shit." I dropped my head to the steering wheel and let out a long, slow sigh. The deer had run out from the woods and I'd panicked, swerved on the rain-slicked pavement, and ended up here on the side of the road, my car facing the wrong direction and halfway down an embankment. It was late, I was already bone tired after the wedding, and now my car was stuck in a muddy ditch. That, plus I would have reacted faster if my head hadn't been elsewhere, namely on Lear I-have-some-skills Campbell. On Lear's lips and his puppy-dog expression when I turned down his request to get a drink, the one he hid quickly behind that stupid smirk. The smirk was all the reason I needed to forget about him. I'd been thinking about his voice, though, how it had been gravelly after our almost-kiss. I lifted my head and let it fall against the steering wheel again, shuddering at the idea of having to call in sick to work because I had been injured while returning from a wedding at a gas station. "Shit."

I was bent over the middle console fumbling for my phone, which had gone flying, when headlights illuminated the car from behind me. Relief and fear overtook me at once: relief at someone helping me, and fear at someone finding me defenseless in the middle of nowhere. I fingered the pepper spray attached to my key ring. My heart rate sped just the same. I could just stay in my car, but that wouldn't do any good, so I unlocked my phone, having it at the ready, and pushed open my door, which lodged against something. A figure emerged from the car, but the headlights obscured any details.

"Are you okay?" The voice made my heart stop completely and then double its speed.

Grabbing my purse from the floor of the passenger side, I tucked my phone into it. There was just enough space between the door and the car for me to slip out, and my foot sank into the muddy ground with a sickening slurp. I closed my eyes as my foot slipped into the muck, trying to ignore the vile sensation. "I'm not hurt," I called out. The next step left me sliding to the ground, my butt sinking into the wet earth, and I shuddered at the squishy feeling.

"RJ? Is that you?"

It wasn't a murderer.

It was worse. Lear stood on the edge of the ditch, inching forward.

"In the flesh," I said, clearing my car door and sludging up the embankment.

"Let me help you," he said, stepping down enough to hold out a hand.

Pride made me want to ignore his hand, but my sheer exhaustion and the ankle-deep mud won. I let him help me the last steps.

His smirk was gone, replaced with a look of concern, and he grasped my hand and steadied me with his other arm against mine. Minus the car wreck, the mud, the grease stains—and that we hated each other—it was almost like a slow dance. "Are you sure you're okay? You didn't hit your head or anything?" His hand traveled up my arm and his gaze moved over my face.

The touch, the look, the words: They were all utilitarian, how I'd expect any decent person to act in this situation. What surprised me was how comfortable I was with his touch and his concern, the latter being something I never wanted, not since I'd learned concern could turn to pity and resentment fast. I took a small step to the side. "Thanks," I said, glancing down at my mud-caked shoes. "I'm fine. My car is stuck, but I'm not hurt."

Despite my step to the side, he was still holding my hand, his fingertips still brushing my biceps. He seemed to realize it then, too, and let his hands fall. "Did you call for help already?"

"Just about to." I pulled my phone from my purse, thankful it wasn't dead. One small bright spot in the night.

He nodded, glancing over my shoulder at the car. With a better view now, I saw how close the rushing water was to the edge of the embankment. "The creeks out here flood fast when it rains," he said, returning his gaze to me, his brown eyes once again sweeping my face in this intense and sexy and annoying way. Lear motioned to the sky. "This system will go until one or two in the morning."

"Why do you know that?"

"Because I was running an outdoor event tonight." He motioned to his car. "I think I have a few towels and a change of clothes in my trunk. Let me check while you call."

Of course he would know the weather. He got under my skin and on my last nerve, but I knew he was actually good at his job. I wasn't sure why being nice was so difficult for me when I was around him. Roadside assistance answered quickly but warned me it might be hours before a tow truck could arrive, and might not be until morning. By the time I'd hung up, raindrops had hit my nose, and Lear returned with a beach towel.

"Thanks," I said, awkwardly trying to clean myself. "It's going to be a while, so the towel will come in handy."

"How long is a while?"

"Hours. Maybe not until morning, but I can just call for a ride. You don't have to stay."

"RJ, I'll give you a lift," he said, glancing up as the raindrop frequency increased.

"No, it's fine."

"It's raining, it's the middle of nowhere, and you're still refusing my help?" He cocked an eyebrow, the gesture losing and gaining something as that same brow twitched after a drop of rain hit his forehead. "Will you just let me give you a hand for once?"

He was right, of course, and I had no idea how long it would take for a ride to get out here. His warning about the creek flooding also left me worried about being so close to the water. So why was I resisting his help so ardently? It had a lot to do with the way his hair was blowing in the wind and the urge I felt to smooth it down. "I'm not stubborn," I said, defensive. "I don't want to put you out. Besides, I'd get your car filthy."

He looked me up and down, which was infuriating, and also hot, which was doubly infuriating. "I have some clean gym clothes. Do you want to borrow them? I wouldn't feel comfortable leaving you out here alone."

"I'd have to change in front of you," I said, motioning to the space between us.

The corners of a grin returned, and my entire body heated, but he spoke again before I could respond, holding out his palms. "I won't look. C'mon. It's coming down harder. Can you continue to despise me from inside the car?"

"I don't despise you," I muttered, stepping forward to join him near the open trunk of his car, where several boxes, totes, and bags were organized with Tetris-like precision. The trunk provided a small shelter where we could both stay dry, and I was certain he must have a few umbrellas back there, but the intimacy of the space was kind of nice.

He pulled a T-shirt and basketball shorts from a gym bag and handed them to me, along with a plastic bag he'd grabbed from the side pocket of a toolbox. He nodded to my feet. "For your shoes. And you could have fooled me." He turned, facing the empty road where the intermittent light shone off the forming puddles.

I stepped out of my heels and tossed them in the bag, wiping at my legs as best I could with the towel. I shimmied the basketball shorts up my legs, pulling the dress up to my waist at the same time. I reached over my head. Muscle memory had me expecting the high zipper of the dress I often wore for weddings, only to brush the goose-bumped skin of my upper back. *Dammit. This red dress.* I fumbled for a moment before clearing my throat. "Could you help me with the zipper on this? I have a hook at home, but I can't . . ."

Lear turned slowly. "Did I hear you correctly? Are you actually asking for help?"

I rolled my eyes. "Forget it. I'll wear the shirt over the dress."

"I'm just giving you shit," he said, motioning for me to turn. "I'll unzip your dress." His voice was normal, maybe even playful, but I still closed my eyes against the sound of those words from his lips, because I'd had fantasies of him ripping a dress from my body. He rested a palm on my shoulder and fiddled with the hook before dragging the zipper down my back slowly, the sound and vibration a subtle reminder of his mouth. As he pulled it down, I had a moment wondering if he was checking out my butt and then remembered it was caked in mud. "There," he said, stepping back. His hand fell from my shoulder, the pad of his thumb ghosting down my spine as it fell away.

"Thank you," I said before pulling the shirt over my head and pushing the dress to the ground in a way everyone who went to middle school with breasts knows how to do. I tossed the dress in with the shoes. They were probably both ruined anyway. "I'm done," I said, picking up the bag from the concrete.

"Wow," he said, taking the bag from me, his eyes not leaving my body.

"What?"

"I've just never seen you dressed down. You look nice."

I scanned his words for sarcasm. Finding none, I just glanced away.

"Sorry, uh, it's unlocked if you want to climb in. I'll stow this back here."

I hadn't realized I'd been cold, but sliding into the car and closing out the rain and the wind, I was comfortable, despite my bare feet. A second later, Lear climbed in the driver's side and started the car, fiddling with the touch screen. Immediately, warm air blew onto my toes.

"You've got a little mud on your face. Hold on," he said, reaching across my lap. Though he couldn't see me, my eyes went wide in surprise, but he didn't touch me. Instead he opened the glove compartment and pulled out a package of wet wipes. "Here."

"You're more prepared than my friend who has a toddler," I remarked, taking the wet wipe and pulling down the mirror.

"Thank you . . . ?" He signaled, despite there being no cars, which made me suppress a grin as he pulled out onto the highway.

I cast a glance at my car, which would hopefully not be washed away by the time a tow company could contact me. "It's a good thing."

"Just part of the job." He didn't say more, and we drove in silence.

"Thank you," I finally said, breaking the bubble of background noise. "You didn't have to be so nice."

"I don't think making sure you weren't stranded in a ditch really qualifies me as nice," he said, reaching for the touch screen. His gaze flashed to me before returning to the road. "But it's no problem."

I looked out the window, the rain pelting down. I hummed along with the song, letting my mind wander. "Lear," I said, slowly turning my head. "Is this the soundtrack to *Hamilton*?"

"Yeah. So?" He gripped the steering wheel and didn't look at me. "It's good."

"I know. I just didn't expect you to be listening to musicals."

"There's nothing weird about it. It's a wildly popular show." His tone hardened, and the defensiveness was kind of cute.

"Not weird." I laughed. "If anything, it humanizes you."

"You were thinking of me as nonhuman?"

I took in his profile, the half of his face nearest me illuminated only by the ambient light from the dash. "Sometimes."

"Has anyone ever told you you're kind of mean?" The question might have hurt were it not for the corners of his lips tipping up. The little baby smile highlighted the cut of his jaw, and I remembered with sharp clarity what it felt like to touch him.

"I've been told that my entire life." I bit my lower lip, taking in his face again. Lear had a good body, but he was handsome, even more so when the cocky swagger front he put up crumbled. I had the most nagging urge to reach for his thigh. The few times I'd touched him, there'd been a spark between us, and I still felt the ghost of his touch up my back from when he'd helped with my dress. "I can be nice sometimes, though."

His expression was one of surprise before adjusting back to aloof, which made me want to make him lose control a bit. "I don't know if I believe that."

I shrugged and looked back out the window, letting the familiar songs from *Hamilton* comfort me as the warm air on my feet kept the chill away. "Maybe that's for the best."

"Probably," he said.

The idea of a no-strings thing with him was ridiculous. Not only did we work together, but he was my mentor's friend. Still, when he agreed, my chest squeezed. *Lear Campbell could have been my new Corey minus the struggling YouTube channel.* I studied his profile and imagined he would be good at uncomplicated, that he might be down for something fun. I needed to think through the idea and decide if it was worth it. I could be nice sometimes, but I was rarely impulsive. The rest of the drive, I weighed out pros and cons in my head.

Chapter 16

I WAS ALMOST at my place across town after dropping RJ at her apartment when I heard the buzzing from the floor in front of the passenger seat. The rain pounded on my window and lightning flashed across the sky. *This fucking day will never end.* After spending most of the drive in awkward silence, I'd dropped off RJ at her place, watching with far too much interest as she sprinted from the car to her door, holding my umbrella in one hand and her clothes and bag in the other. She lived in a four-story apartment building in a nice area of town and had waved awkwardly once she got inside the security door. I would have waited for anyone to get in safely, but I wouldn't have watched anyone else's body so closely.

I felt around on the floor and found her phone almost immediately where it rested halfway under the seat. I let out a slow sigh while paused at the red light with my blinker flashing, ready to make an illegal U-turn to drive back across town and pretend I didn't want to devour this woman.

I tapped the button to buzz her unit when I arrived, lamenting for the first time in my life the loss of the landline phone.

"Hello?"

"RJ, it's Lear. You left your phone in my car." I could hardly hear her with the rain falling in sheets behind me. With all my skills in preparation and planning, I hadn't thought to grab another umbrella from the back of my SUV, and I'd ended up waterlogged from the quick jog to her door.

"Dammit," she muttered. "I just got out of the shower. Can I buzz you up? I'm in 3F."

I shook some of the water off my shirt as I walked down her hall. The building was completely quiet—it was nearing midnight—and it looked expensive. Classy and maybe a little pretentious in the way I always thought of RJ. I knocked on her door, brushing the dripping water off my face.

"Hey," she said, eyes widening at my appearance. "Oh, God. Did you get soaked running in here?"

I shrugged and pulled her phone from my pocket, trying desperately not to let my eyes roam over her body wrapped in a thin white robe. I was sure that was the last thing she wanted. "No big deal."

Our fingers grazed when she took it. "Come in. I'll get you a towel. It's the least I can do." RJ hustled to a closet in the hall and returned, holding a fluffy red towel to her chest. I should have been taking in her legs or the gap in her robe that showed a sliver of skin leading down from her neck, but my attention was drawn to her bare feet. It was so casual, so comfortable to see her like this in her home.

"Here," she said, handing it over. "Thanks for bringing my phone back. I felt so gross once I got inside, I just went straight to the shower."

I rubbed the towel over my head and down my arms, feeling her eyes on me. "Thanks," I said, handing it back.

She smiled, the unguarded smile I'd only seen once or twice. "I told you I can be nice."

"Yeah." I didn't mean to stare at her body. The entire elevator ride up, I'd reminded myself to drop the phone, turn around, and leave, but I found myself gazing at her legs and then following the lines of her robe.

She coughed, drawing my attention up.

"God. Sorry." My face heated, and I glanced away. "I didn't mean to be a jackass."

"You're always a jackass," she said, taking a half step forward and tossing the towel aside.

I felt the grin tip my lips up. "What was that about being nice?"

RJ crossed her arms over her chest, which really just made her breasts more pronounced. "You were imagining me naked."

"You *are* practically naked."

Her eyes were narrowed, but then her face broke into the most unexpected laugh. She'd looked like a powerhouse with her arms crossed. Even in the robe, she was formidable. And then she laughed, and she still looked like a powerhouse, but in the most captivating way. I was mesmerized. "So, my dream . . ."

"I know." I raised my palms. "You said to drop it. I will. I have."

"Well . . ." She stepped forward and sank her teeth into her lower lip. "What if you didn't drop it yet."

I glanced around her entryway, my gaze once again snagging at the dip of her robe. "What?"

"It was a stressful night after a long day. I could use some stress relief. Couldn't you? We're clearly attracted to each other." Her expression told me my dumbfounded response was unwarranted, and she pressed on. "So, prove it."

Did I hit my head or something? She paused and I nodded. "Attracted to" was probably not a strong enough phrase, but I wanted more. "Prove what?"

"Your . . . skills."

My brain short-circuited, but I reminded myself to attempt cool. I folded my arms over my chest and leaned against a nearby column. "Which skills do you want me to prove?"

Her expression shifted from badass energy to annoyance. That was a look I was used to seeing from her. "You want me to spell it out?"

"Yes, I'm going to need you to spell it out."

"I can't with you." She growled and paced her small living room, which was as cute as it was sexy. "I'm inviting you to stick around and we can . . . you know."

"I don't *know*. You still haven't said."

If my dick hadn't been straining in my pants at the idea of peeling the robe off her shoulders, I might have continued trying to get a rise out of her.

RJ stopped pacing and turned as I neared. Her gaze dropped to my belt. "Looks like you know." RJ met my stare again with a cocked eyebrow.

Challenge. That's what this was. That's why this was new and exciting. She challenged me and she liked it when I challenged her back. I reached her in two strides, resting my arms on either side of her head and caging her against the wall. *Damn, she smells good.* Her breath caught as I leaned forward, grazing my lips over her ear. "I know what skills I want to show you." I edged closer, the puffs of her breath on my neck sending electricity through my body. "Because I think you'll kiss like you want to win, and I haven't been able to get that out of my head. But what do you want? Because I don't know what we're doing here." I dragged a finger gently down the other side of her neck as my lips lingered. The almost-kiss at that wedding had been fast and stolen. This moment felt like it stretched.

RJ let out a gasp when I grazed her earlobe, and I was already fast-forwarding to how that moan would sound a hundred times louder. Pressing my body to hers felt like weights coming off my shoulders. It felt like an eternity before she slid her palms up my chest, her fingernails lightly scratching the fabric of my shirt.

I stilled, worried I'd scare her off, but her hands kept moving, lingering on my chest, her fingers grazing my nipples through the fabric. I had to close my eyes against the rush of sensation, and I nipped her ear. "Did you decide?"

"Shut up," she said as her fingers tangled in my hair to pull my face to hers.

We paused for a second, but all I could focus on was RJ's mouth, her slightly parted lips, and the sensation of her pulling my mouth to hers, her eyes flicking to mine moments before we touched. "Can I?"

"Yes," I said, my body on autopilot, and our lips met.

Her soft, full lips made contact with mine, and she pulled my face toward her. She sucked on my lower lip and my body and mind finally caught up.

Wrapping an arm around her waist, I pressed into her, her body melting against me. We wrestled for control, our lips and tongues clashing just like we normally did with words, but I didn't care if I came out on top as long as this kiss kept going.

RJ moved one hand from my shirt to the back of my neck, her nails grazing my skin, and I moaned against her lips. RJ kissed like she did everything, and I couldn't get enough of her mouth. I was lost in her taste and her constant need to take the upper hand. I let my palm slide down her back to feel the swell of the ass I'd noticed from day one, forgetting how much this woman drove me nuts.

"I'm serious," I panted after pulling apart and meeting her eyes. "Tell me."

Despite the haze of arousal clearly on her face, her eyes narrowed. She shifted to the right like she would walk away, but I stopped her, locking eyes.

I let one hand fall to her waist and guided her toward me, my erection pressing into her stomach. "I want to know exactly what you want. I won't guess when it comes to pleasing you." I pushed memories of Sarah out of my head, of her admitting too late she'd wanted more than I gave her. RJ's body was intoxicating, and I didn't intend to waste this buzz on the past. I bent, my lips and tongue caressing her neck as I waited for her response.

"I want . . ." Her breath hitched as I lowered my hand to squeeze her ass. *Dear God, this ass.*

"Say it . . ." My lips slid along her collarbone. "It's probably the only time I'll let you tell me what to do, and I'm a good listener."

She laughed then, her throat elongating as she tipped her head back. It was the best sound and, if it was possible, my cock swelled even more. When she met my eyes again, her eyes had that brightness I'd noticed before.

"In my dream you were . . ." RJ bit her plump lower lip, her teeth sinking into the skin, and on instinct I kissed that spot, pulling that lip between my own. RJ wasn't exactly acting timid, but I'd never seen that softness in her before, the sweet bewilderment, and it was addictive. Her breathing was hard when I pulled away, her breath hitching. "In the dream you were on your knees."

Chapter 17

NOT ONCE IN my life had anyone described me as shy, so when I snapped my mouth shut, my cheeks heating at the words I'd just spoken out loud, it was an unfamiliar feeling. I hadn't finished my pros and cons list when he buzzed, hadn't weighed out the value of a night with Lear's body against the potential for problems. But when he looked at me like he couldn't not look at me, I lost my head. There was no danger of him hurting me. There was little danger of me even wanting to hear from him again. How else to explain how I was standing here like this? Lear left me off-balance, as I both hoped he made the man from my dream a distant memory and prayed he'd be a disappointment so I could get back to my regularly scheduled life.

He didn't kiss like a disappointment, though.

"On my knees, huh?"

"You don't have to." I tried to keep my voice steady and didn't like the breathy quality it was taking on or how his gaze hadn't strayed from my mouth. "Obviously, you know you don't have to. I mean, we can do something else or . . ." I paused when he met my eyes. I'd never really noticed Lear's eyes before, not like this. They were brown, but up close, there were flecks of gold, and they were lighter than I expected. *What am I doing noticing his eyes?* "You know," I said, letting my hands fall from his shoulders, "this was a bad idea. Forget it."

"Whoa," he said, taking a small step back. "What just happened?"

I missed the warmth of his chest immediately but appreciated him giving me space without hesitation. I stood there, my brain telling me to walk away and my body telling me to stop talking. When we got serious, Case stopped going down on me. He told me once he'd do it if he had to, but there were too many variables and it made more sense to do something else that was more certain to work. When I told Britta that, she'd frowned and said, "'More certain' like you took care of yourself?" She'd been right.

Lear was still looking down at me, confused.

"You didn't look like . . . Some guys don't like . . ." *Get it together. You are RJ fuckin' Brooks.*

Lear cocked his head to the side before he dropped to his knees in front of me, his hands skimming over my outer thighs. "I like." His fingertips slid under the hem of my robe and brushed the skin on the backs of my knees. "I'm used to you being bossier. Are we doing this?" He inched my robe higher, hands still exploring. His thumbs made circles on the insides of my legs, and his middle fingers danced behind my knees.

I sucked in a breath at the sensation. "I'm not bossy. I just know what you're supposed to be doing most of the time."

He smirked, toying with the hem of my robe. "So, we are doing this?"

When I nodded, he slid his palms up my thighs slowly until he reached the lace lining of my underwear, and he guided his fingertips along the edge, moving closer to my center and then away. "What should I be doing now?" He dropped his lips to my thigh, kissing the sensitive skin as his fingertips slid under the fabric and up the backs of my thighs.

He moved so slowly, and I pulsed with the desire to grab his hair and hurry him along. I hadn't expected slow. I'd assumed it would be hard and fast, something I could walk away from. But this was maddening, and I was at his mercy.

"This?" He rubbed his finger in circles over my clit, the fabric of my underwear an unwelcome barrier. "Or this?" His lips brushed over the spot he'd just rubbed, the suction just strong enough to make me inch my pelvis forward.

"Yes," I said, no longer caring that my voice was breathy. "More."

"That's the RJ I know," he said, sucking lightly one more time before pulling my panties down my legs.

I stepped out of them and Lear guided one leg to his shoulder. I should have been concerned about several things, namely my body open to my mentor's childhood friend, but his hand on my thigh and his tongue making a first incredible pass over my slick folds left me forgetting everything. Lear did this like he kissed, and my back arched at the flurry of sensation—the gentle lapping and slow circles, the pace slowing each time I neared orgasm. I moaned, grasping at the wall for balance, or maybe counterbalance, as I shifted my pelvis against his mouth. The edging made me want to cry out and promised a powerful release.

Lear pulled away, catching his breath and looking up. His lips glistened and my skin tingled even more. "This?" He dipped into me with a long finger.

My eyes closed against the feeling and he slid in a second finger, finding my G-spot.

"Or that?"

"Shut up," I said, reaching for his head, no longer concerned at all. I guided his face back to me and cried out when he began to suck and lick while his fingers pressed against my G-spot. My thighs trembled, and a rush of intense anticipation flooded me. I might have fallen, but Lear's other arm held me tight against him and his mouth. I cried out, telling him not to stop as the throb built inside and out and my body finally exploded, my head tipped back and eyes closed as wave after wave of intense pleasure ripped through me.

The world slowly came back into focus and I realized my fingers were still wound in his hair and my leg still rested against him. "Oh. Sorry," I said awkwardly, sliding my leg down and pulling my hand away, leaving his hair mussed.

"It's not a problem," he said, sitting back on his heels and wiping the back of his hand over his mouth. His eyelids were hooded and his tongue peeked out over his lower lip. "It's the farthest thing from a problem."

Why is that so sexy?

I pulled at my robe. The bareness of my still-sensitive skin felt awkward as the orgasm faded and I covered all the places he'd kissed and touched. Raising a hand to my temple, I pushed back the hair I assumed was wild and out of place, though it felt like it had before. It was my mind that was spinning out of control.

He looked up at me. "So?"

"So . . . what?" I took a step back, my spine hitting the wall. I needed a few more inches between us, but then realization struck me. "Let me take care of you." At this angle, I could see the outline of his erection and I wasn't unimpressed, not that I hadn't felt it against me earlier. I was looking forward to making him lose control.

He shook his head. "I meant . . . did my skills measure up to the dream?"

I paused my calculations of how I wanted to touch him. After a beat, I caught up, regaining my bearings. "You were okay."

"Just okay?" He handed me the underwear that was sitting discarded at my feet, the cotton garment hanging off his finger. "I'm pretty sure the people at the bar three blocks away heard you crying out my name."

I snatched the underwear from his finger, shoving it in the pocket of my robe, knowing he was probably right and hating that smirk that was seconds away from crossing his face. This was a tremendously bad idea, except that I could still feel the slight tremors following the onslaught of his mouth. "Fine. You have skills—well, you have *a* skill."

"I used at least a few," he said, rising to his feet in a smooth motion.

I took another step away, not wanting the temptation of him so close to me, needing a few more moments to catch my breath, because I realized with a daunting clarity that I wanted to kiss him again. "Do you want me to stroke your ego or stroke your dick?"

He looked less cocky than I expected, but just for a second before he shrugged and mirrored me, taking a step back. "Ego is good for now." He glanced over my head, where a clock ticked on the wall. "I should probably get home."

"Oh." A little surprised, I glanced at his crotch again, where there was definitely still a very erect penis. "Of course. Thank you for bringing my phone back, and . . ." I looked around for something to do with my hands and awarded myself the prize for the strangest sexual encounter of all time. "Tonight. Good to get that out of our system. Are you sure you don't want . . ."

He nodded, putting his hands in his pockets and walking with me toward the door, where we, once more, stood awkwardly looking at each other, and I fought the annoying desire to kiss him again. "I'm sure. Will you need anything with the tow?"

I met his eyes. "No, I'll get my friend to take me," I said with my hand on the doorknob. "But thank you."

He nodded again, flipping open the lock on the door.

"I guess I'll see you around." I held the robe closed, still curious why he was leaving without letting me return the favor, an unfamiliar sensation nudging me closer to him.

"Oh, and, RJ?"

I needed to get away from Lear and these wayward thoughts, because the last thing I needed was to get fixated on the guy who I wanted to strangle ninety percent of the time, even if he had made me see stars. "Yeah?"

Before I finished the word, his hand was cupping the back of my neck, pulling my lips to his, and his body was crushing me to the door frame. His lips and tongue caressed mine, insistent and like the best kind of punctuation mark at the end of the sentence of this night. I sank against him immediately, and when he pulled his lips from mine, he dipped his head close to my face. His grin tipped up in a cocky way, and he winked. "Next time you can stroke my ego *and* my dick."

I glowered at his back as he sauntered to the elevator, admiring the way his muscles moved under his shirt and flashing back to how he'd touched me. "Wait, next time?"

Chapter 18

LEAR

RJ'S EYES SPARKLED when she made someone laugh—her face shifted from this serious, imposing presence to something bright. A couple weeks after the gas station wedding and the subsequent late night, we were at a rehearsal and seeing each other for the first time. She'd said something to make the groom and best man crack up on the other side of the room. I wanted to grin along and then reminded myself it was RJ, who hated me, and that I wasn't supposed to be admiring her smile. If that night in her apartment was an invitation, it *was* permissible for me to be checking out her body, admiring the swell of her ass. Admittedly, I'd done that, too, but the feeling I knew was jealousy wasn't about those guys being near her body. It was that she was laughing with them, and I wanted to make her laugh.

"Lear?" The bride's mom's voice pulled me back.

"I'm sorry. I thought the altar was off center for a moment. Do you mind repeating that?" She smiled sweetly at me, and I should have felt bad for lying, but I didn't. The altar was exactly center—I'd measured. Twice.

"How wonderful of you to check that." She touched my arm and smiled again before launching into a series of questions about the caterers.

Internally, I let out a slow breath. I needed to get my attention off the hot divorce attorney who was having sex dreams about me and put them where they belonged: on this sweet middle-aged woman asking about cream puffs and salmon tartare. I shouldn't have spent the night imagining how it would feel to kiss RJ again, or what kind of underwear she was wearing. Or wanting to punch myself in the gut for having turned down her offer to take care of me. I definitely shouldn't have been sneaking glances at the way the dress she was wearing hugged her hips when she walked toward the exit. Her leaving should have put a damper on me wanting her, but it didn't. And her laugh . . . *Focus.*

I glanced at my watch as the couple gathered their family to head to dinner. As predicted, we'd run an hour long, and I patted myself on the back for encouraging them to plan a buffer between rehearsal and dinner. At the exit, RJ and the couple spoke as everyone else filtered out, and I pulled my tablet from my bag. I didn't need to check anything—even the contingency plans for the contingency plans had been checked and rechecked, but I wanted to be occupied when RJ finished.

I'd been jumpy all week, unable to focus on anything except work, and looking for excuses to text RJ. I hadn't found any, so I sat there night after night with my phone in my hand like a high schooler, typing and deleting messages. That wasn't the new me, and I needed to get a few things straight with her.

"Bye, Lear!" The couple waved and walked out into the cool night air.

RJ strode toward where I stood, her heels clicking on the wood floors. "That went well," she said in her professional voice. That one differed from the one she used when she was bickering with me. I liked the bickering voice better.

"Do you—"

Her phone blew up when she pulled it from her pocket and turned it on. "Dammit," she muttered, tapping something quickly.

"Everything okay?"

"Just work," she answered without looking up. A crease formed between her eyebrows until she tucked the phone away. "Were you going to ask me something? I already adjusted the order for the ceremony readers. No need to remind me."

"Reminders never hurt."

She shoved her things into her bag. "And yet, they are unnecessary, since you watched me write the change in the ceremony."

I shoved the tablet in my bag. "I would think you, of all people, would appreciate me dotting *i*s and crossing *t*s." I hadn't even been planning to remind her, so I didn't know why I was getting into this with her, except that her sniping at me was normal and I liked it.

She leveled me with a stare.

"Anyway, now that's squared away. Do you maybe want to get a drink or something?"

RJ's cocked eyebrow was a work of art—a somehow perfect mix of sexy and derisive. "So you can give me more reminders?"

My instinct was to apologize and wait for her to bring it up, but I reminded myself my instincts had led to a lot of regret in California. I stepped closer to RJ and ghosted a finger down her bare biceps. "I could remind you of the other night."

Her arched eyebrow lowered, and her full lips tipped to the side. "To remember my phone and avoid back roads in the rain?" Her voice was always a challenge, a push, like every verbal exchange was a match to win.

I could play that game, though, and I dropped my lips to her ear, enjoying the hitch in her breath. "About you telling me not to stop."

I bit the inside of my cheek and waited for her to volley back. RJ would.

She didn't move closer, but she didn't move away. "You know I don't leave things to chance."

"Neither do I. Get a drink with me." I wished I had a wall to lean against or could shove my hands into my pockets. I was pulling off the impression of a confident, collected guy, but not well. "Please."

She tipped her chin up. Her eyes were so deep, a brown I could get lost in. *Focus.* This was RJ, so letting my guard down would be a mistake. We just stood there for a beat, then two, but when she spoke, they weren't the words I wanted. "I don't drink before going into work."

I glanced at my watch. "Dinner, then? Unless you're planning another meal of coffee and donuts."

The eyebrow returned, and her words sent a shot straight to my groin. "Danish. And what I put in my mouth is none of your concern."

"It's not a concern," I said, grazing her soft skin again, the backs of my fingers sliding over her arm. "Just a recent interest."

I expected that to land one of a few ways. While her pulling me into a supply closet for a repeat performance was unlikely, I thought her slapping me or agreeing to a drink had roughly the same odds. I didn't expect her to laugh.

"That's the line you're going with, huh?" She stepped back and so did I, but when she looked up, she held her fingers in air quotes. "'Recent interest in your mouth,'" she mocked. "Your game has to be stronger than that, Campbell. I expected more."

"It was a perfectly good line," I said, crossing my arms. "Who goes back to work at eight on a Friday night?"

"You realize you're *at* work, right now?"

"Good point. Forget I asked, RJ." I grabbed my bag and pushed the taste of her from my memory. "No problem."

"Hey," she said, her laughter subsiding. She wrapped her delicate fingers around my forearm, her touch warm and more gentle than I expected. She met my eyes. "I'm the type of person who is going back into work. I don't have time for drinks or dinner or any other seduction techniques you have in mind. I don't have time to date."

"Message received," I said, heat moving up my spine. *So much for that plan.* "Loud and clear." I didn't want to date her, anyway. I didn't want to date anyone.

"So," she said, smoothing down her dress, "if there's a back room or something, let's get to it."

A record screeched in my head and I had no smartass response. "What?"

RJ's features were set, the slight tip of the edge of her lip the only crack in the wall. "Your sad lines aside, you have some skills I'd like to partake of."

I uncrossed my arms and straightened my shoulders. "Is that lawyer speak for 'I want you in my pants'?"

"It's lawyer speak for 'This will go better if you don't say anything.'"

"What's RJ for 'It doesn't cost me anything to be nice to people'?"

She grinned, her white teeth showing behind her dark lipstick. "I don't have a phrase for that."

I couldn't help but return her smile. It was just so jarring to see a real, unguarded one from her. "So, you want my skills but not to spend any time with me outside of being naked?"

"Oh, there won't always be time to get naked." Her eyebrow was up again, and it felt like a challenge. "I can be very efficient with the right partner."

I thought back to the night in her apartment and how she'd reacted to me, how she'd responded to my touch. "Fair enough. Like, friends with benefits or something?"

She tucked her phone into her bag and stepped closer, resting her palm on my chest. She smelled faintly of cocoa butter and cherries. "We're not friends."

I rolled my eyes. "Enemies with benefits, then?"

She patted my chest. "You're smarter than you look."

The dip of her waist was a perfect fit for my hand. "You're meaner than you taste."

"Don't you forget it." RJ's breath puffed against my neck. "If either of us finds someone else or it just isn't working anymore, we're done."

"Sure," I said, making sure we were alone in the room and then lowering my lips to the side of her neck, figuring out the rules here as we went. I kissed below her ear.

The breath that escaped her lips was motivation enough to kiss her there again.

"You've been tested?"

That familiar prickle at the back of my neck rose at her question. I remembered the smell of the clinic and how numb I'd felt asking for everything. "I'm disease- and virus-free."

RJ didn't notice the shift in my tone. "Me, too." Her voice was all business, except for the breathy way she continued when I reached the base of her throat and my hand tightened at her waist.

My entire body wanted to connect to hers as I inhaled the scent of her neck. "Birth control?"

"I have an IUD. Condoms?" RJ's voice was low against my ear, seductive and somehow matter of fact.

"I have one in my wallet."

RJ pulled back and met my eyes. "No drama."

"Wouldn't think of it."

She nodded and wrapped her hand around mine. "C'mon."

"Where are we going?"

"To find a supply closet."

Chapter 19

RJ

TODD, MY ASSISTANT, had flagged things of interest in the research I'd asked him to gather and I read through notes, communication, and reports on the Avente Foundation, headed since its inception by Andrew Mayfield. I skimmed over the summary and then clicked between documents. Mr. Mayfield had put all of his energy into the foundation and it seemed to be a priority for him, but both Mayfields were emotionally attached. If there was going to be a weak link in his chain, it was there, but so far everything was all about helping kids of color go to college and making dreams come true.

"You're early." Lear strode toward me, his gait cocky, a half smile on his lips.

When my meeting ended, I'd decided not to drive back across town but to use the wedding venue as a makeshift office. "No sense wasting billable hours driving back to work."

"Mm," he said, reaching me, resting a shoulder against the wall to my left, his arms crossed loosely over his chest, sleeves rolled. His gaze dipped to my lips and my lower belly clenched in anticipation. "Couple won't be here for an hour."

I glanced at my watch and set aside my phone. "I can give you fifteen minutes."

His smile quirked. "You'll want more."

Brushing my palms down my skirt, I glanced around the small space. "Not if you're efficient."

"Is that how this enemies-with-benefits thing will work? I take what time you'll give me?"

Lear wore a black shirt that fit over his sculpted chest and highlighted his shoulders.

"Yes." I traced my fingers over the buttons, enjoying the way his smile faltered. "That's how it'll work."

He studied my face, not making a move to touch me. He was silent for two beats longer than I could hold on to my cool, not that I let him see it. I wondered if he couldn't handle this or would change his mind, but he stepped away. "Follow me." He walked toward a closed door on the opposite wall and opened it up to reveal a supply closet, the shelves lined with boxes of tissue and cleaning supplies. "It's not . . . romantic."

Lear smelled good, and I ran a palm up his chest again, wanting to feel the firm muscle. "We don't need romance," I said, pulling him toward me in the cramped space.

"You're right. Romance gets messy." Lear's mouth lowered close to my lips but dipped to my neck instead. His lips worked over my throat as his fingers teased the nape of my neck. "Complicated."

I panted, dragging my nails across his back, turned on and interested in what in his past was so complicated, but I didn't want to open doors to sharing stories. "Don't mess up my hair."

"I'll be careful." Lear's hand moved lower over the fabric of my skirt. A promise and reminder of his powerful hands that slid to the zipper on the side. "Better take this off so it doesn't wrinkle."

I shimmied out of the fabric and draped it over a stack of chairs. "You're so considerate." I kissed him, enjoying the give of his lips and the soft heat of his tongue.

"I'm a nice guy," he said, sliding a hand down my belly and between my legs. "If you give me a chance." His fingers teased me through the fabric of my underwear, soft pressure over my needy flesh.

I palmed the bulge in his pants through the fabric, the rigid length tempting and hot. "I don't care about nice, and you only have twelve minutes left."

Without warning, he slid his fingers into my underwear, teasing and stroking, his movements quick but intentional. "You're going to want more time."

I already wanted more time. An image of spending all night under those touches flashed through my head, but I pushed it aside.

"But I'll follow your rules," he said, dipping a finger and then two into me, moving in and out of my slick heat, finding an angle that made me groan against his neck. "Are you getting lipstick on my collar?"

I slid his zipper down and reached into his pants, palming him skin to skin, loving the heat of him. "I'm not wearing any."

"You came prepared." His breath hitched as I stroked him, and he nudged me backward until my back hit the edge of a small table. "Did you plan this?"

"I plan everything. Do you want to talk or make the most of the next eleven minutes?"

He had me perched on the edge of the table in seconds, and I pushed my underwear down as he pulled a condom from his wallet. I had to give him credit for bending to my time limit. I wasn't even sure why I'd pulled that number out. I had work to do, lots of it, but I'd never put a time limit on sex. I watched Lear roll the condom down his length, squeezing it in his broad fist and letting his pants fall down his thighs. The rush was kind of hot. "Nine minutes and thirty seconds," he said, moving between my thighs. I thought he'd push in—I wanted him to, to take me to the edge, hard and fast, but he teased me instead, moving his length up and down my sensitive flesh. "There's so many other places I want to touch you," he said into my neck, still teasing me. "I want more time in the future, time to find out how you like it."

I stifled a whimper at the way his words skated over my skin. I would not whimper with him. Instead, I grazed my fingers over his shoulder. "Let's see how you do with fifteen minutes and then I'll decide if I'm open to negotiation."

"Eight minutes more," he said, ignoring my reaching for him.

"Stop making me wait." I inched forward, trying to guide him to where I wanted.

"RJ." He ghosted a hand over my breast, palm barely grazing the nipple though the thin fabric of my shirt. "You have a lot of rules."

"And?" I wanted more of his hand there, even though it would wrinkle the top.

Finally, blessedly, he slid into me, filling me, slow at first, pushing in and then pulling back out, but picking up speed, developing a hurried rhythm. "I have a rule, too."

My breath came in hitches as he pumped into me, finding the right angle, and I leaned back on the desk until he hit me just where I needed. "What's your rule?"

He settled his fingers over mine and guided my hand to his shoulder, the weight of his hand an odd mix of comfort and anticipation. "You finish first. Six minutes left, RJ."

I rolled my head back, and he nudged my fingers away and began making slow circles over my swollen, pulsing bundle of nerves. My body heated and my thighs shook. I wanted to pull his hair, to climb on top of him, to kiss his soft lips again, but I couldn't do anything but roll my hips and force my noises to mute. Lear knew how to touch me, and me finishing first would not be a problem.

An orgasm coiled like a spring in my belly and I rolled against him harder. I expected a smirk, but his gaze was intent on me as the table made sharp noises against the wall behind it. He continued the steady, sliding pressure against me and I broke, thighs shaking and my groan strangled as I came, the rush of pleasure like blinding light and then being wrapped in a sweet-smelling blanket.

Lear's expression changed, and he gripped my waist, thrusting into me harder before letting out his own groan, the sound muted against my neck and his eyes squeezed shut.

We stayed there, both catching our breaths, the closet silent around us.

He pulled out of me, taking care of the condom and swiping a box of tissues from the shelf. He looked at his wrist. "Four minutes left . . . can I bank those for next time?"

I grinned and pulled my panties up. "Depends . . . what would you do with them?"

He handed me my skirt and our fingers lingered, the contact somehow more intimate and personal than what we'd just done. "Could I get that shirt and bra off you in four minutes?"

We both readjusted and, out of habit, I looked him over, making sure he didn't appear rumpled. "You could try."

Lear stepped toward me and tipped my chin up. His gaze was more intense than I expected. "I would." His hand at my neck was possessive, firm without being rough, and it felt like he wanted to kiss me.

I didn't like that I wanted to kiss him, too, so I placed my palm on his chest. "We'll see what happens next time, then." I took a step back and smoothed down my skirt, my center still heated from his attention. I opened the door and stepped out into the still-empty hall. When I didn't hear his footsteps, I looked over my shoulder to find him leaning on the door frame. "I'm going to get back to work," I said.

"Don't mind me. I'm just watching you go."

I laughed and returned to my phone and laptop, fairly certain he couldn't see how wobbly my legs felt. "Enjoy the view."

Chapter 20

LEAR

ONE OF THE grooms' father slapped a wide palm on my shoulder and I winced. "Not gonna lie. I didn't know what to think of a man doing all this over-the-top, fancy wedding planning stuff, but you're a good guy," he said, his voice loud in a uniquely dad sort of way. "I think you're taking good care of our boys. It's gonna be a real nice day." He motioned to his son and soon-to-be son-in-law and his eyes sparkled a little, blinking back tears. He was a contractor and kind of reminded me of my dad, who would have looked at this expensive wedding to a business mogul's kid and shaken his head in disbelief. Hal didn't seem to need anything, but his hand landed on my shoulder again. "We just love 'em both so much. You got kids?"

I shook my head.

"Well, you worry about your kid finding someone who loves 'em, really loves 'em right. Then it happens, and it's like a piece is added to your heart . . . Well, anyway, you'll know when you're a father."

I smiled automatically, schooling my expression, and reached out to shake his hand. "I'm happy to be part of their day." His wide palm fell on my shoulder again, hard. I bit the inside of my tongue to keep from crying out. *Please, for the love of God, take your hand off my shoulder.*

"And that minister, well, not a minister, the lady up front, she is a straight shooter. I tell ya." He motioned to RJ, who was talking with the couple. "I like her."

She wore a sleeveless white shirt, and the fabric looked silky, like it would slide over her skin smoothly, with blue cigarette pants that hugged her body. She flicked her eyes up and they narrowed when she caught me looking, but her lips curled in the sexy, irresistible way I couldn't get enough of as she gave me one of those secret smiles. It was a lot easier to focus my attention on her secret smiles than linger on what Hal had said.

I returned my attention to him. "She's definitely something."

"I'll leave you to it," he said, wrapping his large hand around my own. "Just wanted to say thanks and that we're really lookin' forward to tomorrow." He walked back toward his wife in the late afternoon sun. I'd had a few weddings in a row where I wasn't needed for the rehearsal dinner. Those were the best, because I got to spend time with the woman walking toward me casually, like it wasn't all I'd been wanting all week.

I slid a hand in my pocket, knowing if I was as confident as I was pretending to be, I'd be able to do something natural with my hands, when all I wanted to do was reach for her. "Everything good with the couple?"

"They're all set." She looked over my shoulder at the building that housed the rain location for the manicured garden. "You have somewhere in mind?"

"Venue manager is going to be here for a while. I was thinking go back to your place—it's close by, right?" I didn't need to ask. I remembered everything from the night I'd driven her home after her car accident.

"Yes, but not my place." She slid her own hand into her pocket, averting her gaze. "I need to do something later across town. Your place?"

A heat I didn't enjoy spread up my neck, and it had nothing to do with my sunburn. While it was nicer than a supply closet, I wanted to impress her, and I was certain my place wouldn't. "I'm staying with Penny and her wife right now. Uh, in their basement."

A small smile quirked at the corner of her mouth.

"I'm not embarrassed about it," I lied. Gretchen was helping me untangle things with Sarah and the small house we'd bought together outside the city in California. Until that was settled, my finances were as unimpressive as my social life.

"You shouldn't be." Her smile fell, some private joke with herself. "I wasn't laughing at you. You have a bed in the basement?"

"Yes."

She nodded toward the exit. "Sounds perfect. Your place in half an hour, then."

I OPENED THE door. "Hey. Your errands go okay?"

"Sure," she said, glancing around the entryway in a way that made me wonder if there really were errands she had to run or if she just didn't want me in her place. The house was small and cozy, with photos of Kelly and Penny on all the walls. There was an empty frame set aside on an end table. I was pretty sure that had held a photo of Sarah and me last time I'd visited. "Are you redecorating?"

I inhaled, smelling the distinctive odor she had picked up on compared to the fresh air from outside. "We can head this way," I said, motioning to the basement door. "I was painting," I said unnecessarily as we walked by the stack of cleaned brushes and rollers drying on the kitchen floor.

The stairs creaked slightly as we walked into the finished basement. "What were you painting?"

"They hadn't done the nursery yet. I didn't want them to have to worry about it when they brought the baby home." I led her through the small open area where I'd stacked boxes and into the bedroom.

I'd told her I wasn't embarrassed, but I noticed everything as we walked, taking it in through her eyes. There weren't many boxes and almost no furniture. I also avoided how I'd felt painting the nursery, the unexpected flood of emotion when I rolled the pale yellow color they'd already picked out onto the walls.

I closed the door behind her and watched RJ walk around the small room. "That was nice of you to paint for them."

I shoved my hand in my pocket again. "They've done a lot for me. It wasn't a big deal. So . . ."

I'd had my mouth all over RJ's body. We'd had quick and dirty moments in hidden spots and supply closets, but having her in my bedroom, in my life, was uncomfortable, and I felt uneasy only because I didn't know what to expect. I'd imagined her in this bed with me a hundred times.

RJ stepped toward me and slid a hand up my chest. "You don't want to talk about it?"

Her hip was familiar and comforting under my palm. "It's just not that interesting."

She looked up at me, her fingers working the buttons of my shirt. Her gaze wasn't exactly soft but soft adjacent, and she spoke in a quiet voice. "I think you're interesting."

"Is that a good thing?" I dragged my hand up her ribs, confirming the softness of the fabric of her shirt, and dipped my head to slide my lips up her neck.

She let out a tiny moan when I kissed the spot she liked. "It's an interesting thing. I usually know what to expect from people." Her fingers ran over my chest and down my abs, and the way she moved slowly, making it clear we had time, had me wanting to savor her touches and also throw her onto the bed. "Sometimes you surprise me."

"I didn't know paint fumes were a turn-on for you." I pulled her shirt from where it was tucked in, sliding my fingers under the silky fabric. "I—" The joke froze in my throat as she slid my shirt off my shoulders, sliding her fingers over my sunburn, her short red nails digging into my skin in a way I normally liked. This time, I made a noise that was mildly inhuman. It was a yelp mixed with a growl.

RJ jumped back, her eyes wide. "What's wrong?"

"Just a sunburn." I winced, breathing through my nose and waiting for the pain to fade. "It's okay." I reached for her hip again, but she gently pushed my hand back.

"Let me see."

"It's fine. I'll just be careful."

RJ's hands came to her hips, her lips pursed, and I relented.

"Fine," I said, turning around and letting her finish sliding my shirt off. I'd spent the morning outside, focused on the work I was doing, and now the burn felt developed and painful.

"Lear," she said, touching a cool finger to the back of my shoulder, "this is bad." The cool touch felt good as she traced over my skin, barely touching me. "How long were you out there?"

"A few hours. I wasn't thinking. Forgot sunscreen."

"What was so important?" She tugged the sleeves over my hands and set the shirt aside.

"The nursery furniture they bought a while back just in case—the rocking chair and dresser and stuff . . . it's all secondhand, and the paint was faded and not great to begin with, so I was outside sanding and staining that, too." I'd gone into autopilot mode, wanting to make it all look perfect while ignoring my thoughts. Following along with YouTube tutorials was easier to focus on.

RJ was quiet for a moment. "Do you have aloe?"

I turned. "No. Don't worry about it. Let's get back to this . . ." I reached for her hip again. "We had plans."

RJ pushed my hand away. "I didn't know your entire body was sautéed when we made the plans."

"Not my whole body," I said with a shrug I regretted immediately.

RJ noticed, and her expression was self satisfied. "You're right. Just the back half of you. Please go take a cool shower. I'm going to find you aloe." She snatched her bag off the floor.

"You're telling me to take a cold shower . . . now?"

She pressed a finger to my lips. "Shrugging causes you pain. What did you think you were going to do with me on that bed?"

I hadn't thought that through, the burn a distant second thought to kissing, touching, and tasting RJ, and I finally relented.

The cool shower felt good on my back and shoulders, and I stood under the spray in my tiny basement shower until the chill of the water got to me. Goose bumps were really not how I'd planned for this evening to play out, but when I stepped out of the shower, a towel around my waist, RJ was already back, sitting legs crossed on the bed, holding a bottle of bright green aloe vera gel.

"You really don't have to do this," I said, trying to read her. Uncomplicated and unattached was our thing. We made each other feel good and then went back to veiled contempt, and she had to be looking for an opportunity to flee.

RJ waved off my words, though. "Do I seem like the woman who does things she doesn't want to do?"

"For someone who ardently resists help, you're really insistent in other people accepting yours."

"I'm an enigma." She patted the bed next to her. "Stay in the towel, though."

"So you can access my body quickly?" I lowered to the bed, wincing.

"Yeah, I've always wanted to use aloe as a lubricant. You are very much misreading this situation." RJ's laugh was low and warm, and I wanted to hear it again.

"What about your clothes? Shouldn't you avoid aloe stains?"

She laughed again, kind of a free laugh, and when she squeezed aloe onto my shoulder, her hand sliding over the liquid, the coolness of it felt like immediate relief. "That was nice of you to get things ready for them."

"I guess," I said, letting my eyes fall closed at the sensation of her hands, knowing she couldn't see the vulnerable movement. "They're family."

"Two weeks ago, you gave that bride's great-aunt a crash course on Instagram so she could see the wedding posts."

I dipped my chin to my chest, and she stroked aloe over my neck and down between my shoulder blades. "It's not like hashtags are that hard to explain . . ."

"I'm saying you're a nice guy," she said. "Why are you pretending you're not?"

She swiped the cool goo across my back, gently working it over my skin. With my back to her, it was easy to ignore the emotions rising in my chest at the idea of being a nice guy. "Not that nice-guys-finish-last BS, is it? That's tired."

I ignored her question and she gave a little hum, and I savored how her fingers gently glided over the same areas, making sure my skin was covered.

"Can you lay on your stomach to let this sit a little?"

"You don't have to take care of me." I slid onto the bed, the towel still wrapped around my waist, the air-conditioning blowing across the aloe, the combination making me want to sink into the bed.

"I know."

I turned my head, resting it on my forearm.

She stood by the bed, staring at my body, but not in the way she normally did. She was inspecting and assessing, and she wiped her hands with a tissue.

"I'm fine, RJ. I'm sure you want to get going if we're not going to hook up."

She lowered to the bed next to me, stretching out on her back. Her shirt was tucked back in and she looked like she had at the rehearsal, but everything about her lying there, the scent of her perfume and the aloe all around me, felt right. "Soon." She kicked off her heels and settled her hand behind her head before glancing at me. "Why are you looking at me like that?"

"Like what?"

"Like I just did something altruistic. This is completely selfish." She stroked a finger down my arm, careful to avoid the burned skin. "I prefer my benefits to come from human men and not grilled lobster. I want you back in fighting shape next time."

"Maybe you're just nice, too."

"I'm not." She looked at the ceiling, her finger still moving over my skin.

We lay in the house's silence for a few minutes, her fingers not leaving the stretch of unmarred skin. "I grabbed Tylenol, too, when you want it." She said it quietly, like I was asleep or she just didn't want anyone else to see this glimpse into a softer RJ.

I could have fallen asleep—her touch and the give of the mattress and the long day in the sun painting before the rehearsal were hitting me. I was exhausted and I wanted to pull her close and kiss her in a way that really conveyed what it meant to lie next to her and not talk. I couldn't really move, so I just said, "Thank you."

Chapter 21

LEANING AGAINST MY car, I reread my email to Gretchen, making sure no wayward typos made it into my answer to her question regarding the latest challenge with the Mayfield case.

I hit send, and a notification flashed across the screen a moment later.

LEAR: Stop working.

RJ: I never stop working.
RJ: How did you know I was working?

"You get this crease between your eyebrows when you're focused on the job." Lear strode toward me, hands in the pockets of his jeans, looking handsome in a blue T-shirt that stretched over his chest, the sleeves accentuating his toned biceps.

"I do not," I said, tucking my phone into my pocket. Seeing him out in the world, in the middle of the day, was unsettling except for the way his forearms flexed, reminding me of how he'd relaxed under my touch the weekend before when I smeared aloe on his skin.

He laughed and placed the tip of his finger between my brows. "Right here."

"Whatever." I nudged his arm away, but the warmth of his skin briefly made my palm tingle. "Why are you watching me, anyway?"

"I wasn't watching you. I saw you when I walked out of the pharmacy." He leaned one arm against my car. "You think I'd spend my only day off following you around?"

As soon as my eyebrow went up, he laughed again, the slight breeze blowing his hair across his forehead. "I'm just running errands. How about you? Besides working in the parking lot."

"I'm on my way to get a manicure and pedicure, if you must know."

"That's good—your feet were looking a little rough last time I saw them." He jumped out of the way before my hand could make contact with his abs, his smile easy.

I fought my grin and swatted his stomach. "Like you've got room to talk."

"Maybe I should go with you."

"You get pedicures?"

He crossed his arms across his chest. "Are you calling me unevolved?"

I matched his posture, giving him what Britta called my lawyer eyebrow.

"Fine. I don't normally drop money on it, but I'll get one if it will make your sexual experience better."

I rolled my eyes and strode toward the nail salon. "I guess if you won't stop talking during sex, smooth feet are a consolation prize."

The nail salon wasn't crowded, and I inhaled the clean, slightly perfumed scent as I greeted the staff member at the desk. "Hi, Tom. I have an appointment."

The man at the front smiled and made a note on his computer before looking over my shoulder. "And you?"

"Any chance you have an opening?"

"Pick a color," he said, pointing to the wall of nail polish behind us and returning to his screen.

"Decisions, decisions . . ." Lear rubbed his chin and I nudged him with my hip.

"You're not going to get a color."

He shrugged. "I can't on my fingers. Penny has a strict no-nail-color rule, lest it clash with some couple's color scheme."

"Oh." I reached for a bottle and my hand collided with Lear's, him grabbing the bottle of That's My Jam, my unfortunately named favorite. "I thought you said you didn't want color."

"On my fingers," he said, holding the bottle out of reach. "This might look good on my toes."

"That's my shade."

"I know—you wear it all the time."

I huffed, but he only grinned in response. "Is that still the color of your back?"

He pointed to a bottle of light pink polish. "Closer to this now."

Mai and Laura led us to the pedicure chairs, Lear following behind me. We didn't have a lot of money growing up, but I remember thinking getting a pedicure was the height of luxury the first time my mom took me. As I sank my feet into the hot water and Mai started the massage feature in my chair, I stifled a groan and closed my eyes.

Laura looked up at Lear. "Is the water okay for you?"

"Perfect. Thank you." Lear's deep voice stood out in the space filled with mostly soft voices, and I glanced at him. His jeans were rolled up to his knees as he flashed his annoyingly charming smile at Laura.

They left us to soak, and when I rolled my head to the side again to take in Lear, he was already looking at me. "Why do you know what color I pick?"

He handed me the bottle and lifted one shoulder. "You always wear it, or a color that looks like that."

I closed my eyes again, not wanting to see the dimple pop when he inevitably smirked. "No one ever pays attention to my fingers unless I'm flipping them off."

"You flip me off a lot."

I smiled without looking at him. "I guess I do."

"You also have nice fingers. They're . . . pretty."

My eyes snapped open at the compliment, but Lear had let his eyes fall closed, and I admired the curve of his jaw, looking for sarcasm.

"Thank you." I looked at my own hands, examining them. No one had ever complimented my hands before, but it was the part of my body I loved most. "My fingertips are curved like my grandma's."

"No way. Let me see."

I held out my hand, and he took it, examining my three middle fingers on each hand, all of which curved slightly inward. He'd never held my hand, not outside of gripping it during one of our hookups, but it was nice, warm, and for a minute I had an insane fantasy he'd kiss my knuckle. "I don't know how I never noticed that. Were you close with her?"

I pulled my hand back. "Yeah." She'd lived with us after my dad left. She'd been one of the largest constellations in my sky for a long time—caregiver, disciplinarian, comforter. "We were close."

He nodded, maybe sensing I didn't want to talk more about it. Maybe just not interested. "This is nicer than the nail salons I've been to before."

Around us, people chatted under the soft lighting and airy color-coated walls. This was the one place where I totally relaxed. Usually I put my phone away, and even if I looked at emails, I didn't answer. My mom got on me about self-care, the same things my grandma used to say to her, and I listened, if for no other reason than it reminded me of her. "I would have thought LA would have a lot of nice nail salons."

"I never went in LA. My mom would take me when I was younger, though. We lived a couple hours west of here."

"I can't picture you young . . . All I imagine is a mini version of you in OshKosh polo shirts." I wiggled my toes in the water, moving toward the jets. "If your mom visits you, bring her here. They're the best. So good, she might forget what a charming jackass her son is."

I expected him to volley back, but he was quiet. When I turned my head, I caught a flash of a pause before he gave me a small grin. "She actually died when I was a teenager. Both my parents did. She would have liked it, though."

Shit. I felt the blood drain from my face, and I desperately tried to pull back my words.

"It was a long time ago. Stop searching for something to say." He leaned his head against the padding of the chair and closed his eyes, leaving me to fumble privately, though Mai gave me a raised eyebrow of acknowledgment.

"I'm sorry I said that, about you being a jackass." I looked away, too, sinking into the awkwardness. "I didn't mean it."

"You call me a jackass all the time." I heard the smile in his voice before I saw it. "It's almost a term of endearment."

"Don't go that far." I stole a glance at the side of his face. "I don't really mean it, though. I mean, you're not really a jackass."

He chuckled, and we let our conversation fall away as Laura and Mai went to work on our feet, scrubbing and clipping, moisturizing and massaging.

My gaze never strayed far from Lear, taking in how long he looked in the chair, how comfortable. Guilt still niggled at the edges of my thoughts at what I'd said, but his slight yelp at the hot towel around his legs and the pink that crossed his cheeks made me stifle a laugh and call him a lightweight.

"Can you do my toenails in the same color as hers?" He motioned to the bottle in Mai's hand.

"That's my signature color," I protested.

"It's a publicly available shade."

I motioned to his sneakers tossed on the floor. "No one is even going to see your feet."

"Who sees yours besides me?"

Laura and Mai exchanged a look.

"Don't encourage him. He's not cute."

Laura waved her hand at me. Mai and her daughter had the same smile. "I think he's kind of cute."

"Thank you," Lear said with an elaborate bow. "She's so mean to me."

"No, she likes you," Mai said, fanning my big toe after the first coat of polish. "I can tell."

Lear pointedly ignored me, joining in the conversation with Laura and Mai. "You think so? She's kind of difficult to read."

"RJ?" Mai waved him off and expertly moved the brush over my toenails, never a drop or line of polish touching my skin. "RJ is easy to read. She's a softy on the inside."

Lear leaned forward conspiratorially. "See, I think you're right, but she doesn't want anyone to know."

"I am sitting right here," I said, arms crossed. "Why are you butting in on my pedicure time?"

Lear grinned. "You invited me."

"You invited yourself."

Mai handed Laura the bottle, and she began painting Lear's toes, which I begrudgingly had to admit were nice. After his cold shower was the first time I'd ever seen him barefoot, and though I wasn't a foot person, it annoyed me that even his feet were handsome.

"Let this dry," Mai instructed. "Don't wiggle your toes while you flirt with this boy."

"I am not flirting with him."

"Lies, lies, lies," she said with a laugh over her shoulder as she walked away.

Lear watched Laura, following her quick, precise movements before swinging his gaze to me. The smirk on full display. "She thinks you're flirting with me."

"She's inhaled too many nail polish fumes," I said, glancing at my overturned phone on my lap and suppressing a grin.

"She comes almost every other week. You should come with her again," Laura said.

Traitor.

Lear dropped his smirk and just gave Laura a smile. "Her nails always look really nice, and this was very relaxing. Maybe I will."

I risked a glance at him again, though he was looking at Laura working. He looked good in casual clothes.

His eyes were closed, head resting against the chair. "You're staring at me."

"I am not."

Lear rolled his head to the side. "You can't help yourself."

"Believe me. I can."

He laughed, his flat stomach moving with the force of it, and when he caught me looking, he met my eyes, his lips in a playful smirk.

Laura fanned his toes, shaking her head at us. "I never thought I'd see RJ here with a date."

I rolled my eyes, inspecting my own toes. I didn't hate the idea of doing this again with Lear as much as I thought I might.

Chapter 22

LEAR

I STOOD MAKING small talk with a groom's grandmother, scouting a space RJ and I could escape to later. My sunburn had faded, and she hadn't been back to my place, but every time I fell into bed, I thought about her soft touches and how the mattress dipped slightly with her next to me.

"Excuse me," I said to Nana Mary as I saw the photographer step in, glancing around. He was from out of town and I hadn't worked with him before, but Penny said he was a big deal and could be a good contact. As I strolled toward the man, I made eye contact with RJ across the room. She looked like she'd come from court, wearing a gray suit, her hair pulled back. I loved getting her out of the suits that made her look so formidable. I got a peek into this soft corner of her life and it was a nice study in contrasts. Not that she wasn't formidable naked.

RJ, of course, rolled her eyes at my grin.

"Hi. I'm Lear Campbell. Good to meet you." I stretched out my hand to greet the photographer, who eyed the space skeptically.

"Garrett Parker," he said, not returning the smile and squeezing my hand harder than necessary.

"We'll get started soon," I said, glancing at my watch. The bride was wiping at her eyes in the corner, so I knew we had a few minutes. "What do you—"

"I'm known for capturing unique angles, so I'll be moving all around. Is there anything you need to adjust to accommodate that?"

The guy reminded me of people I worked with in LA who believed they were the most important person in the room. The skill of keeping my expression and tone neutral came in handy more than I would have expected. "No, but . . ." I glanced up, motioning for RJ to join us. "Let me introduce you to the officiant. We've not been in this space before, but she usually has a few notes for photographers."

RJ strode toward us and I swallowed, wondering what was under that simple, professional suit.

"Notes?" Garrett Parker's face twisted into a smirk. "I don't really take notes."

"Excellent, then you must be good at remembering," RJ said as she reached us, adjusting her glasses on her face. "RJ Brooks," she said, holding out her hand.

"Garrett Parker, Parker Studios. The couple likes my style, so that's what I'll be doing—moving around, getting the important moments from unique angles. Ones I won't be able to capture tomorrow. Questions?"

RJ tilted her head to the side, a look I knew well, though it was usually pointed at me. "Perfect, just stay off the altar."

"That's not my style." The guy adjusted his camera bag on his shoulder and looked past RJ. "I'll stay out of your way, and other officiants are always fine with it for a rehearsal. I'm a professional."

"Excellent. I'm a professional, too, and I'm telling you I don't want photographers on the altar. The couple knows that, and now you do, too. Questions?"

The man heaved a labored sigh, looking at me. "I have a certain style and it involves catching moments from the altar, sometimes during the rehearsal. This is ridiculous."

RJ straightened next to me, and I didn't need to see her face to know the look that was coloring her pretty features.

"Let's pause," I said, trying to play Switzerland. "There is a second level." I pointed to the loft space overlooking the altar. "Could you use that space instead of being on the altar? RJ, would that work?"

The guy swore under his breath, hoisting his camera bag on his shoulder again. "I'll try it."

"Good," I said, stifling the urge to push the guy back, schoolyard style. "RJ?" I said, turning my head to face her, and saw her expression was twisted into a stiff, icy glare.

"As long as you stay out of my space, I'm good." RJ didn't meet my gaze but kept her focus on the photographer.

"Um, alright, then. Garrett, why don't I show you how to access the loft?" I said, motioning to the inconspicuous door behind him. "RJ, can you give me a few minutes and then we can get started?"

She nodded wordlessly, still keeping her expression trained on Garrett, who sighed again and turned.

"You should have a good vantage," I said, making small talk as we climbed the stairs to access the loft.

He grunted in response, surveying the space and looking over the railing at the altar. I wasn't a photographer, but I knew enough about it to know this space was great. He pulled a camera from the bag and took a few test shots. "It's fine. Part of the job is working with people like that sometimes." His demeanor had thawed and apparently we were having a bro moment.

"RJ is good. We all have our nonnegotiables, right?"

"Of course," he said, taking a few more shots, "but some women think theirs are special, you know?"

I ignored his question, checking my watch to give my hands something to do. RJ didn't need me to protect her, but I wanted to speak up against this guy's bullshit. I bit my tongue, remembering

Penny's note that, despite what looked a lot like posturing, this guy was a big deal, and having him as a good contact was important. Still, I wanted to tell him what I thought. "You ready?"

"In a minute," he said, crouching, camera trained on where the bride and groom were laughing with some family members. "I'm just saying thanks for calming her down."

Protectiveness. That's what was coursing through me, even though RJ would be the first one to tell me she could fight her own battles. "I didn't *calm her down*, I just offered a solution." I crossed my arms over my chest, dropping the Switzerland from my tone. "We need to get started."

THE REHEARSAL WAS going smoothly. RJ and I had found a kind of balance in who ran which part, and compared to the first wedding we worked together, it was a well-choreographed cakewalk. A lot of our time together felt like we were in sync. Sex with RJ was always incredible, but joking with her, texting with her, all of it was starting to feel important to me.

As we neared the run-through of the ceremony, the photographer crept behind RJ, camera trained on the couple. I gripped my tablet. He was quiet, and I wasn't sure RJ even knew he was there, which made me even angrier. *Dick*. RJ finished going over the ring ceremony, her voice like honey in the room as she turned from bride to groom to make sure they were clear on what to do, something I noticed she always spent time on.

In that next moment, three things happened almost at the same time. The maid of honor cracked a joke and everyone laughed, Garrett swung his camera to capture the moment, and RJ turned her head as the best man responded. Garrett's lens made contact with her face, the momentum of both of their movements resulting in a crash. RJ's sudden jerk made me think it probably hurt, but then the guy didn't move right away, just nudged forward and snapped a few shots before stepping back. It all happened in seconds, everyone else still laughing at the jokes between the best man and maid of honor.

RJ's hand went to her face, and she stared at her fingers for a moment, presumably to see if she was bleeding. I couldn't hear their exchange, but it was short and terse before she turned to the couple and finished the rehearsal without incident. Garrett Parker of Parker Studios had stepped back quickly, and I balled my fists at my sides for the rest of the rehearsal.

"I have what I need here," Garrett said, pausing on his way out. We stood near the exit, the hall where everyone else had lingered only partially visible from where we were positioned. "Ten tomorrow at the bridal suite?"

"Yes. Ten." I kept reminding myself that Penny wanted this contact for future business, but I glanced back at RJ, whose fingers gently tapped at her face where he'd hit her. "And what were you doing up there? She asked you to stay back."

"It was a good shot. I took it." He gave a passing glance behind me. "She'll get over it."

"Jesus, man. Can you show her a little respect? She asked you to stay off the altar."

"Listen, *man*," he said, stepping forward. He was a few inches shorter than me and a thin guy, but his step was clearly meant to intimidate. "You know they're paying me a lot more than they are her, so I'm going to do what I want. You're the event planner. Figure out a way to appease her." He looked behind me again, a smirk crossing his face and his tone lightening. "She needs to relax. Friend, I'd do it myself, but I don't have time to get her drunk enough."

Well, Penny's gonna be pissed. I stepped forward, using my size to force him backward. "Listen, motherfucker, they are paying you a lot and you'll take great photos, but if you ever make a joke like that in my presence or deign to disrespect a woman in front of me like you did tonight, you'll be developing those photos from the ER, understood?"

Our voices were low in the alcove. "You're threatening me?"

I took a step back, crossing my arms over my chest. "I'm a professional. Just making sure you have all the information you need for tomorrow, *friend*."

"Of all the amateurish . . ." He took another step back and pushed open the door. "Have a good night, asshole. Good luck booking me for anything again."

Shit, shit, shit. I turned slowly, taking in a deep breath and composing the necessary email to Penny in my mind. Most of the wedding party had left for dinner, a barbecue at the groom's parents' house, which was perfect because they didn't need me there. After confirming a few details, I waved the last of them away and looked for RJ.

Chapter 23

RJ

I WAS RUNNING out of excuses to hang around after wedding events to "casually" run into Lear, but tending to a facial injury was a new one. I brushed my finger over the scraped and tender spot on my jaw where the jerk's camera lens had made contact. It was minor and had only bled for a moment, but I was pissed. I dropped my hand and took in my face in the bathroom mirror. *Severe.* That was the face I tried to convey, and it's what I thought I'd made clear to the photographer. Of course, I'd made it clear to Lear, too, and look how that ended up. I inhaled slowly and tried to relax the line between my eyebrows. It wasn't like it was the first time I'd had to deal with cocky assholes in my line of work. The guy had reminded me of Case, though. When I told him I wanted more affection between us, for us to take time to really build our relationship, he was dismissive. When I called him on it, he acted like I was at fault for changing the rules. Maybe I had. That's why the thing with Lear was better. The rules were clear and neither of us was interested in changing them.

Resting my palms on the sink, I inhaled and exhaled a deep breath. *Let it go.* I'd been looking forward to the rehearsal all day. More accurately, I'd been looking forward to afterward all day. "I'll feel better after I get off," I said into the empty restroom, ignoring the niggling thought that I'd feel better once I was with Lear. My quiet voice echoed around me. I'd spotted Lear and the photographer near the exit as we finished up. They'd been almost toe-to-toe, Lear looming several inches taller. My heart had fluttered when I saw that, wondering, maybe hoping . . . was that about me? I rolled my eyes at my reflection in the mirror. "Ridiculous." Pushing off the counter, I stepped into the hallway.

"Hey," he greeted me from where he stood leaning against the doorway into the hall where the ceremony rehearsal had taken place.

I walked toward him, admiring the lines of his long body, his sleeves rolled up to reveal his forearms. "Hey."

He glanced at my jaw, then scanned my body shamelessly. "I was hoping you'd stick around."

His eyes flicked down again, following the lines of my suit. I flushed. It was a nice suit, but I'd bought it for court, for a space where I needed to be sharklike, severe RJ, and I had a moment of regret that that was all Lear would ever see in me. I shook away the thought. "You're a fan of my suit?"

A slow grin spread across his face, but he didn't move from his spot along the door frame. Lear shrugged one shoulder. "It's alright."

"No smart comment about getting me out of it?" I stepped closer, leaning against the opposite door frame and matching his pose.

He dragged his thumb over his chin, his voice low. "Do you want me to get you out of it?"

"Obviously." I crossed my arms over my chest. "But I expect some wit from you. A little tête-à-tête."

He pushed off the wall, reaching me in two steps, his eyes following his finger down the buttons on my blouse, grazing each with the back of his middle finger. "Something like, I'd prefer it in a pile on the floor?" He finished the question with his finger resting on the waistline of my pants.

My breath hitched as he played with the closure before meeting my eyes again. "Something like that."

"You'd make fun of me if I said that," he murmured, dipping his lips to my ear as he continued teasing at the button, an errant finger trailing lower over the fabric.

I smiled despite myself. "Yeah, I would."

"Because you're mean," he said, dragging his nose down my neck, the light pressure tickling me as the anticipation grew.

"You wouldn't know what to do if I was nice to you," I said, the last few words breathy as his lips grazed the sensitive skin near my collarbone. Him touching me, teasing me out in the open, was exciting, and my breath hitched.

"I'd figure out something to do," he said, and I felt his smile against my neck, his thumb trailing the button near my navel and his scent surrounding me.

"Like what?" My breath came quicker as he left my skin tingling with every swipe of his lips, and his fingers slid under the waistband of my pants, tracing the edge of my panties.

"I guess you'll find out when you're nice to me," he murmured near my ear.

"The world may never know, then." I tipped my head to the side, stretching my neck. "Is there anyone here?"

"Building manager," he said, glancing down the hall. "C'mon." He stepped back and took my hand. I missed the constant, teasing pressure of his finger against my shirt, but his hand encased mine as he led me across the open space toward the door he'd taken the photographer into.

"The loft?" I followed him up the dimly lit back stairwell. The building was refurbished industrial space, and I wondered if this used to be a foreman's office back in the day. At the top of the stairs, the space opened up into the lofted area, looking over the ceremony space and a back room with a few chairs.

"Back here," he said, guiding me into the small room and pushing the door closed.

I took in the small space, eyeing the worn and stained chairs. "What—"

He cut me off, his fingers curling behind my neck and his other hand at the small of my back. Our lips and tongues tangled, and I felt the anticipation from the hall return under the pressure of his insistent kiss, and I let my hands roam over his obliques to his back. Our bodies pressed close to each other, and I shimmied out of my jacket with his help, tossing it on one of the worn chairs. Apparently the banter-and-teasing portion of our night was over—and I was fine with that. Lear's hips pressed to mine, his unmistakable arousal nudging my stomach, and I reached between us to stroke him.

"Yes," he said, fingers curling into my hair and his kiss deepening at my touch.

I winced when he cupped my chin. The unexpected pain when he made contact with the spot where the camera had grazed me felt startling.

He froze. "What's wrong?"

"Sorry." I brushed my fingers over the tender spot. "Just where that guy hit me. I'm fine."

Lear's featured shifted, his expression darkening and warring with something else. "That dick," he muttered. "I'm sorry. Does it hurt? Let me take a look." He cupped my chin, careful not to touch the injury, and stared intently.

"It's fine, just tender."

His fingertips held my face so gently, it was hard to reconcile this touch with the searing embrace from a few seconds earlier. Lear studied my face like he was inspecting a surgical field and not the minor cut with the surrounding swelling. "Asshole," he muttered under his breath, brushing a fingertip at my temple, his face still so close to mine, as close as if we'd been about to kiss, but the energy had shifted and I suddenly didn't know how to act. His touch was reverent, gentle, and I was experiencing an overwhelming sensation of being cared for that was unfamiliar.

"I'm fine." I shifted my gaze, avoiding his intense inspection and tipping my head away. I felt relief and loss at the same time. "I mean, he is an asshole, but I'm fine." I strategized how to get back to where we were a few minutes before. That moment seemed to be gone, though, because Lear was still casting quick glances to the spot on my face. "What were you two getting into it over, anyway?"

"What?" He looked up abruptly, like he'd only been half listening.

I brushed my hands down the front of my shirt, smoothing the mussed fabric. "It looked like you two were going to fight before he left."

Lear ran a hand through his hair and rocked on his heels. "Just a disagreement."

Dammit, all I wanted was a quickie and now I was stuck in this awkward sinkhole. "About what?"

Lear assessed my expression. "I told him he needed to listen to you."

I froze my ministrations. "Why?"

"Because he was acting unprofessionally, and I didn't like it. The guy hit you with a camera."

"On accident." I did not know why I was defending Garrett Parker, douche photographer.

Lear stepped back, his expression skeptical. "He was saying inappropriate stuff, and I let him know I didn't like it."

My hackles went up. "I don't need you to fight any battles for me."

"I worked in professional sports. It's not like I don't know what sexual harassment looks like. I wasn't fighting a battle for you. I told that guy I didn't appreciate him being a dick."

I reached for my jacket, flustered at the feelings of anger and the tinges of something softer rising in me. I didn't like the softer. It felt too close to caring that he'd stood up for me. "I deal with ten guys just like him every week. I can handle things myself when they need handling."

"Well, I didn't like it. I don't think that makes me a bad guy. Are you seriously mad I told him to get his act together?"

No. Yes. I glanced at the door we'd just crashed through. I took a measured breath. "I'm not mad. I just don't want you thinking you have to protect me or whatever." I motioned between us. Him protecting me, or feeling like I needed protecting, was changing the rules. "That's not what this is."

"Noted," he said, features tight. "Let me add it to your list of guidelines."

"What does that mean?"

He stepped past me, opening the door into the main loft space. "No kissing after sex, no planning, no actual conversation. No telling guys who ignore your instructions and injure you they are in the wrong. Anything else?"

I huffed, ignoring the way he seemed to see everything I was tormented over. "I think we're done here."

"Yeah," he said, stepping into the hall. "Clearly."

Chapter 24

LEAR

I WIPED MY hands on a dish towel after packing leftovers into the fridge. The small kitchen always made me think of my aunt's waffles on Saturday mornings. She gave us whipped cream and chocolate chips, stuff my mom never let me have, and said dessert should never be optional. I folded the dish towel how she used to, something I'd watched her do a thousand times in that kitchen, and glanced over my shoulder. Uncle Harold was snoring softly in his easy chair, the evening news playing loudly on the TV.

The phone buzzed in my pocket.

RJ: Hey.

I stared at the message, surprised. I'd seen her the day before at the wedding, of course, and she'd barely made eye contact with me. Luckily the photographer stayed out of her way, but she seemed to be making it a point to stay out of mine. Maybe I was staying out of her way, too. I ignored the message and shoved my phone in my pocket. I'd been so pissed on Friday night after she did a one-eighty on me. It was another example of why getting involved with her, with anyone, was a stupid idea. When they walked out, and they eventually walked out, it left you feeling helpless.

My phone buzzed again, and I sighed, telling myself to ignore it as I pulled it from my pocket and unlocked my screen.

RJ: Can we talk?

LEAR: I'm in Sybel, helping my uncle.

RJ: I can call you when there's a good
time.

Uncle Harold would turn in soon, I knew, and he didn't need me to help him into bed. He was pretty self reliant, getting annoyed with Penny or me when we overstepped while trying to help him. I was staying the night only because I'd promised to help him with the lawn the next morning.

RJ: I owe you an apology.

I was certain anyone watching me would have known how surprised I was to read those words.

I looked up to see Harold stirring in his chair. "I think I fell asleep," he muttered, looking around.

"You still snore the same as ever," I joked, walking into the living room.

He laughed, this belly laugh that brightened his entire face. "Too old to change now."

"Hey, a friend is going to call—I might be out on the porch if you need me."

He winked. "To call? Boy, you're too old for me to care about you sneaking girlfriends up here. I didn't much care when you were a teenager and I sure don't give two figs now."

I laughed. Looking back, I was probably not as stealthy as I thought I was. "Just a phone call and just a friend. I'm steering clear of girlfriends for a while." Maybe forever. Sarah had come with me when my aunt Bette died, and I hated that she'd met my family, hugged my uncle Harold, and made me feel like she was always going to be part of things. I shrugged it off.

He waved a hand. "I'm going to bed, anyway. Have fun with your friend." He stood, and I pushed my thumb down on my middle finger, cracking the knuckle and stopping myself from helping him up, which would piss him off. He creaked to his feet and pulled me in for a hug. "You're a good boy, you know that, right?"

I nodded but said nothing, his question hitting me in the chest in an unexpected way. "Good night," I said, voice rough before I managed to control it. "We'll get a jump on the lawn in the morning."

He patted me twice on the shoulder and shuffled down the hall to his bedroom. I heard his door click shut and wandered out onto the patio, where the cool breeze was rustling through the trees. Shoving my hands in my pockets, I ambled toward my car, looking up at the stars. I'd been in LA a long time, and it wasn't like I couldn't see the stars there, but not like this. The mountains made it feel like I was the only one in a valley, the only one looking up. I scrubbed a hand through my hair and prepared myself to talk to RJ.

Chapter 25

I TOSSED MY phone on the empty passenger seat next to me and dropped my head to rest on the steering wheel. The plastic, cool from the air conditioner, felt good against my skin, which was dappled with light reflecting from the gas station's glowing signs. When I woke up, I hadn't expected my Sunday to go the way it had.

I'd played soccer with Eric and some of his friends in the morning like always, working up a sweat and getting to be aggressive without being called some sexist or racist term that showed me the true colors of yet another person around me. When I finished the game and grabbed my things from the sidelines, I had a series of missed texts from Britta, Kat, and Del, our token man and the perpetual graduate student in the group chat.

KAT: RJ, did you see the news on social media?

DEL: That Case is getting married?

BRITTA: Why would you say it like that?

DEL: Like what? He is.

BRITTA: It might be hard for her to read.

BRITTA: RJ, it was on social media today in a kind of very public way.

Kat: Are you okay?

Del: FWIW, you're cuter than his new fiancée, and her name is Feather, which should make it easier for you to make fun of her.

Britta: Stop helping.

Britta: Del, we're going to kick you off this chat.

Del: Promise?

Kat: RJ, please text us when you get this.

I'd glanced up from my phone, watching the others wave and head toward the parking lot, but I dropped onto a park bench. Case and I had been over for years. I'd always assumed he'd move on, find someone he wanted to be with who fit what he wanted, someone consistent and polished. Someone nice. Instead of replying to my friends, I opened my browser and searched for Feather, Chicago, and proposal. Case didn't do social media. That's how he'd say it, like it was recreational meth. *I don't do that kind of thing.* The story came up on the account of what looked to be a petite woman with long braids. She wore artful and colorful makeup, a brush of a bright purple across her lids. She was stunning, and her brief bio said she was a massage therapist and poet.

The post was a thread.

C and I were interviewed by a local news crew after yoga in the park. Here's the video!

Yoga in the park? I hit play on the video, fairly certain this was a different Case and my friends had gotten it wrong. That was one thing I'd offered we could try together and he'd all but rolled his eyes. Sure enough, there was Case in a tank top and basketball shorts, his arm draped around the woman. Her hair was pulled back, and she wore a sports bra with yoga pants. The reporter introduced some potential legislation that would affect that section of the park and asked them their opinions. I waited for the Case I knew to emerge, for, even in a T-shirt, the shoulders to go back, his chin to go out, and for him to speak as if his words were the only and last ones anyone needed to hear. Instead, he looked at the woman beside him. "Go ahead." Two simple words that would have knocked me over like a two-ton truck. Not once in the entirety of our relationship had he encouraged me to go first. Even in bed, it was up to me if I wanted to finish ahead of him. The competition had been fun sometimes—not in the bedroom—but I stared at the interview as the woman spoke for a few minutes about the magic of the space and how the legislation would ruin the vibe.

The vibe? I shifted my gaze to a besotted-looking Case again. *Is he high? Did he suffer a traumatic brain injury that affected his personality?* Nothing I knew about the man fit into the image I saw before me. When the woman finished talking after sharing how she was sending good energy to the legislators, Case spoke up. "I couldn't agree more. This place is special. We met here and . . ." He looked down at the woman longingly before glancing at the camera. "Is it okay if I go a little off topic?"

The crew must have given him the okay, because he dropped to one knee and took her tiny hand in his. "Feather, I was going to ask you to marry me in this park, but since we might not get that chance, I'm asking you now. You've changed my life. You know, the last person I was with was cold and competitive and wore me down. You breathed life into me, showing me it's not about winning but about living, that if I am around a happy person, I can be happy, too; that a special person will make me want to break my own rules. I want to feel sunshine on my face with you in a hundred parks, a thousand parks. I don't have a ring yet, but will you marry me?"

Tears streamed down her flawless cheeks, and she nodded, a wide smile crossing her face.

What struck me first wasn't the romance of the moment, it was that he did that on the fly. He'd never done a spontaneous thing in his life, especially not in public and especially not involving a major decision. He was a planner. *He didn't have a ring? He just decided, yep, gonna marry her?* The video continued, and they kissed, him swinging her around and the small assembled crowd cheering. He had teared up, too, his eyes wet and his face red. He turned to the camera. "So, please vote to keep the park. It's a really special place for us." The reporter appeared on screen again and the video paused on her wide smile.

I continued scrolling to the next thread, where Feather—seriously, her name was Feather?—added more. Obviously, I said yes!

I looked up from my phone and watched two women with strollers walk along the path near me.

BRITTA: I know you saw our texts. Are you okay?

RJ: Just watched it. I'm fine.

KAT: What he said was so far out of line, RJ. No one thinks those things about you.

I flashed to the night before, to Lear, to getting mad at him for sticking up for me, to the photographer's eye roll when I told him how things would be. *The last person I was with was cold and competitive and wore me down. You breathed life into me, showing me it's not about winning but about living, that if I am around a happy person,*

I can be happy, too. I went into hype-woman mode, psyching myself up. Case *wanted* someone like me. Maybe he thought I wasn't a happy person, but he hadn't walked away until I needed something from him. Like my dad, who walked out when he was asked to step up. Case had stuck around until I asked him for some kind of emotional support. Then, poof. Gone.

> RJ: Well, obviously someone thinks it, but it's fine.

DEL: I think I've read her poetry before.
It's not bad.
KAT: Del! Not the time.
BRITTA: You are the worst.

> RJ: Don't be mad at Del. He's majored in every possible thing. I am sure he was in a poetry program for a couple of weeks.
> RJ: And I'd hate to see Case end up with a bad poet.

DEL: I know it.

I'd brushed off their concerns for a few more minutes and lied, telling them I needed to get into the office. Instead, I'd gone home, showered, and fallen onto my couch, going over and over my relationship with my ex. When that grew tiresome, and after I'd watched the video of his proposal to another woman for the third time, I'd tried to do some actual work, only to get pulled into a bitter divorce case. The vitriol between the couple was cutting and dark, and my mind wandered to asking Case if we should get married, of broaching the subject and his shaking his head, saying he didn't believe we'd be compatible long-term, that it was too difficult to love me and he didn't want to commit to having to do it forever. The fact that maybe he was right left me distracted, and I finally closed my laptop, deciding to grab my keys and drive to clear my head.

After an hour of getting lost in the mountains, following random exits, and then tracing my steps back to the interstate, I found myself in a gas station feeling three inches tall and like whatever was going on with Lear, I was ruining it. Not that I wanted to marry Lear. I didn't even want to talk to Lear most days, but I was realizing Case had found it difficult to care for me, and Lear had fought with that photographer, wanting to protect me, as if on instinct. There was something meaningful there, and my anxiety coiled at the idea of letting that go.

I glanced at my phone, where he'd replied that I could call whenever. I had no idea what I was going to say or why I'd even insisted on apologizing. Case's sunny smile from the video flashed in my head, and I pushed it away. Unexpectedly, Lear's expression from two nights ago came to mind, the look he'd had on his face before he admitted to fighting my battles for me. *For standing up for me.* I put my car in drive and pulled back out onto the road leading to the highway. Lear had said I was mean before he dragged his nose down my neck in this way that drove me nuts, like he was inhaling me and stroking me at the same time. I hadn't felt cold when he called me mean, though. I'd kind of liked it. I'd liked it in the way I liked a lot of things about Lear, and I knew he deserved more of an explanation for my response last night.

I merged onto the highway, still unsure why I felt this sudden need to apologize. But I was certain it would be easier to do while driving.

Chapter 26

LEAR

WHILE I WAITED outside, I leaned against my car, still looking up at the stars with an eye on the highway in the distance.

Excited to hear RJ's voice and annoyed that this woman clearly had me twisted up enough to need to remind myself to calm down, I navigated to her contact information and tapped the phone icon, not wanting to wait for her. I didn't move off the car. There was a full moon that lit the sky just enough for me to trace the lines in the concrete while I waited for her to answer.

"Hi," she said, and I could make out the ambient sounds of the road in the background. "Thanks for talking when you're with family."

"It's okay. I try to help my uncle out when I can." I paused, kicking myself and realizing that playing it cool and telling her my life story were not compatible. "He's asleep, though. Um, what's up?"

I strolled into the land behind the house. The only place to really sit was the patio, but I didn't want to risk waking Harold, or having him hear me crash and burn at whatever this was if he still had his hearing aid in. I started toward the back of the property where a small clearing at the base of a rocky ridge was lit by the moon and surrounded by lush grass.

As I walked, I could see the ridge beyond this part of the mountain, the hillsides dotted with the light from expensive windows inside very expensive homes. Uncle Harold was approached often about his land, and he'd gotten good offers, just none good enough yet, he'd always say. "So, what did you want to talk about?"

I imagined following the line of her neck down to that perfect bare shoulder, the soft skin interrupted only by her bra strap, and wished she was sitting next to me in the moonlight. I picked at a few blades of grass and waited for her.

"Listen," she said, voice quiet but steady. "About the other night. I suck at apologies."

"I shouldn't have stepped in."

"I'm trying to get better at owning up when I'm in the wrong. Not that it happens often, but I was in this instance." I wished I could see her expression. "I was wrong for snapping at you. I'm sorry."

"It's fine," I said, keeping my tone even. "You're independent. You handle stuff on your own. I get it."

"I do. That guy . . ." She sighed. "He reminded me of someone from my past, and it got me out of sorts. It wasn't just about you."

A guy steering clear of emotional entanglements would have inserted a "Cool" there effortlessly. Instead, sitting under a gnarled tree, I went the other direction, because I couldn't not ask. "Old boyfriend?"

"Yeah. I mean, he never hit me with a camera or anything else. He wasn't violent or abusive."

"Just an asshole?"

"Just . . . absent." She let the word hang for a few moments, and I heard the *tik tik tik* of her turn signal. "Anyway, it doesn't matter. I wanted to apologize because it was actually very noble that you wanted to set him straight. I think coming to my rescue, however unnecessary, is above the call of duty for a sex buddy."

"Are we buddies now?"

"You know what I mean."

It bothered me that it rankled how she hadn't answered the question. "Just so you know, I would have confronted him if he treated any person I was working with that way. I wasn't trying to save you." Except, I kind of was, if I was honest with myself. I would have told the guy off if he was a jerk to the other officiants I worked with, but I wasn't sure I'd threaten a fistfight if he got in Father Dominic's or Judge Cooper's way.

"That's really all I wanted to say. You deserved an apology and it felt like a cop-out to text it."

I racked my brain for something to add to keep her on the phone. "You're forgiven. I mean, you don't need to apologize, but we're good," I added, with no better options. "It's too bad it happened, though," I blurted when I heard her intake of breath like she was about to say goodbye. I liked hearing her voice in my ear.

"Why?"

"I was looking forward to Friday night. I mean, you've been on my mind." She didn't respond and I hurried to fill the silence. "Not in a weird way," I added quickly as a cool breeze blew around me. "Just, you know, we have a good time together."

I wished I could see her expression. I knew her flirtatious, annoyed, and ready-to-strike expressions, but I didn't know which one she might be wearing now. "We have a good time," RJ said finally. "And sometimes you're on my mind, too."

The old tree was solid against my back and I relaxed. "More dreams?"

"You'll never let me forget that, will you?"

I wasn't forgetting it anytime soon. "Probably not."

"You're telling me you haven't had sex dreams before, Lear?"

"Recently, they're usually about you." I didn't mention the non-dreams, the fantasies of making her laugh or holding her hand that plagued my thoughts when I wasn't careful to direct my brain elsewhere.

RJ chuckled, and when she spoke again, her voice sounded breathier. "Good dreams?"

I imagined lowering my lips to the spot on her neck that seemed to always make her let out a small moan, and I felt myself growing hard behind my zipper. "You want me to tell you about them?"

"Yeah, I think I—" She stopped suddenly and a horn blared. "Shit!"

I straightened immediately, my pulse rocketing up at the change in her tone. "What's wrong? Are you okay?"

"Fine, sorry," she said with a sigh, voice returning to normal.

"What happened?"

She was quiet for a minute while I pictured her in a ditch somewhere. "I got distracted and veered into the other lane."

I could only blame my dumb response on my body's still-tense reaction. "Distracted by what?"

"Seriously?" Her tone implied she was giving me a patented RJ look. It was comforting. "The impending phone sex."

"We weren't having phone sex," I said, relaxing against the tree again. "Not yet."

"Well, I had already skipped ahead to the inevitability of it."

"Always so impatient," I chided her, once again picking blades of grass with my free hand. "There's something to be said for living in the moment."

"I've always lived three steps ahead of the moment, or tried to. When I was a kid, my grandmother would say, 'Ruthie, you got your feet right here and your head an hour into next Tuesday.' Always Tuesday." Her tone was wistful, and I wished I could see her face, the way her features relaxed.

"Ruthie?"

"My given name is Ruth. My family calls me Ruthie."

I rolled the feel of the name around in my brain. Despite our arrangement, it was maybe the most personal thing I knew about her. "It's pretty."

"Thanks," she said. "Anyway, yes, I am impatient, but I don't think phone sex is worth a car accident."

"Probably not." The tree above me rustled in the breeze. "Do you want me to stay on with you while you're driving, though? Just to have someone to talk to?"

"I'm good, but I'm glad we talked."

"Me, too." I stood, shoving my free hand in my pocket. "We're . . . uh, we're good?"

"Definitely good," she said. "The best of sex buddies."

"Friends?" RJ was a puzzle I was having a hard time putting together, and I really wanted a label to affix to this.

"You don't want to be my friend," she said, her voice cutting out for a moment. "I'm better at what we have than friendship."

"Give yourself more credit," I said, following the line of the trees against the sky. "I think you care more than you let people know."

My words hung there. I imagined in a text exchange, I'd see the bouncing dots as I wondered how much I'd overstepped on the phone. The pause kept going. "Maybe," she said finally. "I better go, but I'll see you next weekend?"

I nodded, though she couldn't see me. "Drive safe, Ruthie."

I stared up at the stars and wondered what the hell I was doing and why I'd really wanted to hear her say we were friends, that something existed between us beyond just the mind-blowing sex. She hadn't, though—so I needed to focus my attention elsewhere and get my head on straight before the destination wedding the following weekend.

Chapter 27

RJ

"FANCY MEETING YOU here."

I glanced up from my laptop. "Is it? You texted asking where I was," I said, kicking out the chair across from me as Lear strode forward. I'd been responding to emails and reviewing a motion at the hotel's rooftop bar before the rehearsal. We hadn't seen each other since we'd fought and made up. He looked good in slacks and a pressed black shirt, the sleeves rolled over his forearms.

Lear slid into the chair and leaned back, his hair blowing slightly in the summer breeze. "Maybe I just meant that you tickle my fancy."

I bit my lip to stop the giggle from escaping. An honest-to-God giggle. *Who am I?* "I don't even know how to respond to that, other than to promise saying things like that is a solid way to make sure I never *tickle your fancy* or anything else again."

He took a tortilla chip from the bowl I'd been snacking on and flashed one of those grins I pretended bothered me. They were still cocky, but maybe in a sweeter way now. Maybe he was just wearing down my defenses, which, admittedly, I realized weren't fortified enough. I'd told him my real name, the nickname almost no one knew or used, and I hadn't thought twice about it. Eric used it sometimes to tease me, but only because he'd won it when we bet on the outcome of a case. With Lear, it had just come out, like one more piece of me I'd been comfortable with him seeing.

"Help yourself," I said wryly, motioning to the chips and finishing the last line of my email before hitting send. I grabbed my own chip. "Everything's ready for tonight?"

"Of course," he said, eyes intent on me. "I'm always ready. You know that." He raised his eyebrows suggestively. "And I'm always *ready*."

This time I did laugh. "You're in rare form today. We don't have time to explore whether you're *ready* or not." I glanced at my watch and tucked my laptop into my bag. "We're supposed to be downstairs in ten minutes."

When I agreed to officiate this destination wedding, I had thought a little time on the beach and a few cocktails would be the best part. A quickie in an actual bed without worry of being caught hadn't been part of my expectations for the trip, but with his hint, I thought about it. Maybe that kind of thing would be the reset button to put us back in the safe friends-with-benefits territory versus this confusing intrusion of feelings.

Lear didn't move from his spot across the table and took another chip from the bowl as I stood and put my bag over my shoulder, checking my watch. "We changed it to accommodate Grandma Florence, remember?" He tucked an arm behind his head and motioned me toward him after looking at his own watch. "Come back."

"You never told me you changed the time." I rested a hand on my hip and bit back the smile I felt rise when his eyes dipped, lingering on my breasts for a second, the heat in his gaze making me want to pull him into the elevator.

"I did tell you," he said, returning to my face.

"You never—"

"RJ." He wrapped his hand around mine and tugged me back to the table, the warmth of his fingers on my skin so familiar.

"You think I'll let that slide because you're cute?"

When he laughed, and I remembered how his breath against the back of my neck felt, a shiver ran through me. We weren't strangers to each other's bodies, but just sitting and talking . . . this was new.

"You think I'm cute." He still had my hand as I returned to the seat I'd been occupying. "I emailed you last night, and you're going to read me the riot act about not communicating and then check your officiant email and have to eat your words." He kissed my knuckles and then let my hand go. "I'm saving you the trouble."

"How very thoughtful." I'd never had to convey sarcasm when my mind was spinning from a kiss to my hand, but there I was, pretending the act hadn't thrown me.

"Plus, if we start fighting, you won't be smiling like that anymore."

I tilted my face toward the railing surrounding the rooftop, the sky beyond a brilliant blue. "What makes you think arguing with you wouldn't make me smile?"

"True." Lear's long fingers grazed the table, and I thought about the feel of them on my body, at the back of my neck. "Do you want to get together after the rehearsal?"

"Maybe." Of course I did, but I didn't want him to know how much I'd been looking forward to it. How much I'd started looking forward to him. "I have a big case I'm on now and I might need to get some work done, so we'll see." Did using work as the rationale soften the noncommittal response? I didn't usually care if I let a sexual partner down, but I didn't want to hurt his feelings.

Lear leaned one elbow on the table and dragged an index finger over the inside of my wrist. "Sure. I know work comes first."

I met his eye, enjoying his smiling expression and ignoring how the stroke of his finger on my wrist felt like foreplay. "It doesn't always leave time for fun. Have to stay on top of everything."

"You don't have to explain, RJ. We're not that different."

"Yes. I mean, I'm more type A than you, but still . . ."

He tickled my wrist, making me yelp. "Take it back."

"Never," I said.

Our eyes met, both our smiles wide. The heat was rising between us, and my body tingled in anticipation. "Lear, I own three label makers."

"That's just prudent," he said, snatching another chip from the bowl. "And kind of sexy."

"My label makers are sexy?"

"Yeah." He bit his lower lip, expression darkening. His eyes flicked to my lips, and I wondered if he'd kiss me there in the open. We didn't kiss outside of sex. That had been my line to draw, because it felt wise and like a way to make sure we didn't get confused. I wanted him to lean over and kiss me now, though. "Your custom tabs for each ceremony are enticing, so, yeah, I think your label makers are sexy."

"Lear," I said, lifting my arm to glance at my watch.

"You know, it's considered rude to check your watch when a man is telling you things about you he finds sexy," he said.

"We don't have a lot of time."

He stroked his finger along the inside of my wrist again. "We have forty-four minutes," he said, not taking his eyes off me. "You think I didn't check?"

My breath hitched at the soft touches. "You thought I wouldn't double-check?"

"No, I knew you would."

"If I didn't need to get ready and review my notes, I'd say we could do our thing now," I said, still enjoying the feeling of his fingertip tracing over my skin. I thought about the Mayfields. I'd been working that morning and again after arriving at the hotel, and the case was always on my mind. It was one of the biggest in my career, and the more involved I was, the more I wondered if I wasn't a little like Dina Mayfield. She was to the point, confident, and logical. I wondered how she'd react to this position, if she'd lean into how good it felt, knowing it wouldn't last.

He flashed a genuine smile and leaned forward, his forearms on the table. "We can hang out later, Ruthie."

I was lost in the sensation of his finger moving along my sensitive skin, and I almost missed the nickname, almost let it flow over me.

I gently pulled my hand away and ran it over the front of my shirt. "Don't call me Ruthie."

"Why not? It's your name."

"Only . . . special people get to call me Ruthie. I don't even know why I told you about it."

He held a hand to his chest in mock indignation. "You're saying I'm not special?"

"Lear, you're the farthest thing from special." It felt wrong coming out of my mouth, but that was exactly why I needed to say it. When our bodies weren't connected, when his hands weren't on me, it was easier to know what to do.

His cocky smile fell for a split second, though maybe I imagined it. Before I could think too much about it, he glanced across the rooftop at a group of kids screaming. "Sure. No problem."

I looked away from him, taking in the sight of the other patrons, families and couples lounging in the sun. "What about you? You said Lear is a nickname. Nickname for what?"

"Can't tell you."

I cut my eyes back to his. "Why not?"

He smirked and pushed back from the table in a fluid movement, holding a hand out to me. "Only special people get to know."

I rolled my eyes and stood, brushing chip crumbs off my clothes. I should have expected him to say that, but it still stung. "Fine. I'll see you downstairs."

I started to walk past him toward the bar's exit when his hand brushed my wrist. "You're not even going to say goodbye?"

"I thought 'I'll see you' was sufficient." We walked together into the lobby and hurried through the already open elevator doors. When they closed, we were alone. "You don't have to tell me about the name."

Lear stepped closer, backing me gently against the wall of the elevator car, and his hands fell to my waist. I had that feeling again, the one where I wanted him to kiss me against all reason. Instead, he spoke. "I chose to be in a production of *King Lear* in high school instead of going out for football. Nickname stuck."

"You were a theater kid? I guess that tracks. What with the musicals and all."

"*Hamilton* is a wildly popular show," he insisted. "And I'm named after my dad's father, Richard, who ended up being kind of a dick. I like Lear better."

The elevator dinged with each passing level as we neared my floor. I rested a palm on his chest, surprised at the honesty, the lack of sarcasm or playfulness. "Lear it is, then."

We stood near the mirrored wall, bodies tucked together, swaying in a sort of dance. His gaze fell to my lips again. "RJ it is," he murmured. "I'm glad I joined you on the roof."

"I'm glad, too." I was a few moments from pushing the emergency stop button and challenging him to go as fast as he could again, but reason took hold. "I'm not saying goodbye, because I'll see you downstairs in—" I glanced at my watch.

"Thirty-three minutes," he said, not taking his eyes off me.

"Show-off."

Chapter 28

LEAR

THE NEXT DAY started out so well. The wedding preparations were in full swing, vendors arrived on time, and there hadn't been a single hiccup, which should have prepared me for a major one.

I pushed a thumb between my eyebrows, surveying the small group of people gathered in the bridal suite. The destination wedding on the Outer Banks was small, and about fifty people sat on the beach outside, enjoying a beautifully timed sunset that would have aligned with the couple saying *I do*.

I'd been looking for the best man but gotten distracted when RJ smiled at me from where she was checking things at the makeshift altar. The breeze blew her curls, and the warm glow from the sun made her skin even more tempting to kiss and taste. I was imagining the feel of her lips when the bride's dad pulled me into the bridal suite, his mouth in a firm line.

This isn't good.

The bride sobbed into her mother's shoulder, and her father paced, the slight man looking like a caged animal. "How could he do this?"

"I don't know, honey," the mother of the bride said, stroking her daughter's hair.

"I'm gonna kill him," her dad muttered, fists at his sides. "I'm going to chop off his balls."

The groom had shown up, taken pictures with his attendants, and then left, texting that he couldn't do it. I might have killed him, too. The young bride's choked, hysterical cries filled the room, and I didn't let myself connect with what she was feeling, because as much as I thought I was getting emotionally untwisted, seeing her this raw left me feeling like my skin was scraped and bleeding. I made a mental checklist of tasks I would handle.

Notify the DJ.
Have hotel staff take down monogrammed decorations.
Cancel honeymoon suite.

The list went on, and I motioned to her dad that I'd begin taking care of things. Stepping out of the room was a relief, and I immediately looked around for RJ. I needed to tell her, but I also wanted to be next to her right now. I shook away the thought and found the hotel staff first. I knew it would take time to reset everything, but the last thing the bride needed to see was the lovely scripted version of their initials on every surface when the B in J&B was MIA. I texted RJ, hoping she'd have her phone near her since we hadn't begun yet.

LEAR: Groom is AWOL.

RJ: I knew that guy looked skittish.

LEAR: One point for you.

RJ: I didn't mean that to sound so cold.

LEAR: I know. Meet me in the bridal suite.

I hurriedly filled in the hotel's event manager and rushed back to the suite, where the scene was unchanged. The bridesmaids loitered outside looking green, and Jayda, the bride, sat inside with only her mother, who rubbed her back, and her father, who continued to pace, presumably planning the castration of one Benjamin Mercer.

I cleared my throat. "Would you like me to say something to the guests?"

The bride's parents shared a look across the room. "Maybe we should do it," her mother said, looking to me for confirmation. They were very proper people—concerned about which rules of weddings should be followed and how things were done, especially the mother of the bride. It felt good to know the answers. Penny had made me read books on wedding etiquette before I started, and though I'd balked, I was glad she had. My phone buzzed in my pocket and I had a feeling she was calling to check in on things. I thought about ignoring it, but given the number of vendors I'd just quickly asked to pack up, I had to check. It was her, and I shoved my phone back in my pocket. The bride's mother still looked at me for the answer.

"There's no one way to handle it. It's up to you." *Please don't make me be the one who has to do it.* There were many moments where I missed working with a professional football team, but never as much as this one. I'd seen powerful, hard-as-nails people tear up when their team won or lost, but I'd never had to watch the team's owner sob because the commissioner wasn't coming to the party.

RJ stepped into the room, her posture as poised as ever, but her expression looked uncertain as she met my eyes. Jayda sobbed loudly again, and RJ's expression shifted to something more flat. I wasn't sure what I expected—for her to offer the woman comfort or exchange sympathetic glances.

"We'll do it," her father said. I wondered if he was just jumping at the chance to do something, but I stepped aside and nodded, letting him and his wife take a moment to convene, their hands clasped. I wasn't sure why I noticed the clasped hands, but it's all I could focus on. They somehow clung to each other and held each other up.

"I've already asked them to shift to just dinner in the reception space, and they're making the changes they can now. People can head that way for drinks and appetizers if they want," I said in a low voice. He nodded grimly and held his wife's hand. I thought I should follow them, but Jayda looked lost, and it tugged at my heart. I met RJ's eyes, wondering if she'd have some feminine instinct to comfort the girl or say something profound, but she stood still. It was not like RJ to have nothing to say, to not step in, and I waited a few extra moments, hoping she would.

Finally, I stepped across the room and dropped to one knee in front of the bride in her white dress, the miles of fabric surrounding her like a darkly ironic marshmallow. "Do you want me to get your bridesmaids?"

"I'm so embarrassed. I don't want to see anyone." She shook her head, and then the silence hung around us, only her small sobs punctuating it. She looked up from her own clasped hands, eyes red, black eye makeup smeared. "What am I going to do?" Her voice was small. "He was going to be my whole life. What am I going to do?"

I shifted my weight, remembering asking myself that question. Remembering crying when no one was around because I had to let it out, and then getting angry that I had to show weakness, even to myself. "I don't know. I think today probably feels like the worst day of your life, though."

She nodded.

I wiped my palms down the legs of my pants. "It maybe feels hopeless and black, like you're drowning?"

"Like I can't swim," she said, voice hitching as another sob ripped through her.

I nodded, swallowing. I set my hand next to hers, where she held a handful of material from her full skirt. I tried to remember what Penny and Caitlin and eventually Uncle Harold told me. I remembered ignoring it and brushing off their platitudes, but I channeled them anyway. "You *can* swim, though. You will."

"How do you know?"

"I've been there. Had everything pulled away from me by someone I loved. Not exactly like this, but I was left alone." My chest tightened, and I bit the inside of my cheek hard.

"What did you do?" The woman looked up miserably, eyes already swollen from the crying.

"I took time to be sad and mad, and then . . ." I searched for the word, wishing I'd followed her parents out to the reception. The back of my neck heated, knowing RJ was listening to this. I didn't want to tell the bride that I was over it, that it just stopped sucking, that I didn't stay up at night getting angry, because I did. I rested my hand on top of hers. "I started thinking about swimming to the surface, and then eventually I started swimming."

She pressed her lips together, eyes plaintive. "Did you get there? To the surface?"

I sensed RJ shifting from foot to foot behind me, but I didn't turn. The bride's dad's voice carried down the hall as they returned, and I stood. "I'm working on it." I squeezed her hand and stepped back to make room for her parents.

I swallowed again, not sure why I was needing to do that so often, as her dad pulled me aside to go over a few details. I blocked out the conversation with his daughter while we talked about logistics, but I kept letting my gaze wander to where RJ had been standing. She'd slipped out, and I didn't know if she'd heard what I said to Jayda, or what she thought. I realized as I left the suite to take care of about two hundred details that I didn't know if I wanted RJ to have heard me or not. On one hand, I wanted her to know me.

Increasingly, I had this urge to tell her things I didn't tell other people, to make sure she saw all of me. On the other hand, she'd made it clear she wasn't interested in drama, and I had a sinking fear she'd see me, all of my drama, and leave. I didn't like the idea of one more thing being in the air unsaid between us, but I had to focus on the job in front of me.

THREE HOURS LATER, I closed the door to my room and leaned against the cool surface. Since everyone had traveled to the destination wedding, no one had much to do besides hang out. A surprising number of people had stuck around for the party, and though the mood was somber, the bar was stocked. I'd been on the phone, putting out fires and trying to help undo a honeymoon Penny had helped to plan on top of the wedding. I was exhausted from all that, not to mention that I couldn't get my conversation with the bride out of my head. I'd been bogged down in memories since stepping out of that room and feeling alone. I hadn't seen RJ for the rest of the night and hadn't had time to text her. I assumed she'd left, since there was no reason for her to stay. I wanted to be the reason she stuck around, though. The portable battery pack had made a valiant effort, but my device sat at nine percent.

LEAR: You make it home?

If there hadn't been things I needed to do the next morning, I would have driven home, too. I pushed off the door, pulling my shirt from my pants and unbuttoning it. My phone dipped to five percent, and I was digging for the charger still plugged in next to the bed when I heard a knock at the door.

"It's me," a voice said from the other side, a smoky, sexy voice I'd wanted to hear all evening.

When I opened the door, RJ stood there in yoga pants and a T-shirt that hung off her shoulder.

"I thought you left."

She looked up at me through thick but unadorned lashes, her features soft. "I didn't."

"Why?"

RJ stepped into my room and wrapped her arms around my neck, pressing her lush body to mine, and I pushed the door closed behind her, hugging her back. "I thought . . . It seemed like you might need someone." She squeezed me tighter, pressing her face into the crook of my neck, clutching me, pulling me in.

I held her, inhaling the scent of her hair product and pushing back against the tide of emotion. "RJ," I said, flattening my hand against her shoulder, unsure of what to say and wanting to say a hundred things at the same time.

"That thing today . . ."

I stiffened. "Yeah."

She settled her hands against my chest and tipped her chin up. "Do you want to talk about it?" She bit her lip in a way I knew meant she didn't want to talk, didn't want to hear the sob story I wasn't eager to share. She slid her fingertips through my hair, and my body warmed, despite the mental and physical exhaustion.

"Can we not talk?"

She kissed my throat, sliding a hand under my shirt and along my stomach. "We could not talk."

She finished unbuttoning my shirt, her fingers dexterously moving over the buttons with laser focus. Her silence in that room came back to me, and I wondered about things some more. "RJ?"

She pushed my shirt off my shoulders, the graze of her palms like a balm.

I missed the heat when she pulled them away, but didn't mind when she tugged her own shirt over her head, and I was rapt as she reached back to unhook her bra, the move awkward and sexy. I finally pulled my senses back. "RJ?"

"Yeah?" She shrugged away her bra, standing in front of me with her perfect breasts begging for my touch, my mouth, but my eyes kept drifting to hers. "What?"

"Thank you for coming over."

She took my hands and guided them to her pebbled nipples. She let out a sigh at my touch. "Let's not talk."

Chapter 29

RJ

"WOW." I COLLAPSED onto the bed, Lear's chest heaving against my back. "That was good."

His breathing was heavy when his arm wrapped around my waist. "Good is underselling, don't you think?" He spoke into my skin, his breaths puffing against my shoulder.

"Be happy with your A minus."

Lear rolled me to my back in one fluid motion, pinning my arms over my head. "I don't get A minuses, and we both submitted assignments."

I pulled my arm free from his grasp and traced his jawline with my fingertip. "Peer review. The minus makes you work harder next time."

Lear's hair was sweaty, and some longer curls framed his face. "You're . . ." He propped himself on an elbow next to me, letting his forearm rest over my stomach again, the weight familiar and comforting.

I let my head loll to the side and studied the stubble on his chin. It was so rare to relax like this after sex, to have time to notice things like the scar under his chin or the small chip in his front tooth. "Difficult? Hard to please?"

He shook his head while his fingers grazed my waist, swirling an invisible pattern on my skin. "Pleasing you is fun. You're hard to read."

"I like to think I'm an open book." The hairs on his forearm tickled my palm until I reached the smooth expanse of his biceps.

"Unless you don't want to share something."

"Like I said, smarter than you look."

Lear seemed tired. The lines of his face were still as handsome and chiseled as ever, but he looked like he could sleep for days. I turned from his face and glanced at the ceiling. I didn't need to concern myself with Lear's sleep schedule. Worrying about that led to caring too much and the inevitable moment when I realized I cared more than he did. "What about me are you trying to read? I know you know it was good for me."

"Twice, I believe." His palm flattened against my belly, and he stroked up to my ribs and then back to my hips in slow movements. "What bothered you earlier in the bridal suite?"

I thought about his question and the soft way he'd asked it, like he was requesting the information versus assuming he should have it.

His slow sweeps continued, as if warming me and protecting me at the same time. "It's okay if you don't want to share. I just wanted to ask . . . you know, in case you wanted to talk about it."

"It's not a big deal." I focused on the path of his palm over my skin and not the way my heart rate ticked up. *It shouldn't be a big deal.* Like I always did, I tamped down those emotions that might get in my way. If something could make me feel like that, it could hold me back. "My dad left my mom and me when I was in high school. She got really sick, and he took off. My best friend, Michael, he . . ." The sentence caught in my throat before I thought about saying the words. I hadn't talked about Michael in years. I wondered if he was the last man I'd truly counted on to be there for me. "Um, he ghosted me shortly after. Said I was too sad."

I expected him to say "I'm sorry," or some other platitude. Years ago, I had decided I could be with Case when I told him about my dad leaving us and he asked immediately about child support. If I'd brought up my old friend Michael, he would have rolled his eyes, so I'd kept it quiet. His questions were simple to answer, factual. He didn't ask how any of it made me feel, and I never shared. Lear didn't say anything but kept moving his hand in that long arc. I didn't like the silence. "So, people peacing out just . . . gets to me sometimes."

Stroke. Stroke. Stroke.

"You don't tell people that often, do you? Things that get to you."

"I tell you that you annoy me all the time."

He smiled but didn't laugh or otherwise respond, giving me time to steer the conversation.

I let out a sigh. "But, no. I don't. I've never seen the point. Do you?"

He shook his head. "Not so much anymore."

"You still don't want to talk about what you said to her?"

He shook his head again, in a slow nudge of his chin against my temple. The air conditioner in the room kicked on, filling the silence with a low hum. I'd heard a lot of his story when he'd talked to the jilted bride, heard in his voice how someone had broken him. I didn't want to ask him to share that. I wasn't sure I was someone who even could respond the right way. "I should go," I said, not moving from under his touch. "It's late."

"You could stay." He slid his hand up my ribs, the tip of his thumb grazing the side of my breast, but kept going to my shoulder. "Give me a chance for extra credit."

"We never spend the night."

He stroked my shoulder. "We don't."

"But . . ." I held my breath as his fingers moved up my neck and across my nape, not wanting to move away from his touch. "It's a hotel room, so not home."

Lear's lips dipped to my neck, nose brushing my skin. "It is."

"And it's technically morning already, so it's not spending the night . . ."

Lear's palm slid lower down my belly. "And we're not going to sleep."

"You should sleep." My breath stuttered when he rolled, the length of his body pressed to mine. "You're tired."

Lear's fingers inched down the crease where my thigh met my hip, and he spoke against my jaw. "Do I feel tired?"

When his hand ghosted over my clit, the sensation of barely being touched rocked me, and he chuckled against my chin.

"Stay." His fingertips dipped lower, circling my tight bundle of nerves, and I groaned.

"Okay," I said with a sharp inhale, letting my thighs fall apart. "Only so you can earn your A."

Lear pulled his head back enough to look into my eyes, his grin making a dimple pop. "That's generous."

"I'm nicer than you assume."

His mouth was on mine, pulling my lower lip between his before he began to kiss a trail down my body. "No, you're not, but I like you mean." He kissed my belly and then met my eyes with a raised eyebrow. "Can you let me do this now?"

The pillow cradled my head as my eyes fell closed at the feel of his mouth. My entire life, I'd always told men exactly what I wanted. It wasn't a hardship—if I thought about it, I didn't trust them to get it right, so I gave lots of direction, every time. I groaned when he spread my thighs wider, his tongue moving in perfect wide circles.

I clutched the pillow above my head and my breathing sped. At some point, I'd stopped giving Lear direction, stopped getting distracted with worry that he wouldn't get it right. I didn't want him to know he knew me so well, didn't want to admit he could anticipate my responses, but he did.

He shifted, increased his pressure, and I squirmed, but his hand was there, already resting at my waist to hold me in place.

"More," I huffed, meeting his eyes.

"I know." He spoke over my skin, the words muffled. His fingers filled me, his pinky finger tracing against the spot that made me groan at the sensation.

My thighs shook and my muscles tensed. Lear's hair was soft under my fingers as I slid my hand over his head, gripping his hair, and the coils in my body tightened. I whimpered toward the ceiling, too gone to be bothered that Lear Campbell was making me whimper and it was normal. My body always reacted to him this way.

He held my thigh and gripped my waist, tightening the circles of his tongue a moment before I knew I wanted him to focus right there.

"Yes, yes!"

He pressed his fingers deeper, crooking to nudge my G-spot in a slow, steady rhythm, filling me, taking me closer to the edge, where my body and mind were ready. I paused on the precipice, the tension building so slowly that I teetered on the edge. He didn't stop. He kept going in that maddening slow rhythm until the first string was pulled and my body unraveled in a flurry of sensations and heat, my hips rolling under him.

I was still moaning when Lear moved up the bed and stroked my neck. "Minus?"

I needed more contact, needed more touch, as the edges of the orgasm rippled through me. I pulled Lear to me, slanting my lips over his and tasting myself on his mouth. "Plus. Definitely plus."

He kissed me again, his arousal evident against my leg. "Always good to have the highest grade in the room."

I stilled. "Wait. Are you saying I've earned only an A minus?"

Lear dragged his lips across my shoulder. "Let the minus motivate you."

I rolled to the side, pinning him to the bed with my leg over his and my forearms on his chest. "You think I'm so competitive that will work on me? That just because we're friends, I'll let you sucker me like that?"

"So, you do want to be my friend." His grin was cocky, but the real smile underneath showed through.

"Shut up." I kept him pinned, dropping a kiss to his lips.

"And I didn't try to sucker you. I just said I have an A plus."

I hated that he knew me so well.

Chapter 30

LEAR

BEFORE I OPENED my eyes, I felt the warmth of RJ against me, her soft waist under my forearm. The bed smelled like the hotel's detergent, like sex, and like RJ's lotion. When she'd run out to her room after round two, I didn't think she'd come back, but she'd returned with a small toiletry bag she toted to the bathroom, walking out saying "If you think I'm going to fall asleep without lotion and my sleep bonnet, you're out of your mind." I'd helped her apply the lotion to every inch of her skin.

In the morning light, the pink satin of her sleep bonnet rested on the pillow next to me, covering RJ's curls. I liked it, the familiarity of it, as if she stayed with me overnight all the time, like we were an us. I slid my arm lower, pulling her against me.

"Motherfucker," she muttered quietly, and I froze. The light from her phone filled the dim room, casting us in a circle. "Not you. Sorry."

I kissed her shoulder. "Work?"

"Client's soon-to-be ex-spouse playing stupid games." She tapped hurriedly on her phone. "Play stupid games," she said, tapping her screen forcefully, "win stupid prizes . . ."

"Are you taking someone down at 5:42 in the morning?"

She kept grumbling under her breath, something about a deposition canceled at the last minute again and sanctions. "I started at five thirty."

I slid my lips over her soft skin, kissing the side of her tense jaw. If the sun wasn't up, we could still claim it was part of the night before. "I always assumed you rolled out of bed with victories already under your belt."

She laughed, this soft breathy sound escaping her lips. "I should have seen this coming."

"You want to talk about it? It's criminal to be out of bed before six if we don't have to be."

"I can't." She tapped a few more things on her screen and dropped her phone on the nightstand and rolled to her back with a huff.

"Okay," I said.

"I can't because of attorney/client privilege, not because I want to keep you away from other parts of my life." She stumbled over the words a little, clearly unused to feeling a need to clarify herself. I nodded and kissed her shoulder.

The sheet covered her chest, but just barely, and my eyes dropped to the swell of her breasts. "You really love the job, huh?"

"Are you asking me or my nipples?"

I stretched, feeling the lack of sleep but not much caring. "Both." I flicked my eyes back up to her face. "Sorry."

"My breasts have little to do with my law career other than men seeing them as an excuse to underestimate me, but yes, I love the work." RJ looked soft in the diffused light from the window, and I played with the sheet to stop myself from reaching for her again.

"What do you love about it?"

RJ arched her brow and flipped down the sheet. Her plump breasts were tempting handfuls, nipples pointing to the ceiling, and she arched her back. I traced my eyes over her curves, not noticing she'd moved her fingers into my hair. "We don't really need to talk."

"We don't *need* to talk, but I'm curious." I folded the sheet back in place on her chest and rested my palm at her hip. I could have stopped touching her altogether—I should have—but I couldn't make my hand move away from her curves. "You obviously love your job. Tell me about it."

She gave me a raised eyebrow when I covered her chest with the sheet, but didn't move away from me. Her hand even rested near mine on top of the sheet. "It's a challenge." RJ's big brown eyes shifted, and she looked at the ceiling. "People are complex, and there's always some obstacle to overcome to get to a win for your client."

The tips of my fingers grazed the tips of hers. "And you win?"

"Of course I do." She slid her hand into mine, positioned for a thumb war.

"My thumbs are bigger," I said, stretching it over hers, pausing before I took the win.

RJ moved fast, though, and the sweep of her finger over my skin had me fumbling to regain the upper hand.

We continued the thumb war. In my life, I'd done a lot of things in bed with women, but this was a new one. "So, the winning is what you like best?"

"That, and . . ." She slowed her movements and lowered her thumb, waiting for me to strike.

"You think I'm going to fall for that?"

"You're delaying the inevitable." We returned to our thumb standoff, the side of my palm stroking against the sheet covering her stomach. "What I was saying, though, is it's the winning, and that when my dad left, my mom didn't really have anyone to fight for her." The sides of our thumbs rubbed against each other, the movement closer to a stroke than a battle. "I thought that was bullshit as a kid. I couldn't fight for her, but I can fight for people now."

Her brow furrowed, just for a moment.

"You like to help the underdog, stand up for the wronged?"

She nibbled her lower lip. "Most people have been wronged by someone."

My heart sped up, and I thought about Sarah and leaving LA. I thought about him, too, not knowing how to imagine his face. RJ's thumb slid over mine, but I didn't move, wondering if I should tell her. If RJ Brooks, wearing only a sheet and engaged in a thumb war with me, was the person I'd finally talk to.

She pressed down on my thumb, and her expression cracked into a grin. "Gotcha."

Her expression was so cocky, her thumb still pressing down on mine. *No, I won't tell her.* "Lucky strike," I said, swirling my thumb around hers. "So, what happened this morning? Someone's threatening your win?"

"I'm assisting on a case where I believed someone I shouldn't have. People are awful, and relationships make people exponentially more awful." She pressed my thumb down once more for good measure and then pulled her hand away.

"Yeah. I guess so." My hand felt strange suddenly without her fingers intertwined. "Not everyone, though. You're not awful."

RJ rolled her head to the side and met my eyes. Her lids lowered. There was a hint of a smile at the corner of her lips. Her hand slid over my chest. "What time is it?"

"Another response could be, 'Lear, you're not awful, either.'"

"And yet . . ." Her face broke into a full grin. "You're not awful, but we're also not in a relationship. Those are messy and someone always ends up getting hurt."

"Did you get hurt?" The skin on her back was smooth, and I ran my own hand along her spine, studying her expression and the way her lips twitched. It was a flash and then gone, but it made me want to know everything.

RJ avoided my question, shot me a wicked grin, and pushed the bedding out of the way, straddling me, her thighs on either side of mine. "We don't have much more time." She reached between us to stroke me. "So, we can talk about relationships or make better use of our fifteen minutes."

She handed me a condom from the bedside table, but I held it out of her reach with one hand and held her hip in place with the other, my finger sinking into her curves and my cock jumping. I raised my eyebrows, expectant.

"You want to talk about old relationships?"

"You can't always avoid conversation by mounting me."

"It's worked so far." She slid her slick folds over my bare cock, and I groaned at the feel of her heat, soft against me. RJ pressed her palms to my chest and held herself above me, giving me just enough to want to sink into her. "And didn't you say I wasn't awful just so we could do this again?"

I was so lost in the sensation, imagining what it would feel like to be bare inside her, that it took me a moment to catch up to her words. "What? No. 'You're not awful' is not a line I used to seduce you."

She snapped the condom from between my fingers. "I don't require sweet nothings."

I held her hips, inhaling sharply at her touch. "Doesn't mean you don't deserve them."

Chapter 31

RJ

I PACED MY office while reading through a motion. The summer sun shone through my window and cast long rectangles of light on the gray carpet as it lowered in the sky. The act of walking around while I read put me in the right headspace: focused, but like I was ready to be in motion, to act. It was something I'd done since college.

On my desk, my cell buzzed, and I turned it over, Britta's face flashing on the screen. "Hey," I said, resting on the corner of my desk and sliding my feet out of my heels. "What's up?"

"Wanted to check on a few details with you for your trip in a couple weeks."

I glanced at my calendar, where I'd marked myself out of the office to head back to Chicago. It was a quick trip, a Friday through Sunday, but it was the most vacation I'd committed to since starting at the firm.

"But first . . ." Britta moved from somewhere noisy with the low hum of conversation in the background to a silent space. "Sorry, Wes has a study group over. How're things with the guy?"

I rolled my eyes, but I caught myself smiling at my fingers, thinking of Lear's laugh and how he'd known my signature polish color. "Things are fine."

"Sounds like there's a 'but' or 'and' coming," she said with a laugh. "You're still just banging it out?"

"How old are you?"

"Old enough to want details."

"Then, yes, we're still banging it out." I grabbed the iced coffee sitting on my desk; the condensation had left a wide ring around the law school insignia on my coaster. "Why do you ask?"

"You seem a little different lately. I was just wondering if something was maybe evolving with him."

A feeling like butterflies, or maybe wasps, flitted around in my stomach. I'd felt something familiar and unfamiliar lying in bed with Lear. The familiarity was being next to a man, close to him in a way where I trusted him to know my body. The other thing . . . For a few minutes I'd just told him things, private things, without thinking it through first again, without remembering to keep him at a distance. "I don't think I can handle anything more evolved than banging it out."

"He's not your type?

I bit my lower lip, glad we weren't on a video call. "No, of course not. I'm not looking for anything anyway."

"I feel like there is something you're not telling me."

"There is." I settled behind my desk, debating what I wanted to tackle after the motion I'd been reviewing. "That pink bridesmaid dress was hideous."

Britta laughed, and I smiled on instinct. I loved my friend's laugh. "You've told me that already."

"Well," I said, hearing the distinctive *click-clack* of heels on the hardwood in the hall, "you know everything, then." I squared my shoulders at the sound, relieved there wouldn't be time for Britta to figure out Lear maybe *was* my type, and also concerned that I was beginning to think of him that way. "Hey, I'll call you later. I gotta go."

"RJ," Gretchen said, stepping into my office after a double knock on the door. "I figured you'd still be here."

"Of course." I straightened.

Gretchen nodded toward her office. "You want to have a drink with me?"

When I pictured being an attorney originally, I didn't have many references except reruns of *Ally McBeal*, *Suits*, and *Law & Order*, but I imagined a glamorous existence where every workday was wrapped up by sharing a drink with the boss. "Sure," I said, following her down the hall. Gretchen's corner office was all white leather and chrome, with touches of color in orchids. They were such an unexpected thing in her office, I noticed them every time. I settled into one of the chairs and accepted the glass of Scotch.

"There's a training seminar on trusts I'd like you to attend. It's in Boston at the end of the summer," she commented, settling into the chair next to me.

"I'll get the dates from your assistant." I sipped the smooth drink. "Carl asked me to speak at the biannual firm training retreat in the fall."

Gretchen's eyebrow raised slightly. I didn't know all the politics between the senior partners, but I'd seen her raised eyebrow regarding Carl more than once. "About what?"

I met her gaze with my own slightly raised eyebrow. "Diversity." It wasn't the first time I'd been asked to be the expert on the topic as a, or often *the*, Black woman.

"No," she said with a wave. "I'll tell him you'll be presenting on concealing assets and electronic spying."

"Thanks, Gretchen."

She raised her glass. "No thanks needed. You're skilled in asset valuation, and Carl can hire someone to speak on diversity. Better yet, he could enroll in a class himself."

We both glanced out her window, where the sunset had the sky shifting from orange to a relaxing shade of blue.

"I spoke with Dina Mayfield tonight," she said. "We're going to slow down our work."

I mirrored her demeanor, taking a sip before responding. "Oh?"

"They're attempting to reconcile," she said. We weren't facing each other, but I heard the eyebrow lift in her voice.

"For real?"

"Apparently. They want to try one last go at counseling, see if they can save the marriage." Gretchen shook her head. "She said they bonded over something with the foundation. She said she forgot how much his passion meant to her, and I don't think either is quite ready to let go of the foundation."

I nodded. "That sounds . . . touching. You believe it?"

"I believe they're going to try." She leaned back in her chair, stretching and sipping her Scotch again. "What do you think?"

I thought through her words. "I think she's asking us to slow down but not to stop."

Gretchen flashed me a rueful smile and held up a hand. "Give the woman a drink."

I smiled and settled back into the chair. "It would be something, though, if it worked. I mean . . . once they get to this place, accusing each other of cheating . . . it's not likely, is it?"

Gretchen finished her drink. "In my experience? No, but she's paying to retain us, so who knows."

I finished my drink. "Who knows?" I tried to imagine the Mayfields' eyes meeting across a room full of kids receiving college scholarships. Gretchen was right, it was unlikely. We'd keep working, but the idea of their possible reconciliation, mixed with the sunset and the good Scotch . . . I let the idea of me and Lear float around me without swatting it away.

Gretchen's voice cut into my unformed daydream. "How is it going wrapping up the wedding thing?"

It was delayed, but I mentally pushed away the sappy feeling about Lear. "Good. I'm committed to five more in the next month and a half. Three of them for our biggest clients' kids and grand-kids."

She nodded. "You know why I want you out of it, right?"

"It's the right move. I agree." Still, I wondered if I'd miss it at all after the last ceremony . . . and if I'd have any opportunities to see Lear, and if I wanted to keep seeing him.

Chapter 32

LEAR

"HEY, ABEL. WHAT are you doing over here alone?" The kid, who was fourteen or fifteen, was the bride's younger brother I'd gotten to know the night before, and we'd bonded over a shared interest in anime. I felt for him sitting alone. I'd been there, and he kind of reminded me of myself at that age.

"No one to dance with," the kid mumbled. His attempt at cool indifference didn't convince me at all as his gaze followed a group of teenage girls making their way to the dance floor.

"I see," I said, sitting back in my chair, my gaze landing on a familiar body at the bar just past the dance floor. RJ was talking to an older man and glanced at her watch in a way I knew she thought was subtle. I returned my attention to the kid. He was maybe a buck twenty soaking wet, a few pimples dotting his forehead. I remembered being there. "You ever asked someone to dance before?"

The kid snorted. "Are you kidding? Look at me. What girl would say yes?"

"Plenty. It's confidence. You need a little swagger." I leaned forward, resting my forearms on my knees and casting a quick glance in RJ's direction again. The group of teens had stopped near us and Abel's eyes followed a blonde in a pink dress. "That's someone you like?"

He shuffled his feet, his ears turning pink. "She's in my class. Her name is Faith."

I glanced at the girl, who was paying Abel no attention. "Ah." I let the music fill the silence. I wasn't sure what I was doing, trying to mentor this kid.

"What do you mean by swagger?"

"It's . . . you know. Being confident. Women like someone who believes in themself. Most people are drawn to others who are confident."

His voice dipped low. "How do you do that?"

"Feel confident?" *Hell if I know.* "You walk into a situation thinking *I've got this.* What's the worst that could happen?"

"Besides tripping and falling, having her turn me down in front of everyone, and then the entire school knowing I'm a loser?" His expression was serious, the sarcasm and derision sharp in the young guy's voice.

I chuckled, rubbing my hand over my neck. "I think that's unlikely, but, okay, I get it. You gotta practice." I glanced across the bar again, and RJ met my eye, just for a second. I thought there was a hint of a smile, but she looked back to her drink quickly. The conservative black dress she'd worn to officiate was high necked and fell to her knees, but the subtle way it hugged her curves was completely distracting. I glanced back to Abel. "You see that woman over there? The one who married your sister and her husband?"

"Sure."

"Go ask her to dance." I nodded in her direction. "She doesn't go to your school."

"C'mon," he scoffed.

"I'm serious. Walk over to her, tap her shoulder, and ask her if she'd like to dance. Just be confident, like you know she'll say yes." *God, I hope she will.* RJ put up a tough front, but I'd seen a few soft moments.

"I can't do that," he said, resigned, looking up at Faith again, his puppy-dog longing not subtle.

"Sure you can," I said, patting him on the shoulder. "Practice. Plus, I bet it's a slow song coming up, so you really just have to sway. Look at what other people are doing and do that."

"You really think she'll say yes?"

I shrugged. "Never know if you don't try." RJ turned again, her back to the bar. "Plus, she's pretty. Maybe Faith will get a little jealous."

Abel snorted again but stood. "Okay. Just tap her on the shoulder?"

I nodded, raising my fist to bump. "Confidence."

As he walked slowly around the floor, I pulled out my phone and sent a quick text.

LEAR: The kid needs a win. Please
say yes.

Across the room, RJ glanced at her phone, then looked up, confused. I gave a little wave, but Abel reached her before she could respond. He was attempting swagger and, though I couldn't hear him, the expression on RJ's face gave away a little of how awkward the exchange must be, but she nodded and followed him to the dance floor as the chords of a cover of "Can't Help Falling in Love" began to play.

RJ met my eyes over Abel's head as the song played, and he rested his hands stiffly at her waist. She gave me a sardonic half smile, and I shrugged. I was sixty percent sure it was good natured, and she returned her attention to her partner, whose expression was nothing short of adoring as he gazed up at her. He also looked panic stricken, and I tried to catch his eye as they turned, mouthing

"Confidence" with a pumped fist. I hoped I wasn't scarring the kid irreparably by sending him to RJ.

He said something then, and RJ's face transformed into a genuine smile, her eyes kind of dancing and her lips, her full lips I loved to kiss, spreading in a wide grin. Abel's posture relaxed, and I smiled, too, like a proud dad or something. I was still smiling when RJ caught my eye again. I couldn't read her face—I wasn't used to her looking at me with such an open expression. Her gaze was softer than usual, and she laughed a little at herself, her lids lowering for a minute before she looked back to Abel.

I couldn't take my eyes off her. I didn't want to. They swayed awkwardly, but the way her neck curved and her defined calves in her high heels got to me, even more so when I looked back to her face. My smile faltered when she looked up again, catching me staring, but she didn't look away, just held my gaze over Abel's head for a few seconds. It was how she looked at me when we were arguing, challenging each other to break first, only this time it felt different. When I rubbed the back of my neck and looked away for a moment, giving her the win, she smiled. *God, that smile.*

I knew the song—hell, they played it at every single wedding—but I'd never really listened to it before. It swirled around me and I straightened my shoulders, shrugging off the feelings it stirred. Her next smile was shyer—well, shyer for RJ—and I returned it. She raised an eyebrow that I interpreted as *What's next?* I had a lot of ideas, and it troubled me how few of them involved getting her naked. That we'd spent our entire relationship either arguing or having sex, that she was exactly the opposite of what I wanted in a woman, seemed to fall away as the song continued. I didn't look away, and neither did she. I didn't know her well enough to have a conversation without talking. *So why does it feel like I just opened up my chest to her?* The sex was always amazing, but this was different. This was a connection, and I hadn't felt anything like it in a long time. She lowered her eyelashes only to look back up, her expression vulnerable just as the chorus flowed around us. *"I can't help falling—"*

Her expression changed immediately, and she snapped her attention to Abel. My trance broken, I saw the little perv had slid his hands down to grab RJ's butt. I was on my feet in an instant. *Oh, shit. You just swung from swagger to assault, kid.*

When I reached them, RJ had stepped back and was finishing saying something to him. Her regular expression was back, and Abel looked like he was about to be flayed and quartered.

When his wide, panicked face swung to me, I said, "Not okay. Never grab a woman without her permission."

"I'm sorry." He looked stricken. "Ma'am, I'm so sorry," he said, turning to RJ. "I didn't mean to . . . I wasn't thinking." His face turned beet red, and he looked like he might wet his pants. Though maybe that was good—he'd never do it again. "Oh, God. Please don't tell my parents. I'm so sorry."

"Lesson learned. Don't do it again," she said. "But before that, the dance was nice."

"Really?" He forgot his fear for a minute.

"Solid swagger," I said in a low voice. "If you can keep your hands at the waist, maybe try asking Faith." I nodded in the girl's direction, where she was standing apart from her friends.

He took a deep breath and walked away from us.

"Your protégé?" RJ raised an eyebrow again.

"Something like that. Are you, um, okay?" I hadn't been grabbed, but my head was still spinning. In my mind, we'd had this entire exchange about how much we cared for each other, but we hadn't actually said anything. My body was tense because I wanted to reach for her, but I knew better than to rush into it.

"Yeah. That's not the first time a guy has grabbed my ass." She rested a hand on my biceps. "I seem to remember you have."

Resting my hand on her lower back, I pulled her into me to finish the song. "Never without you wanting me to, though." I winked. "Begging, if memory serves." This was normal, this banter, our verbal thrust and parry, but I couldn't shake the thoughts from a few minutes before.

"I've never begged you for anything." She smiled again, her playful, flirty smile that was still a little guarded. It was a lie, and she knew it before I raised my brows. "Okay, maybe a few times."

When she laughed, her body vibrated, and I pulled her closer, an automatic response, just wanting her near me. "A few?"

"Don't push your luck," she said, her hand sliding up my arm to my shoulder, the friction through my shirt electric.

"I have pretty good luck, though." My hand on hers tightened as her fingers brushed my neck. With her in her heels, we were close to the same height, and her brown eyes met mine. "Dancing with the prettiest woman in the room and all."

She rolled her eyes, but the gesture was accompanied by her smile, the real one, emerging on her lips. "Let's find somewhere private and see how that luck pans out."

I brought her hand holding mine to my neck and wrapped my other arm around her. I dipped my head to speak near her ear. "Slow down. I like dancing with you."

"We don't dance," she said, relaxing against my fingers again, grazing the side of my neck. "We find supply closets."

"We could dance." The song was nearing its end, and I noticed Abel still talking to a giggling Faith. "Maybe we could try dancing."

RJ pulled back, raising her eyebrow. "When you say dancing, what do you mean?"

My life with Sarah flashed into my head, the things I missed that I'd never admit to—cuddling, doing the dishes together, grocery shopping, those everyday pieces of sharing a life with someone. Only RJ would wrestle me for control of the remote and make some kind of competition of clearing the table. We'd come home from the store with the weirdest mix of healthy and junk food and bicker about what to cook for dinner. *Why does that sound even better?*

Dancing. I wanted it all. The song continued around me like a taunt.

I opened my mouth to put that into something that made sense, that she'd understand.

I didn't get a chance. "Lear. Thank God. I couldn't find you." The mother of the bride took my arm. "There's an issue with the photographer and they'll be ready to leave soon."

"Sure," I said, turning back to RJ. I wanted to drop a kiss on her lips, a promise that we'd come back to this, to pull her into my arms and just say that by dancing, I meant we become an us. I meant all of it, including arguing about what show to watch or dinner to make before we fell into bed together, but she gave me a knowing look and shooed me away with Mrs. Huerta.

The song ended as I stepped away, but I couldn't shake our dance from my head for the rest of the night.

Chapter 33

RJ

THE BOARD FLASHED *Delayed*. I'd hoped it would read something different than it had ten minutes earlier, but no luck. I returned my eyes to the text chain with my friends.

> RJ: Flight delayed again. I won't be there until after midnight.

> > Britta: Doesn't the airline know who you are?

> RJ: Apparently the fuselage doesn't care.

> > Britta: Do better, fuselage. We miss you.
> > Kat: Do you want to FaceTime with us so you don't feel left out?

> RJ: Do I want to FaceTime you guys from the airport while you get drunk at a club?

I did, except I had a mountain of work to catch up on, and I knew once I set foot in Chicago, I wouldn't get anything accomplished.

RJ: I should work, but text me later. I
don't want to hear about your amazing
sex life, though. You get real sharey
when you drink.

> BRITTA: I make no promises. I have a great
> sex life.
> KAT: I'll make sure she's all shared out by
> the time we call.
> KAT: Not that I want to know about
> Wes's . . . stuff.
> BRITTA: Wes has excellent stuff. It's the
> stuff of legends. 😉

I laughed to myself, earning side-eye from the older woman perched next to me reading a paperback.

> DEL: I wish you guys would take me off this
> group chat. I have my own stuff.
> KAT: Sorry, Del.
> BRITTA: I'm not. You know you love us.

RJ: I'll talk to you guys later, but have fun!

I set my phone aside and glanced around the seating area for an open outlet. I'd checked in, breezed through security, and settled at my gate hours ago. Between a late plane, a late crew, and the mechanical difficulties, I was wondering if driving might have been faster. A casualty of the wait was my laptop sitting at twelve percent battery life.

To my left, six kids sat in a tight circle, each with a device held to their faces and the cords running into the three closest outlets.

Across the way, two large men had spread out so thoroughly as to take up five spaces between them, and their gear was blocking two more, but I didn't have the fight in me to get between them.

With a sigh, I closed my laptop and tucked it in my bag, standing at the same time as my phone buzzed. I smiled, sure it was Del complaining more about how we treated him like one of the girls. I started walking, passing a coffee kiosk and a candy shop. Gate after gate was full, and my stomach rumbled as I neared the food court.

After ordering some fast food, I stepped to the side to wait, the tempting smell of fries in the air, and pulled my phone from my pocket.

LEAR: Weddings are more fun with
you here.

A smile tugged at my lips, and I glanced around as if someone in the space would, first, be paying attention to me and, second, care that I was grinning at a text from a man I claimed to not like.

RJ: Why?

The person behind the counter called my number, and I tucked my phone away to claim my paper bag filled with French fries and a cheeseburger that would be the highlight of the next several hours. Balancing the food with my luggage, I wheeled out of the area and saw an open outlet at a nearby gate. I pounced into action, speed walking to the spot before anyone could take it. Unfortunately, a man took the seat before I could reach it, but I persevered, and in my slacks and the silk camisole I'd worn with my long-abandoned blazer, I plopped down onto the floor sitting crisscross applesauce and plugged in my laptop.

My phone buzzed again and I unlocked it, grabbing a few fries from the bag.

LEAR: This minister isn't as good a kisser
as you.

I smiled, pausing with my fries halfway to my face.

RJ: They must like you too much.

LEAR: That's probably the issue.

RJ: Maybe you should tell them to smile
more.

The dots bounced as I settled into my new work space, laptop on my knees and food next to me. I wrangled my suitcase into a desk of sorts and ignored the man who'd stolen my seat watching me curiously.

LEAR: I'll try that.
LEAR: I do feel bad that I told you to smile
more. You should have slapped me.

RJ: I wanted to.

LEAR: What stopped you?

RJ: I was on the ground and you were
standing over me. I couldn't reach your
face.

LEAR: I did offer to help you up, but you could have kicked me in the shin.

RJ: I should have kicked you in the balls. I'll keep it in mind for next time I see you.

LEAR: Kinky. I'm not usually into that, but I'll try it. My safe word is Motownphilly.

I settled against the wall, giving up on returning to work for a few minutes.

RJ: You think you're so funny.

LEAR: I am funny. It's one of many things you like about me.

I did like him. Along the way, he'd stopped getting under my skin and wormed his way into my head.

RJ: Sometimes. Where are you now, anyway? Still at the wedding?

LEAR: Home. You?

I took a quick video, scanning the terminal and ending on my face.

LEAR: Where are you going?

RJ: Chicago, if my flight ever takes off.

LEAR: What's in Chicago?

He didn't know I was from Illinois. There was a lot we didn't know about each other, and something about that was comforting, safe. Normal, instead of whatever I'd been feeling since he'd asked me to dance after that kid grabbed my ass. The dance was nice. Before the dance was . . . weird. Nice. Weird. I still couldn't decide, because it felt like we'd said things we'd never actually uttered. Things I hadn't said to anyone.

RJ: My friend's bridal shower.

LEAR: You just can't stay away from weddings. Here I thought it was me.

RJ: I can stay away from you.

LEAR: No, you can't. I'm the best you ever had.

RJ: Cocky much?

He replied with an eggplant emoji and I rolled my eyes, but the phone rang and his name flashed on my screen before I could answer.

"Tell me I'm wrong." His voice was rumbly in a relaxed, delicious way. I imagined him spread out on the couch, shirt tossed aside, sweatpants riding low on his hips. "I want to hear you say I'm wrong."

"You're wrong." I ignored the flutter through my core at hearing his voice. "I tell you you're wrong literally all the time."

"A guy can dream." It sounded like he was stifling a laugh. "And we both know about your dreams."

"I'm hanging up on you." I shifted my impromptu desk and

stretched out my legs in front of me after deciding I didn't care if that put me within a few inches of Mr. Seat Stealer.

"No, don't go," he said as his voice evened out, the laugh gone along with the charming voice he'd put on sometimes. He sounded tired, and comfortable, and sexy in a new way. "I like talking to you."

"You like giving me a hard time."

"Yes, but I kind of missed you today."

I bit the inside of my cheek. He'd said that so openly, without a hint of the sarcasm or one-upmanship I was so used to. I didn't know how to respond.

"I guess you've gotten used to getting lucky at weddings, huh?"

The seat stealer gawked at me, and I returned his gaze, eyebrow up, wishing I didn't need this outlet so badly or that this guy's flight would board soon.

"Sure, but, you know, other stuff, too. Joking around with you."

"Are you drunk?"

"I have to be drunk to tell you I like spending time with you?"

"Well . . ." I searched for the words. "Kind of. I think you got bored with that other officiant not putting you through your paces."

"You're deflecting," he said, clearly stifling a yawn, and the words stretched between us, but it wasn't an uncomfortable pause. "My sister tells me that all the time."

"Is she a therapist?"

"Gynecologist. And a know-it-all."

"I'd probably like her."

"She'd love you."

I bit the inside of my cheek again, glancing at the flurry of activity as the seat stealer and those around him stood, gathering their things. *Love?* Why was he now bringing up love?

I yelped when a kid tripped over my leg, leaving my ankle throbbing.

"What's wrong?"

"I just got stepped on. I'm on the floor next to an outlet." I rubbed my leg, happy for the distraction.

"I can't quite picture it. Describe what you look like."

"You can't be serious." I smiled at his ridiculous come-on and shielded my mouth with my hand, dropping my voice. "I'm not going to have phone sex with you in the airport."

Lear's laugh reverberated through me, that familiar warm sensation making me cross my legs. "I'm not trying to have phone sex with you. I was just trying to picture you camped out on the floor in one of your dresses."

"I'm wearing pants." I rolled my eyes. I should have ended the call and grabbed my laptop to tackle the most recent swath of motions. "What about you?"

"What am I wearing?"

"Yeah."

"I thought you didn't want to do this," he said, and I could picture the smug expression, that little smirk he'd give me sometimes.

"Call it curiosity. How do you look at home?"

"What if I told you I was naked?"

I swallowed, the memory of my fingers sliding over his hard stomach filling my head. "Are you?"

His voice grew lower. "Would you like it if I were?"

"I'd worry you were cold." I lowered my voice, too. "Shrinkage and all."

His chuckle was low. "I'm still in what I wore to the rehearsal," he said on a laugh. "Sorry. Nothing too sexy."

My mind flashed again to his slacks sliding down and the buttons on his shirt as I undid them. "So—um—what's up? Why did you text?"

"I already told you. I missed you tonight."

"Lear, c'mon. You missed hooking up with me."

"Yeah . . . That's not all, though."

I felt antsy, the temperature around me suddenly rising, and my fingers got twitchy at the return of his softer tone.

"It's not that weird, is it? We've gotten kind of close."

I looked around as if someone in the seating area would give me the right answer. "I don't know," I said finally.

He was quiet, and I rushed to fill the silence, a silence bracketed by the creeping anxiety at this shift. Was it even a shift? Whatever it was, it scared me, because I'd missed him, too, and that wasn't acceptable. Letting "maybe" linger in my brain wasn't acceptable. Missing someone, wanting them, thinking about them outside the tightly drawn boundaries I'd created was a recipe for getting hurt.

"I mean, no. It's not weird, it's just . . . you know what we are."

"I kind of thought after last weekend . . ."

I let my eyes fall shut and read between the lines of that sentence. I'd been thinking about that night—the way his eyes locked on me from across the room, the way his hands felt on my body that left me flushed and excited but that wasn't exactly sexual. It was just a dance, but apparently it hadn't been just me thinking about our time together when we were apart, wondering what it would be like if there were more. I knew I'd been sending mixed signals, making him think there was more, but I couldn't go through it again. "Lear . . ."

"No, it's cool. My mistake. You're right." His tone brightened, but I could hear the lie in it, the smile he was faking.

I bit my lower lip. "It's not you. I just don't do . . ."

"RJ, it's fine. Get back to your mobile office and I'll talk to you later."

After we hung up, I let my head fall back against the wall, regretting it immediately as who knew what child had smeared who knew what against the surface. *What was that?* I gave myself only a few moments to linger on the awkward conversation before forcing myself to open the laptop. It was no use, though; my mind wandered, and I couldn't focus on work.

It wandered to the way his voice changed when he said it was fine.

It wandered to Case's indifferent expression, and my dad's roses, and realizing the old friendship with Michael that I thought was stone was made of sand. I thought about all the times I'd expected a man to be there only to find he'd gone.

My mind wandered to how much I enjoyed kissing Lear. I wasn't an indecisive person, and I didn't spend a lot of time worrying about people's feelings. I knew we couldn't be more than sex, maybe friendship, but that was all I could give him. I had the sinking feeling that if I let myself have more, it would ruin me.

Still, my mind wandered back to Lear and how he'd looked at me when we danced.

No matter how many times I shook it off and leaned into work, my mind wandered back to what it was like when we were together, and I had to decide if I could leave things with him saying "It's fine." It was much harder to shake off than I wanted.

Chapter 34

LEAR

I GLANCED AT the clock on my nightstand, the numbers a taunt. I had to be out the door by eight a.m., but I'd tossed and turned, wide awake, and now it was almost three in the morning. I'd gotten twisted in my sheets, and Harold's familiar phrase came back. I was all twisted up. Only this time it was over RJ and our phone call.

The weekend before, the morning in the hotel, the slow dance . . . I'd been certain it was something, but my radar was busted, my tools to detect what the hell was going on needed calibration. I hated making a fool of myself and I'd done it in a big way. I rolled to my other side, hoping if I didn't see the time, I could ignore it. The other side of my pillow was cool against my face and I willed myself to go to sleep, but every time I closed my eyes, I imagined RJ's real smile, the one where she bit her tongue between her lips, and the way the slightly crooked fingertips I loved twitched when she was annoyed, and the way she sighed after a deep kiss, unaware she was doing it.

My phone buzzed on the nightstand and I reached for it, assuming it would be Caitlin checking in. She'd grown up here and she knew the time difference, but she never seemed to care when she wanted to tell me something. It wasn't her name, though. RJ's face along with You up? sat on my lock screen.

I set the phone back down. *I don't need this. She's not interested, and I've already embarrassed myself tonight.* I rolled over again. This time the pillow was warm, though, leaving me tossing again and staring at the still-illuminated screen on my phone. Now she wanted to do this? I groaned, my dick reacting to the idea of dirty texts from RJ, despite knowing I should resist the temptation. I reached for the phone, then set it down. "Dammit," I muttered into the dark room, sitting up to rest my back against the headboard, the cool air hitting my bare chest.

LEAR: Yeah. Make it to Chicago?

RJ: Eventually. Why are you still up?

Even through a text, she sounded accusatory, and I was tempted to set down the phone again.

LEAR: Can't sleep. Did you text me just to lecture me about being awake?

RJ: No.

LEAR: "You up?" at 2:30 a.m. usually has a pretty clear meaning.

RJ: I know, but I wanted to tell you something.

I waited, hating how rapt I was when the three dots began blinking, how eager I was to devour whatever she was going to say next.

RJ: It's not just you.

LEAR: What do you mean?

RJ: I think about you, too.

I sat rigid, rereading the text. It wasn't what I had expected. A few hours earlier it had been what I wanted, but now it felt like she was playing some game. Still, I waited for more dots, like a sucker.

RJ: I think about kissing you . . . I think about it a lot.
RJ: Kissing you, and other stuff.

My dick was, once again, on full alert.

LEAR: Other stuff?

RJ: You were there, you remember the other stuff.

LEAR: I remember vividly.

RJ: Yeah. Too vividly.

My thumbs flew over the keyboard, drafting a reply. I wish I could kiss you right now.

RJ: But even though I think about it . . .

My stomach dipped and I erased the message.

RJ: The thing is, that's where it needs to
stay. I like kissing you and I like the other
stuff, but that's all I can manage.
RJ: That's a me thing. Not about you at all,
but I want to be clear. I don't want you to
get hurt or be disappointed. I can't give
any more than that.

Those words were so RJ—direct, specific, and honest. I should
have anticipated them. I slammed a fist against my bed, the gesture
ineffectual, my fist making a dent in the soft sheets because I hadn't
anticipated them. My face burned and my erection deflated at her
words—for the first time in a long time. The hurt and embarrassment
had nothing to do with Sarah or what had happened in California. It
was a crushing awareness that I'd made myself the sap again.

LEAR: Got it. Enemies with benefits.

RJ: We're really good at that. Maybe even
friends sometimes.

I glanced at the clock again and groaned. I wanted to ask her
why this fuck buddy arrangement was all she could do, why she was
so resistant to trying anything else or even dipping her toe in the
water of something more. I had a wild hair to tell her what happened to me and how I ended up back in North Carolina, but that
thought luckily never made it to my fingers. It was a late-night text,
not therapy. Feelings hour never led to anything good, anyway, but
not caring could serve me well.

LEAR: *Really* good.

RJ sent a winking emoji before asking, What are you wearing? I settled back against the headboard.

LEAR: You first.

The dots bounced, and I committed to not caring.

AFTER I'D GOTTEN only a few hours' sleep by the time RJ and I got off the phone, the next morning was a nightmare. Not only was I sleep deprived and horny—because phone sex, even with RJ, was not as good as the real thing, not even close—the couple I was working with was high maintenance and dissatisfied with every decision they'd made, remade, and confirmed. So the day dragged on. When I finally got a break between the first dance and cake cutting, I eagerly pulled my phone from my pocket, expecting missed messages. I'd promised RJ I would delete the photos she'd sent me, and I had, but I wished I had her to look forward to at the end of this day that wouldn't end. I wanted her in my arms. We hadn't gone back to the real conversation after—we'd shared the same kind of casual goodbyes we usually shared in person, and I'd fallen into a restless sleep.

I crossed my ankle over my knee and did a quick scan of the dance floor before giving myself permission to dive into whatever she'd sent.

There were plenty of missed messages, but they were all from Sarah. I cracked my neck on instinct, bracing myself for the hurt of her betrayal to creep up my spine as it always did, accompanied by an overwhelming sense of rising dread.

SARAH: Please don't delete this. Caitlin won't tell me anything, and I'm worried about you.

SARAH: Please just let me know you're okay.
SARAH: I still care about you. I know this
is a hard day for you.

I scoffed, annoyed and relieved that my sister hadn't told the liar anything about me. I reread the message, angry that she could pretend to still care. I gritted my teeth at her last message, rage simmering in the back of my head at her remembering this was the anniversary of my parents' accident. I'd known the day, but after so many years, the reminder was an ache. The day was hard, but not unbearable. My heart surged in my chest that she still cared, though, even while my thumb hovered over the delete icon as it had so many times. I could tell her off. I could say all the things I'd wanted to over the last year. I could call her all the names I had in my head or go for those insults that would needle her, the ones that would really hurt her. We'd been together long enough that I knew where her insecurities hid, but what was the point?

LEAR: I'm fine.

SARAH: I can't believe you answered.

LEAR: Did you want something else?

SARAH: To talk. We never talked. You just
left.

The day that I had walked out on her was still vivid in my mind. It was raining when I got in my car to leave. It rarely rained in Southern California, and the drops had been heavy on my windshield, traffic moving slowly as I inched out of LA, away from Sarah, and into a fog. A fog that had finally begun to lift.

SARAH: But you're okay? Have you talked
to someone?

LEAR: My mental health is none of your
business.

SARAH: I deserve that.

I imagined her brown eyes narrowing slightly, the way they did
when she wanted to say more. I wanted to hate everything about
her, but I remembered the kindness that usually accompanied whatever she'd say next. That annoyed me more than anything else.

SARAH: I just wanted to say I'm sorry. I'm
sorry I hurt you. I'm sorry you found out
like you did. I'm sorry for all of it.

LEAR: Okay.

She'd texted, emailed, and DM'd all of that many times. I hoped
to look up and see the last rotation of the Electric Slide, which
would mean my respite was over and I'd have to get back to work to
make sure the end of the reception went well, but the line dancing
was just beginning.

SARAH: Do you . . . want to know
anything about us? Do you want to see
some photos or hear updates?

On instinct, I bit the inside of my cheek and set my jaw. I shook
my head, even though she couldn't see me. What kind of person
would ask that?

LEAR: No.

SARAH: I thought it might be good closure.

LEAR: It wouldn't. Do you need anything
else?

SARAH: I won't keep you. I'm sorry,
though, Lear. I need to say it again. I'm
sorry, and I do still care about you.

The lack of sleep hit me like a pile of bricks and my body wanted
to sag and brace, a juxtaposition that made me want to climb out of
my skin. Instead I stood quietly and strode toward the front door,
needing fresh air and space immediately.

SARAH: And I'm glad you're taking care of
yourself.

I breathed in the cool evening air with a slight breeze that felt good
against my face after the energy and heat of the reception and the
stress rising from Sarah's texts. Her apologies echoed in my head, and
I once again considered poking her where it would hurt, letting her
believe she'd broken me, giving her more guilt to pile on, but that was
childish. I didn't want to hurt her; I didn't want to care about how she
felt. Yet I was there pacing like a caged animal because she still made
me feel like this, and I hated that she had any kind of power over me.

My phone buzzed in my hand and I was one breath from throwing the damn thing to the ground. This time it was RJ, though.

RJ: Remind me to never text you so late.
I was a zombie today.

RJ and Sarah texting me at the same time made me pause my pacing. Sarah was more than two thousand miles away and was still holding part of my heart. RJ was in Chicago and wanted nothing to do with my heart, and maybe that was better. I needed to get myself in check and stop acting like a lovesick teenager around RJ. It was sex and work and nothing more, and I wasn't going to give up more of myself than that.

SARAH: Are you still there?

LEAR: No.

I shoved my phone in my pocket and cracked my neck again, really not wanting to walk back into a wedding. With my hand on the door handle, I resolved to not answer RJ right away, to leave her text on read and make sure this thing between us stayed casual. That would be safe, which was exactly what I needed.

Chapter 35

RJ

I WAS STRETCHED out on the sectional in Britta and Wes's living room. Her feet met mine, both of us exhausted after the bridal shower. Between Britta's sister keeping everything moving like a highly choreographed dance montage and her mom bursting into tears constantly, we were exhausted. Kat had gone home, and the two of us lounged, surrounded by gift bags and leftover center-pieces.

"Red wine for RJ," Wes said, handing me a glass. He'd been saved from the headaches of the day, and Britta said he and his best friend, Cord, had played video games all afternoon. "And water for you, Bubs," he said, handing Britta a tall glass. He dipped his head to steal a kiss, and with anyone else I would have stifled a gag, but I just sipped my wine and smiled at their naked affection.

Wes sat on the edge of the couch. "How much space do you two need to catch up? Should I leave the room, the apartment, or clear the building?"

"You can stay," I said. "You're not so bad." I liked Wes. More importantly, I liked Wes for my best friend.

"High praise, RJ."

I raised my glass to him. "You know it is."

"I actually have some studying to do." He stood, stretching, and

I didn't miss how Britta still openly stared at her fiancé's body. Who could blame her? Not only was he an aspiring teacher after leaving his role as CEO of a successful company, but he worked out . . . a lot. "Let me know if you need anything. I'll be in the bedroom."

"You are not subtle," I said, pulling Britta's attention back as Wes walked down the hall.

"What?"

"You were practically drooling at your fiancé's ass."

"It's a nice ass." She shrugged, sipping her water. "He'd do the same to me."

I smiled, both at her response and at how true it was. Those two acted like the other was a first crush, even after a year together. I loved that he needed no convincing to know my girl was a queen, and he never had. "You're right. He would." I glanced at my phone, sitting faceup next to me on the back of the couch. I'd texted Lear a few hours earlier, casually. Never mind that I'd gone back and forth in my head on what to say to sound so casual. What I'd sent was my fourth draft, but he didn't need to know that.

I knew he had a wedding, but it still surprised me he hadn't replied. There were always breaks here and there, unless all hell had broken loose. I stretched to wake up my phone. Nothing.

I motioned to Britta's water glass. "Is there something you need to tell me? Do I need to prepare for a baby shower?"

Britta snorted, almost spraying that same water all over me. "Are you kidding me? Between FitMi and Wes being in school, we barely have time for each other, let alone a kid."

"Yeah? It's been rough?"

I will not look at my phone. I will not look at my phone.

"It's just work." She settled back onto the couch. "When we first got together, it was like we couldn't be apart, but now we have to plan things to make sure we have time together. It's still good, though, just different, you know?"

I nodded, though I didn't really know. It had always been that way with Case—date nights, sex, hell, sharing a meal: It was all on a schedule, the intimacy level predetermined. Predetermined by him, usually, and I just assumed that it was doomed to fail, that maybe that's why he couldn't love me. It was working for Britta, though, so maybe it had been me. "Worth it?"

"Yes." She said it with a dreamy look on her face, the smile automatic. She lowered her voice conspiratorially. "We've gotten good at quickies."

I set my glass aside, which just happened to require looking near my phone, which still showed no new messages. "Never doubt the joy of a good quickie."

My belly fluttered thinking about the text exchange with Lear the night before and how it had turned into us on the phone, listening to each other. It hadn't been a quickie, though; we'd talked for over an hour, the heat rising, teasing each other with words. I clenched my thighs at the memory and tried to push away the awareness that he'd known what to say to turn me on and keep me going, even in a text.

"What was that look?" Britta's eyes narrowed.

"What?" I cut a quick glance at my phone. "Nothing."

"Do you have some thoughts on quickies you'd like to share?"

"I do not."

"Thoughts on making relationships work?"

I laughed. "Certainly not. That's you and Wes's domain."

Britta narrowed her gaze. "What are you not telling me?"

"Nothing. Stop trying to read me."

"Did something else happen with that guy?"

I glanced at my phone, which I knew she saw. *Rookie mistake.* "What guy?"

"'What guy,'" she said, mocking. Lowering her voice, she said in a hushed tone, "The hot guy from the coffee shop. The one you kissed. The one with whom nothing was evolving."

"Why are you whispering? Will Wes get upset at you calling another guy hot?"

She laughed, her smile taking over her face. "No. He'd want to hear all the details, come out here all nosy, and then you wouldn't share any of the good stuff. So . . . spill."

"There's no tea here," I said, settling back against the couch. *Don't look. Don't look.* "I go to work, I do weddings, I repeat."

"But I know what you're *doing* at these weddings, or rather *who* you're doing." She waggled her eyebrows.

I rolled my eyes. Britta wouldn't judge a casual fling. She was in her love bubble, but I wasn't worried she'd look down on the sex-only arrangement with Lear. I bit the inside of my cheek, debating what to tell her, because I was pretty sure she'd see through any of my deflections. Turns out I didn't have to.

"You're still sleeping with him, right?"

A flash of memory hit me from our morning in bed at the hotel: us thumb wrestling and how he'd made me want to share things about myself. It had really stuck with me, even though I'd played it off. There had been other moments like the one in the hotel when he'd looked at me like he saw me. When he'd said we could dance, I'd been tempted to agree.

"Are you dating?"

"We're not dating. It's casual."

I sipped my wine. *Don't look at the phone.* "To his credit, he's not the dude-bro I initially thought. He's funny and kind of quirky. He's helped me out a few times and can be sort of sweet when not being aggravating." The thought of his hyper-organized trunk and how he secretly listened to musicals in his car brought a smile to my face.

"You like him," Britta commented, sporting her own smug grin.

"I do not. He's hot and good in bed."

"Funny, you didn't mention any of that when you were telling me how he was funny and quirky." She pointed to my phone. "Is he whose text you've been looking for all night?"

My cheeks heated. Not only had I been caught, I'd been caught waiting for a text that hadn't come. "We were exchanging messages last night. I just thought he might reply."

"Oh, that's all? Just late-night texting like you do with everyone? Debriefing upcoming wedding ceremonies, I'm sure. Definitely sexting within an inch of your life . . . or maybe . . . eight inches of your life?"

"I'm not taking the bait, and I really don't know why we're friends."

"Yes, you do. Everyone else is scared of you."

"They are," I said with a laugh I didn't fully feel. My blank phone screen taunted me from the back of the couch. "They should be," I said before taking another sip of wine.

"Hey, I was just kidding." Britta scooted toward me, expression more serious. "You're the good scary, like don't-fuck-with-me-because-I'll-end-you kind of scary. You're the most badass person I know."

I nodded. "I know. I am, I just . . ." I glanced at the ceiling and shook my head. "I know."

"What were you going to say? Seriously, what is going on with this guy?" My best friend's expression shifted again, this time to concern.

"The sex is good. It's fantastic."

"Okay, and . . . ?"

"And . . . good sex has never made me feel like this before."

"Like what?"

"Like I want to talk afterward and I care about how he hasn't texted me back. He told me he thinks about me, wants to spend time with me. Britt, I think about that stuff, too."

Her smile spread. "Well, that's a good thing. Good sex and you both like each other. What's the problem?" She examined my face, and that same smile fell. "Seriously? You broke up with Case years ago."

Britta had liked him at first; Kat had, too. He was charming, successful, good looking—we fit together. We were both driven and had similar goals. After three years together, we had a rhythm. Dinner together Monday, Thursday, and Sunday. Sex Tuesday night and Saturday morning. Date nights once a month. I hadn't wanted the messiness I grew up with—the fighting, the drama—and Case was drama-free. Problem was, it was boring. I was boring, and I was bored. When I tried to change things up, he resisted. It wasn't until the end that I looked back to see that I'd become hesitant to step outside the lines of what we'd fallen into, thinking it would make things too dramatic, too difficult, and then he told me I was still too hard to love. I smiled weakly at Britta. "I know, and it's not just him."

"You never had good sex with Case anyway. Tell me I'm wrong."

"It wasn't . . . bad."

Britta pursed her lips. "As a new resident of Good-sexville, I feel confident saying 'not bad' is not the same as 'good,' and that applies to more than just sex."

"He was steady. He was reliable. He was a good match for me, and yes, it bothers me that he broke up with me."

"You were more upset that he did it before you did."

I paused to consider what she'd said and sipped my wine. "He did it before I thought to."

"You wanted to make it work." Britta petted my calf, which would have annoyed me from anyone else. "There's no shame in that."

"He told me it was too hard to love me. I'm never going to be that woman who willingly makes herself vulnerable again. I took all that energy and put it into being the best I can at work. You know

I hate to not be the best at something, and I'm horrible at relation-ships."

"Practice makes perfect."

I ignored her very logical response. "Anyway, I told Lear all I can do is this physical thing. I don't want to set myself up for that again. He also knows Gretchen, my mentor, and she hates the wedding thing. Everything would just be too messy. It's not worth it." I woke my phone to see the blank screen and tossed it to the other side of the couch with a sigh.

"It might be worth it."

"It's not." I sipped my wine. "That's okay. The sex is good. I don't need more. He hasn't responded to my text from this morning. I'm just . . . He needs someone nicer than I am. I think he'll realize he's fine with just sex, too."

I glanced around the room, looking for a natural way to shift the focus from me, but she was relentless. "What if he's not okay with just sex anymore?"

"Lear's not that complicated. It's why our arrangement works," I said, the lie bitter in my mouth as soon as I said it. I'd seen hints that Lear had shadows.

Britta nudged my knee with her leg. "If he wants more and you don't, how will you feel about letting him go?"

The lie that I'd feel fine was on my tongue, but I swallowed it and washed it down with a last drink of wine. "Stop knowing me so well," I said, nudging her back. I wouldn't be fine, but I would walk away if I had to.

Chapter 36

LEAR

"ARE YOU SURE you have everything you need?" Penny's words came through between the baby crying on her end and the noise from the crew laying the dance floor on mine.

I gritted my teeth. "Yep. I'm good." This was a big-deal wedding and she had checked in a lot this week. "Don't worry. I know what I'm doing, and you left good, very extensive notes in addition to hourly phone calls all week."

"I know, just don't forget the—"

"The bridal suite. I know." I held up a finger to the man finishing the dance floor. "Penny, there's a lot going on here."

The baby cried again, the sound muffled and then louder, like someone was pacing with him. I bit the inside of my cheek, cracking my neck.

"Yeah. Of course. Just don't forget to—"

"Check the napkin rings. I got it, Penny. Will you let me do this?" Across the room, Tina and the lighting technician were toe-to-toe, and the two people delivering the cake were trying to balance the massive base layer while steadying a wobbly table. "Go take care of your kid and trust me. I'll check in later."

I shoved the phone in my pocket and jogged across the room, helping to balance the table before disaster struck. I glanced at my watch. I didn't need Penny in my ear, because this entire day had been cursed since the beginning. Vendors were late, family members were fighting, and it was raining despite a forecast of sunny with a light breeze, so everything was shifting to the rain location at the last minute.

"Thanks," the baker said, wiping his brow with his sleeve. The cake would be huge, five tiers covered in fondant and what looked like edible lace. He and his assistant were already unpacking the delicate sugar paste flowers to affix to the surface, and I admired their work as they began the cake's construction, staring at the creation that was what the couple wanted down to the last detail.

"Yeah," I said. "No problem." I glanced at my watch again, because RJ was supposed to arrive in ten minutes. I set my lips in a firm line and checked on the progress the hotel staff had made in getting the secondary ceremony location all set.

I pulled my phone out of my pocket when it buzzed, a stupid hope that it was RJ texting. It had been a week since we'd spoken, and I had almost replied to her zombie text three hundred times, but I couldn't bring myself to do it. Every time my finger hovered over the send icon, it was like my memories hit me in the chest with a hammer.

CAITLIN: You okay?

I shoved it back in my pocket, really tired of people checking up on me. But the text helped as a reminder of why it was good I hadn't replied to RJ, no matter how much I'd wanted to. The emotional entanglement wasn't worth it. The night before, at the rehearsal, she'd been efficient. She'd smiled at me and it made me want to wince—it was a fake smile, a stiff, professional one, and we'd both found reasons to be busy at the end of the evening. I'd taken a deep breath when she'd walked out, but I hadn't relaxed since.

The lighting tech jogged toward me. "Hey, Lear. We got a problem with the power." I nodded and followed him away from the entrance where RJ would come in, glancing at my watch again.

I hate this fucking day. I spent fifteen minutes with the guys trying to figure out the issue with the power, only to get pulled into a new crisis with the caterer. My phone hadn't stopped buzzing between vendors, my sister, and Penny. Now I reached for the door handle to the bridal suite. I raised my knuckles to knock but heard a panicked voice from inside.

"Hey, it's okay. It's not a big deal." RJ's voice was calm and kind of throaty.

"No, you don't understand. This thing means everything to him. This will gut him." The bride's voice was the frantic one. I shook my head, about to knock again. RJ always met with the couple before things got started. I'd forgotten she was meeting with them separately.

"Here," RJ said in a hushed tone.

"He'll know it's not the real thing," the bride said, voice rising. "This means so much to him. Oh, God. How can our marriage make it if I can't even keep one promise?"

I narrowed my eyes, knowing I shouldn't be listening in.

RJ spoke next. "It's fine. What he doesn't know won't hurt him. It's a little lie. If he finds out, you can confess, but otherwise, he'll never know."

Her words rattled in my head, and I clenched my jaw as I knocked on the door. The two women were standing close together in the middle of the room, the bride's eyes wide as her fist closed around something. "Everything okay?" I asked, stepping inside and striving for an even tone.

The woman nodded quickly, tucking whatever she was clutching into a hidden pocket in her dress.

"I think we're good, right, Mina?" RJ gave me her professional smile again and patted the woman's bare shoulder.

"Yes. Yes." She nodded again, eyes still wide. She looked to RJ again, who nodded, and my jaw ticked. The secret between them and whatever RJ had talked the bride into hiding from her fiancé made an uncomfortable sensation linger in my chest.

"We're all set and guests are seated. Tina will come down to get you in a few minutes with your dad and you can get married, okay?" I bit back the edge that threatened to creep into my tone. "RJ, shall we?"

She gave Mina an encouraging smile and followed me into the hall.

"What was that all about?" I tried to sound casual as we walked toward the ceremony location, RJ's black heels clicking on the tile.

"Nothing, just nerves."

I nodded, pushing back the increasing unease in my gut at her lie. I glanced at her face, her expression cool and calm, the lie rolling off her like it was nothing. My phone buzzed in my pocket and I reached in to silence it. My sister's name flashed on the screen and I clenched my jaw again. "Sure," I said as we reached the entry. "Game time." She smiled, the stiff smile I'd come to hate in the course of twenty-four hours, and walked in the other direction to get the ceremony started.

Despite the innumerable issues that had already come up, the ceremony started without incident, and I stood at the back of the room watching RJ. In her heels, she was still shorter than both the bride and groom, and she stood on a platform I'd had placed there. Her voice filled the room, and while everyone else was focused on the grinning bride and the smitten groom, I couldn't take my eyes off her. I couldn't make myself move on from whatever had gone on between Mina and RJ and what they were hiding from the groom or push away the gnawing feeling that grew every time I saw the date on my phone.

Chapter 37

RJ

I CAUGHT LEAR near the DJ after the couple signed their marriage license. "You've been busy this afternoon."

Lear looked up from his phone, startled. "What?" His posture was tense. He'd looked that way before the wedding, too.

"I said you've been busy this afternoon." I motioned to the elaborate reception. "Which makes sense. This is a big event."

"Yeah." He glanced over my shoulder, but I knew the only thing behind me was a blank wall, so he was just avoiding eye contact. "I've been busy."

I narrowed my eyes, and he looked over my shoulder again. This was a big wedding—the bride's father was an oil tycoon from Texas and a client of Carl's. It was an expensive event, but I'd never seen Lear like this. He was normally so unflappable, and as many times as I'd enjoyed ruffling his feathers, I didn't like seeing him like this. "What's going on with you?"

He finally met my eyes, but he looked suspicious. "What was going on with the bride before the wedding? I heard you say 'What he doesn't know won't hurt him' before I came in."

"It was nothing. The wedding went off without a hitch." I'd found it kind of endearing that the young bride was so beside herself over her something old, a quarter. There were so many problems in my life and in the lives of others I couldn't fix, it felt good to give someone a win. From one look at his stiff posture, I knew Lear wouldn't get that, though, and I didn't feel like taking the time to explain the complexities of why I wanted to help people, why someone looking at me like I'd fixed everything that was wrong was special. Someone I casually hooked up with didn't need the ins and outs of my psyche. "She was going to memorize her vows and didn't. I told her I would suggest they both have the cards in case they got nervous, which I would have done anyway." The lie came out of my mouth easily.

Lear searched my face, though I did not know what he hoped to find. I also wasn't sure why he cared so much about this. He opened his mouth and would have possibly shed light on the topic, but his assistant walked hurriedly toward us and took him by the elbow to manage some crisis.

I leaned against the bar and raised a finger to the bartender. I wasn't going to stay, but I wanted to find out why Lear had such a stick up his butt, and a glass of chardonnay sounded nice.

After my trip to Chicago, I'd returned to a busy week in the office with court appearances, continued research on the Mayfield case, and three cases with complicated custody issues, not to mention the many calls from Penny to prepare for the day. The only person who didn't seem to want any of my time was Lear. I'd been excited the night before to figure out how to sneak off somewhere, but he'd avoided eye contact like he'd done today. I refused to believe he was pouting. On the phone he'd said he was fine with the arrangement and that he understood how things stood between us. I rolled my eyes and sipped the wine. Maybe Britta was right to ask, because it seemed like I might have to walk away.

From the front of the room, knives tapped glasses. "Thank you, everyone." The groom stood, a smile wide across his face and his cheeks dusted with the blush of alcohol and young love. "Mina and

I just wanted to say a few words of thanks." He began thanking their parents, and I glanced around the hall. They were a nice couple, but I was really only still there for one reason. Lear stood off to the side, talking in a hushed voice with his assistant and someone who appeared to be from the hotel staff. Lear stood taller than the other two, his broad shoulders filling the fabric of his button-up shirt. It was navy today, and the gray slacks he wore fit him well. I glanced at his hand. He was always so calm and collected, but his fingers were twitching, like he wanted to reach for something.

The groom's voice cut into my thoughts, his tone changing from boisterous to a little emotional. "And of course, Mina."

I pulled my gaze from Lear and watched the groom smile at his new wife. It was endearing. I did like that part, the part before the bad stuff came in and they were just happy, the part where they boldly and publicly expressed their love in words. It didn't last long, in my experience, but I liked these moments.

"I met her at work. She was on the twenty-third floor and I was on the eighth." The bride smiled and the people in the room shifted, as if many had heard this story before and were eager for its retelling. "In the basement, there was this vending machine, and it was the only one in the building that had cherry Pop-Tarts. Anyway, one day, I scrounged some quarters from my desk and headed down there and ran into the most beautiful woman I'd ever seen." He looked at Mina, who met his eyes adoringly, and the gathered crowd let out a reverberating "Aw."

I sipped my wine, knowing anyone looking at me would see what I wanted them to, but even I, the cynical divorce attorney bent on avoiding feelings, had to look at the couple and hope they made it.

"She was buying cherry Pop-Tarts, too. I was smitten immediately when she politely smiled at me and walked away." He held Mina's hand and spoke to her. "I went back to that vending machine at the same time for weeks, hoping to catch you again. I ended up with an actual bucket of quarters in my desk, and I probably gained ten pounds after eating those Pop-Tarts every day."

The crowd laughed, and I glanced back at Lear, who had finished the conversation with his assistant and was watching the couple. His expression was . . . flat. I couldn't tell whether Lear actually liked weddings. I was pretty sure he didn't, but he usually faked it well, and he wasn't now. I glanced down at his fingers, still moving around restlessly.

"Anyway, one day, I ran into you again. You were wearing a black-and-white dress and red heels and you took my breath away. I'd always thought that expression was a cliché, but I actually forgot to inhale for a moment. You were that captivating."

Mina's face lit up, and even from the back of the room, I could see her eyes welling with tears.

"I had to think fast. I'd never thought about what I would say, so I asked to borrow a quarter for the machine. I can tell you this now," he said with a grin. "I had, like, six dollars in change on me, and I never got around to spending that quarter you lent me or buying Pop-Tarts that morning, because I didn't want to waste any time not talking to you."

Again, the *aww*s filled the ballroom, and I let my eyes dart across the room once more to Lear, whose expression hadn't changed.

Mina stood, leaning into her husband so they could both speak into the microphone. "So, I have a secret, too. You wanted me to have that quarter with me today. It was my something old, but I accidentally left it at home." She held his hand, and the two of them seemed to forget any other people were in the room. "I planned to give it to you after the ceremony like I did back then," she said, looking around the room. She pointed to the back of the room, and the gathered crowd all turned in their seats to look at me. "RJ, are you still here? RJ gave me this one to use instead until I found the original."

Heat rose on my cheeks. Even though the crowd had returned to watching Doug and Mina, I felt one set of eyes still on me.

"She said you'd never know, and maybe you wouldn't." She pulled the quarter from the pocket in her dress. "I know how much the original one means to you because it was the start of our story, but, here." She held out his hand and placed the quarter in his palm. "Our story is just starting out, and I want us to have lots of quarters, old and new." Her voice wavered, and embarrassment prickled on the back of my neck.

Mina's father was solidly in the top one percent, and she'd grown up in lavish wealth. Watching her and her husband talk about collecting change was still moving.

The groom slipped it in his pocket. "I already feel like the richest man in the world."

Mina smiled. Doug smiled. Everyone applauded, and the two kissed as the sound of silverware hitting glasses filled the room.

I sipped my wine, reminding myself I didn't have to feel bad about helping her out, even though she ended up confessing. I also reminded myself I didn't want someone spouting cheesy lines at me like that. But something still made the hairs on my neck stand on end, and I looked to my right to see not everyone was focused on the happy couple.

Lear's gaze met mine, just for a second. His expression was blank. It was off-putting, but he looked like he didn't even know me. The inkling I was feeling was guilt. Guilt at having been complicit in trying to deceive the groom and lying to Lear. And it shouldn't have mattered, but it still unsettled me.

I don't have to tell him everything. I repeated it to myself. *Friends with benefits doesn't require confessing all of our secrets.* Still, the uneasy feeling didn't leave me as I watched the couple onstage kiss a second time. Now guests were tossing quarters onto the dance floor.

I wished Lear were nearby. He'd be grumbling about how he'd

have to get someone to sweep up the coins before someone's stiletto slipped and they broke an ankle. He would have already planned for someone to do it, though. I was a planner, a type A, I-know-what-you-should-be-doing planner, but Lear put me to shame. I sighed, since that was probably what he was doing at that moment, and sticking around was beginning to make me feel pathetic.

I spotted him again across the room. He glanced at his phone and cracked his neck in this annoying and weirdly sexy way he had when he was stressed. He didn't notice me watching, and my irritation grew. I hadn't moved, so he knew where I was. He knew we always hooked up after rehearsals, and he'd avoided me the night before. I flashed back to our conversation. He'd agreed to keeping things just physical, said he understood. I felt like the bad guy and I didn't like that, because I'd been up-front with him.

Another few moments of him looking around and avoiding me had me gritting my teeth, and I pulled out my phone.

Chapter 38

LEAR

PENNY: So?

I blew out a slow breath and glanced around the reception. All the events were done, and now the evening would coast for a while with people dancing and drinks flowing. Tina was checking in with the caterers about the s'more and nacho bars the couple had requested to be ready at nine, and I took a moment to rest against a wall.

> LEAR: Happy bride. Happy groom. Happy oil magnate.

PENNY: I love you. Get an expensive bottle of something tomorrow. I'm buying.

> LEAR: You already did. Thanks.

I cracked my neck, a headache threatening to cut through the Advil I'd taken. I'd dismissed three texts from my sister and deleted one from Sarah without reading it. I'd been able to push away a lot in the last week with my focus on preparing for this event, but I had a feeling things were going to crash down on me soon. A very nice bottle of bourbon was waiting for me at home, and I had plans to spend the next day forgetting it had been a year since I'd found out the ground beneath me was actually water. I was about to tuck my phone into my pocket again when the screen lit with an incoming text.

RJ: Something wrong with your neck?

She was at the bar across the room, nursing a glass of wine. She never used to stay for the receptions, always leaving once the marriage certificate was signed or her duties were otherwise fulfilled. She leaned against the corner of the bar from her perch on the stool, one leg crossed over the other. I returned her text, only flicking my eyes from her for a moment.

LEAR: Long day.

RJ: You look tense.

Her hair was pulled into a tight bun, her curls restrained and tamped down, and I had an urge to mess it up. She traced a fingertip down her neck and across her collarbone, her teeth just barely sinking into her bottom lip.

LEAR: You don't.

RJ: How do I look?

She met my eyes, and she looked . . . predatory, like this was a contest she was gearing up to win. I'd gotten used to her real smile and her jokes. This was something different. *Of course it is. She re-*

minded you what she wants. Not smiles, not jokes, just pleasure. I glanced down at her body, letting my eyes trail slowly back up, knowing she was watching me look. She slowly—achingly slowly—uncrossed and recrossed her legs, and I wanted to groan.

> LEAR: Like you want to meet me in
> the bathroom down the hall from the
> coatroom.

Her lips tipped up in a grin, and she finished her wine, setting it gingerly on the bar top. I tried not to notice the lines of her throat when she sipped or think about how she liked to be kissed along the slope of her shoulders, how she was soft and cuddled in those moments after we'd had sex. *No.*

RJ: Maybe so.

Across the room, Tina gave me a thumbs-up and motioned to her watch, showing she had things handled. I normally took a break to sit down or return emails or just get off my feet. Tonight, I planned to make better use of the time. RJ had already stood and was making her way out of the hall, hips swaying. Beautiful, round hips swaying, and I couldn't shake the tension at the base of my neck, the awareness of what she'd said, of the deleted messages on my phone, and the edginess I'd felt all night.

I pushed off the wall, loosening up, shaking off the cobwebs. I wasn't some touchy-feely, emotional guy. I left that guy in California, and if RJ Brooks wanted sex with no complicated emotion, I could do that. Hell, maybe it would help get my head on straight.

I knocked lightly on the door of the single-stall bathroom, an out-of-the-way place I'd scouted earlier. Spacious, tucked away, and clean. It was ideal for brides in enormous dresses.

"Come in." Her voice was low and smoky, and when I pushed open the door, she was sitting on the vanity, legs crossed again. Her palms gripped the edge of the marble surface, arms outstretched, which pushed her breasts together. "You have an answer for me?"

I licked my lip and reached behind me to flip the lock. "Yeah."

Her eyes met mine as I closed the distance between us. "We usually meet after rehearsals. You made me wait."

I stopped just an inch or two from her, noticing how her knee shifted toward me.

"I don't like to be kept waiting."

I dragged my forefinger from her kneecap up her thigh, the fabric of the dress soft under my touch, the heat from her body radiating toward me. My voice came out sharper than I'd planned, deeper and more clipped. "Too fucking bad."

RJ's body almost shivered at my touch, like a ripple of want passed through her. She wanted me to go faster, but I continued the slow pace of my finger up her thigh until I was at the top, and then I slid it across her lap, watching her squirm. "You've never talked to me like that before." Her teeth sank into her lip again, deeper this time.

"You lied to me." I stepped closer, my erection pressing against her leg. Her eyes glinted at this change in our behavior, but I spoke honestly. "It made me mad."

RJ uncrossed her legs, taking time to rub one against my dick, and her expression shifted, like she was calculating something. "You made me mad, too. You ignored my messages. You know I hate that."

I continued to slide my finger back up, then down, her thigh, grazing under the hem of her skirt, itching to move my hands up under her dress and feel her heat. "But you want to spread those beautiful legs for me, don't you?"

RJ's fingers slid into my hair and slowly curled against my scalp, waking up all my senses. "I told you I don't like waiting."

I pulled my hand away from her dress and stroked up her bare arm, seeing the goose bumps rise and the frustration flash on her face. "And I told you, that's too fucking bad."

Her fingers tightened in my hair and I inhaled sharply. She spread her thighs, and I stepped between them, our eyes meeting and her dress riding up. "Why is it so hot when you talk to me like that?"

I wanted to slide further, to dip my hands between her legs and give her what she wanted, but I knew this was driving her crazy and I clung to that iota of control. I shrugged. I couldn't mess up her hair, not here, but making her agitated was enthralling. I reminded myself I didn't have to be gentle and romantic. She'd made it clear she didn't want that. "I haven't decided if I'm going to have sex with you."

RJ pressed a hand between us, stroking me through my pants. "Yes, you have."

She hadn't touched me in two weeks, and I clenched my jaw against the sensation of her palm. RJ's expression was smug, and she looked up at me with those big brown eyes, and *damn*.

I pulled her lips roughly to mine and her fingers tightened in my hair again. I needed to kiss that infuriatingly smug smile off her face, that smile that meant she thought she knew me, that she could call the shots and I'd follow along. The flood of memories washed over me at the thought of another woman thinking what I didn't know wouldn't hurt me, and I deepened the kiss, pressing myself between her legs and swallowing her sighs when the head of my dick pressed into her wet panties. I pulled away from her mouth, nipping her bottom lip. One arm rested on the wall behind her, the other cradled against her neck, my thumb gliding over her throat. "You lied to me." I heard the strain in my own voice.

She was silent for long enough that I pulled back to look at her face as she searched mine. "I'm sorry I lied to you. I don't know why this bothered you so much, but I won't do that again." She pressed a soft palm to my face. "We're honest with each other, above anything else."

I flexed my jaw, so frustrated with myself that I wanted to walk out of the room just to prove how little she meant to me, but I knew RJ didn't apologize easily. I wanted her like this—angry and passionate—and I wanted to revel in the feel of her soft hand on my cheek. I wanted both, and I wanted to ignore the voice in my head that wanted even more from her. "Then tell me the truth now. You want this?" I pressed against her. "Because it's been a long damn day, and I'm not in the mood for games." I was in uncharted waters. I'd never said anything like that to a woman before, never come close, but no woman had frustrated me as completely as RJ before, frustrated me and left me wanting.

She swallowed and met my steely gaze with her own. "I didn't ask you for games. In case it's unclear, I'm asking you to take me."

I unbuckled my belt, but RJ slid down my zipper, stroking me. I had to close my eyes against her touch, and I pulled her wrist away. "Not yet." I pushed her dress up her thighs, my thumbs pressing up the insides of her thighs until I could hook into her panties and pull them down her legs. Her skin was so soft, I wanted to kiss every inch. *Focus.* "So, we need, um, a safe word or something, since we're both feeling rougher?"

She smiled, a laugh escaping in one breath, and heat rose on my face.

I didn't like the embarrassment that wrapped me up, that this was more ammunition for her to use against me. That I didn't know how to do this. "Forget it," I said, shifting to take a step back. "I'm leaving."

She reached for my arm. "No, Lear, wait." Her expression softened in an instant, leaving my head spinning. "I wasn't laughing at you, I just . . . I don't normally do this either, being rougher." Her eyes widened, and I watched as she carefully pulled back the smile and the openness, swallowing whatever she was going to admit and reminding herself what I was to her. "Cubicle. Cubicle means I want you to stop. That's all. I wasn't laughing at you. I was just nervous."

I didn't ask what she had been going to say. I didn't want to care. I didn't want her to think I cared. *Because it doesn't matter. Because it's just sex.* And it wasn't just sex because she'd said that's all she could do, it was just sex because that was probably all I could do, too. The weight of my phone in my pocket filled with missed messages of concern and reminders of the date were proof of that. I wanted RJ—her scent and taste and the feel of her against me filled my brain—but I also needed to prove to myself that I could have RJ's body without demanding her heart.

I pulled her face to mine, letting our lips and tongues clash before nipping her bottom lip again, the yelp and moan she let out pushing me on as I nipped at her earlobe, my fingers pressing between her legs. "Don't lie to me again," I said, sliding a finger into her, then two, pushing them in and out of her slick entrance.

"I said I wouldn't." She rode my hand, pulling my hair as I sucked the skin over her collarbone and rubbed a thumb roughly over one of her hard nipples pushing at the fabric of the dress.

I pressed my fingers in harder, fingertips finding the swollen bundle of nerves. "Good."

"But you're not in charge," she said, but her voice wavered on the last word. I hated that I knew she was close to coming, not because of that but because of the way her eyes widened and her mouth opened, and I'd dreamed of that expression for months.

"Feels like I'm in charge," I added, my thumb brushing over her clit.

RJ pulled hard on my hair. "Will you stop talking and make me come? That's all I need you to do."

Her words hit me somewhere primal and I pressed hard against her G-spot, watching her writhe, so close, her mouth opening, and then I pulled my fingers away.

"Why did you stop?" Her voice was pitched low, but her tone was frantic, and I felt her still rolling against my hand as I pulled back, reaching for my wallet.

I'd made sure I had a condom there, even after avoiding RJ the night before, despite my resolution to get this woman out of my head. I ripped open the foil and almost dropped it when RJ pulled the dress over her head. The fabric rubbing against her bun made several curls spring loose, and I, once again, wanted to pull them all free. I was desperate to be inside her, but also desperate to have her be as messy and out of control as I felt. I unhooked her bra instead, letting the fabric fall and rolling one nipple between my fingertips, increasing the pressure when she arched into me.

"You're making me wait again," she gasped.

I pinched her nipple more firmly, lips closing around the other, teeth grazing the sensitive flesh. "Deal with it," I said, teeth grazing her again, testing to see if she liked it, then nipping and teasing, feeling her hips roll toward me again and again. I sucked hard as her fingernails dragged over my back. She reacted in this breathless way each time and I wanted to do it over and over.

"All your clothes are still on," she said, scratching my back.

"And yet you're bare to me." I didn't need to say it—it was obvious—but her eyes lit up and she rolled her hips to me again. I let my eyes trail over her body and dug my fingers under her ass, holding the pliant flesh.

"You only see what I show you." She leaned against my hand and settled her own grip on my shoulder. "Don't forget that."

That was all I needed to push my hips between her thighs. "Ready?"

"Yes," she said, spreading her legs wider.

I pushed into her, all the way and hard, watching her eyes widen.

I still paused, letting her adjust, but she dragged her nails down my back, rolling into me, and I pulled out and thrust again, my muscles tensing as I drove into her, giving her everything I could because that's all she wanted. She cried out into my shoulder, saying "Don't stop" and "Harder." With each thrust, it felt like I was unleashing the tension that had been coiling in my body all day, all week, and I pushed further, harder, shifting her hips so I could go deeper.

RJ's nails dug into my back through my shirt and I winced as she bit down on my neck, sending pain and pleasure through me. She spasmed around my dick, her thighs trembling against me. I couldn't hold out and I finished with a roar into her shoulder. We stood there wrapped in each other's arms, both reeling and panting. Finally, RJ slumped against me. "Dammit, Lear."

"Did I hurt you?" I didn't pull back to see her face. If I was honest with myself, it was because I knew she wouldn't have the soft, dreamy expression I loved. I didn't want to see her efficient half smile, not yet. Didn't want to see that *Thank you and goodbye* in the set of her jaw.

"No." She rested her head on my shoulder, one of the loose curls brushing my cheek, her warm breath against my neck in the moments of silence. "Did I hurt you?"

I stroked her bare back, the tension that I'd pushed away gathering again because her tone was soft. We'd only been in the bathroom for ten minutes, but it felt like an eternity. An eternity where she'd reminded me that if I didn't get my own feelings in check, I would get hurt. I shook my head and inhaled against her neck. Still, I stroked her back a few more times before stepping back, steeling myself to watch her efficiently pull on her clothes and walk away like I knew she would.

Chapter 39

RJ

GRETCHEN AND I sat across from each other at the hotel bar near the office on a Friday night. When she'd suggested I grab a drink with her after work, I'd jumped at the chance, and we sat with glasses of wine and a cheese plate between us, discussing the Mayfield case. "Maybe" had fallen apart quickly; after a couple weeks back in counseling, the couple had decided to move forward.

"Has the game plan changed?"

Gretchen shook her head. "No. The public line is conscious uncoupling, but our client wants to win, and she wants him to have distance from the foundation."

"I kept working on the foundation. It's the only thing he seems to care about, and given her other charitable endeavors . . . I think if she'd give up the foundation, he'd give on a lot of other assets, leaving her ahead."

"I agree, but she's set on this point." Gretchen sipped her wine.

I studied the cheese plate for a moment. "It's kind of a shame, isn't it? That their decision to try again fell apart so quickly."

Gretchen tipped her head. "I suppose, but not unexpected. There doesn't seem to be a lot of trust between them. A charitable foundation wasn't very stable glue to hold two people together, not from my vantage point, anyway."

"You're right," I said, uncomfortable with the tinge of sadness I felt. It wasn't for the Mayfields. It was for the loss of possibility that love could persist. It had been a silly hope, one I never would have entertained in the past. "I'll get on it."

"I'm glad you're on the team, RJ. When I get back from vacation in a few weeks, let's talk about what's next for you." Gretchen was married to an orthopedic surgeon I'd met a few times. I'd expected her to be with someone serious, severe, someone who mirrored her, but her husband was funny, laid back, and kind of a nerd.

"I'll get on your calendar." I toyed with the stem of my glass. "Can I ask you a personal question, Gretchen?"

"Sure."

"How do you balance this? Being around the relationship acrimony every day and then going home to a marriage. Seems it would be challenging."

She considered my question for a moment, then raised the glass of chardonnay to her lips before she answered. "The job doesn't get in the way for me. My marriage isn't those marriages. My marriage isn't the Mayfields' marriage." A small smile crossed her lips, one I couldn't read. "We should know better than anyone why marriages fail. But I also had practice."

"At marriage?"

She nodded. "Seven years. I really loved him, but you know as well as me, love alone isn't enough. We didn't talk enough, didn't communicate about what we wanted, stopped giving each other the benefit of the doubt. It spiraled from there, like we hear from a lot of clients. There's a lot of things I regret from that marriage. A lot of ways I messed up, but he's happy now. I'm happy now, and we both probably learned a lot."

I rearranged what I knew about Gretchen in my head and made a note to smack Eric on the arm the next time I saw him for not telling me that bit of information.

"Why do you ask?"

Well, I came dangerously close to falling for someone and letting down my defenses. "No reason, I guess."

Gretchen raised an eyebrow but didn't acknowledge my BS response. "It's easy to get jaded in our line of work, but I like to think it just makes us more careful with who we trust and how we ask others to trust us." She glanced down into her glass before finishing it. "I don't have any expert advice, though. My first marriage was a mess, and I didn't like who I was by the end of it. If you're looking for balance, make sure you pick someone with your same desire for equilibrium."

I glanced over her shoulder and spotted a familiar form at the bar. I thought about pointing him out since they were friends, but I didn't want Gretchen to suspect what was going on between us. A small part of me wanted him to myself.

"I need to get going," Gretchen said, checking her watch. "You'll be prepared to share Monday afternoon with the team?"

I brought my eyes back to her face. Ten years earlier, Gretchen wasn't the mentor I would have chosen, but she was the one I needed now. We'd talked about strategy for the Mayfield case but shifted to my career. She didn't mince words, she never sugarcoated anything, and she'd reminded me that eyes were always watching powerful women. She had ideas, though, and I'd listened. She looked at me with confidence, like she knew what I could achieve. "I will," I said.

She dabbed her napkin to her lips. "Do you want to walk out together?"

I glanced over her shoulder again. I thought again about telling her he was there, but something in his posture gave me pause. Other than to raise his glass, Lear hadn't moved. "I think I might stay and have another glass of wine at the bar. Don't want to turn in quite yet."

Gretchen nodded and walked toward the exit.

I strode to the bar and slid into the empty seat next to Lear. "This seat taken?"

He looked surprised to see me but didn't smile like usual. I never thought I'd miss the way he always had that annoying grin on his face. "Hey. What are you doing here?"

"Late meeting." I glanced at the Scotch in front of him and noted his flat demeanor. "What about you?"

He held up his drink wordlessly.

I couldn't tell if that was supposed to be a joke. "No wedding this weekend?"

He shook his head and sipped from his drink.

"Me, either." I signaled for the bartender and asked for water. "What are the odds, huh?"

"Pretty slim, I guess." He didn't elaborate, just continued to sip from his glass, and the silence between us grew awkward.

An unfamiliar insecurity gripped me. "You want me to leave you alone?"

He shrugged, not looking at me but tossing back his drink. "Do what you want. You always do."

My stomach clenched like I'd been punched, and my cheeks heated. "Okay." I stood, pulling my purse onto my shoulder and taking a step away, wanting to leave this interaction and the brief kinship I'd felt for him behind. That last time with him had been hot, and I'd had it in my head that it would make it easier to delineate what he was to me, but by the time we'd had to pull apart, I hadn't wanted to. I'd spent every day of the last week wondering if he felt that, too, but his dismissive tone said differently. "Okay. See you later."

"RJ." He turned and grabbed my hand. "I'm sorry. Don't . . ." His eyes trailed down to his hand, still wrapped around mine. He paused there for a moment before opening his fingers slowly, like it pained him. "Don't go. I'm an ass. I'm sorry."

I bit the inside of my cheek. The embarrassment from his dismissal still stung, but for some reason I felt uncertain, too. For starters, Lear was apologizing, which was something we rarely did. More than that, his hair was kind of messy, like he'd run his fingers through it over and over. His eyes were a little glassy, and he looked . . . sad. I glanced at the empty tumbler on the bar. "How many of those have you had?"

He slid his fingers through his hair. "Too many."

"Settle up. Let's go for a walk."

"You want to walk with me?"

I rolled my eyes, falling into safer territory. "No, but if you get so drunk you fall off a stool and break your arm, I'll have to deal with some other wedding planner next weekend. C'mon." I nodded toward the exit.

We stepped out into the warm night. The area around the hotel was busy, and we walked side by side for a few minutes without saying anything. Crossing the street a few blocks away, we strolled into a park, the bustle of traffic fading as we wandered in the moonlight.

I glanced at him, only to find his expression inscrutable. "Do you want to talk about it?"

"About what?"

"About why you were downing Scotch alone at a hotel bar in the town where you live." We passed a group of teenagers practicing some skateboarding maneuvers on a small set of stairs. Lear didn't reply until we'd passed them.

"It's been a bad day."

We stopped at a railing separating us from a drop-off where a small creek gurgled below. I watched him, taking in how he set his forearms on the railing. I searched for a quip, something to make him elaborate. Ten ideas popped into my head, but I bit them back. I wasn't sure he needed sarcastic RJ tonight.

"You don't need to hear about my . . ." He trailed off, glancing out over the water. "About it."

"I haven't wanted to push you into oncoming traffic yet tonight, which is weirding me out. I know I'm not always . . . nice, but if you want to talk to me, you can." I stumbled over the words, nudging his forearm with my own. I half expected him to jerk away, but he didn't, and we stood, arms touching in the breeze. "I'll listen."

Finally, Lear pulled his phone from his pocket and tapped it before handing it to me. I wasn't sure what I was looking at for a moment. Blurs of white and black, but then I saw it and my eyes shot to his face.

"He turns one on Sunday," Lear said without looking at me.

"You have a kid?" I glanced between him and the sonogram image, picking out the details in the grainy photo—the outline of the nose and hand.

"Nope," he said, taking back the phone and shoving it in his pocket. His words were a little slurred, and for the first time I questioned if I knew what I was doing. We were miles outside the carefully drawn borders we'd erected around our relationship.

Lear glanced at me, then back into the darkness. "I told you I was engaged?"

"Yeah. You said it didn't work out."

"She was pregnant. I tried to play it cool, but I was . . ."

"Excited?"

"I never wanted to be a dad. Never wanted someone to need me and risk leaving them alone." He met my gaze. "I worked through a lot of shit with my own parents dying, and I was still scared. Terrified, but I got excited. I fell in love with the idea of being his dad. Fell in love with him."

The kids on skateboards crossed the path behind us, their laughter and the sound of wheels on concrete pausing our conversation.

"What happened?"

"We'd just finished the nursery. I remember it was her birthday and I'd gotten her a little cake, and when I brought it in, she started crying. She told me she'd had an affair and didn't know who the father was. Just . . . said it." He seemed to search the surface of the water, his shoulders tense. "She'd had blood pressure issues during the pregnancy and had to be on bed rest, and I couldn't leave her alone, so we lived in this uncomfortable . . . miserable middle point between anger and anticipation for a week, and then she went into labor."

He was quiet, his jaw working back and forth, and I bit my tongue to keep from pressing until he was ready.

"Fifteen hours later, he was born, and he wasn't mine." He said it so matter-of-factly, someone might have missed the pain in his voice. "She said she'd had a feeling with the timing . . . Anyway. Lots of red hair, same as his real dad."

My jaw dropped, and I set a hand on Lear's without thinking about the intimacy of the gesture. "My God," I muttered.

He nodded, jaw ticking and mouth in a set line. "Turns out, the other guy was excited to be a father, too, and he was the one she wanted. So, I had a son for a couple minutes; then I didn't. I had a family I'd promised myself I'd never leave, and then they left me."

Nearby, a group of crickets chirped, and the laughter from the teenagers faded into the night. "What's his name?"

"I don't know," he whispered. "We were going to name him Eli after my dad, but then . . . I didn't talk to her. I don't know his name." Lear's jaw ticked again, and his eyes were wet.

I wasn't sure what to do, so I linked my fingers with his, edging closer so the sides of our bodies lined up.

"He's out there in the world and growing and learning and he's not mine, but he was mine and I don't even know his fucking name." His voice cracked, and he wiped his free arm across his face.

I squeezed his fingers, resting my head on his arm. "Lear. I'm so sorry."

"No. I'm sorry," he said, taking in a deep breath and wiping at his eyes again. "I'm drunk."

I squeezed his hand, stroking my thumb over his.

"Anyway," he said, taking a shaky breath. "That's my sob story. I fell in love with a woman who I trusted and lost a son who was never mine to begin with and Sunday is his birthday and . . ."

"And it's going to suck," I offered.

"Yeah. I thought I'd have an event this weekend to be busy with, to take my mind off it, but I'll be alone all weekend. You know, it's so stupid. I found this shirt I thought was funny and Sarah teased me because he wouldn't fit into it until he was in twelve-months clothes. I keep thinking about how big that damn shirt looked and how he could probably wear it now." He took another breath, this one steadier, but he didn't pull his hand from mine as he scrubbed his face with his free hand. "I know it's pathetic to react like this. You'll probably never let me live this down."

"No. It's not pathetic." I unlinked our fingers, the punch-in-the-gut feeling from earlier returning, horrified that he'd think I'd . . . well, that he'd think I'd do something like that. I rested my hand against his cheek, guiding his chin so he faced me. "Lear, it's not pathetic, and I'd never throw it in your face," I said, examining his expression. Our eyes locked. For a moment—really, a split second—he rested his cheek in my hand. "I had no idea." I thought about him getting so sunburned getting the nursery ready for Penny and her wife, what it must have been like for him while he painted that room.

"Thanks for listening," he murmured. "I don't talk about it." He dragged his face away from my hand and returned his forearms to the railing.

"Maybe you should." I was frozen, our tender moment leaving me feeling as confused as ever. I simultaneously felt like comforting him and avenging him, like finding his ex-fiancée and lawyering her into submission, to try to take away the pain he was obviously covering up.

"Maybe I should," he said into the air, the sentence almost wholly swallowed up by the breeze and the crickets and the creek gurgling below. "I thought being like this—like a guy who didn't care—would work, and it hasn't. It still hurts. I still care."

I thought back to meeting him, to despising him, and I followed the tense line of his jaw. Truth was, I'd wanted to think he was a jackass, but I'd changed my mind early on. For a long time, I'd known he was something kind of special. "I never thought you were a guy who didn't care."

He grunted in acknowledgment, and we both stared at the water. Torn between wanting to comfort him and not having any idea how to do it without putting myself and my heart somewhere dangerous, I just stood next to him, listening to the lapping of the water below.

"What can I do?"

He pressed his palms to his forehead. "Nothing."

Chapter 40

LEAR

I SCRUBBED MY palm down my face and shuffled into my kitchen, squinting against the sunlight and peering into the fridge. *I can't believe I told her all that on Friday night.*

Looking between a bottle of orange juice and a six-pack of beer, I scratched the back of my neck. *July twenty-fourth.* I reached for the beer. *Fuck it.*

I paused with my hand around the neck of a bottle when someone rang my doorbell. I was going to ignore it, but they kept ringing, the sound reverberating and setting my teeth on edge. "Dammit," I muttered, taking the bottle with me to the door. When I whipped it open, I froze, seeing RJ standing there, two cups of coffee in her hands.

"About damn time," she said, pushing past me. Her pale blue T-shirt stretched across the swell of her breasts and she sported leggings that hugged her thighs. Her hair was pulled on top of her head, and I must have been gaping.

She set down the coffee and crossed her arms over her chest, lips pursed to the side, and her gaze fell to my beer. "Breakfast?"

I matched her posture, crossing my own arms, but the beer was in the way. "What are you doing here?"

"Get dressed," she said, leaning against my couch and sipping from one of the cups. She nodded toward where I stood in a pair of sweatpants that hung low on my hips.

"You usually tell me to take my pants *off*." I set my beer aside and tried to forget about opening up to her the night before.

"I'm usually bored when I tell you that," she said, smiling behind her cup. "I'm up at seven a.m. on a Sunday. Your dick is not impressive enough to be up this early. Get dressed. We're going to play soccer."

"Soccer?"

RJ set down her cup and placed her palm on my chest, pushing me down the hall. "A guy I work with plays on Sunday mornings. He invited us to join."

I stared down at her, still trying to piece together her words with her hands on my bare chest. The fog was clearing from my head, and I met her eyes, feeling their warmth, seeing her soften for a moment before she replaced that expression with one that was more classic RJ. "Shut up. If we're friends with benefits, this is the friends part," she said.

"I didn't say anything. I'm just shocked when you're nice to me."

"Well . . . don't get used to it." She gave me a last push toward the basement and walked back down the hall, her hips swaying in those leggings. "We have to be there in thirty minutes, so hurry."

THE PARK WAS mostly empty, the grass still dewy, and clouds hung low in the sky. RJ waved to a group of men gathered on the field, and a prickle of jealousy rose in me when she jogged toward one of the men, a tall blond, and gave him a wide smile and high five.

"Wedding planner. This is my friend Eric," she said, motioning between us.

The guy stretched his hand out for me to shake. "Wedding planner. I'm sure you have a name Ruthie has decided to ignore?"

"So, people *do* call you Ruthie?"

"Lear, this is Eric, who is going to regret so many things on Monday."

He laughed, and I took his hand. "Nice to meet you."

RJ looked around, pausing on another man with a baby strapped to his chest. "There she is," RJ said. She waved in my direction before walking toward the guy and the baby. "Entertain each other."

"Our girl does not want for any social graces," Eric said with a laugh, motioning to where RJ stood with the guy and the baby. "That's my husband and our daughter."

I eyed RJ turning into the gooiest version of herself I'd ever seen, making faces at the baby. I braced myself, but it didn't hurt, not much. I pushed the thoughts of babies out of my head and turned back to Eric, who introduced me to the other guys. We were almost done picking teams when RJ returned, Eric calling out her name before she even reached the circle of players.

"You ready to lose?" I asked.

She took the ball from Eric and bounced it between her knees. "It's probably good you're asking yourself that question. It's important to be prepared."

"Big talk, *Ruthie*," I said, mimicking the nickname Eric had used. The breeze blew around us, cooling the already hot and humid weather, which made it easier to forget everything I'd told her the night before. "Want to up the stakes here? Loser buys breakfast?"

Her face scrunched, eyes narrowing. "I'd love to have you treat me to breakfast."

She dropped the ball and dribbled it to the other side of the field and left me standing there, a half smile on my face. *Damn, this woman.*

"THAT WAS A cheap trick, and you know it."

RJ smiled, raising her palms in the air. "I didn't say it wasn't, but you still fell for it."

"You feigned injury!" I held the laminated menu in my hands after we settled into the booth at the restaurant. With every option available to her, since she'd won, RJ had chosen a hole-in-the-wall breakfast place on the edge of town.

"I . . ." She smiled wider, an open smile, and her laugh almost overwhelmed me. "Yeah, I did. But you still fell for it."

"Remind me to ignore your cries of pain next time the opportunity arises." I pretended to study the menu but was instead taking in her face while she read the options, a line between her brows deepening.

"I'm just saying, you could have scored *before* checking on me, that's all. Then you wouldn't have ended up such a sucker."

As I ran for the goal, RJ had pretended to trip, crying out, and when I'd stopped to help her, she'd popped up, stolen the ball, and earned the winning shot. "I should have scored and then checked on you? Do you know how much of a jerk that would make me?"

RJ shot me a plaintive look over the top of her menu. "Would you rather be a nice guy or a winner?"

I glanced back at the menu, ignoring that question. "So, why this place?"

"They make the best waffles in the state," she said, setting the menu aside. "And since you're buying, I thought I'd order extra."

"I'm sure they're good, but the best waffles in the area are at Molly's."

She shook her head. "Compared to here, those taste like frozen waffles that weren't heated long enough."

"Not possible."

The waitress approached our table to take our order, giving RJ a warm smile. "You've been gone too long, girl. Thought we'd never see you again. The regular?"

RJ nodded. "And he'll have the same."

The waitress nodded back and walked away.

"What did you order for me?"

"Don't you trust me?" RJ's curls fought against the tie she had holding back her hair, a few escaping the tight hold and framing her face.

I tucked my fingers against my palm at the urge to brush them off her skin. "You literally just told me I was a sucker for trusting you."

Her head tipped back, and I admired her throat, the way her muscles flexed in her shoulders when she laughed. "You're right, but I never lie about waffles." She cringed just for a second at the reference to lying, and I jumped in, moving the conversation forward before she could stumble into some awkward apology I didn't want.

The night of the quarters wedding had been incredible and confusing. I watched RJ sip her coffee and tried to put all of that out of my mind. I'd been so angry at her when she'd lied, so furious, and then she'd texted me, and the sex was good and so raw. I couldn't get her out of my head, and I didn't know what to do with that, because she'd been clear about exactly what we were, but sitting here, it felt like more. "Where did you learn to play like that?"

"High school," she said, setting the cup down, crossing her arms over each other, and leaning forward. "What about you?"

I matched her stance. "Same. Wasn't good enough to go beyond that."

"To be fair, you're not that good now."

"See," I said, sitting back. "We were having a moment, and you ruined it."

"I didn't ruin it." RJ thanked the waitress as she approached our table, and looked adoringly at her plate. She glanced up at me and winced, her nose scrunching in a way I tried hard not to notice was adorable. "Maybe I ruined it a little. I'm not good at moments."

"I don't know." I looked down at my plate, where a stack of golden waffles sat next to a ceramic dish of butter. RJ had ordered the same thing for us both, and even though the three carafes of syrup seemed excessive, it wasn't by much. Sarah had usually avoided carbs, and even though I didn't want to think about her, the comparison popped into my head, and I glanced up to see RJ again admiring her food. "You're not so bad."

RJ emptied what had to be half the syrup over her plate, and I bit back a laugh.

She motioned to my plate with an expectant expression. "I'm telling you. They're the best. Just get ready to eat your words," she said, with the fork poised between the table and her mouth.

I dragged the knife across the waffle slowly. "Don't rush me, woman. I have a process."

She rolled her eyes and took a bite. I immediately forgot my process when she let her eyes fall closed and moaned. "So good. It's like . . ." RJ paused, eyes snapping open.

"No, keep going. It's like . . ." I motioned for her to continue, enjoying how the embarrassment shifted her features subtly.

"Shut up."

"No, I'm really interested." Under the table, my foot bumped into hers. "What are they like?"

"Just taste it." RJ pointed to my plate. "You'll see."

I left my foot where it was, the gesture feeling so bold, despite my having enjoyed so much of her body. I still glanced away instead of maintaining our eye contact, waiting for her to pull away or shut me down, but she didn't.

"Okay, I'm ready," I said, setting my knife aside. "Is eating this in public appropriate, though? You looked like you were really having a moment."

She shifted her foot then, but it was to kick me, and I laughed. RJ's reaction had not been unwarranted. The waffle was good. Really good, and it was only me refusing to give her the satisfaction that stopped me from moaning just like she had.

"Told you so." RJ's smug smile returned, and I couldn't stop focusing on the pressure of her foot next to mine. "When will you learn not to question me?"

"I bow to the queen." My mock bow earned me a shift from her smug smile to a real one. "How did you find this place?"

She shrugged. "I drive around sometimes, just to get out of my head and think. I never know where I'm going, never plan to be anywhere, and I found this place."

"You were driving around the night you called me at my uncle's place. You seem like someone who always has a plan, but maybe not."

"Not always," she said, voice dipping lower. "I needed to think that night."

My heart rate sped up because I knew I was asking for trouble, and today of all the days, I should have known better. "Needed to think about me?"

She met my gaze, and her mouth opened like she was about to say something. She hadn't moved her foot. Her expression didn't look pinched or pained, and despite my resolve to play it cool, I hoped she was going to say something real.

The waitress's voice cut between us, and RJ's facade snapped back into place, her foot suddenly gone from the space next to mine. "How's everything tasting over here?"

"You know it's perfect," RJ said, turning her smile to the server.

"More syrup?" She eyed RJ's plate and laughed.

She was a lovely woman, and yet I'd never wanted someone to leave as much as I did in that moment. When she finally did, RJ looked down at her plate and took a big bite into her mouth before looking back up.

"Were you going to say something?" I took my own bite, trying to appear casual, like the last two minutes hadn't left me picturing the way RJ's lips parted.

She shook her head, mouth still full.

"Did you take a big enough bite there?"

RJ still chewed, but held up a middle finger, earning a pointed cough from the woman with three small children at the table next to us.

"Nice. Really nice," I said as she pulled back her hand. "Corrupting young children now?"

She flipped me off again, this time shielding her hand with the other and covering her laugh.

"For shame, Brooks. For shame." I sat back in the booth, enjoying my bite. "The youth of America just wanted breakfast, and now . . ."

"Jerk," she muttered when she finally swallowed. "I didn't know the kids were there."

"I'm shocked at this poor behavior." I clucked my tongue like my aunt Bette used to do. "Were you going to, um, say something before, though?"

"Nothing important." She reached into her bag and pulled out an envelope, handing it to me across the table. "Here, though."

"What's this?" It was a nondescript white envelope, but it was sealed. "Are you serving me a summons or something?"

"No." She set her fork down and leaned forward, resting her elbows on the table.

I was about to call out her avoidance of my question and guide her back to answering, but she spoke again.

"I wasn't sure you would want to know, which is why I sealed it."

I glanced down at the envelope, noticing her foot was against mine again.

"I found his name. Your, or rather . . . the kid." She searched my face, her speech speeding up. "It just seemed like you wanted to know, and I thought if I could find out for you, you wouldn't have to do the searching, and then you'd know."

I rubbed a finger along the edge of the paper.

"But if you don't want to know, or if I overstepped . . ." She reached out and grabbed the envelope. "It was probably a dumb idea. I'll throw it away."

"No," I said, pulling it back from her.

"It's fine," she said, gripping it more firmly.

I countered her force, sure the children at the next table were wondering why two adults were playing tug-of-war over waffles. "Will you let go?"

"Will you?" Her eyes flashed, meeting mine and staying there.

Why am I fighting with her for this? The envelope wasn't large, and our fingers butted against each other, threatening to rip the paper in half. I softened my voice but didn't ease my grip. "RJ, I want it."

"Are you sure?" Her voice also lowered, the smoky quality I knew from other contexts coming into it. She also did not relax her grip.

"Why would I tell you if I wasn't?" *And why does the fact that she won't let go make me want to jump over this table and kiss her?*

RJ finally relaxed her fingers, and the force of my grip brought the envelope to the table in front of me.

"Thank you." I hadn't actually been sure I wanted it. I could have looked on Sarah's social media anytime and found out, but I hadn't. I'd blocked her and anyone connected to her, leaving my digital social life as dismal as my actual social life. I looked at the envelope, aware of RJ's gaze on me. Her lips were pursed and pulled to the side, like she was considering snatching the envelope up again. "I know it's stupid that this one thing bugs me so much," I said, folding the envelope and tucking it into my pocket. "I appreciate you finding out. I'll look later."

She let her eyes drift away from me, and her posture stiffened, her fingers twitching like she didn't know what to do with her hands. "It didn't take a lot of work, but, I'm glad it's . . . rather, I hope . . ."

"Hope that I forget you did this kind thing and don't bring it up again?"

"Exactly."

I brought a forkful of waffle to my mouth, saying "Okay" through the bite. Her shoulders relaxed before she took her own bite. With the scent of syrup teasing my nose and the comfortable silence between us, I was overtaken, once again, by the urge to kiss her.

RJ checked the time on the clock over my head, and my chest tightened at the idea of not spending more time with her. I asked, "What are you doing the rest of the day?"

"Not much. I should stop at the office for a few minutes. Why?"

I drank the last of my orange juice, knowing I wasn't going to make more of a dent in the stack of waffles. I wanted more time with RJ, and I didn't want to go back to the empty basement. "We could hang out, if you want. Go see a movie, or find some game to play where I can have a chance at redemption."

"Bring it on. There's no game in existence where you could best me."

I'd smiled more today than I'd thought possible. "So cocky."

"So confident. There's a difference."

"Yeah," I said, reaching for my wallet. "I guess there is."

Chapter 41

RJ

THE BOWLING ALLEY smelled like popcorn and wood polish, and the hits of the 1980s and 1990s flowed from the overhead speakers. I'd been surprised when Lear asked to spend the day together, and even more surprised when I agreed. After we both had time to shower, he'd picked me up, and I grinned but didn't say anything when the cast recording for a musical played through his speakers. Well, I didn't say anything for a few minutes, which showed a great deal of restraint on my part since he was humming along with a song from *My Fair Lady* when I buckled my seatbelt.

I bent to test the weight of the different bowling balls on the rack, lifting them to see which was best, and felt his eyes on me. "Are you staring at my ass?"

"Yeah." He said it casually, and I glanced over my shoulder to see him at the rack next to mine. "You have a perfect ass."

"Oh?" I wiggled a little.

"It's not like you don't know," he said with a low chuckle I felt deep inside. "Did you take me bowling to seduce me, Ms. Brooks?"

"Seduce you?" I held up a purple ball, checking out the swirl of glitter as I turned it. "That implies you need tempting."

Lear chose his own ball but didn't step toward our lane. Instead, he moved his lips near my ear. "So you're not trying to seduce me?"

His whisper in my ear made butterflies flutter in my stomach in the most comfortable way I'd ever been uncomfortable with. For a second, I lost myself and considered sinking against him, because it was kind of sexy, but it was familiar, too. I took a small step back, because we were in a bowling alley and not a dark corner. "If I wanted you, I could have you anytime and anywhere, and we both know it. My only goal today is to provide you with another embarrassing loss."

His lips grazed my ear, and his fingers brushed my lower back before he whispered again. "Will you seduce me if I win?"

My face heated, but I shook it off. Not even Lear was worth attempting a sexual encounter in this bowling alley's bathroom. The idea of negotiating a prize was tempting, though. I stepped back and placed my hand on his chest, meeting his eyes and willing my heart to stop whatever it was spinning. "I've never thought about the possibility of you winning." I pushed him gently and strode toward the ball return for our lane. When I looked over my shoulder, he hadn't moved, but he grinned. "But on the off chance that happens, maybe."

AFTER EIGHT FRAMES, it was clear no one was going to be scouting us for a bowling league. He was up to throw, and I watched him size up the pins, letting myself drink in his bent form as the ball careened smoothly into the gutter. He clapped his hands together the same way he did after every frame, like a disappointed punctuation mark. "How are we both so bad at this?"

"Speak for yourself," I said, gently pushing his shoulder as we passed in the lane.

"Oh, your forty-three speaks for you *just* fine."

I glanced over my shoulder and narrowed my eyes. I really didn't enjoy others seeing me not succeed at something, but this felt so low-stakes, I couldn't bring myself to hold the scowl. Lear wasn't someone I worried over seeing me not at my best. "I wasn't sure it could be heard over your thirty-seven."

Lear was leaning against the score console, arms crossed, revealing his forearms under the rolled sleeves of the button-up. He looked so good when he leaned like that, the muscles along his torso stretched. He smiled at my gibe, lifting his shoulders in a shrug. I'd had more fun than I'd thought I would. When he smiled, I smiled back—it was automatic, and it was genuine. Even when I turned to the lane and lined up my shot, I was smiling. *My God. Lear makes me smile.*

I rolled my shoulders, uncomfortable with the realization, and stepped forward to launch my ball down the lane. I waited for it to veer into the gutter, but it stayed center.

"You're gonna get a strike," Lear called out from behind me.

"Yeah, right." Still the ball kept going down the center line. "No way."

"You're gonna get a strike!" Lear was on his feet and behind me.

The ball struck the middle pin, and the others toppled, all save one. "C'mon," I hissed, moving my hands to the right as if I could create enough wind to move it.

"C'mon," Lear said near my ear. "Fall over."

Through our sheer force of will, or maybe just physics, the pin toppled, and I threw my arms in the air, but before I could spin, Lear's arms were around me, lifting me, pulling me close, and he smelled like soap and beer. His voice was light and happy and so close. "I can't believe you did it!"

He set me down but didn't move his hands, and I took in his goofy grin, his eyes soft on mine. The feeling I'd had in the diner of wanting to kiss him came back to me.

"Never seen two grown-ass adults so excited about a strike before," an old guy a couple lanes over called out in a good-natured tone. His group of four had been well into a game when we arrived.

Lear and I pulled apart like we'd been caught. "She's never gotten one before," Lear called back.

I smacked his stomach with the back of my hand. "Like you have," I said, returning to the chair by the scoring computer.

"A smart man lets his woman win," the guy pontificated, shining a spot on his ball. "Especially when she's as pretty as her."

His buddy called over his shoulder, "A smart man finds a woman who lets him win!"

An older woman who was maybe his wife playfully smacked him on the back of the head. "Like you ever got the best of me."

I smiled at their banter, this group of strangers probably in their seventies.

The first man didn't look at his friends but spoke over his shoulder. "Don't be like that, Sherry. You know he ain't a smart man!" He nodded toward the two of us again. "Just some advice from those of us who have been around awhile."

Lear laughed and moved closer to me, standing right next to me so I could feel the puffs of his breath over my ear. "We'll keep it in mind."

I turned to catch Lear's gaze and smiled at his easy expression. "Don't act like you have the option to *let* me win."

He squeezed my hand before taking his turn. "Yeah, yeah." Lear sent the ball hurtling down the lane, managing to take out three pins. "Now all I need is a spare."

I sat back and relaxed, letting his hope linger for a moment and checking out the way his muscles rippled under his T-shirt. "Keep your fingers crossed."

"My dad used to say that all the time. Fingers crossed." Lear kept his eyes trained on the ball return, and I studied the lines of his jaw. "I know it's a common phrase—everyone says it." He dipped his long fingers into the holes and smiled to himself, turning back to the lanes, shaking his head. "Don't know what made me think of that."

He glanced at the pins, then back at me. Lear didn't talk about his parents, or he never had with me. All I knew was they'd died when he was a teenager. I'd been struck when he talked about never wanting to leave his family, how that was the worst thing he could imagine doing, how it physically pained him to have to walk away.

He launched the ball, and it took out most of the pins but left a few standing. He strode back toward me with a shrug. "Guess it didn't work."

"I don't know." I stood to take my turn but paused, letting him slide past me to sit. I settled my palm on his cheek, patting his stubbled face. "That's the best shot you've had all game."

He laughed, and I couldn't tell if he actually leaned into my touch or I imagined it. "You're probably right."

"So, keep the fingers crossed. Maybe your dad was onto something." We were standing too close, and it felt natural to hold his face in my hand. I patted his cheek twice and stepped away to get my ball. Lear was quiet at my back as I took my first throw. Gutter ball.

He was studying his beer when I glanced back, but he raised his eyes and gave me an encouraging smile. He looked like he wanted to say something, the way his eyes flicked over my face, but I turned away before he could.

"Enjoy the view," I called over my shoulder before taking my next shot.

The ball hugged the gutter but stayed in the wood, and one pin fell over.

"You two can't bowl for shit," the old guy nearby said with a hoarse laugh.

I flashed him a wide smile before strutting toward Lear. "We're good at other things."

Chapter 42

LEAR

RJ HELD HER hand to her stomach as we pulled away from the diner. "I can't believe we had waffles twice in one day." After bowling, we'd gone to a movie, some new superhero epic, and after our hands brushed a few times, lingering next to each other, she'd twined her fingers with mine, and I'd spent the rest of the movie lost in how good it felt when the pad of her thumb brushed my palm. Another round of waffles hadn't dulled the way her hand in mine made my heart beat faster.

I grinned at her contented smile. "That gallon of syrup was pretty filling, then?"

Watching RJ Brooks drown her waffles in syrup had left me laughing harder than I could remember.

She pushed my shoulder gently. I could only assume the gentleness was because I was driving and she didn't want to veer off the side of the road. "You're right," I said, glancing over. "Most people use half a container. I think that's the recommended serving size."

"Oh, thanks for the lecture, Mr. I-Need-Butter-In-Every-Waffle-Groove."

"Who wants uneven butter distribution?"

She tipped her head back as she laughed, and I had to drag my eyes back to the road. "Who has ever even uttered the phrase 'uneven butter distribution' before?"

"I don't know. I'm sure Ina Garten says it."

It was too dark to confirm, but I was sure she'd raised an eyebrow. "You watch *Barefoot Contessa*?"

"Ruthie, you haven't let me cook for you. If you had, you wouldn't have to ask. I am a Food Network superfan."

"You're kidding me."

"Hand to God." I'd always loved to cook, and for a while, I'd had a lot of time to kill. "I'm good."

"Lear, sometimes you surprise me," she said, glancing out the window, her face in profile, the moonlight highlighting her soft features. "I like that about you."

She's beautiful.

She relaxed against the seat, taking in the slow-moving scenery and seeming not to focus on anything at all. I'd never seen her like that before. RJ fully at ease. She was at ease with me, and she had been like this all day.

I had the sudden urge to link our fingers again and hold her hand and feel the stroke of her soft fingertips against mine, but it was different somehow in a dark theater. Coughing, I shot my eyes back to the road, lest we crash while I admired RJ's lips and fantasized about holding her damn hand. I shook my head, dismissing the thought. Instead, I rested my palm on her thigh. The thigh was both more and less intimate. It was more sexual than sweet, I hoped. "You liked it when I surprised you after that rehearsal a few weeks ago. My scalp is still healing from how hard you pulled my hair."

"Your surprises are sometimes quite nice," she admitted, voice soft.

I flicked my eyes toward her, and our gazes caught for an instant. That moment, though only a second or two, felt interminable, and I had to force my eyes back to the road as we neared city limits and traffic increased.

"I had fun today," she said.

"Me, too. Maybe we should just stay away from love and matrimony," I said, going for a joke, but it fell flat.

A distant smile crossed her lips. "Probably."

We fell into a silence, relying on the sounds of the road and the music from my car speakers as background noise. When I pulled into the parking lot at her apartment complex, I cut the engine.

"I won at bowling. I hope you're not still waiting for me to seduce you," she said as I reached for the door handle.

"Yes, you've mentioned that you won a time or seven. It's late. I'll walk you to the door." I didn't wait for her to protest. Instead, I hurried to her side of the car, and we walked together toward the building, slowing as we reached the sidewalk leading to the main door. "Thank you," I said, breaking the silence. "For today. I didn't know I needed that, and it really took my mind off . . . Anyway, thank you."

She looked up at me, those pretty coffee-colored eyes meeting mine. "It wasn't anything." When we both stopped walking, I rested my hand at her waist when she didn't step back.

"It was." Our gazes remained locked, the light breeze swirling around us. "You're . . ." *Everything. Amazing. The woman I want to be with. The person who makes me feel like I'm finally reaching the surface.*

RJ's hand slid up my body, resting over my heart. The light weight of her touch, the warmth through my shirt, had me leaning my chin to hers.

"Lear," she murmured, the sound intoxicating and filled with question marks. RJ never spoke with question marks in her tone. This was unfamiliar territory.

"Yeah?" I inched closer to her face, our breaths mingling. She smelled different from normal—not like the perfumed, made-up version of RJ that I knew from the weddings. Whatever product was in her hair smelled faintly floral, and my hand tightened at her waist. "What is it?"

RJ bit her lower lip and lowered her gaze, pausing before she said in a voice just above a whisper, "Do you want to come upstairs? Stay the night?"

"Stay here?"

"Maybe I was wrong about not being able to do more than sex. I think I'm a little better when I'm with you, and maybe you feel the same way. I don't let people in often, which I think you know, but I want you to stay with me." Her expression was open, those invisible walls she kept up so high were down, and a chord in my chest thrummed. "Tonight and . . . well, maybe we could do this, we could dance."

I'm falling in love with her.

In that instant, in the soft glow of the building lights with the breeze around us, I wanted to follow her up the stairs. I wanted to lay her down on her bed, to go slow and hold her all night. I wanted to open my eyes in the morning, sure she'd be there with the scent of her on me. I wanted to protect her and keep her safe and wake up to do it again as I learned all her secrets and she learned mine. Even as I stared into her eyes, though, a chill wound down my spine as I remembered that the last woman I'd wanted to protect and keep safe had been going to be my wife. After an entire day of almost forgetting, it came back to me in a rush. The smells of the hospital, the chill of the air conditioner, and the OB's voice telling her it was time to push.

Sarah cradling the baby, tracing her fingers over his shock of red hair in the delivery room.

Sarah looking at me and shaking her head, holding the baby so close because she loved him, and letting me know with every inch of her body language that he was hers and not mine.

The doctor and nurses worked, things beeped, and the baby's cries quieted, and everything went in slow motion for me.

It's all I could see, and those feelings of pain and betrayal rushed right back. I let my hand fall from RJ's waist, taking a small step back and a ragged breath, unable to find my equilibrium again because that's what falling in love led to. I wouldn't risk that again. "It's late. I should probably go," I said without meeting her eyes, though in my periphery I saw her straighten. "I don't think me staying is a good idea."

She took her own step back. "Okay." Her voice was unsteady, and she stretched out the *ay* sound.

I shoved my hands in my pockets to stop myself because, despite the cold-water effect at the memory of Sarah, I still wanted to touch her. "I want to, it's just that we're . . . you know . . ."

"Got it," she said, turning away and rooting through her purse for her key. "Of course. We're not stay-the-night people."

"Ruthie . . ." I reached for her arm, and she shrugged away.

"Don't call me that." Her tone was sharp, but she shrugged again. The wall was back up, only higher this time, and fortified. "Just RJ."

"I thought maybe . . ."

"No," she said, pulling open the door without looking at me. "RJ is better. It helps keep things clear."

Again, Sarah's stricken face saying "I'm sorry" filled my head, and it was like being slapped. Every instinct told me to turn on my heels and get the hell out of there because I couldn't put myself through losing someone again, but the flash of a wounded expression weighed on my shoulders. "It's not you, it's—"

"You're right. It's late, and it's been a long day. I shouldn't have asked." She plastered on a stiff smile, a fake smile. "Good night, Lear."

"Good night." The door closed softly before my words were all the way out. I'd expected a slam. A slam was definitive, like an angry exclamation point, and RJ's anger always faded. Without it, the door was just closed.

Chapter 43

RJ

I CHECKED MY phone one more time before silencing it and storing my things. My email and social media were blowing up again after a local news outlet connected the dots between my officiating duties and Dina Mayfield being represented by the firm. Still, Lear's texts from hours before sat unread along with his email. He'd approached me when I arrived, but I'd taken a phone call to avoid him. I had three texts waiting from him, only the most recent visible.

LEAR: Can we talk after the ceremony?

My body tensed reading it again, knowing he was nearby. After I'd invited him to stay and he'd turned me down, I'd never needed to get away from someone so fast. I was embarrassed and hurt, and angry with myself for thinking there was something there, for admitting I wanted him in my bed and in my space and in my life.

He didn't contact me afterward, and I didn't contact him, either. Making the call would mean giving up some power, and the lack of power I felt in the situation already left me unsteady. Even Gretchen had asked if I was okay. I'd pushed aside everything I'd always believed in and made the move that would leave me vulnerable, and when he said no, I hadn't been expecting it. I reminded myself that only someone without power could be left behind. I still felt left behind, though.

The night before, at the rehearsal, I'd given him a wide berth, only speaking to him when absolutely necessary because the sight of his stupid face reminded me how many butterflies I'd felt inviting him to spend the night, inviting him to be more in my life. Shame burned my cheeks, a feeling I was tired of, and I tapped a reply before tossing my phone in my bag.

> RJ: I don't think we have anything to talk about.

THE COUPLE HAD been indecisive the entire time, and the number of last-minute changes should have surprised no one. I'd kept my head down and my mouth shut unless it dealt with me, and they'd effectively rewritten half the ceremony the night before. Now, with everyone gathered, the music was supposed to begin, but the crowd was met with silence. At the back of the hall, I saw the bridal party looking at one another. The sound system controls were to the left of the door, so I couldn't see what was happening but saw Lear sprint over. Nervous chatter began, people eager to fill the silence, and I glanced around. Finally, the music began, though far too loud. "What a Wonderful World" played at a volume to rival any club, and several people covered their ears as the groom and his mother made their way down the aisle. The volume evened out with the start of the processional music, and I stood at the front of the room trying to keep my expression neutral.

The rest of the entrances went well until it was time for the bride and her father. As they neared the front of the room, the bride's father tripped on her train, sending him sprawling to the floor and her veil pulling back as it caught on his arm. The man climbed to his feet, and the bride approached me, her face soured as she tried to rearrange her headpiece.

"Well, that was a fucking disaster," she muttered.

Her groom's eyes widened, and he motioned to where I stood, fully miked. In the back of the room, I caught Lear wincing, and knew the sound system had picked up her words perfectly. I looked from him to the couple quickly and gave them what I hoped was a reassuring smile.

I began the ceremony, reading more than normal with all the last-minute changes from the night before. The couple relaxed, and I read the passage they'd selected to open the ceremony, something from a book they'd read together in college. It was offbeat but moving, and the crowd seemed to forget about the earlier issues. I shifted to the next thing the couple had added the night before, the reading of a poem by a family friend. I followed my script, noticing the bride's eyes widen and tears well as I read the friend's name and asked them to come forward.

In the back, Lear was waving his arms and shaking his head, and the room fell into another moment of hushed and awkward silence. "We took that out this morning," the groom hissed, leaning forward. I had the forethought to cover the mic this time, but my heart hammered. I was used to navigating the unexpected. I was even used to people crying in my presence—it happened often—but the combination of Lear trying to signal me from the back of the room, the bride's tears, the groom's concern for her, and the shift in the room because of what I'd said made me anxious.

For the second time that evening, heat burned my face at the embarrassment as I walked back and jumped to the next portion. I'd examined my notes, going over everything they'd changed the night before, and they'd added that poem. In the back, Lear threw up his arms, his mouth in a firm line, and I went from my normal reaction to his presence—wanting to kiss him—to wanting to punch him, to not wanting him to look so disappointed in me. I knew how to improvise, and the ceremony went on, but I clenched my toes until I was offstage and could let my anxiety show in other ways. I'd messed up, and I didn't know how exactly, but a thread of guilt wound through my veins. It wasn't a feeling I was used to.

Lear was in the alcove when I went to retrieve my things after the ceremony ended. His broad shoulders made him look imposing, and his jaw was set as I walked toward him. "Hey," I said quietly, my brain still pinging. I was pretty sure I'd messed up big-time, and I felt something crack when I approached him, something I didn't try to hold together. I waited for him to read my face or uncross his arms so I could hug him and apologize. I bit my lip because I didn't just want that, I needed that. I parted my lips to say it, to admit I was upset, but he spoke first.

His voice was pitched low. "What the hell was that?"

I stiffened at his tone and at the one-hundred-and-eighty-degree difference from how I'd wanted this to go. He was poised for a fight, and if I knew how to do one thing, it was that. I tucked away the thread still niggling my brain, and I closed off the idea that I wanted to find comfort in Lear. "You'll need to be more specific. I seem to recall a lot of things going wrong." I crossed my arms over my chest, staying as far back from him as I could in the small space, my mind running back to all the small spaces we'd crowded into since we'd first met.

His eyes narrowed, but the hushed tone of his voice sounded more powerful than any yell. "Maybe we start with you asking someone to walk to the stage who is currently in the ICU."

"What are you talking about?"

He took a step closer to me, the smell of his aftershave filling my nostrils and my brain with the sense of him, of his body heat so close. "I texted you and emailed you and tried to talk to you before the ceremony. Their friend was in a bad car accident this morning, and you brought it up in the middle of their damn wedding ceremony."

Blood drained from my face as the bride's twisted expression suddenly made a lot more sense. "I didn't know that," I said, uncrossing my arms and stepping closer, shoulders back and on the defensive. "I didn't read your texts or emails. I didn't want to hear your excuses or pity. Why didn't you bring it up in person this morning?"

His eyes were hard when they met mine. "Because you've made it very clear you don't want to talk to me, and I thought a grown professional would read their damn emails."

"Don't take that condescending tone with me."

"You don't get to police my tone. Do you even feel bad about this? You're so set on putting me in my place. Can you step outside your ice palace long enough to even accept an iota of culpability?"

"My ice palace?" We were almost toe-to-toe, the sounds of the crowd around the corner. "I didn't say I wasn't at fault. I should have checked the messages. I didn't want to deal with your apologies, so I didn't look."

"You think I was going to apologize for not playing your endless game of hot and cold on the worst day of the year for me? You make it so hard to—" He held up his palms, stepping back and leaving the sentence unfinished.

"I make it hard to what?"

Lear let out a slow breath and his expression was tight, features dark and severe in a way I'd never seen before. "Forget it, RJ."

"No, say it." I stepped closer and into his space, daring him to confirm what I already knew.

"I said what I needed to say about the ceremony." He took another step back. "The rest doesn't matter."

"That's never stopped you from saying something before." I crossed my arms over my chest, wishing they could cover all of me. I felt naked, as if the only way to stop his words from sinking in was to stay on the offensive, even though I heard the words coming out of my mouth and tasted how wrong they were.

When he stepped forward again, the movement took me off guard, his body centimeters from mine, our faces so close I could kiss him if I wanted to. I didn't want to. "Fine. You're so afraid someone else is going to leave you that you push everyone away." His features were sharp, more defined than usual, and his jaw was set as he stared at my face. "I didn't come up to your place because I couldn't trust you'd want me the next day. It's like you need me to be small so you wouldn't miss me if I left, and maybe you wouldn't, but I can't subject myself to those games."

"I was clear about what this was." I pressed my finger to his chest. In the small space, our voices were hushed but felt loud and permanent. "You caught feelings after I told you not to." *And gave them to me.* "The endless game of hot and cold? That was me reminding you what we agreed to and you pushing for more."

"You're going to stand here and tell me you didn't feel things?" Lear motioned between us. "That I imagined what it was like when we were together?"

"Believe me, I regret entertaining those feelings." My heart beat heavy and fast as if this were fight or flight, and I wanted to flee, but I couldn't back down. "Feelings lead to pain and betrayal. You might remember that better than anyone." I bit my tongue hard after I said it, seeing how the hit landed like a slap and his eyes widened. I regretted it immediately.

"I guess I should." He gave a small shake of his head. "Is this when you drag me into a back room to fuck while you tell me how little you care about me? Give me a few minutes. I can't turn off my heart as fast as you."

I held his gaze, commanding my face not to give away any sign of how much his words had cut me.

"I thought there was something special about you, but you make it impossible to—"

"Care for me?" *Love me. Like me. Take a chance on me.* Familiar heat and anger and embarrassment prickled over my skin. I held his cold stare, heat behind my eyes at his silent response. He didn't say anything. I'd asked him to love me, indirectly, in my own way, but I had asked, and now his mouth was set in a straight line. "Don't worry. I will never ask you to again. In fact, I'll ask you to forget you ever knew me."

I walked fast to get out of there before the tears broke through my armor. Between the wedding ceremony and the mounting shame and regret I felt over opening up my heart to Lear, I needed out. I needed to be away from the maybes this wedding stuff had made me consider. I was almost to the exit when I caught the eye of Dina Mayfield standing near a tall man, their hands brushing casually, fingers grazing in a flash, but in the intentional contact only ever found between lovers. I doubt anyone else would have noticed it, but it was one of those clear milliseconds, and the man was not Andrew Mayfield. It was the chairman of the board for the Avente Foundation.

And in that moment, with everything Lear and I had just said to each other, the possibility of something romantic to believe in had never felt like a bigger illusion.

Chapter 44

LEAR

MY PHONE BUZZED on the nightstand like an incessant fly in my ear. I finally rolled over to silence it. My mouth tasted like I'd slept with an old gym sock in it, and my head rejected the movement. The bottle of Jack I'd finished the night before clattered to the floor, and I groped for my phone without moving my head from under the shade of the blanket. I had a brief recollection of stumbling to the bathroom, which was probably the only reason my bladder wasn't joining the party of body parts cursing me. *I'm drinking too much.* I knew it was true, and I made a promise to myself to get my head back in order.

CAITLIN: If you don't pick up your phone
so I know you're alive, I'm asking
Gretchen to check on you.

LEAR: I'm alive. Go away.

CAITLIN: PICK UP YOUR DAMN PHONE.

It buzzed again in my hand, this time with a phone call, and I considered ignoring it and going back to sleep. Shutting my eyes didn't help, and my head still swam in an attempt to quell the churning in my stomach. I tapped the green icon. "I'm too hungover for this."

"Then you should have answered a single message from me in the last week." Her voice was louder than normal, and I winced. "I was worried about you, jackass."

"I'm a grown man." I rolled to my side, where a cool spot on the pillow was a welcome sensation against my skin.

"Debatable."

I had a high tolerance for my sister, even in the worst of times, but it was in short supply right now. It had been two weeks since I'd turned RJ down, and a week since she'd told me to forget I knew her and stormed out. I'd watched her go in shock, but also with righteous indignation firmly in place. Standing in the alcove, I'd reminded myself that she wasn't that different from Sarah, and that I didn't need the hassle. I'd tried to hang on to that feeling, but even after a bottle of Jack, the sinking sense that I missed her was still there. "What do you want, Cait? I'm alive. I'm fine."

"You're hungover on a Monday morning."

"I work weekends and today is my day off. Don't make it sound like I skipped work."

"Why are you hungover on a Monday? Penny said you haven't been around all week."

Penny and Kelly, along with baby Connor, were finally home and settling into their new life. Coming back to work didn't mean catching up on anything, since she'd been all over me about every event she'd missed.

"Penny has a big mouth," I grumbled.

Caitlin's voice softened. "I knew I should have come out there on his birthday. You're not okay."

I sat up, legs hanging off the side of the bed, and regretted it as my head spun, countering the relief of being upright. "I'm fine. It's just been a long week. It's not that."

"Well, what is it?"

RJ. It's RJ. "Nothing."

"I swear to God, Lear." She used the same tone our mom had growing up. It was uncanny, and I would have teased her about it normally. "I'm not letting this go. You're the only brother I have, and you had a hard year, but you're drinking a lot, and you need to let me in because you won't let anyone else in."

"I did, okay?" I fell back against the pillows.

"You did what?" Her voice returned to normal. "You let someone in? Who?"

I let my eyelids fall closed again and saw RJ's smile in the murky darkness: the smile she flashed me over waffles; the shy smile when she handed me that envelope, the one I hadn't opened yet; the smile she gave me after she came down from a powerful orgasm. I saw all her smiles. "It doesn't matter. It was something and now it's nothing."

"A woman?"

I rested my hand over my heart. "Yeah."

Caitlin was quiet for a few moments. "She broke up with you?"

"Do we need to talk about this?"

"No, we don't have to." In a very Caitlin way, she let her statement hang in the air until I spoke.

"We weren't really dating. It's complicated."

"Hm." She drank something on the other end of the phone, probably coffee. The slurping grated on me, and I glanced at the clock. It was only six in the morning her time, so I forgave the coffee. "But you were in love with her."

"What?" My eyes popped open at her assertion. "No. What makes you say that?"

"Probably just the hiding and moping and being hungover on a Monday thing. And you're a guy who falls in love."

"I don't love her. I don't even know if I like her. She makes it impossible to love her. We're completely wrong for each other, which I should have seen from the beginning."

Again, my sister was quiet. "What did you see in the end?"

The question threw me in unexpected ways. What had I seen? I'd been furious with RJ, on top of being annoyed with all the problems at that wedding. She'd avoided me all week and then gotten mad when I didn't spoon-feed her some information I'd sent her via email. I wanted to say that, but when I closed my eyes, all I could see was her expression, the hurt in her eyes. I couldn't shake from my head the way her eyes looked afterward, when it seemed she might cry after I told her she was heartless. I remembered the way she hid the hurt in the twitch of her eyebrow, the tiny movement of her mouth. When she asked me if it was too hard to care about her and I didn't respond. Truth was, I hadn't regretted something more than when we met and I told her to smile. I'd been a split second away from reaching for her, from pulling her into my arms and laying myself bare. "I didn't see anything."

I'd felt bad after refusing her offer. I'd thought about calling her and turning back a hundred times, but I'd second-guessed myself. I'd wondered when she'd go cold again, and then I'd gotten angry when she said she expected me to apologize. My body tensed as I lay back down on my bed, thinking about it all over again. "I didn't see anything," I repeated. "The best advice you ever gave me was to date nice people who don't bring drama to my doorstep."

"When did I say that?"

"When we moved in with Uncle Harold and Aunt Bette."

Caitlin sounded amused and incredulous. "When I was sixteen?

What the hell did I know when I was sixteen? That's not why you stayed with she-who-shall-not-be-named, is it?"

It was, at least in part. Sarah was a nice person who avoided conflict, and she shied away from drama. RJ wasn't the opposite of Sarah, but she was different, and the ways I would find myself concerned about being bored with Sarah never existed with RJ. I always felt excited, invigorated, and alive.

Caitlin read my silence as a yes. "Lear, no . . . that's horrible advice. Nice is good and all, but just nice is . . . flavorless. We need sparks in our lives."

I pictured RJ's cutting glare, the way she turned on a dime when I rejected her offer and how she looked like she wanted to slap me. "Sparks I have, but I need to pee, so unless you want to stay on the phone with me, I need to go."

"What would you do if I said I can stay on the phone?"

"Hang up. Never take me in the bathroom with you."

She laughed. "Okay. You know I'm here if you need me, right?"

"I know."

"And you'll think about talking to someone?" I agreed and we hung up. I set my phone aside and let my eyes fall closed again before climbing out of bed. RJ had been a mistake from beginning to end, and I needed to figure out a way to remind myself of that. I stepped out of the bathroom a few minutes later, determined to fall back onto the mattress and start this day over again. I scrolled through trending news on my phone, eager for the distraction, and stopped short on something a local paper had picked up. I stopped scrolling at the photo of RJ standing next to me. I didn't understand the connection to the headline, "Mayfield Uncoupling Complicated by Longtime Affair," but the photograph had captured the moment when she'd asked if I thought it was difficult to love her and I hadn't said a word.

I didn't need to see her face in the photo to remember how she'd looked, how I knew the silence would hurt her like she'd hurt me. It had been crystal clear to me in that moment that we were wrong for each other. We weren't the focus of the article, though. We were only in the background of a middle-aged couple smiling at each other, their fingers linked.

Chapter 45

RJ

I'D SPENT ALL day on Sunday in the office with my phone turned off. Work was predictable, familiar, and something I could manage. It was cold comfort after everything had fallen apart with Lear, but cold comfort in a place where I shined and where I knew the rules. After talking with the team, I'd explored the best potential loopholes, strategies, and angles to get Dina Mayfield what she wanted. I ignored my reaction to seeing her at the wedding, to seeing the intimate gesture between her and the board's chairman. I'd already known the Mayfields' attempt to reconnect hadn't worked. It didn't matter. Monday came early, and I was in the middle of reviewing the final settlement for a client when Eric poked his head in the door.

His normally easy smile was gone, replaced by a tense line.

"What's up?"

He took a seat across from me, studying my desk. "I just left a meeting. Gretchen pulled me in with Dina Mayfield and the team."

A chill slid up my spine. "I didn't know we had a meeting scheduled."

He scratched the back of his neck. "It was scheduled without you."

"What the hell?"

"I'm sure Gretchen will be down in a bit. Did you see the thing in the paper this morning?"

I shook my head as I clicked to open a browser window. I'd buried myself in work so I didn't have to see messages from Lear, or more likely, no messages.

"I guess you're still a draw for the press . . . someone attempting to get a shot of you at a wedding this weekend found Dina Mayfield instead."

I skimmed the results, the emotions from Saturday night feeling raw again at the memory. "I saw her there, but what does that have to do with the case?"

"Photo revealed her there with the head of the Avente Foundation's board." Eric leaned forward and glanced at my screen just as I clicked on the article. He didn't wait for me to finish reading. "The paper got the photo and uncovered a source saying they've been having an affair for almost three years."

I kept skimming and muttered, "Shit." The article went on to cite a source that said Ms. Mayfield had pretended to reconcile with her husband to gain leverage for their divorce, wanting to be the sole connection to the foundation. I looked up and met Eric's gaze. "It's bad, but I don't understand why you were in the meeting and I wasn't."

"She blames you for the photo. You doing the weddings and drawing press interest." Eric's expression softened. "Which isn't fair, but she insisted you not be involved in her case anymore."

That chill expanded from my spine to my entire body, and I returned my gaze to my screen, ashamed. I'd poured so much time into this case, invigorated by the complexities, interested in the couple, and felt proud Gretchen had picked me, and now the client blamed me. On some level, I knew that was bullshit, but on another level, I still knew I was off the case.

"I knew you'd want a heads-up," Eric said, tapping my desk. "I'm going to step in with Gretchen. Can you catch me up later this afternoon?"

Gretchen knocked on my door, her silhouette imposing outside the wall of frosted glass, and I nodded at Eric.

"Come in," I said, steadying my voice. Gretchen looked professional, composed, and pissed. It was in the set of her mouth, which was different from her normal assessing expression.

"I'll leave you to it," Eric said, giving us both a nod.

The definitive *click* of the door was the only sound in the room besides my pounding heartbeat, and Gretchen took the seat across from me, letting the silence hang.

"I assume Eric told you what happened," she said. "Please catch him up on your work this afternoon. We'll be pivoting our strategy now."

"Sure." I swallowed. "Gretchen, I'm sorry. I didn't know press would be anywhere near that wedding."

She held up a palm. "You didn't make Dina Mayfield have an affair, lie to her husband, or touch the man in public where a photographer could catch it. Like me, you advised her to tell us everything. She didn't."

I knew what was coming.

"But we don't represent people because they do the right thing."

I added, "We represent them because they're our clients."

Gretchen nodded. "And this wedding officiant thing has compromised your ability to represent her. I know you agreed to do this to keep some of our other clients happy, and that you're winding down, but this needs to end immediately. You've asked me to help guide you in your career. My guidance is to wrap up what you need to in the next week and get out of these weddings."

I nodded. "I will. I have a small one on Saturday—it's not for a client—but I'll cancel the rest."

"Good."

"I'm sorry, Gretchen."

"I know, and you need to fix it. You're off this case, but you're a talented attorney." She leveled me with a stare. It wasn't cold, but she was studying me. "Normally, I don't involve myself in the personal lives of our attorneys outside of it affecting the firm, and this does not affect your work, but that photo revealed more than just Dina Mayfield. Are you seeing Lear Campbell?"

I flushed, and heat spread across my face.

She shook her head. "Never mind. You don't need to answer that, and I shouldn't have asked. But, for what it's worth, I've known him for a very long time. I'd hate to see him hurt." She stood and rapped the corner of my desk. "You're tough like me, I think. Sometimes we hurt people we don't mean to."

The sound of her delicate knuckles against the polished wood added an emphatic punctuation to the sentence.

When the door closed again, I pressed my fingertips to my temples.

No Lear. No Mayfield case. And I had given the person I looked up to most at work reason to believe I would hurt her friend. Her friend I *had* hurt.

That thread of guilt I'd felt at the wedding grew thicker in my veins.

"SHE LIVES!" BRITTA'S smile filled my screen later that night, though her voice was hushed.

I winced and glanced at the clock on my wall. It was after ten, and I hadn't left the office all day. "Sorry, is it too late?"

"No, just give me a minute." The phone fell to her side, and I listened to the bedding rustle and then heard Wes's muffled, sleepy voice. "It's RJ. I'll be in the living room," she said softly.

"Hi, RJ." The end of my name trailed off, and I imagined Wes had already gone back to sleep. Minus three friend points for not thinking before calling at ten at night.

"Sorry," I said when she held the phone to her face again, their living room in the background, the floor-to-ceiling windows behind her. "I forgot he has to be up so early."

"He's already back to sleep. He's been getting up early to train with Cord. Lately he's passed out by nine." She pushed a curl off her face, eyes bright. "I don't think he even fully woke up. What's going on? Haven't talked to you in a few days."

"It's been a week." That was an understatement. "You remember I told you I was on a big case?"

"Sure," Britta said. "Something happen?"

"I'm off the case." No one enjoyed making their client mad, but it was chilling when Dina's anger turned to me specifically, hearing her accusation that the spectacle of the weddings on the side had taken my focus and attention from her case. When I talked with Eric, he told me more details. I had asked him to, but every new piece of information was an added papercut.

"I know you can't give details, but are you okay?"

The breath that escaped my lips was shakier than I wanted, and my chest felt tight.

"I'll rephrase," Britta said, searching my face on the screen. She, Kat, and Del always joked about how I lawyered them—made use of silence and a stony expression to get them to talk—but Britta never needed to do anything to get me to talk. "Tell me why you're not okay."

"It's stupid," I said, pulling in another breath I wished were steadier.

"Okay." Over her shoulder, a framed photo of Britta and Wes hung on the wall, taken after a race. They were both sweaty and smiling ear to ear, holding up matching medals. Theirs was the only love story I had total faith in.

I'd seen the photo a hundred times, telling her I appreciated cheering from the sidelines when she invited me to run with her. They were so happy together, and they just seemed to get each other. I'd thought I had that with Lear, that maybe there was a possibility he was worth taking a chance on. "It's a hit at work, but I think it will be okay eventually. I have to quit the weddings early, but I can live with that. I liked the weddings, but I love the law."

"So why do you look like you're about to cry?"

"I'm not about to cry," I said, my eyes prickling with budding tears.

"Okay."

"I don't cry." She was my best friend, so she knew that wasn't true, especially since two teardrops trailed down my face as I said it.

"I know." She gave me a half smile. "Tell me what's going on. Do you need me to fly to North Carolina to kick someone's butt?"

I laughed, wiping at my face. "Wouldn't you just send Wes?"

"Nah, I'm way tougher than he is. Is this about the guy?"

Lear's razor-sharp, perfectly aimed words from the wedding came back to me like ice water. "That's done." I gave her the highlights, ending with him calling me out as cold and heartless.

Britta listened, continuing to search my face while I spoke. "So," she started, tucking a curl back into the scarf around her head. "You fell for him."

"Rookie mistake . . . I knew better than that."

She rolled her eyes and ignored my cynicism. "And let me guess. Then he didn't call, and you didn't call, and you both ended up resentful?" *Maybe Britta is the one who should be in the courtroom.*

"I can't speak to how he feels." Though of course I could. His voice had dripped with resentfulness. "He said I enjoyed making him feel small, that cold is my default setting."

"Don't take this the wrong way . . ."

"No one says that before anything nice," I pointed out.

"They don't." She brushed a curl back that wasn't there, her nervous tell. "You're good at making people think that's true. You only let people see the emotions you choose to show them, so the people in your life don't always know how deeply you feel. In that way, you're a good liar. It's always worked for you as a defense mechanism before, I think."

"I don't do that." *I do that.* I thought about my breakup with Case, fallings-out with former colleagues or friends who had hurt me or crossed me. I thought about my old best friend. "I don't." I flashed over all the moments with Lear where I had shut down the possibility of anything more, telling him he only saw what I let him see.

I sucked in a breath, wiping my face again and willing my body to get it together. This was probably hormones and lack of sleep and stress, and not missing Lear Campbell. "For a while, it seemed like I could be the real me with him. The real me I am with you guys, and it would be . . . safe."

"Girl, I love you, but it took a long time for us to get the real you. I spent our entire freshman year trying to crack my roommate's shell, getting held at arm's length and coming back for more."

"I know. It's hard to love me," I acknowledged. "It's hard to like me."

"No. You're not hard to love at all, but you don't make it easy for people to figure that out. Maybe Lear hasn't quite figured it all out yet."

"I stayed with Case for so long because he didn't try to change me. He didn't mind that I was laser focused on work. He didn't mind that I didn't care if people thought I wasn't nice. He didn't mind all the things about me I really love. I mean, he didn't mind until he did, but when I was with Lear, it was different. It's like . . . it's like he doesn't just tolerate or ignore those things. It wasn't that he just didn't mind—I thought he genuinely liked those things about me, but he didn't."

"You said that was a hard day for him, right? The night you invited him up?"

I nodded, because mixed with my anger and shame was definitely guilt, knowing I'd made that day harder on him instead of easier. "Probably the worst day of his entire year, so maybe he's right and I'm insensitive." I shook my head and wiped my eyes again. "I'm just not cut out for the relationship stuff. It's probably good it ended when it did."

Britta was quiet for a moment and pressed her teeth against her lower lip.

"Spit it out."

"I say this with love," she said.

"No one says that before anything nice, either."

"They don't."

I set my tissue aside, having forced my tears back into submission.

"Maybe you need to bite the bullet and use your words. You're good at words, and your current tactic is to avoid communicating."

"We talked at that last wedding."

"Sounds like you didn't so much talk as snap at each other after not talking."

She was right, but the idea of opening up, of talking about my feelings and risking him shutting me down again, made my skin crawl. Being mad was easier. "What would I even say?"

"I don't know. 'I love you and I want more than just your body'? 'I'm sorry I made you think I didn't care'?"

I laughed. "I don't love him."

She didn't respond but met my eyes through the screen, one eyebrow slightly raised, the same way I'd looked at her when she and Wes were first getting together.

"I don't," I repeated, butterflies in my stomach flitting about aggressively. "And I don't like that you're trying to lawyer me."

"Is it working?"

I tapped my fingernails on the desk and then flattened them, looking at the polish, my signature color and the one he'd committed to memory. I glanced around my office at where the carnations had sat for weeks on my desk. "It might be working. So, what do I actually say?"

Chapter 46

LEAR

THE PUZZLE PIECES were spread across the table between us, and I mindlessly tried to sort the edge pieces by color, making piles, while my head was everywhere besides Uncle Harold's dining room. It was on RJ and Sarah and the envelope I hadn't opened and the feelings I'd kept bottled up that were threatening to explode.

"Somethin' on your mind, son?"

"What?" I looked up, pulled from my thoughts. "No, nothing. Why?"

He pointed a gnarled finger toward my pile of pieces. "You seem distracted."

I glanced down at the table where he pointed—I'd begun piecing together green edge pieces, part of the grass, and had wedged a bright orange and pink in with them. "Oh, yeah." I shifted the piece away and looked down, searching for a green one to take its place. "I guess I have a little on my mind."

"Penny's running you ragged at work?"

"Would she run me any other way?"

He chuckled, moving his own pieces around, his section of the puzzle coming together a lot faster than mine. "No, I don't suppose she would. We don't get too many shrinking violets in our family. My Bette taught the girls to speak up."

I flashed him a quick smile I was sure he didn't buy, but we fell back into silence, the room filled only with the sounds of sliding puzzle pieces on the lacquered wood of the table.

"Been about a year since everything happened in California, hasn't it?"

Hairs rose on the back of my neck. "Yeah," I said. "About a year." Cait and Penny kept pushing me to talk to a therapist. If Aunt Bette were there, she would have had me talking months earlier, but Harold just waited. It surprised me when he changed topics.

"I ever tell you how scared your dad was before Caitlin was born?" He didn't look up, just spoke while moving the pieces around. "Never seen a man so worked up. You know your grandpa, well, he wasn't that great a father. The times were different, but your dad . . ." He smiled, a wistful expression, his eyes crinkling at the edges with memory. "Well, he worried a lot, wanted to make sure he could do right by your mama and you kids. I think maybe you get that from him—wanting to make things easy for other people."

"I don't remember him being a worrier," I said, mirroring Harold, moving my pieces around like this was a conversation we always had.

"Course you don't. Sometimes we don't see things in people they don't want us to see, and he was good at keeping it hidden."

I nodded. "What made you think of that?"

Harold lifted the water glass to his lips and then met my eyes, his gaze unrelenting for a moment. I was fourteen again and waiting for the punishment to come, knowing I'd messed up. Looking away wasn't an option. "'Cause you got the protective and worryin' parts down but never had time to learn the hiding part from him—you're not good at it. So, you gonna tell me what's really bothering you, or are we gonna keep dancing?"

We held the gaze for another moment, and my stomach churned. "You sayin' I'm not a good dancer, Uncle Harold?"

His laugh bounced off the walls and shook his thin frame. "I'm sure you don't embarrass yourself, if I taught you anything."

"Haven't done much dancing lately." The chorus to "Can't Help Falling in Love" threatened to take up residence in my head. I took a swig from my beer, returning to the puzzle. The picture was of a lake, a boat floating in the middle and sunlight dappling the surface. "The kid's birthday was about a week ago," I finally said, not looking up. "It's . . . been on my mind."

"That makes sense." He moved a few pieces into place and reached across the table. I thought he was going to take a piece he wanted, but he rested his hand on mine instead. "I've been around a lot of years. There's no shame in missing someone, missing something you thought would last."

I swallowed. "I know."

"And there's nothing wrong with bein' sad. Maybe you should talk to one of those counselors. I did after your aunt died. It was kinda good to talk about things."

"I know I should."

"But." His eyes met mine again, thin white eyebrows lifting. "At a certain point, you got to start dancing again."

The silence hung heavy, and I didn't know how to respond or what to say, because he was right.

"I can teach you some moves," he said with a wink. "My dance card is pretty full over at the senior center. I'm one of the few fellas left, and I can still cut a rug."

I laughed, the tension breaking like it always did.

"How's that friend of yours who called when you were up here that time?"

"She's good."

"She's a girlfriend?"

I shook my head. "Not a girlfriend."

"One of those women from the phone program? Grinders or Tindlers or something? The swipers?"

I choked on my beer at the idea of my sweet uncle Harold reading about hookup apps. *God, I hope he was only reading.* "No, no swiping involved. We work together."

"Ah," he said, fitting the last piece in the middle of a section of blue sky.

"She's an officiant at some of the weddings I've worked. She's kind of infuriating. Drives me nuts."

He smiled, not looking away from the puzzle pieces. "Oh?"

"Just always has to be right, can't let things go." I imagined the way RJ had the most intimidating, icy stare I'd ever seen on anyone and how she sometimes stroked my neck in the softest way when I kissed her. "She's difficult." "Difficult" wasn't exactly right. She had these walls I never seemed to fully make it over.

"That so?"

"What's that look for?"

"Same as I always look." He chuckled to himself and fit together two sections of the puzzle. "So, she puts you through your paces, huh?"

"She makes me feel like I'm walking a plank."

Harold laughed, a loud one this time. "Sounds like quite the woman."

"Yeah." I sat back, resigned. "She is quite the woman."

"In my experience, if that kinda gal pays you attention, you try your damndest to keep it." He went back to his pieces but spoke again without looking up. "What'd you do?"

"You assume *I* did something?"

"Well, did ya?"

The way RJ had looked at me when she asked me to come up, the openness of her face, the way the softest part of her felt accessible to me, the way she'd hardened immediately. All of it was burned in my mind. "I wanted more, and she didn't, and then she did, but I . . . Well, it went south, and I said some not so nice things to her and she walked away."

"What did you say?"

The words flashed back to me. I didn't regret that I'd called out her hot-and-cold approach to us, her armor, but I also couldn't forget the way her face looked when I said it. I'd hit nerves I didn't know I was aiming for. "I probably deserved her walking away."

He nodded and gave a *hm*. "You're still twisted up over that other woman and the baby."

"It's not that. I mean, yes, I kind of am, but RJ and I . . . we're just not right for each other. You and Aunt Bette . . . I want something like you guys had. I've made enough mistakes . . . I don't need to be with someone who makes me feel so uncertain all the time."

He nodded, not looking up from the puzzle. "I ever tell you how I met your aunt?"

The second sudden subject change threw me. "You met at her dad's company, right? Courted the boss's daughter and all that?"

A faint smile crossed his lips. "Yeah, that's part of it. She worked in the front office and would be on me all the time about my paperwork and reports. I started turning them in late, just to get a rise out of her, and ooh, she'd get so mad." His expression took on a wistful, boyish look, eyes dancing. "One day she said, 'Harold, what will it take to get you to stop making my life so difficult?' and I told her she could go out on a date with me."

"And she agreed?"

He tugged on his suspenders. "No, sir. She told me where I could stick my hat."

I tried to picture my kind, charming aunt clapping back at anyone. "No way. Aunt Bette?"

"Oh, yes." He rubbed his jaw as if the response were fresh. "I deserved it, of course. I think these days you'd call it sexual harass-ment. You kids now know better than we did, but after that I kept turning in things late and making her mad. I'd ask her out, and she'd tell me where I could go."

"So how d'you get from that to getting married?"

"Well," he said, stretching in his chair, "one day, she said, 'You know, Harold, you're a good-looking man. I might consider going out with you if I wasn't so mad about your late work all the time.'" Harold smacked his knee. "Boy, let me tell you the model employee I was after that. No *i* left undotted, nothing turned in even a minute late."

"And she agreed to go out with you?"

"Two years later." He smiled again, glancing over my shoulder to where their wedding photo hung near the mantel. "She outsmarted me. In my experience, you marry the girl who outsmarts you, and you always have someone smart in your corner."

"Yeah, but Aunt Bette was nice and sweet. RJ is like trying to date a python. I'm not going to marry her."

"Course you're not. You let her walk away."

"I—"

He held up a hand, and I stopped short. "I'm not telling you what to do. You know what's in your heart. If she's treating you bad, if it's just not right, much better to get out. Maybe she doesn't want ya, or maybe she's scared of something. All I'm sayin' is if you can't get someone out of your head, maybe you gotta get your head outta your own backside and think about why it is you can't stop thinkin' about them in the first place." His words hung in the air until he pointed at the piece in front of me, and I handed it over.

I thought about those moments where I got to see her—when she rubbed aloe on my back or let me hold her close while she talked about work. I thought about her searching my ex's social media to give me peace of mind. I thought about what I knew about emotional baggage and the temptation of putting up walls. "So, your advice is to get my head out of my ass?"

"I think I said it a li'l better than that, but yes."

I glanced at my phone buzzing a few feet away.

PENNY: RJ quit. This Saturday is her last wedding with us.

Chapter 47

RJ

MY LAST CEREMONY was unlikely to garner much media attention. I was back at the Outer Banks, but this time it was for a small wedding on the beach. No celebrities, no oil magnates, just two besotted accountants who loved nineties R & B. They'd forgone a rehearsal, so everyone milled about in their formal wear, ready to begin, and I inhaled the ocean air. *My last wedding.*

I read the group text again as Penny finished talking to someone.

BRITTA: Did you chicken out?
KAT: Did you talk to him yet?
DEL: Did you know the phrase 'chicken
out' gained popularity in the forties, but
chicken has meant cowardly since the
14th or 15th century?
DEL: And RJ definitely chickened out.

                    RJ: The 14th or 15th century, huh?

Penny stepped toward me with her arms out.
"Motherhood looks good on you," I said when we broke the hug.

"You mean I look tired and frazzled and like a human the size of a Chihuahua controls my life?"

"Exactly." She looked happy, though, and I returned her smile. I'd even mostly forgiven her for hiring Lear and then making me work with him and fall in love with the jackass.

Rowan and Jordan stood with an older couple, one of their parents, presumably, and a small crowd gathered near the altar. I subtly looked around for Lear, unsure if I wanted my eyes to trip on his familiar height or the shape of his shoulders under a lightweight shirt.

I didn't see him, though, and returned my attention to Penny. "What's the plan?"

"Lear will get them lined up once the guests arrive, and then it's your show."

His name made my pulse speed, because I still didn't know what I was going to say. I simply nodded in response to Penny, and she gave me a few more notes, reminding me of the couple's pronouns, that there was a small tweak to the sound system from what we'd discussed, but I was only half concentrating, because over her shoulders, I saw him approach the couple with a smile. His hair was a little long, but he looked good. He looked happy and relaxed, and my stomach dipped at the realization that maybe he'd already let this thing between us go.

"Their parents decided on a reading, and I emailed you a copy. The friend who is singing 'Can't Help Falling in Love' decided to save it for the reception, and we did a sound check earlier," Penny continued, and I returned my full attention to her.

"I like that song." I remembered dancing with the kid Lear sent over, the little groper who I was fairly certain would never do that again. My neck heated, and over her shoulder I saw Lear's gaze trained on us. Our eyes met for a moment, but he looked away.

"Me, too," Penny said. "You ready?"

I nodded and shook away the prickling sensation at seeing Lear, at remembering so many moments with him. The couple were all smiles, and we started the processional, but I couldn't help but feel more than I wanted to, knowing Lear was nearby.

When the processional was almost done, the small number of attendants flanking the altar, Jordan made his way down with his parents, and two little kids took tentative steps down the sandy aisle, one holding the rings and the other tossing red rose petals on the sand. Both were kind of dancing, the petals making uneven piles on the ground, and the ring bearer started swinging the pillow from side to side. Everyone's smiles grew by thirty percent when cute kids made their way into a wedding, and this was no exception. Even I smiled and, on instinct, looked for Lear at the back of the crowd before remembering we weren't friends anymore, not friends or whatever we'd been before. He wasn't looking at me, though. His eyes had widened on the kids.

Sure enough, when I glanced back, it was in time with a collective gasp from the crowd. Both kids had frozen and the little pillow was on the ground, no rings in sight. Though I didn't see it happening, I envisioned a dancing kid and no one paying attention to where the rings flew. The processional song was still playing from the speakers, a nontraditional choice—"On Bended Knee" by Boyz II Men—when the first guest dropped to the sand to look for the rings. The small but very thorough crowd fell like dominoes, everyone digging in the sand in search of the symbols of love. I looked from person to person, and soon the small strip of beach was completely covered with searching hands. I'd been to a lot of ceremonies and worked with a lot of couples, enough to fear looking at Jordan to my left or Rowan about to walk down the aisle with their parents, but when I did, they were smiling, laughing, really.

Jordan leaned closer to whisper, "The real rings are in my best man's pocket . . . those were just for show."

"Do you want to say something?"

In front of us, someone's grandma was elbowing a middle-aged man out of the way. "They're already in the sand, and it makes for a memorable day, right?" His gaze trailed to Rowan, whose expression was similarly amused. "Plus, I told my mom Charlie was a little overenergetic for this and she insisted I was wrong, so I'll be happy to bank the 'I told you so.'"

At that moment, the only one out-searching Grandma was Jordan's mom.

Lear met my eyes over the writhing and searching crowd and gave me an incredulous smile, the kind he might have given me before, like nothing had happened. I flashed the same smile back, covering my mouth to hold in the laugh, like the couple was doing. Lear's eyes were bright and locked on mine. It wasn't the kind of moment I considered romantic. We were trying not to laugh about subterfuge that ended with a woman in her sixties digging like she was building a sandcastle. People were panicked. Lear pressed his lips together, his full, kissable lips, and I did the same. Like the couple, we weren't panicked. With striking clarity, I realized Lear was my match. He was infuriating and obnoxious, and every time I was near him, I felt more *me* than I ever knew possible. We were laughing at this, almost uncontrollably, and he was my person. I was sure I'd never feel truly panicked if he was nearby.

His head tilted to the side, a small gesture, but I mirrored it. *I think he feels it, too.*

"I found them! I found them!" Jordan's mom held the rings over her head. Her hair was mussed and her dress askew on one side of her chest, but she beamed, and everyone cheered.

Lear's lips turned up in a half smile, and that same odd feeling from before, that we'd had an entire conversation without saying a word, struck me. Jordan's mom handed him the rings, and everyone slid back into their seats, but Lear kept his eyes on me, his half smile in place, and my chest continued fluttering. I thought about doing something completely out of character—running up the sandy aisle to kiss him, yelling "I love you!" across the open space—but I subtly held my finger to my cheek and mouthed, "Smile more."

He did, a wide grin that softened his features and had me reconsidering the run up the aisle to kiss him. Instead, he winked before turning to Rowan to send them down the aisle toward their future and two sandy fake gold rings.

Chapter 48

LEAR

I WIPED MY palms over my thighs and watched the ceremony from behind the last row of seats. Penny didn't really need me, since it was a small wedding, but I checked in with her anyway. It was nice having her and Kelly back in town. I'd been so wrapped up with my stuff and with everything with RJ, I'd forgotten how good it felt to spend time with them.

Penny nodded along with the ceremony, subtly checking her watch. She didn't need to. RJ was on time. I had worried my cousin would be weird around me, knowing what happened with the baby in California, but I underestimated her. She'd thrust baby Connor into my arms and told me she and Kelly were going out. He was a cool little guy, and we were already tight. I never opened the envelope from RJ. After a while of looking at it on my counter, of questioning all my decisions, I realized it didn't matter. The child had Sarah and his father, he had people who loved him, and I'd left, but I hadn't abandoned him. After hanging out with Connor for the first time, I tossed the envelope with the kid's name in the trash. I had people here, and I could leave him and Sarah in California. I'd also finally taken everyone's advice and called a therapist.

"The couple asked me to say a few words of my own," RJ said, her voice catching in the breeze and the ocean crashing behind her. She wore a simple black dress like she always did. I was sure I'd gotten her out of that one before—the zipper ran down the side, and I'd been fumbling for it on her back until she batted my hands away. She grinned at the couple before continuing, and I felt my own smile stretch for no other reason than that she was here, and it felt good to be near her. Even to myself, I sounded like something clichéd from a wedding ceremony, but I couldn't bring myself to care.

"That was a bold move. Jordan and Rowan are so in love, they forgot you should never give a lawyer a microphone and free rein." The crowd chuckled, and they got her professional, kind smile, but her eyes flicked up and met mine. "Love isn't always easy. It's not always what you necessarily expected." Her gaze lingered on mine before she looked at the couple. "Sometimes it knocks you down and makes you mad, but sometimes it helps you up, too. And sometimes, if you're lucky, it gives you a new home in another person's heart. I think it's safe to say here that home is what we're seeing between these two."

Jordan and Rowan exchanged a look and laughed, some inside joke tickling them both, but I thought about RJ on the ground in that parking lot, her butter rum Life Savers and the bottle of syrup on the grass, the scowl on her face and how I'd been so dedicated to her thinking I was an asshole, so allergic to being the nice guy again.

"Rowan told me the first time they talked to Jordan was while waiting for police to arrive after Jordan ran a red light and they were in an accident. Rowan said their first instinct was to sue the irresponsible driver, but something changed between the crash and the arrival of the police. Something sparked, and luckily it had nothing to do with the vehicles. So, we're gathered today to celebrate sparks, and the years of sparks to come."

I was nodding when RJ looked up and caught my eye. I didn't realize it until her eyebrow quirked up this tiny, barely recognizable amount.

Penny's hushed voice pulled me away. "Why do you have that look on your face?"

RJ continued speaking as the sun lowered, the sky shifting to darker shades of orange and purple clouds. "Though, Rowan, speaking as an attorney, are you sure you don't want to take legal action against him?"

Everyone laughed, and Rowan shook their head emphatically, kissing Jordan's fingers clasped in their own before the couple began their vows.

I leaned into Penny and whispered, "I think I'm in love with RJ."

"I thought you two couldn't stand each other."

"We can't . . . most days." I flicked my gaze back to the altar. Her curls were pulled to the top of her head and blew in the breeze. I hadn't figured out what I was going to say or how any of this was going to work, but I didn't want to leave this wedding without a plan to see her again, to keep her in my life.

Penny gave me a sardonic smile, but it fell when she met my eyes. "Wait, are you serious?"

"For the first time as a married couple, Rowan and Jordan Marshall-Caine!" The couple kissed and raised their clasped hands, and everyone was on their feet, cheering and clapping.

"Serious," I said, dragging my eyes from the couple to meet Penny's. "She makes it hard to get to know her, but I think whatever it takes for her to let me in, it might be worth it."

"Well," she said, blowing out a slow breath, "I owe Tina twenty bucks. She called that the very first wedding she saw you two together."

Penny checked her clipboard before giving me another smile,

this one softer. "If this is your last chance, you better figure out what you're going to say."

I watched RJ step back, giving the couple room to embrace friends and family, and her eyes found mine again, but I didn't look away this time. "I know."

Chapter 49

RJ

I TUCKED THE signed marriage license in my bag and shook hands with the couple again, wishing them well. Penny handed me the pen we'd used and shook her head. "Are you sure you want to leave all this?" She motioned around to the reception, already bouncing with music and drinks after just forty-five minutes. The terrace was beautiful, and the waves crashing against the shore provided the perfect backdrop for the party.

"Yep. I'll miss some of it, though."

"You mean some people?"

"The text I've received from you more often than anything else was 'You're killing me.'"

"I meant Lear."

I glanced around, looking for him by the bar or near the DJ, but he was nowhere in sight.

"You're not going to say anything?" She lightly punched my arm and laughed, but I inspected my nails.

I didn't know what to say to her. Hell, I didn't know what to say to Lear, but the way he'd looked at me during the ceremony . . . it was something. "I don't know what you're talking about."

Penny stepped forward and held out her hand. I loved that she didn't dive into a hug. "I expected nothing less. I will miss you, RJ."

"Hey." Lear's fingers grazed my bare shoulder, and Penny winked before stepping away.

I rolled my shoulders back before facing him. "Hey."

He smelled good, like sandalwood and sunscreen, and I wondered if we could fast-forward through this, go find a supply closet, and let things play out.

"Can we talk?"

"We could pretend we talked and then not talk," I said, my fingers itching to reach for him, to stroke his forearm and find a hidden spot somewhere so we could skip this part, the talking part, because a lingering fear rippled through me that I'd mess this part up and he'd say no again.

His eyes dipped to my lips, and I was pretty sure he was thinking the same thing, but they flicked back up. "I think this time we need to actually talk."

I nodded toward the beach, and he motioned for me to lead, his fingertips brushing my lower back. "We're better at not talking."

His chuckle next to me as we moved away from the music soothed some of the anxiety within me, and we took the short staircase down to the beach. "I know. We're great at not talking."

Memories of kisses and touches, of him covering my mouth to stay quiet, and the way his hands felt traversing the lines of my body—"great" was really an understatement. I'd swapped out my normal heels for flat sandals, and I missed the advantage of the added inches. When I was standing up straight, my eyes were only level with his chin. It was a nice chin, but I looked out to the ocean instead, waiting for him to talk.

"I'm sorry I said those things," he began, and I noticed him shoving his hands in his pockets. "I . . . I don't have a good excuse. I was scared."

I held up a hand. "I think this is actually where I need to apologize. Not you. I actually don't think I deserve a second chance. I was hot and cold with you because . . . well, hot was too scary. Hot was too big, and cold was familiar. It's what I've gotten used to."

The sky held on to the last vestiges of orange as sunset faded into night, and the stars twinkled over the horizon. "I'm sorry I ignored you. That's always worked for me." I ignored men, and they went away before I had to care about them. "Maybe it didn't work. Maybe it was just easier."

"Maybe we both have some stuff to work on." The wind picked up, and Lear slipped out of his jacket, handing it to me.

"Probably." My instinct was to decline, accept being a little cold instead of taking the help, but instead I thanked him and slipped my arms into the sleeves. We paused, nearing the edge of the wet sand, where the surf rolled in, a cool breeze blowing off the water.

"When you invited me up, I wanted to say yes, I just . . ."

I shook my head and placed my palm on his chest to stop him. "I shouldn't have done that. You had a lot on your mind. I got caught up with what I was feeling."

A tiny grin crossed his face. "Is that your way of saying defeating me in soccer and bowling turned you on so much you couldn't think straight?"

I took in the warmth of his hard chest under my hand, the way my hand looked over his heart. "No, I'm used to winning. It was the waffles."

The wind whipped around us, along with the sounds of the surf crashing against the shore and the hum and low bump of the speakers in the distance. Lear's jacket surrounded me, and his smell—spicy and clean—filled my nostrils. "I've missed you, RJ."

I examined the long shadows on his face and the way his lips quirked when I bit my lip. It was the Lear I'd had in front of me for months. The Lear I hadn't always seen. "Call me Ruthie."

He didn't respond, his expression unchanging.

"Lear," I said, touching his forearm.

He dropped his gaze to my fingers and followed their path as I slowly dragged them over his arm, the tiny hairs tickling my skin until I reached the back of his hand.

"You can call me Ruthie."

Our fingers intertwined, and he drew me closer to him. "You told me not to. Almost no one calls you Ruthie."

"I know. I know I said that, but . . ." I looked out over the ocean, searching for the right words. There were none, though, just the moon reflecting in a million glittering spots. When I looked back, his soft brown eyes were still intent on me.

"But?"

"But . . . almost no one calls me that because Ruthie is sweet and nice and gentle, and I rarely want people to see that. You're special, though, Lear. I know a lot of people have led you to believe you're not, including me, and I'm sorry, but you are." I rested my hand on his chest, tipping up my chin to take in his inscrutable expression as I stepped closer. "You can call me Ruthie, and maybe that will remind you that you get parts of me most people don't get. That you're special, even when I forget to tell you, and, despite my best efforts, I think you see a lot more than what I plan on you seeing. Or maybe I've just gotten comfortable with you seeing all of me."

I kept talking, afraid that if I quit, I wouldn't keep saying all the hard things. "I should have some grand gesture in mind here, something that shows you I know I was wrong and that I'm sorry, that I want you in my life. I wish I did, because I *do* want you in my life . . . standing here now, well . . . I don't know how to prove to you I won't push you away again, because I might try, but I have this." I pulled the printed confirmation from my pocket and handed it to him, studying his expression until his eyes met mine again.

"You prepaid for bowling lessons?"

"For both of us. I never let people see me doing things at which I might fail. But I want to bowl with you, and I want a relationship with you, because even though you'll see me fail left and right at both things, I want to be the person who lets you in. All the way." I spoke faster and faster, pulling the words from a raw place in my chest, and I gripped his shirt. "I fell in love with the way you double-check details, and your maddening attention to butter, and that you sing along with musicals, and I fell in love with how you look at me like I can do no wrong even when I'm messing up all the time, and I fell in love with how I feel when I'm with you. So . . ." I finally stopped for a breath after speaking like I needed to get all the words out at once. I'd spent most of the time I'd known him comparing Lear to other men, but I wasn't the same person with him that I was with other men. I was more me with Lear Campbell than anyone I'd ever been with. "Please come watch me be a horrible bowler, because I trust you to give me crap when I'm awful, and I know you'll still love me when I make fun of you for the same."

He still didn't say anything, and the sound of the waves crashing was the only sound between us. "I'm in love with you, Lear."

Slowly, so slowly, his palm slipped from mine, and I worried I'd made a mistake. Maybe he wasn't ready for all that. Then he shifted his palm to my hip, fingers gripping me. His expression opened, almost in surprise, but he still hadn't said anything. From the reception on the beach, the music floated down to us. The heavy bass faded out, and the opening lines of "Can't Help Falling in Love" filled the air.

Lear lifted our linked fingers and deliberately kissed each of my knuckles before guiding my hand to his neck and pulling me to him.

"You know I hate silence," I murmured, loving the feel of his body pressed to mine, the warmth intoxicating as the breeze swirled around us.

"I know." A smile tipped his lips up. "That's why I'm making you wait."

"I hate waiting."

"I know." His hand flexed at my waist.

"Are you done?"

"Yeah," he said, as the chorus of the song began. He dipped his face close to mine.

"And?"

He smiled, a real smile that was just a bit of his normally cocky attitude. "Will you stop talking so I can kiss you?"

His lips brushed mine, his tongue gliding along my lower lip and his hand cupping my neck. Our bodies aligned, and I sank into the kiss with the waves crashing behind us. The pressure and sweetness of his lips, of his tongue seeking entry, left me breathless. "I don't want to call you Ruthie, though."

"Why not?"

He lowered his face to mine again, our noses grazing. "I didn't fall in love with Ruthie. I fell in love with RJ." He dotted kisses on my cheek, my jaw, the corner of my lip. "Sweet, nice, gentle, badass, won't-admit-when-she's-wrong, drives-me-up-a-wall, doesn't-want-anyone-to-know-she's-kind RJ." He looked into my eyes, our foreheads touching.

I stroked the skin at the nape of his neck, and my own heartbeat filled my head at his words. "Even though I love you, too, I probably still won't always admit when I'm wrong most of the time."

His face cracked into a smile again, and he kissed me, nipping at my lip. *I love that smile. I love him.* The playful kiss heated, and he trailed his mouth over my jaw and to that spot just below my ear, dragging his tongue along the sensitive skin before nipping at my earlobe. "We'll work on it together."

"So, we're doing this. A real relationship?" I let out a stuttered breath as his lips trailed down my neck. It felt good—it always did when he found that spot below my ear—but it felt right, more right, like those kisses were a punctuation mark on something.

"A real relationship," he said against my skin, pulling my body to his. "If you push me away or if I get scared, we'll make time for each other and talk about it." Of the two of us, he was always more conciliatory, and him drawing this clear expectation squeezed my chest. "I didn't talk about things enough with my ex. I didn't think I could, but you're worth the risk, RJ."

"We'll be honest and talk about things." I caught his lips against mine, relishing the sweetness of the kiss. I'd never come close to this conversation with Case or any other ex. "I like talking to you."

"I like talking to you," he said, dropping another kiss to my lips, this one deeper, his tongue sweeping against mine. "And I like not talking to you."

I grinned against his kiss. "We're good at not talking."

Lear's hair blew in the breeze when he pulled back from my neck. "You want to keep the benefits, then?"

My skin tingled under his touch, and I wanted nothing more than to wake up with him tomorrow, sated and warm. "I do."

Epilogue

RJ NUDGED MY hip with hers at the sink in her bathroom, where we stood brushing our teeth side by side. I nudged her back and we jockeyed for position. "I would kill for two sinks," she said, pulling a tube of moisturizer from the cabinet. I'd grown up with a sister and lived with my ex, but the sheer number and variety of products and creams she owned still baffled me.

"You won't miss brushing our teeth together in a new place?" I set my toothbrush next to hers in the mug by the sink, the one I'd gotten her for Valentine's Day that read *You Bowl Me Over* and pictured pins swooning next to a bowling ball. RJ shot me a rueful look, and I laughed, kissing her shoulder. "We'll make sure the Realtor knows we want dual sinks."

She turned and gave me a peck on the lips, the worn cotton of the law school T-shirt she slept in grazing my bare chest. "You'll add it to the spreadsheet?"

"How did you know I made a spreadsheet for house hunting?" We walked into the bedroom together, removing the pile of throw pillows from the bed and stacking them elsewhere.

"You're not that complicated," she said, pulling out her scarf to wrap her hair. I loved watching her do it, the way her hands worked quickly to tuck and smooth fabric. "Musicals, spreadsheets, and sex, and you're a happy man."

The sheets were cool, and I settled into the comfortable bed, where I would fall asleep in a minute after the long week of events. Penny's business had expanded, and I'd decided to stay on permanently. Sometimes I still missed working for a team, but weddings and the few non-wedding events we did were always a challenge, and I was happy. And every now and again RJ would surprise me at the end of a rehearsal. I really liked those surprises. "Are you calling me basic?"

RJ climbed into bed next to me after turning off the overhead light. We both loved space when we slept, but before that, when she spooned against me, her back to my chest, I was never more comfortable. RJ wiggled against me and linked our fingers. "Totally basic."

"I missed you," I said, tightening my hold around her waist. She'd been traveling with Gretchen, working on some high-profile case. Caitlin told me she'd asked Gretchen to make sure I didn't get my heart broken once RJ and I shared we were a couple. Gretchen responded that RJ was too smart to let me go . . . unless I deserved it.

"I missed you, too," she said, stroking her thumb along mine. "We need a vacation from work."

"My uncle's place tomorrow for Thanksgiving," I said. RJ and my uncle were two peas in a pod, and I joked with my sister that I almost believed he liked my girlfriend more than he liked me. She told me there was nothing to worry about and that Uncle Harold definitely liked RJ better. We'd be staying the night at his place to have Aunt Bette's waffles the next morning. I grinned at the prospect, excited for all the people I loved to sit around that table together.

RJ gave a hum of affirmation. "That will be fun. Harold and I haven't had the chance to beat you and Caitlin or Penny and Kelly at gin rummy in a while."

"So cocky. Holidays don't have to be competitive," I said, knowing I'd not let her hear the end of it if Caitlin and I won. "But to vacations, we'll be going to Chicago next weekend." I traced the edge of her middle finger, feeling the smooth tip of her nail. Her best friend was getting married finally after they'd had to delay the wedding during the worst of the pandemic, and it would be my first time meeting everyone without a video connection between us. "Think it will be weird doing a wedding again? Your pretending-to-believe-in-love skills are a little rusty."

"None of my skills are rusty." She reached behind her and tried to poke my side where I was ticklish. "Anyway. I've had a change of heart about believing in love."

"Ruthie," I said, squeezing her to me. "That might be the nicest thing you've ever said to me."

"Shut up," she said, and I heard the smile in the way she said it. In truth, once RJ decided to let me in all the way, I never had to wonder how she felt about me.

I squeezed her again. "I'm kind of nervous to finally meet all your friends in person."

RJ's body was warm and pliant under my arm. "They're already so shocked I'm bringing a boyfriend, they'll probably be more interested in you than in me."

I smiled to myself when she said "boyfriend," because I'd already picked out a ring with Britta's help, and I hoped to change my title soon to "fiancé." "So, there's Britta and Wes, and then Kat and Del." I kissed her shoulder, pushing aside the neckline of the worn shirt. "Who else is in the wedding party?"

"Wes's friends Cord and Pearl, I think, though Pearl moved for a new job, and I'm not sure if she'll be able to make it back."

"Didn't you say she and Cord had a thing?" I didn't actually need to ask—I'd overheard RJ and Britta trying to figure it out over the phone. I'd heard so much about all her friends, I felt like I knew them. It was a nice feeling.

RJ linked our fingers, sliding hers along mine, back and forth. "I thought so, but Britta said he started dating someone after Pearl moved, so maybe not." She let out a soft sigh when I kissed the crook of her neck. "Without them to gossip over, you might be the topic of conversation."

"Think I'll pass inspection?"

RJ rolled to her side, facing me. "I'm the hardest to impress, and I already like you a lot, so I think you'll be fine."

"You are hard to impress," I murmured, letting my palm slide under her soft cotton T-shirt, feeling the warm, sensitive skin of her stomach beneath. "I keep trying, though. I stocked the pantry with syrup while you were gone, since you'd run out."

She grinned, sliding her fingertips down my biceps. "You did?"

Her neck smelled like her cocoa butter lotion when I kissed below her jaw, my palm skirting higher to cup her breast like we hadn't made love in the living room as soon as she'd returned from her trip a few hours before. "Mm-hm."

"How many bottles did you buy?" Her voice was breathy, and she linked her leg with mine, her skin silky against my calf.

"Twelve." I rolled her to her back, kissing along her collarbone and nudging her shirt over her head. "I figured that would last you at least a couple months."

"Color me impressed," she said, sliding fingers through my hair, her nails grazing my scalp as I kissed down her body. "You're too good to me."

"I kind of am," I said with a grin, hooking my thumbs into the waistband of her sleep shorts. "But you're pretty good to me, too."

RJ stroked the side of my face, her expression soft when her gaze met mine. "I plan to be."

I nudged her knees apart and ducked my head lower, anticipating her first groan. "Me first, though."

Acknowledgments

DEARLY BELOVED, WE are gathered here at the end of the book to celebrate everyone who made this novel possible.

Love is patient. Love is kind. But writers under deadline are often neither. I am so thankful for my family for keeping me motivated, cared for, and sometimes in check! Travis and Tiny Human—you are my rocks. Thank you, Mom and Dad; Jay and Amanda; Bruce and Jean; Mike and Melissa; Barb; Tim; Allison; Kaitlin; Crystal; Aretha; and all my aunts, uncles, and cousins who are basically a mini PR firm working from coast to coast.

With this ring . . . Okay, there aren't any real rings. I wanted to include two bands in the back of every book, but it was cost prohibitive, so use your imagination. With this ring 💍, I take this opportunity to thank the people who helped bring this book to life.

For better or for worse. I'm so blessed to have an editor who makes my work shine, but also crafts my "worse" into something I'm so proud of. Kerry Donovan, you are a delight and a blessing, and I implicitly trust you to make my stories better. Thank you also to the Berkley and Penguin Random House team who brought this book into the world. Thank you, Bridget O'Toole, Dache' Rogers, Mary Baker, Karen Dziekonski, and Lindsey Tulloch. The beautiful cover was designed by Farjana Yasmin.

For richer or for poorer, but let's shoot for the first one if we can, yeah? To my indelible agent, Sharon Pelletier: I feel continually blessed to have such an ardent advocate in my corner and I always appreciate your humor, kindness, and candor. Thank you also to Lauren Abramo, Andrew Dugan, and Sara DeNobrega at Dystel, Goderich & Bourret and Kristina Moore at UTA.

In sickness and in health is fitting since I wrote this book in 2020 and 2021, but I am eternally grateful for the friends who kept me feeling supported, heard, motivated, and laughing. Thank you to my sister, Bethany; Allison Ashley; Katie Golding; Charish Reid; Taj McCoy; Cass Newbould; Alicia Sparrow; Priscilla Oliveras; Jen DeLuca; Libby Hubscher; Regina Black; Rachel Mans McKenny; the 2020 BIPOC Debut family; Kenyatta; Jasmine; Jalen; Aiden; Jacki and the MSA team; Emily; Tera; Haley; Matt; Jen; Brian; The Cardinal Women*; Romance Fight Club members J, Allie, Beth, and Tova; and everyone else who has cheered me on and listened to me drone on about bookish things.

To honor and obey. Even though neither of you obey even basic commands anymore, thank you to Penny and Greta for unconditional puppy love and sleeping on my feet when you weren't being menaces while this book came to life.

To love and to cherish. Finally, thank you to readers who have welcomed my characters into your heads and hearts. It means everything, truly.

Do I know how lucky I am to be surrounded by the phenomenal people above and that my books wouldn't happen without them?

I do.

Continue reading for a preview of
Denise Williams's next new romance!

Chapter 1

PEARL

AS I FLIPPED over my phone, the thin gold bracelet on my wrist caught the light, the chain cutting through the four small stars tattooed on my wrist.

> SHEA: Send a selfie. Show me the dress.

> PEARL: I'm not taking a selfie.

> SHEA: You're too serious. I know you look bangable.

> PEARL: Bangable isn't my objective. I'm working.

> SHEA: Your objective lacks creativity. This is why I'm the fun sister.

My sister was a pain, but a pain with good taste who had found an amazing dress for me. The champagne-colored satin was cool under my palm, and I brushed my fingers against it before slipping my phone into my clutch. The wash of the cool breeze from the air-conditioning swept over the exposed skin at my back, and I straightened at the prickling sensation. The room swirled with people, and before I stepped back into the hall, I surveyed the countless donors and supporters in formal wear.

On the far side of the room, Katrina Dawson laughed with a trio of people in their seventies. The two of us had started a few weeks earlier in our new roles with the company. It was strange being home, both strange and good. After five years in California, the right job had brought me back to Chicago, but I didn't have a good sense of anyone on my team yet, so every day felt like treading water with shields up, especially with Katrina.

I stepped inside and recited my game plan for the evening, particularly who I was supposed to connect with based on our pre-gala preparations. OurCode, like other programs designed to encourage girls and nonbinary kids to take an interest in coding and careers in tech, had support across the industry and a solid reputation. The assembled crowd had paid a thousand dollars a head to attend and would donate more to support the program's growth. Despite some recent setbacks to our inclusion-related programming, we were ready to hit the ground running. Katrina and I had curated a list of potential new relationships we could cultivate, and I made a mental note of names on the list who had arrived. The gala was going to be the launching pad for our new plans, and we'd been working late every night with Kendra. It was odd she hadn't arrived yet.

"Pearl, a minute?" The chairman of the OurCode board touched my elbow. Kevin wore a tux, his entire look put together, but his expression was harried, a deep crease between his brows.

"Sure."

He waved Katrina over as well and we walked toward a corner of the ballroom.

Katrina's dress caught the light, the red fabric dipping low between her breasts and flowing to the floor, giving her a glow. "Hey, Kevin. What's up? I was just talking to the Kellers about increasing their annual donation while you and Pearl chatted."

Maybe it didn't exactly bother me—I wanted us both to do well—but I couldn't deny that I wanted to be the one doing slightly better.

Kevin cut through any pleasantries. "Kendra isn't coming."

To my right, Katrina stilled, her shock seeming to register along with mine. "What?" and "Why?" came from us at the same time.

"I can't get into the details for legal reasons, but she has resigned from OurCode, effective immediately." Kevin's tone was hushed, and both of us leaned forward to hear him better.

"She quit?" Katrina's voice was a hiss, and she shook her head as if trying to slot the new information into existing grooves in her brain.

"She is no longer affiliated with the program." The impatience that bled into his tone made it clear he wasn't planning to give any further information.

I intentionally took a breath before speaking, the combined weight of the bodies behind us suddenly pushing against my back and making me feel claustrophobic. "There are hundreds of people here expecting to learn about the future of the program. Everything is arranged around Kendra making those announcements. What are we going to do?" I pictured the detailed plans we'd spent weeks on, the speech we'd crafted, the hours spent toiling over the right wording and how to frame the strategic goals.

"One of you will have to give the speech."

"That will raise red flags," Katrina said. "Whoever goes up there will be flying without a net. Can you do it?"

My stomach dropped, and I pulled my sweaty palms away from the fabric of my dress. "I know the speech, but . . ."

"Okay, well, Pearl, you give the speech. Come Monday, we'll figure the rest out. You can do it, right?"

I glanced to my left, expecting Katrina to step in, to try to take the spotlight, but she'd literally taken a step back, and I returned my gaze to Kevin. "I could, but wouldn't it be better coming from you or another board member?" *Or someone who isn't petrified by the idea of standing on a stage.*

"You'll do great. You're very articulate." He glanced over my shoulder, a polished expression returning to his features when he made eye contact with someone else. *Apparently articulate and bangable are the descriptors I'm getting tonight.* He held up a hand to whomever had caught his eye. "We'll touch base afterward. Excuse me."

He left us standing in unsteady silence, and Katrina turned to me. "What the hell just happened?"

Just me volunteering to speak in front of three hundred people because our boss is mysteriously gone. I took another quick breath, knowing I didn't get to lose it, not in this space and not in this room.

Katrina's tone was doubtful, our moment of shared uncertainty already over. "Are you sure you can give the speech?"

Even though I wasn't, her tone rankled me and made pride puff up my chest. "I don't have a choice." *And it's not like you stepped up.* I gave her a slight smile and searched the stage for the notebook containing a printout of the speech along with reference materials, everything that I'd need to cram before getting on the stage and coming face-to-face with my fear of public speaking.

Once I was sitting backstage with the binder and eyeing the podium every few minutes, I let myself freak out, now that there was no one around who I needed to think I was bulletproof. I'd never been one to let my guard down at work, certainly not in this new position. The only time was when I worked at FitMi, and even then, really just with one person.

Cord's face filled my mind. His sable brown eyes and long lashes—lashes a lot of women would kill for—and his hair that was always too long, falling over his face and tempting me to brush it back. When I'd admitted my fear of public speaking, he hadn't tried to make me feel better about it, hadn't told me to imagine everyone in their underwear or whatever other advice people usually gave. He'd met my eyes, hair falling in his face, and told me I could speak directly to him and he'd be smiling. He'd added that I could do that any time I needed. I sipped from my glass of wine and grinned at the memory. He'd been so sure that if I ever had to be on a stage, he'd be there to support me. That was before everything happened and before I left without saying a proper goodbye.

He'd been my boss, then we'd been friends, and one night, I'd given in to the urge to brush the hair off his face, and we'd almost been so much more. Now, he was nothing to me anymore, and we hadn't spoken in years. I let my eyes fall closed, the sounds of the bustling hall surrounding me, with the hum of conversation and smatterings of laughter rising over the din. They were all going to be staring at me. My neck heated and the dress felt too small, but there was no choice—I couldn't go back to Kevin and tell him I couldn't do it or that I was scared. Women didn't have that option, especially not women of color.

Not today.

I stood. Soon, the lights would dim, and then I'd be on. I read through the script again. Welcome. Thank-yous. Review successes. Introduce new opportunities. Calls to action. More thank-yous. Goodnight.

I repeated that to myself while the lights dimmed on cue and the volume rose as people shuffled and move toward their seats. I imagined a sea of black, spotted with brightly colored gowns and pastel satin moving between the tables like water, everyone full from dinner and cocktails. I smoothed my hair, making sure my edges weren't the mess my nerves were, then rested a palm on my stomach and took another slow breath. *Okay.*

My fingers shook as I clutched the notebook, and the memory of Cord's too-long hair and baritone voice once again filled my head. *I'll be smiling.*

I decided I could give the speech as if he were in the audience, even though he wasn't there, and I stepped out onto the stage.

Chapter 2

CORD

I RAN FOR the elevator, slipping my hand between the closing doors and hoping the sensor picked it up in time. The Mountain Dew in my Big Gulp cup sloshed and my Chucks slid along the tile floor. Why anyone would willingly choose to wear a suit to work was beyond me, and I'd thrown away every pair of khakis I owned the minute it was official that I owned this business. My best friend and business partner told me I'd regret it, but he was wrong. Throwing away the khakis and polos of my corporate days had been the best decision I'd made. And whether it was luck or talent or a combination of both, things had been going well since then.

Luck was on my side again and the doors sprang back open, revealing a tall woman in a skirt that fell past her knees. Was that a pencil skirt? It went straight down, and my vision snagged on the utter perfection of her calves. I wasn't sure I'd ever noticed a woman's calves before. It felt illicit to find them so appealing and to trace the lines of her legs up to the hem of the skirt. "Uh, sorry about that," I said, stepping inside. "Didn't want to wait for the next one."

She'd glanced back down at her padfolio with a dismissive nod. "Sure."

I didn't recognize her, although she looked like she could be an actress or a model, with skin a shade of brown that looked warm and smooth. Her braids were pulled into a bun I immediately wanted to undo. *Who is this woman?*

I reached for the keypad to punch in my floor—twenty-three—but it was already illuminated, and I glanced back at her. "Are you visiting the FitMi offices?" I sipped from my straw as the elevator inched up. I knew from experience that we'd stop on at least four floors before reaching our destination, and I'd never been so thankful for the delay.

She nodded without looking up, studying her notes closely.

"Interview?" Wes, my partner, had said something about interviewing assistants today, and I wished I'd paid closer attention. Part of me hoped she bombed her interview and didn't end up working for us. I could maybe work up the courage to ask for her number then, but one glance at her set jaw and straight spine and I had the feeling she'd never bombed an interview in her life.

She finally looked up, meeting my eyes briefly as I stepped closer to her to make room for two women entering the car. "Yes, interview." She was, no doubt, unimpressed by my jeans and hoodie, and probably thought I was an intern or lost. "You?"

"Just a normal day for me." I'd never minded looking like an intern until that moment, when I wanted to be the guy she noticed, the guy who looked like someone who should stand next to her. I brushed my hair off my face. I was perpetually overdue for a haircut. "Can't you tell from my three-piece suit?"

A ghost of a smile crossed her lips. "I'm not sure that counts as a suit."

"That's where you're wrong," I said as we waited for the doors to open and close on floor fifteen, where the women stepped out. I pointed to my jeans. "Pants. Jacket." I tugged on the sleeve of the sweatshirt before unzipping it and pointing to my T-shirt. "Shirt."

I'd chosen a black one with the outline of a wagon and oxen, reading *You Have Died of Dysentery.*

Her eyes were back on her notes, but she smiled. "But a three-piece suit has a vest."

"Damn. You're right. Next time I see you, I'll have a vest." I held out my hand. "I'm Cord."

"Pearl." She took it, her shake firm and her skin smooth and soft. Her voice had this breathy quality. It was subtle, like a whisper on top of her normal voice. "It's nice to meet you, Cord." I immediately loved how my name sounded coming from her lips and wanted to hear it again.

Chapter 3

CORD

"THANKS FOR COMING with me tonight." Abby squeezed my hand and smiled, blue eyes bright. She looked pretty in a dress that matched her eyes, and with her hair pulled back in some kind of twisty thing. *Did I tell her she looks pretty?* After six months of dating, I still worried I was saying the wrong thing most of the time and she was too nice to point it out.

"Oh, sure. I mean, of course I came with you. And you look nice."

She smiled wider and looked back toward the closed elevator doors. Two other couples joined us, and relief flooded me when Abby started talking to one of the other women instead of focusing on me. The doors whooshed shut and their conversation filled the mirrored car.

I caught my reflection across the space—hand in my pocket and wearing a tux, I almost didn't recognize myself. Standing there with Abby on my arm, I looked like someone who was comfortable in this kind of environment and not like someone wishing this night was already over. I glanced around. I never stepped into an elevator without thinking about Pearl, and I could almost picture the way her heels would look against the floor of the car and smell her subtle scent.

"Earth to Cord?" Abby nudged me as the other two couples were stepping through the open door, the sounds from the ballroom filtering into the hall.

"Sorry."

Abby slid her arm through mine. "I demand you to stop thinking about work. Give yourself a night off."

It was normally a good guess. Work seemed to always be taking over every thought, even when I was doing things I enjoyed. Even when I was spending time with Abby. Really, every time I was spending time with her. I shook off the inkling that was a telling sign, determined to do better. "Sure. Of course. Sorry, Ab."

We walked into the ballroom, filled with people who didn't need to talk about money because they sounded like money. Abby had volunteered for OurCode for over a year, mentoring a high school student interested in a career in tech. She'd tried for months to convince me to volunteer. She'd pushed me as far as signing up and going through the initial background check, but I always begged off from finishing the training—I didn't have the time, and I didn't particularly like teenagers. I hadn't liked them when I *was* a teenager. The least I could do was attend this ridiculously opulent fundraiser with her and donate, because the donating, I was happy to do.

I brushed my forehead, an old nervous habit, only my hair was shorter now and pushed back off my face. I glanced around and stifled the urge to shove my hand in my pocket. Mingling and cocktail chatter were part of my life now, and luckily my date was skilled at the talking part, moving from group to group, introducing me, and then leading the conversation. Screens hanging from the ceiling showed pictures of girls in the program along with quotes. It wasn't as if the dearth of women in coding and programming was new to me. Before moving into a management role, I'd been in the trenches—usually trenches full of guys who looked like me.

"And Cord is—" Abby's voice cut into my thoughts, and I jerked my head back to the conversation she was having with two women and an older man. She gave me one of her chiding looks—that was about as critical as her looks ever got. This one meant pay attention. "Cord heads up FitMi, the fitness app." She glanced from person to person, reading their faces.

I nodded, unsure if I was supposed to respond. "Yep, that's me."

"I've been trying to get him involved with OurCode for ages, right, honey?"

I hated the pet name, and my tie felt too tight around my neck. "Yeah."

The three people all pounced in a chorus of "Yes!" and "You should!" and I smiled awkwardly, wishing for an escape hatch.

A hand clapped my shoulder. "Matthews, I thought I saw you come in."

Kevin Corbin stood behind me. We'd started around the same time, two green software developers at the bottom of the hierarchy. We'd never been friends, exactly, but we shared beers every now and again.

"Hey, man. How are you?"

"Can I borrow you for a minute, Cord?" Kevin and I stepped to the side, and he held up his glass. "You want anything?"

I waved it off. "What's up?"

"You remember when I took the fall for the issues with the Free-Wall project back in the day?"

I laughed. Four of us had taken some risks that hadn't paid off, and Kevin had taken the bullet when management came down on us for our massive mistake, born of overconfidence and misplaced dreams of glory. "You finally calling in your favor?"

He took a swig from his glass and nodded. "In a big way. I need you to join the board for this thing," he said, motioning around the room.

I followed his hand as if it would give me more information. "For OurCode? Why?"

"Keep this between us, okay?"

I nodded. "Sure."

"I had to fire the executive director this afternoon. She was screwing a board member."

"You fired her on the spot for that?"

"There are . . . additional factors that tipped my hand. I need someone on the board with good connections and who is reliable to make sure the ship sails straight through this."

I took in his expression, the exhaustion around the eyes. I'd been looking for something outside of work to refill my cup, but glancing around at the over-the-top self-congratulating happening around the room, I was pretty sure this wasn't it. "Oh, wow. I . . . don't know if I have time."

Kevin scrubbed a hand over his jaw. "I'm begging. I learned a lot in the last few days about how it's been mismanaged. How can I convince you? The press loves this stuff—being attached to it will look good for you and FitMi." He grinned and lowered his voice. "That most eligible bachelor in tech thing must be wearing off, right? Though it looks like you need no help in that department." He motioned to Abby, and I wished I had a drink in my hand.

"Don't remind me about that article," I joked, ignoring his comment about Abby. That had been the first and last time I ever let our PR people talk me into talking about my personal life. "I'm sure the involvement would be good PR, but . . ." That he assumed the way to get me to support a charity was to tell me it looked good bothered me. I didn't want to be that guy. I glanced down at my tuxedo. *I hope I'm not already that guy.*

"Excuse me," he said, clapping my shoulder again and nodding to Abby, who'd walked toward us. "Think about it, okay?"

Kevin stepped to the stage as the lights fell, and he introduced himself and began a brief history of the program. During the speech, I made mental notes about possible excuses: FitMi was in the middle of expanding, I needed to spend more time with Abby, and Kevin should consider asking a woman. If he was worried about optics, that would be better in the long run anyway. I crafted what I'd say to let him down easy, brainstorming ideas for who I'd recommend in my stead.

Everyone applauded, and Kevin stepped back as the speaker for the evening stepped from the wings. Noticing the line of her calf as it peeked through the low slit in her dress, I froze. Pearl's voice filled the room, and it immediately brought me back to that elevator and being certain I'd just met the one.

AUTHOR PHOTO BY D&ORFS PHOTOGRAPHY

Denise Williams wrote her first book in the second grade. *I Hate You* and its sequel, *I Still Hate You*, featured a tough, funny heroine; a quirky hero; witty banter; and a dragon. Minus the dragons, these are still the books she likes to write. After penning those early works, she finished second grade and eventually earned a PhD in education, going on to work in higher education. After growing up as a military brat around the world and across the country, Denise now lives in Iowa with her husband, son, and two ornery shih tzus who think they own the house.

CONNECT ONLINE

DeniseWilliamsWrites.com

🐦 NicWillWrites

📷 NicWillWrites

f AuthorDeniseWilliams

♪ NicWillWrites

Ready to find
your next great read?

Let us help.

Visit prh.com/nextread

Penguin
Random
House